STUDIO SAINT-EX

STUDIO SAINT-EX

A novel

Ania Szado

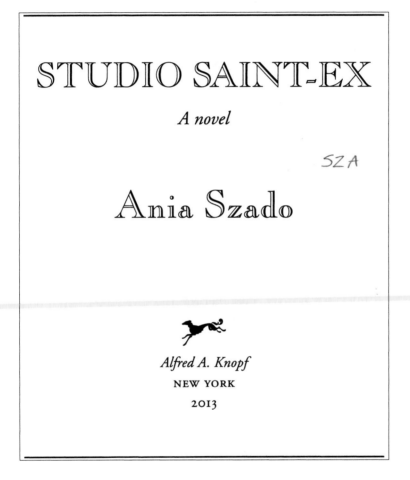

Alfred A. Knopf

NEW YORK

2013

THIS IS A BORZOI BOOK
PUBLISHED BY ALFRED A. KNOPF

Copyright © 2013 by Ania Szado

All rights reserved. Published in the United States by Alfred A. Knopf,
a division of Random House, Inc., New York

www.aaknopf.com

Knopf, Borzoi Books, and the colophon are registered
trademarks of Random House, Inc.

Library of Congress Cataloging-in-Publication Data
Szado, Ania.
Studio Saint-Ex : a novel / Ania Szado.
p.   cm.
"This is a Borzoi book."
1. Triangles (Interpersonal relations)—Fiction. 2. New York (N.Y.)—
History—1898–1951—Fiction. I. Title.
PR9199.4.S99S78 2013   813'.6—dc23   2012032018

Jacket photograph © Estate of Horst P. Horst.
Reproduced by permission of Art + Commerce
Jacket design by Jason Booher

Manufactured in the United States of America
First Edition

For my family

"You will have five hundred million little bells, I shall have five hundred million springs of fresh water . . ."

—*The Little Prince,*
Antoine de Saint-Exupéry

STUDIO SAINT-EX

1

I haven't even brought a book. I rarely do for the flight to Montreal, so short there's hardly time to finish a page without a pert stewardess interrupting with a buckle-unbuckle update or to stuff you with another canapé. While I wait at the gate, I do what I always do at JFK: watch the flow of close-shaven businessmen, triangulated teenagers in A-line dresses or the new bell-bottomed jeans, well-heeled wives with this season's travel bags, exasperated fathers, preternaturally patient mothers with faded eyeliner, cranky children in tow.

Today the tide of travelers, like the rain clouds, has swollen and stalled. The gate is crowded and stuffy. Twin boys chomping Now and Later candy share the seat next to mine. Pan Am Flight 108 is delayed, ladies and gentlemen. And delayed. And we're sorry to inform you that this flight has again been delayed. Due to weather—as though we ever don't have weather. You might as well say due to clouds.

You'd think they would figure out a way. Man has been flying, after all, since before I was born. Even Antoine was far from the first, and he soloed in 1921. Maybe that's him up there, hurling torrents from the sky.

Rain hits the tarmac nearly sideways and skids across, leaping over itself in its hurry to set the terminal afloat. I dig through my bag. As I do so, it catches the interest of a tony woman walking past in Balenciaga. Yes, miss, my bag is a Mignonne NYC. As are the dress and the hat—but not the shoes, which are Beth Levine.

She breaks stride slightly as she recognizes me, then continues, self-satisfaction adding a lilt to her gait. Thank you, miss, yes, I am Mignonne Lachapelle.

Equal parts gratifying and embarrassing. To conceal my habitual blush, I pull out the pamphlet for Expo 67, the world's fair. The twins' mother notices the pamphlet as she reaches across her boys to pin them to their chair.

" 'Man and His World.' " She says the name of the fair's theme as though the words are sour in her mouth. "Can you believe that, in this age?"

"It suffers in translation," I begin, but she goes on.

"I'm waiting for the day there's a fair called Woman's World." She shoves the smaller boy into place with more force than his squirming demands. "Or better, a world called Woman's World."

Even Antoine might have balked at the translation of *Terre des hommes*, the title of his novel that earned the *Grand Prix du Roman* in France and the National Book Award here. Man and his world? I'm not sure he himself ever made a claim upon the earth. He used to say we don't inherit the planet, but borrow it from our children.

Not *our* children. We had no children—except for that which we made.

They say that everything comes around again, to be borrowed, stolen, honored, adored, abused. That fashions—and politics and the songs tucked into babies' ears—lie dormant until the time is right. Is nothing allowed to die? God forbid some of my first works are resurrected. We didn't know how blessed we were to be spared greater notice in our early, earnest days—when I was plowing ahead as boldly as that Amazon strutting there (hip-slung fringe purse pulling up her mini-dress, exposing the muscle of her thigh). Or how lucky we were that the American fashion press was as new and naïve as we were. Or as was I. Clueless about man, naïve about his world.

I'll sit and wait for this flight because in Montreal my mother waits for me. As does Star Pilot, my retrospective collection on short-term display at the fair. Tomorrow, if the heavens dry up, I'll give a talk in the United States Pavilion. "Inspiration and Antoine," I plan to call it—but that's all I have written so far. The studio has been so busy. I haven't had a moment to myself, no time to think.

My toes tap, impatient, unused to being made to stay still. I take out my notebook and my favorite Cartier pen.

I settle the notebook on my lap and gaze at the rivulets that stream down the windows. They undulate, come together, separate. They are sequined snakes. They are runnels, seashores, racing cars, spittle, piping, phone lines, falling jets, falling stars. Let's not point out the obvious: being raindrops, they are tears.

Beyond the glass, an intrepid swallow swoops through the rain, turns sharply at an edge that only it can see, and returns to inscribe its back-and-forth trajectory, measuring the width of a sheet of water, embroidering the span of a panel of sateen.

Let's say it draws a story: of a flower, a little prince, Antoine, and me.

2

In April 1942, I returned to New York. Not to the apartment that had been home to Papa, Mother, Leo, and me, but back to the city after a year in Montreal. Back to stake a claim in the Garment District, where everything had its place: the design studios and showrooms, the fabric, bead, and notion stores, the furriers, the milliners, the shops selling equipment to the trade, the pushers hauling racks of swaying garments, the loading docks holding clues to the concerns of the floors above. And New York Fashion School. The building reached for me with its brass handrails as I passed.

Alma mater. Class of '41. I tried to draw confidence from the thought. It had been a year since I had presented my final portfolio to Madame Professor Véra Fiche and she had ravaged my work. Her performance had been convincing. I had taken it to heart in a way I would never have done had she offered equally vehement praise. It had shaken me deeply. I had been hopeful until then. I had been twenty-one.

A flustered student hurried up the steps and through the doors, likely rushing to his own portfolio ordeal. I would rather have been in his shoes than do what I was about to do.

I walked on, turning the wrong direction automatically before conceding that Madame's building must, in fact, be the other way. Why would she have taken a studio so close to the Hudson River, when just a couple of blocks over she could have been in the heart of the district? Promising designers didn't locate here— among merchants hawking shelving units, pressing machines, and dusty mannequins—and Atelier Fiche was said to be a fashion house to watch. At school it had been rumored that, before coming to teach at NYFS, Madame had had several shows without making even the smallest splash. But if those unremarkable and unremarked-upon collections had existed, they had been excised: *Women's Wear Daily* designated Madame's January '42 collection a notable "debut." At fifty, the designer was no debutante. Still, Véra Fiche's aesthetic, and therefore mine, had been noticed. The American fashion press, obliged to come up with some sort of news in the wake of the vacuum left by Paris—for France had fallen to the Nazis—had begun focusing for the first time on the offerings of domestic designers. The industry had no choice if it was to survive. I suspected the press was pulling at straws or suffering delusions as it found its way.

Regardless: they had anointed Atelier Fiche, if only by dint of a single column inch and one grainy photograph. If Madame hadn't already made plans to find a more desirably located studio or a properly impressive salon, no doubt she would do so when her end-of-school-year tasks were complete. Then, of course, she would give up teaching for good. I was keenly aware that it would take everything she had in her to advance from aspiring to arrived. I was determined to make the same commitment myself.

At 315 West 39th, as if in imprudent solidarity with Madame Fiche, a hat designer had set up shop several blocks from the Millinery District. His street-level storefront displayed miniature masculine hats of the sort ladies were pinning atop their up-dos and rolled tresses in those wartime days—a jaunty, tongue-in-cheek look that managed to simultaneously salute and belittle the men who wore the corresponding full-size versions. There were five-inch top hats like sleek black corks, teacup-sized bowlers, a tiny officer's cap with an optimistic V-for-victory brooch glittering from its band. A pancake-sized beret was adorned with a wide-eyed peacock feather. Its lashes quivered as it watched me.

Beside the display, set back from the sidewalk, the green paint of a metal door was peeling to reveal older and paler green layers. I pulled it open and climbed low steps to the lobby, avoiding the handrail; its varnish was black with grime. At the elevator, I closed the grate behind me and prayed for a swift ascension and a swifter return to ground. The box shuddered upward.

On Madame's floor, walls of brick and dismal plaster disappeared into murky corners and passageways. Industrial whining came from behind closed doors, drowning out the creaking of the floorboards. A heavy, oily smell intensified with each step. Surely Madame doesn't bring clients here, I thought. But here was her studio, "Atelier Fiche" hand-lettered in black ink on a golden card with elegant corner flourishes. Classic and carefully adorned—as expected. At NYFS, Madame had been a fanatic for hand-finished details, fine embroidery, and expensive gilt applied to suits with nipped-in waists or to respectable dresses with long, straight skirts. She had imposed her preferences with a rigid will. I had not managed to stand up to Madame that entire year; what made me imagine I might be capable of doing so now?

"Relax, Mig," my brother Leo had said this morning. "Know your problem? You're still thinking of Fiche as your professor. All she is to you now is a thief and a cheat. What you do is, you surprise her. She opens the door. Bang: lay it on the line. Tell her what you want. And make it good. She owes you big time."

"All I want is an apology."

"You want cash in hand. And a cut of what she gets, now until kingdom come. Think of the future. Future sales."

But what sort of sales could Madame expect? The country had changed since I had designed the line. One minute, the U.S. had been committed to withholding military involvement; the next minute, we'd declared war. Four months later, we were still gearing up for mobilization, but I was certain that soon Americans would be fighting on the European front. Who would wear anything like those flamboyant designs then?

I told Leo about the new fabric use restrictions. I tried to explain how Madame's collection would be hamstrung by patriotic constraint.

"Temporary setback," he said. "Any day now, Roosevelt's going to raise his little finger and start sending in our boys. Bam! Hitler wets his pants and runs home bawling. And just like that, old Fiche goes back to selling whatever fancy clothes she wants." He pointed his cigarette at me. "You got to look out for yourself. Take a lesson from me. When I was building popcorn machines, everyone knew the boss was knocking the bottles off the shelves with his secretary. Good for him; better for me. I figured it was fifty-fifty the guy would promote me out of his way instead of throwing me onto the street."

"You blackmailed him?"

"I just asked him if his wife would like to see some interesting photographs."

"You were bluffing."

"It cost him nothing to give me a better job. But believe me, people will do a lot to save their reputations. Remember that, Miggy. This lady's got a lot to lose. She'd be nowhere without you."

If Leo could see this hallway, I thought as I stood poised to knock on the studio door, he might just wonder whether Madame Fiche was still nowhere. Maybe the designs she copied from my sketches hadn't brought success to Atelier Fiche after all, despite what I had read in the magazine Mother borrowed from the Ladies' Auxiliary of Montreal: "Debut collection takes wing . . . Emerging from the cocoon of NYFS, professor Madame Véra Fiche sets Manhattan society a-flutter . . ."

The *Women's Wear* article had astounded me: it meant I could succeed in fashion. But I couldn't be proud that my designs had been noticed. I couldn't be angry that the credit went to Madame Fiche. It wasn't right that she had taken my ideas for her own, but neither was it right that this collection was being lauded as acceptable, even exceptional.

All I wanted from Madame now was the chance to see the

Butterfly Collection in person, to face it in the flesh, before letting it go and putting it behind me. If it was true that I had talent, I would find a way to make fashion a force for good.

I knocked. The studio was large: faint, sharp footsteps sounded for some moments, growing louder until the door opened. A flicker of emotion sparked briefly in Madame Fiche's eyes.

She still had the same smooth brow plucked entirely bare, the same severe hairdo, the black strands—with some new grey filaments—pulled tight into a flawless bun. Her thin forearms were chalky and damp; they bore the clean heavy smell of plaster of Paris. She still wore the same sort of tailored black dress as always, but in place of her customary belted jacket was an unbleached cotton apron. In an accent even loftier than her usual, she said, "You have interrupted my work."

I squeezed my hands together to stop their shaking. If only I could do the same to my words. "I'm Mignonne Lachapelle."

"*Oui.*"

"I've come about the butterflies. The collection. My designs."

She eyed me, her lips pinched, until my stomach grew so nervous as to almost heave. "*Entrez.*"

I entered.

This was Madame's studio? I had been expecting a space confined and controlled, not a careless expanse that was messily meadow-like in its broad sweep, its glow, its random flowerings. Overstuffed racks dripped garments, two or three to a hanger, with more strewn over the rods. On the floor, bolts of material—some rolls fat with fabric, others just covering their cores—were stacked like colorful, mismatched plates. Long, curling rectangles of butcher paper were fastened to the walls and to the pipes that passed overhead, their surfaces filled with sketches in charcoal or in chalk. From some, silver strings of cobwebs swayed. An oversized sketch pad lay open on a table that was awash in natural light. Sunshine spread across the golden floor. I stepped into it.

II

So much space. So much light. I breathed it in.

I'd become used to the high ceilings of the Lachapelle family home where my mother now lived, used to hilly horizons barely breached by buildings. When I'd emerged from Grand Central Station two weeks before, I had immediately felt compacted to half my height (which was five feet ten—twenty-five years ago). The New York sky didn't curve down to a natural horizon but perched above mile-high rooftops like a distant cap. Leo had walked uncompressed beside me with my trunk on his shoulder. Now he and I lived like mice in his small, subterranean apartment, and Madame's studio was opening like a seashore around me, wide and warmly aglow.

I wanted this.

She led me to the back of the studio, to a cluster of chairs, a coffee table, a sofa. "Sit," she said as she walked on, rounding a worktable beyond the sofa, where buckets and wire armatures waited. "I am constructing a new judy." She nodded toward three headless torsos that stood on posts near a wall of windows—female forms for the fitting of garments, one of them stolen from NYFS.

"In plaster?"

"I try plaster. I try *papier-mâché*." She turned to her task, tearing strips of paper, dipping them into a bucket, fussing over where to fit them on a half-covered armature. Leo had said to let Madame make the first move, but it was as though she had forgotten I was there.

I coughed. Madame looked up with a smile—far more disconcerting than her usual glower—before continuing silently with her work. She turned the armature, inspecting it.

"Madame. I think, I mean I know, you stole my designs. The butterfly-inspired concepts I submitted for my year-end portfolio. I saw the photo in *Women's Wear Daily*."

She slapped a wad of sodden paper onto the judy's bosom. "Silly of me, wasn't it?"

My gut jumped. "You admit it?"

"I admit. I regret."

The most I had expected was begrudging recognition of some sliver of creative debt. Never a swift admission of guilt—not from the most unbending woman I'd ever met. It didn't fit. There had to be more to it.

I stalled. I said, "It was wrong, what you did."

"Wrong?" She leaned over a bucket on the floor to splash water on her arms, then dried them vigorously with a towel before walking around the sofa to perch in an armchair facing me. "It was idiotic. *Stupide.* Can you possibly imagine how much I put into that collection? All my months of hard work. And in service to what?" She gestured with a limp, dismissive hand toward something behind me. "To that." Her voice was flat with disdain.

The skin at the corners of her eyes was crinkling: she was pleased or amused. It had been the same when she'd railed against my sketches. Her tone had hurled disgust as she dismissed my work as misguided, amateur, ugly, a waste of paper, a misuse of time—yet there had been a brightness in her cheeks. On that day, as on this one, there had been a strange intensity in her eyes.

She waited for me to take the cue, to look. I had been thinking about this moment for weeks: when I would see and touch my creation—her creation—the hybrid born from my drawings and brought to life by Madame's hand. I stood up and found it necessary to steady myself on the armchair before turning around.

Hanging high on the brick wall behind my chair was an astonishing garment. It was even more dramatic than I'd envisioned it could be as I was working out its features in my sketchbooks, far more striking and detailed than the black-and-white magazine photograph had conveyed. Madame had constructed the dress of rich silk velvet. It had an asymmetrical hem that rose slightly in the front and fell from a gathered waist to what would be well beyond floor length at the back. On the lower portion, dark beaded flowers glinted subtly against the expansive sweep of velvet, which was itself dark, almost black-blue. On the same velvet backdrop a butterfly—lavishly constructed of beads, sequins, silver cording, and satin insets—inhabited the entire top half of the dress, imbuing it with ruby red, violet, and dark green. The neckline plunged in an angle that contained the antennae and pointed to the ruching that defined the insect's body down the center of the dress. The batwing sleeves draped straight down from the hanger. I walked over to lift a sleeve. Flowing lines of beading and embroidery carried across the full span of the triangle.

I said, "If you were going to copy someone's work, I don't understand why you would ever choose mine. Not this line. How could you even show it? How could anyone think it was appropriate?"

"People need a luxurious escape these days, no?"

The fashions in Montreal had been simple, pedestrian, restrained. They didn't insult anyone with their disdain for the troubles of the times. They didn't make me feel ill. Men were dying; whole families were starving; and Madame was talking about luxury. "People in Canada would never wear something like this. You should see how they scrimp."

Madame's tone was mocking. "You are an expert; you have been rationing with the brave Canadians. Poor you. And here I have been elbow deep in sequins and velvet, stupidly trying to make a living, shamelessly eating my fill. Mind you, appetite is a tricky thing. It is prone to failure when the fate of one's family is unknown."

Her family. Of course Madame Fiche would have relatives in France. I hadn't thought about that.

She drew a watch from her skirt pocket and fastened it on her wrist, then shook her hand briskly to shift the band into position. "If the collection were as inappropriate as you believe it to be, its launch would have gone unnoticed. You would be none the wiser; only I would bear the cost of the effort. But it has succeeded. *Alors*, fate unrolls as it must. You come to extract my penance; I agree to hire you as my assistant; we continue to collaborate to secure ever increasing fame for Atelier Fiche."

"Pardon?"

"There are worse alternatives—for us both."

"You want to hire me?" It wasn't possible. I could not work with a woman who had stolen my designs. But my gaze went involuntarily, longingly, to the studio before alighting again on the dress.

"Listen," said Madame. "In France, that garment would have been a sign of *résistance*. When the men were called to the Front, the wives dressed in pure silk. That's right, even as the Brits and your beloved Canadians went without. The Frenchwomen wrapped themselves in it by the meter so *les Boches* couldn't take it for their own wives. Do you see? That is why I thought the collection was inspired; it is why I did not cancel the launch when Roosevelt declared war. You are wrong about wartime fashions, Mignonne: the most admirable pieces are extravagant in purpose and in spirit—nothing like the insipid styles mandated by this country's pencil pushers."

Resistance, spirit: this was what Madame saw when she looked at my designs? There had been a time, before Montreal, when I had defended the role of fashion in a world at war. I had argued its importance to Antoine. Maybe I'd been right then. Maybe Madame was right. I tried to imagine Frenchwomen wearing the butterfly dress. The hubris of the notion sent a ripple of shame through me—but better to picture the piece on defiant Parisians than on Americans too absorbed in liberty to restrict what they put on their backs.

Madame said, "American society has always followed the Parisian aesthetic, not England's with its colorless sacks. When you brought in your sketches and I saw your butterflies, I thought I had discovered a motif that captured the American spirit: proud and free. I thought that, in all my years of teaching, I had never seen such a perceptive rendering of *l'esprit de l'époque*."

"You really did?"

"It was my first mistake. I let desire blind me to the truth. I let myself forget that you are not really American."

"I am so!" I was born and raised in New York. Only Papa was French: he'd emigrated to Montreal with his parents and brother before both young men moved to New York—first Yannick, to test the market with his locally lauded *haute cuisine*, then my father in pursuit of a career in architecture, accompanied by his Canadian bride.

Madame said, "No child of Émile Lachapelle could be anything but French at heart. No wonder you have no idea what Americans want. I have no idea either, not anymore. I was expecting the theater of war to turn American woman into birds of paradise, not dull, defeated brown chickens like the Brits and Canadians."

But the Canadians weren't defeated—not the ones in Mother's Anglophone neighborhood or the Francophone friends I had drunk with in Old Montreal. After two and a half years of sacrifice, Canadians still believed in the cause that drove the war and took their sons. Among them, I had finally allowed myself to grieve my father's death, after tamping down sorrow through my final school year to impress the likes of Véra Fiche. All of Canada had seemed to understand and share my grief. The proof had surrounded me: in the *Gazette*'s details of slaughter at a beachhead; in the station one day bursting with uniforms and the next day barren of men; in the red-etched eyes of the floury baker's wife; in the intensity with which Mother tuned the radio at night. The Canadian Broadcasting Corporation delivered news with a chairman's precision, but the signal whined in pain, the static crackled loss.

I had returned to Manhattan this spring bearing pride in

my country (*U.S. at War!*) and found an abundance of military recruiting stations jostling like street vendors for a corner spot. The city's dim-out rule was so fresh that New Yorkers were still remarking on the romantic change. It was as though a much-anticipated show had come to town. The city was not under blackout orders, but Bloomingdale's was selling decorative dark shades for those who strove to be fashionably ahead of the times. The neon on Broadway had been replaced with metallic sequin signs that shimmered seductively in the available light, mesmerizing the eye with the slightest breeze. The markets still offered an array of produce—under posters that advocated moderation—and despite the draft, the streets still bore plenty of young men. Yes, we had shipped dried eggs and powdered milk by the boatloads; we had delivered scores of munitions; we had built ships; but why had Roosevelt not yet pitted our troops against the Germans? Thirty-one months after Hitler invaded Poland, American squadrons had yet to be deployed in Europe.

Madame could say what she liked. The butterfly dress could only be an affront to those who were fighting overseas. It was beautiful in a way that was worse than ugly.

"You won't receive a better offer," she said as I picked up my purse. "Not without a portfolio. Not having squandered your chances for an entire year. Think about that, Mignonne."

I had no intention of thinking about it. I was afraid of what I might decide.

3

I knocked on dozens of studio doors with my old sketches and samples in hand. No one cared that I'd graduated at the top of my class a year before; most didn't give me a chance to say a word beyond my name. In some places, among the French expats, it was a name that could open doors—but here in the Garment District, I was just another grad, and of the worst sort: the type that wanted to create her own designs. Wasn't that the nature of the industry now—American designers developing American styles?

Paris had always dictated the look of each season, from the silhouette down to the details, but American women could no longer visit the Continent for hand-fitted originals. There were no new French originals: none for the Rockefeller set to wear, none for the copyists and factory workers to take apart and recreate in quantity for department store racks. And so in July of '41, with First Lady Eleanor Roosevelt at his side, the mayor of New York had proclaimed his city the fashion center of the universe, "not by accident, not by default of the war in Europe, but by the right of creative talent, skilled mechanics and the best dressed women in the world." Yet on the sidewalks in the spring of '42, in the studios and salons, in the backstreet and back alley doors to which I was directed with my portfolio, and in department store after department store where the racks were still fat with made-in-America, faux-Parisian ensembles, proof of the revolution was elusive.

One older gentleman had at least flipped through my drawings. He considered my signature. "Related to Yannick Lacha-pelle, the restaurateur?"

"I'm his niece."

"He's done well with Le Pavillon. You don't want to work for him?"

"I'm not interested in food."

He closed my sketchbook and returned it. "Your concepts aren't half bad. And your technique is sound."

"But you have nothing for me?"

"Want to press seams for three years—or five or fifteen? And then maybe move up to beadwork or piping?"

"You wouldn't make me a junior designer or an assistant?"

"You can get on the cart if you like, Miss Lachapelle, but the wheels turn slowly. You'd be satisfied with tracing and sizing patterns?"

"I want to be a designer."

He steered me to the door. "You'll find a way."

I was a designer who did not design, as Antoine was a pilot who had long been denied flight. When I'd last seen him, a year before, he had still been grounded, decommissioned from the French Air Force, without a posting or a plane. By now, surely, he was airborne again. I was certain he would not still be in New York. There was nothing for him in New York.

I had no cause to think I'd run into him, especially not in the Garment District, yet I looked for him as I had looked for him in the cafés of Old Montreal. I had checked for his letters daily. I'd looked for news of his departure from America in *Le Journal* and for his obituary in the *Gazette*: it was there that I expected to see him if I was ever to see him again.

I had reread his books in my bedroom at Mother's, though I'd made a point of leaving my own copies behind in New York. *Southern Mail*, which I had first read in French as *Courrier sud*. *Night Flight*, the story of a pilot fated to disappear. *Terre des hommes*—a title I would have translated as *Land of People*, not

Wind, Sand and Stars or Expo's "Man and His World." Yet *Terre des hommes* was indeed the story of a man. They were all of them restless dramas of men, romantic loners in search of fulfillment, men who put duty above all.

I had sought Antoine in his novels. I had recalled them as adventure tales. But what I found in rereading them was his testament that the noble man was condemned to wander unprotected and alone, his duties denying him a peaceful existence with a loving wife and the joys of settling in a community for longer than the span between missions or mail drops. By the time I received a letter from Antoine—the only letter he would send me in Montreal—I was half in love with his airborne doppelgängers, with their heart-wrenching ideals and their artless bravery. I wept for them and for myself—for I'd let Antoine go. I had forfeited my chance to ease him away from his pursuit of danger and into a quiet, comfortable life with me.

New York, October 11, 1941

Dear Mignonne,

My pen wishes to speak of your beauty that presents itself to me in poignant images as I lie in bed and cannot sleep: your blond hair that tries charmingly to conceal the emotions of your eyes; your slender fingers that hold your pencil gracefully and loosely even when your mind fights the productivity of your hand; your nose and lips that pout so prettily that I can hardly take seriously your frustrations and your anger.

My pen wishes, but I coax it to behave responsibly. A girl who has left a man should not be subjected to his morose and heartless nostalgia.

I will admit to this, my sweet Mignonne, and damn me for it if you must: not once did I believe that you did not care for me, nor did I anticipate you would leave me here, stranded, alone in New York. Never mind whether or not you expressed discomfort or misgivings about our friendship. It is a young woman's fate to be taken lightly. It is the role of her respectable older gentleman to dismiss his pretty friend's concerns and to give her a little frou-frou to diminish her worries and calm her nerves.

I am not one for frou-frous. I do not play the role you might expect me to play. And you, too, have admirably broken the rules. You claimed that you were leaving to visit your mother because Madame Lachapelle had requested it and a short jaunt was due. When you then posted a letter within the week, from afar, to sever any expectation that our very tender friendship might continue as it had been, this seemed to me to be beyond comprehension. It has taken me months to understand.

But such is man. To find the grain of fault in another being, he will dig as tirelessly as a child with a sand shovel. (A weak analogy, for the child labors only to see what he might discover. Today's man digs in the hope of laying bare a core of ugliness at another's heart.)

Forgive my blindness, Mignonne. It has taken me this long, a full half year of your absence, to understand that the fault lies not in your expectations of me or in my failure to live up to the same, nor in your stubbornness (which I might more graciously call determination, and which I have much admired when it was not directed at my English conjugations or at my refusal to compromise who and what I am). The fault, if there is fault, lies in one simple fact: the world that I have so loved has changed.

It was not long ago that freedom meant more than having a predetermined choice of toothpastes and powders on a drugstore shelf. Soon the sidewalks shall deliver us directly into the store aisles, where shelves laden with mind-numbing extravagances will empty themselves into our complacent hands. Gone are the days when one could rally thirty men from the sidewalks of Paris, as I did upon the fall of France, lead them cheerfully into a stolen plane, and fly to unoccupied North Africa, from whence to stage an attempt to regain our homeland. That the territory proved to be already occupied is immaterial to the point of my story, which is this: all now is rules and technology. Man stripped of choices is stripped, too, of honor.

How is one to act on the convictions of one's spirit? "Of course you must," they tell me, "only first ensure that you meet these criteria"—as they pull out their clipboards. "For your own safety, you understand."

My friends and my peers in the military have colluded to protect me from myself, volleying an endless stream of concerns to impede my reengagement in the war. "He is too old, he'll never survive, do you want to go down in history as the man who sent Saint-Ex to his grave? He is a legend, aristocrat, celebrity, source of commissions, the pet of powerful so-and-so, deluded, irrational, at the height of his creative powers, over the hill . . ." What nonsense they spew in their well-intentioned conspiracy. In preventing the sudden snuffing of my life they only kill me more slowly and painfully from the inside.

If I cannot act, I am not alive. Thought and action must be one—have not I often said so, in one way or another, as we spoke of our beliefs and our dreams? The most worthy of lives can be described without adjectives; the soul of a man can be revealed through verbs alone. If I cannot fly, if I cannot work to free my people, I do not exist.

You did not leave me when you went to Montreal, Mignonne. You left a shell. A man without choices or responsibility is not a man.

I summon the energy to write you now only because life may be starting anew. I have received a letter from a colleague who assures me he will have me reinstated into active duty. He swears the U.S. will join the war before long. I should not allow myself to feel excitement, but it has been months since I've seen even a glimmer of promise. Perhaps I may yet catch up to the world that has rushed so heedlessly and heartlessly ahead of me.

I write in careless haste driven by an impulse to tell you,

after all this time and before I depart, that I have come to see your wisdom. You were right to discard the empty casing I had become, and to not permit falsely optimistic thoughts of me to draw you away from your duty to your mother. And you are right to follow your own path without me now, wherever it leads, for I will at last be on my way, too.

I do not ask when you will come back to New York, or what you will do upon your return. I do not ask that you write to me (though should you wish to upon my departure, simply request my overseas address from Lamotte). I only say remember me, and in doing so, let there be no disagreement between your thoughts and your acts.

Antoine

I remembered him—in Montreal as well as in New York, as I walked the streets of the Garment District wondering what, indeed, I would do now that I had returned.

On West 50th, I found myself in the middle of a string of chatting, shapely girls.

"Almost there," said one, smiling broadly at me.

"Where?"

"Oh! The union office. They're picking the prettiest machine operator. You ain't in the pageant? You don't want to be famous? Gosh, that's lucky for me!"

I almost followed her through the door of the Ladies' Garment Workers building. I had the looks then; I know that now. I had a name, for what it was worth. Beyond that? A stack of drawings no one wanted to see, a stolen collection I couldn't sell, a heart yearning for a man whose own heart was pledged to the stormiest of skies.

Only Madame Fiche had spoken of a real future. Of designing, of talent.

Of success.

4

Madame opened her studio door without a hint of surprise. She had me sit with my back to the butterfly dress again, as if not seeing it would lessen my resentment. Instead, I felt its presence spur me to boldness. "All right, Madame. Tell me: why should I work for you?"

She said, "You went north after final exams last year, yes? Were you in New York in March, when the L-85 regulations were announced?"

"I came back just two weeks ago."

She ticked garment regulations, like grievances, on her fingertips: "Tucks, pleats, sleeve widths, dress lengths. Everything not slender and stingy: gone." She fluttered her fingers as though to say goodbye. "You fancy yourself a designer; I require assistance. I am willing to let you prove your value. To create memorable work within the new regulations requires a master craftswoman as well as a couturier's flair. But as you are here, you will suffice."

Madame Fiche knew exactly what I could do, how hard I could work. At NYFS, I had learned to make patterns, and to cut fabric, and to sew swiftly and carefully, tirelessly. I had learned finishing techniques. I had learned that the harder you work, the harder you are asked to work; the greater your desire and pride, the more the fool. Under Madame, I had worked harder than anyone. She had pushed me, loading me with extra assignments in addition to those given to the entire class. It had been clear that she had been testing me, maybe even grooming me.

I said, "I've already shown my worth by creating the butterfly designs."

"You think socialites today desire to look like insects? Do you? If that is your vision, tell me now. I would very much like to know."

"You tell me, Madame. Did you get any orders?"

"They were immediately withdrawn when the restrictions came down."

"I'm sorry," I said, though I was not; I was relieved there were no women walking around in the dresses I had designed.

"You did not come here to console me, *n'est-ce pas*? I have much to do to get this business back on track, and no time to waste. I have heard there are plans for an event that showcases American designers. It will bring newsmen from all over the country. Fashion Week, or Fashion Press Week, I believe it will be called. We must secure an invitation to participate. We must develop our reputation, our own clientele. First we conquer within our niche. For this, I need you."

"You said I didn't understand American women."

"I am not hiring you to understand them. The less we see of them, the better—until we are so successful that they come begging to wear our clothes. Do you know what they call our countrymen? 'Nazi-lovers.' 'Cowards.' They say these things to me, as I stand in their drawing rooms with a measuring tape around my neck. What do you think they will say when their own sons are sent to die along the Seine? Do you think American mothers will wish to wear a label that says 'atelier' instead of 'studio,' or a dress that emulates the Parisians? No, Mignonne, we will not focus our efforts on Americans. We will focus on the French."

The French? How was even a single Frenchwoman to order an Atelier Fiche design?

Unless she had fled to New York. Of course. Madame had decided to focus on the *émigrés*. This would be her niche: the largest, wealthiest group of French cultural elite outside of Paris. No designer had yet made this clientele his own.

Madame was not a member of the community's exclusive club, the Alliance Française. From the looks of things, she could not afford the fee. Neither could I, for that matter—but my relationship with the Alliance ran deeper than money could reach. She wanted to use my connections as she had used my designs. This from the professor who had driven me to work the skin of my fingers to bleeding, to perfect the details, to never compromise. She hadn't even let her students backstitch to lock the thread at the end of a run; she had insisted we pull both threads to the same side and knot them by hand.

"I thought you didn't go in for shortcuts, Madame."

"And yet I offer you this one."

That wasn't what I meant.

She said, "I suppose I am a sentimentalist. You have so much potential, yet no future in this industry. Your family name won't bring you success on its own; it will take you years to build a fledgling reputation such as I already enjoy. Even if you can afford a workspace and supplies, much of the fabric I have here can't be purchased anymore; just try to find European wools and Oriental silks. It could be years before the shelves are restocked. But shall I tell you why I really pity you? It is because you don't have the character to make it in fashion on your own."

"You're wrong," I said, but I could not hold Madame's gaze. How could she be anything but right? The proof was in the outcome of my portfolio critique: I had let myself be tricked and used. I had been prepared to fail.

"Then perhaps you are too proud to earn your keep?"

"I work very hard, and you know it."

"You used to. I offer you the chance to do so again."

"For pay."

"*Mon Dieu.* You are so pedantic. Naturally there is little salary until we have an established clientele. I expect you to prove your value." She paused. "I will give to you a weekly stipend to start, as a gesture of goodwill, plus a percentage of sales. Not all underlings could hope for as much. Naturally, you must bring in commissions."

"Me?"

"You are expecting to be rewarded for simply showing up?"

The old nervous shaking started up in my knees, but I took a deep breath. Madame might be able to find someone who matched my skills, but none who was a Lachapelle. If she really wanted me, if she needed me in order to gain a foothold with the wealthy expatriates, I wasn't powerless.

I lifted my chin. "I'll prove myself. And when I do, you'll make me a partner in the studio. Promise it."

"But of course," Madame said lightly, as easily as if I had asked her to pass a box of pins.

Leo didn't come home that night—he seemed to have more on the go than just building rides and rails—so I left him a note the next morning: "I got a job. I'm starting today. I'll tell you about it when I get home."

At the studio, I had hardly put down my purse when Madame Fiche handed me a sheet of paper and pointed to a haphazard pile of pattern pieces. "Redraft the pattern to these measurements and sew up a muslin for fitting. My new client, Mrs. Brossard, had her former couturier drop off her measurements so we can get under way immediately. The client is in a terrific rush, a crisis. You'll need to confirm or correct the size tomorrow when we see her. Leave a good degree of selvage on the muslin. In fact, construct a second muslin at least a size larger all around; when we see her we will know which one to work with."

"Wouldn't it be better to take the client's measurements ourselves?"

"She is away until tomorrow; even I have not yet met her.

Shall we proceed immediately, or do you prefer that we render it impossible to meet her deadline? The lady demands speed. She shall have it—if you will deign to apply yourself to that which you have been hired to do. Tomorrow we will go with the two muslins and fit the most appropriate one directly on her. The next day, we deliver the finished coat. It will be fun to work so quickly, don't you think?"

Maybe not, but I felt the exhilaration of having finally returned to the work I was meant to do. I smiled throughout each step: planning, shifting pattern pieces to maximize use of the fabric, tracing shapes onto the muslin with dressmakers' chalk. At one point, I laughed aloud, delighted by the weight and fit of my favorite old shears in my hand.

Madame, who was grumbling through a box of paper on the floor, looked up in surprise at the sound. Her hand stopped clawing through the stack of papers. I thought her mind paused its churning, too. She sat back on her haunches to watch me work, and her face slowly released its tightness. For a moment— it could have been the light; it could have been the odd angle (for I had rarely had occasion to look down on her)—Madame looked vulnerable, open. She looked human.

A few minutes later, she wandered over to critique my work, but her inspection lacked focus and her criticism was without basis or bite. By midafternoon, she took a ring of keys from a nail near the door, removed one, and handed it to me. "Lock up when you leave. I will meet you here at ten o'clock tomorrow; we depart at ten fifteen for Mrs. Brossard's. Ensure that the muslins are what they should be."

I worked alone, relishing the wide-open workspace, content in the relative silence. I completed the pattern and the simple muslins, and then—as the sunlight pulled away from the studio walls—I treated my surroundings to a much-needed general cleaning.

Before drawing the door closed behind me and locking it,

I stood gazing at the space. It was generous and, even in the early evening's slanting light, blessed with a brightness that I had come to crave since moving into my brother's apartment. I could survive living in that dungeon, shoulder to shoulder with Leo, if I could escape every day to this. The immense space that was Atelier Fiche would be, in every hour I could manage to be here in solitude, mine and mine alone.

5

I stopped at a liquor store after leaving the studio, slipping through the iron-hatched door just as the proprietor was ambling over to lock up for the night, and picked out a bottle of wine. I checked the contents of my pocketbook, then bought a bottle of whisky, too, selecting one with a familiar name.

Leo greeted me at the apartment in his work uniform, the shirt open and belt undone. "Hello, Mig!" There were dark crescents under his eyes. The skin of his face was dull and shadowed. He bared his teeth in a slightly frightening grin.

I handed him the paper bag.

"And hello, Jack Daniels!" he said. "Looks like you got your first paycheck already."

"That could be a while coming. But pour us a couple of glasses and we'll talk. Have you eaten?"

"We'll have dinner at the Alliance Française tonight to celebrate. But first," Leo readied our drinks as I settled onto the couch, "here's to my little Miggy. To the success of your new job. Clink, clink." He touched his whisky glass to my wine goblet.

"Thank you." I sipped.

He tossed back his glass and rubbed his hands together. "Okay, out with it. Story time! Going to be a good one, I can feel it."

I swirled my wine and took a drink, and Leo topped up my glass before I could even set it down. "I went back to Madame Fiche's studio yesterday."

"You did? Excellent. Now you're learning to turn the screw. How much did you get out of her?"

"Nothing yet."

"What did you ask for?"

"She hired me."

"Wait a minute. That's your new job? Working for her?"

"It's a good opportunity. She has a big space and all the tools, and fabric stacked up like you wouldn't believe. And she says I can use whatever I need. I can design there. And she's a rising star."

"Christ, Miggy! You're supposed to be the bloody star in this picture, not the *salope* who stole your stuff. Work for some other designer."

"No one will even consider me. Madame knows me; she knows what I can do."

"She better be paying you good."

"She's going to make me a partner."

"When?"

"Eventually."

"Oh, *eventually*. Well, that makes everything okay." He twirled the cap from the whisky bottle on the table. "You said your first paycheck could be a while. How long is a while?"

"I have to prove myself. That's how it works. Besides the regular work, you've got to bring in clients and commissions and help make the studio a success."

"Goddamn it, Mig. There are loads of jobs for girls now. Good regular jobs, nine to five, punch the clock and cash the honest-to-goodness check."

"Not in fashion. If you're trying to make a name for yourself it can be kind of all or nothing."

Leo poured another whisky and downed it, then went to the shotgun kitchen and came back holding my note. He read aloud: "'I'll tell you all about it when I get home tonight.' Notice something? You called this place your home." He flicked the paper close to my nose. When I didn't flinch, he slumped onto the couch and drank. "That's fine," he said. "Stay as long as you want. But you're going to have to make an actual wage—*eventually*—or start digging into Papa's treasure trove."

"You have a mean way with words."

"I'm just telling you straight. I can't keep us in mink on my own."

"I'll get my own place." How could I, though? I couldn't chip away at my inheritance. I had promised myself (typed it up like a contract, signed it, and filed it away) that I'd use that money to start my own design studio one day. Any other use would "expressly constitute and represent" notice that I had given up on my dream—and on Papa's hopes for me.

"Nah, stay. It's not so bad having you here. Besides, Mother would kill me." He opened a drawer in the side table and pulled out a pack of cigarettes and a Zippo. After flicking the lighter and pulling smoke into his lungs, he let his shoulders relax. His head tipped back against the fraying brocade. He spoke through smoke rings. "At least you haven't asked me where I was last night."

"Where were you?"

"Leaving everything but my body on the poker table." He emptied his lungs with a forceful sigh.

"I can get a second job to help with the rent. I can probably wait tables for Uncle Yannick."

"You think so? Because I'm thinking an 'all or nothing' job is 'all or nothing,' if you know what I mean. Put it this way. If you're ever not here when I get home, I'll know exactly where you are. And I get home very, very late sometimes." He picked up the wine bottle and filled my glass. By the time we left for the Alliance, I was woozy.

As I'm a tiny bit woozy now. But mustn't nap in the airport, much as I would like to. A slack, snoring maw is not quite oh-so-Mignonne-NYC. I could catch a cab home, sleep. Or return to the studio, back to the fray.

Or give myself over to waiting, stranded by rain: unreachable, not at work, not at home, not away. Think through my talk for Expo. Inspiration is like reimagining a garment. Parse the elements, recut the pieces, use from the past what resonates today. There's no backstitching in stories. Nothing can be locked in place.

"Tell me a good one, Miggy." That's what Leo used to say. "Use your noodle and lay on the sauce. Can't remember? Make it up. Can't know? Don't tell me so. Borrow someone else's story if you don't like your own."

6

Consuelo starts awake. The days are like this now: either she is all on, a whirlwind, or she is nodding asleep. Once upon a time, she could not have imagined growing sleepy in an airport. Airports were places of drama: of passionate reunion, of desperate waiting for news, of fears so acute they poisoned her veins and made her faint. She had been in her prime then. In her thirties—for love, not age, is the measure of a woman's prime.

Love and passion—and, it follows then, fear.

There is the problem. She has nothing to lose anymore, nothing to fear. So little to stay awake for. At sixty-six years of age, she lives a quiet life in Paris with her gardener, she writes her memoirs, she sculpts. She makes it her life's mission to keep her late husband's stories alive. One above all: the story of their love. Without her love, he would have been nothing. Without his story, she would be nothing now.

An announcement is broadcast: New York–bound passengers, expect delays and cancellations. In Paris, it is a perfectly sunny morning, hot for late May. Consuelo takes off her cat-eye sunglasses, moistens a fingertip with her tongue, and smooths her eyebrows before approaching the counter at her gate.

The counter girl is putting down the phone. She looks more like a tourist than a representative of Air France, her scarf unknotting, her hat askew. Is she allowed to wear dangly earrings like that?

Consuelo loathes the 1960s. Its out-there aesthetic has left her behind. She asks, "There is a problem with weather?"

"A freak system's stalled over New York. Nothing's moving in or out. Could last a couple of days." The girl chews gum steadily as she checks Consuelo's ticket. "The Montreal flight should be fine, madame. Maybe some turbulence. Visiting family in Canada?"

How they underestimate her, these people. "I have an open invitation from the mayor of Montreal to return to the world's fair. I was a guest of honor at the opening."

"Expo 67?"

Consuelo detests the official, generic name. Expo means only exposition, '67 is only the year. "*Terre des hommes*," she says.

"Well, enjoy. Try to catch Expo, too, while you're there."

An hour later, she has finished a scotch and soda on the plane. She is resting her eyes, settling in for the long boredom of the flight. She would rather face a tempest than tedium—and just as well, for she attracts bad weather like a dog attracts stink. She was born in a cyclone and an earthquake. And a volcano. (As she ages, more details of her birth come to her, each more lurid and surreal.) She used to blame herself for the storms that threatened her husband's planes. She suspected floods in India and mudslides in Mexico were somehow her doing. She was like the quake that had birthed her: her tremors spread wide.

She used to pray that the Lord would relieve her of her curse, but today her powers of disturbance have proven their worth. A freak system stalled over New York! Today of all days, when, according to the American fashion news, Mignonne Lachapelle means to fly from New York to Montreal. To the fair, to a podium. To take credit where no credit is due.

Consuelo, if anyone, deserves the honor. It was her husband's book, his art, their life. Mignonne only used him, and her, and the story Consuelo holds so dear. Consuelo had been planning to say so at Mignonne's presentation, speak up and make a fuss, draw the attention of reporters her way. It is why she chose to fly to Montreal this day.

What fun it would have been! Now she wishes Mignonne would make it to the fair after all.

Consuelo would call off the storm if she only could. She would propel the designer from runway to runway, and cross their fates again. But how?

She had done it before, long ago: drawn Mignonne into her path, into her home, into her arms. What powers Consuelo had possessed then! But how had she done it? How had she set the stage and laid her traps?

She has always been her own best teacher. She settles deeper into her seat and casts her mind back.

In the dim evening light of a Checker cab in Manhattan in April 1942, Consuelo glanced seductively at her companion as she nudged her dark hair into place behind her ears, but Binty paid her no mind: he was practicing the words she had taught him for the night's visit to the Alliance Française. She could teach him a hundred languages! Spanish, French, English . . . though he already spoke English . . . and if she concentrated, probably several more. But there were so many demands on her time. And why should she bother to educate him? He couldn't even summon the decency to look at her. He was mouthing French words as he examined his manicured nails.

"*Bonjour*," he muttered, as though it were two words. Bone juror.

She snapped open her compact and dabbed at the tip of her nose, at her delicate nostrils and charming chin, and at the goddamn hollows below her eyes. Consuelo's supple skin was her South American birthright. It had been the envy of her friends in Paris, and used to make her husband crazy with desire—but already, just four months after her arrival in New York, the city was sucking the life from her skin. She examined the compact's applicator pad. Even in this light, she could see it was yellowing. Just like her! The natural oils that kept her looking so much younger than her forty years were being sucked from her skin and absorbed into the cake of powder. The makeup had lost its delicacy; its pinkish bronze surface was becoming mottled and slick. Even the mirror turned against her. It didn't reflect her beauty. It hated her. It glared.

Her old compact, gold-plated, bought in a tiny perfect Parisian store, had shown her features softened through a shimmering, translucent film. Too bad her husband had deflected it with his arm when Consuelo had flung it at him last week.

It was he who put the dark hollows below her eyes. They would be gone if she could sleep, if he would only let her lay her head upon his furry chest.

She raised her voice to speak to the cab driver. "It's at the corner of East 52nd, with the flags."

"I know it, ma'am."

"Countess," she corrected as the car drifted across lanes. She might have let his error pass if he'd called her miss instead of ma'am.

"Driver," said Binty, "can't you push it any faster? The comely countess and *moi* are dying for a drink."

Consuelo giggled. Thank God for her little lover. He was so carefree compared to the men she had been with in France, especially when it came to his pocketbook. She had only to ensure that Binty was never bored. He was up for any excitement. As long as Consuelo was "happy, titled, and entertaining," as he had said when they met, he would be happy too. She had slapped him once and kissed him twice, and taken him to her bed.

It was impossible for Consuelo to be boring. She had tried it once and failed.

"Are you nervous, darling?" she asked.

"I'm never nervous."

"Tonio's not the violent type. He's probably not going to hit you. Especially not at the Alliance Française."

"Another good punch-up thwarted."

"It would be no joke if he did hit you. He's very strong, you know. He's awfully tall."

"I've seen your husband. Several times."

"Actually, he might hit you. Especially at the Alliance. He's desperate to salvage his reputation there."

"To hit or not to hit: which would you prefer?"

"If you take off your glasses, he might hit you." The truth was, if Tonio loved her he would hit Binty either way; that's what it came down to. Even his detractors would find that noble. Unless, of course, they thought the two men unfairly matched.

"It's too bad you aren't taller," she said.

"I don't need to be tall." He held up his wallet as the taxi waited in traffic.

He was right. Tonio would never win over those who had become hostile to him if he hit Binty. So what if Binty was a *nouveau riche* American while Tonio was a French national treasure? If the expatriates had shown Consuelo anything, it was that neither literary awards nor an aristocratic name could protect a man from the venom of his countrymen. Wealth, on the other hand, was the great magnetic unifier—and Binty was moneyed in fabulous and intricate ways.

As for Tonio, the Germans had blocked access to his bank accounts, which were likely empty anyway. His royalty checks never lasted long. Back when he and Consuelo had lived together in France, they had burned through his checks faster than he could write. And his inheritance? Too small, and long gone. Tonio's father had died young and his *maman* seemed bent on living to an old age. God bless the mother, though: if it hadn't been for her horror at the prospect of a son's divorce, Consuelo's claim on Tonio would have vanished in a court of law. In fact, if it hadn't been for the matriarch's saintly closed-mindedness, they might never have gotten around to legalizing the marriage at all. But now Consuelo maintained every right to demand her share of her husband's heart—as well as his new celebrity.

He had become a phenomenon here, the man the *New York*

Times called upon to explain the nature and vagaries of France, the only modern Frenchman to have his novel on every shelf. How trying it must be to have the Anglos clamoring for pieces of him, while his own elite compatriots seethed with jealousy. His life would be sweeter—and much easier—if only he would return to the bosom of her love.

What communion of souls they had known in their early days! In the stretches when he was not off flying over heathen lands, they had immersed themselves in all-night, wine-soaked dinners with delightful friends. She had insisted they surround themselves with beauty in their every hotel and home. An artist needed beauty: expensive antiques, closets glistening with fine French fashions, exquisite perfumes and cosmetics that were a woman's duty to acquire. Such marvelous times. Consuelo had hoped against all odds to rekindle them in New York.

So much for hope. Tonio had sent a friend to fetch her from the gangplank. True, they had both long since given up on faithfulness, but that didn't excuse a man from the requirement to serve his wife. He had claimed his absence was to avoid the ever-ravenous photographers. And there had indeed been photographers waiting. Before disembarking, she had run back to her cabin twice to check her makeup and hair. Imagine wanting to avoid photographers; it was absurd. It was an outrage that he hadn't wanted to be seen with her at the port—and worse that in the months since her arrival, he had not yet changed his ways.

Did he think she would just roll over and slink back to her cave? She squeezed Binty's knee.

He asked, "You're sure your husband is at his club tonight?"

"He's there." Probably with some fawning Fifth Avenue socialite.

"It would have been a lot easier to invite him to join us at your place. That could be good for some raving and pummeling. I might even pick up a dashing scar or two."

"That's not the point, darling. Why should I stay out of

his way if he's taking his friends out on the town?" The other evening, Consuelo had seen Tonio leaving Le Pavillon with an attractive girl. Even as he scorched his wife's heart, she had felt the tug of desire. "Let him see how it feels to face his spouse's darling in public."

"As opposed to seeing me in the lobby of the apartment, as usual?"

"It isn't the same, and you know it." She kissed Binty's cheek as the taxi stopped. "How do I look?"

"Gorgeous," he said, without glancing at her. He returned his wallet to his inside jacket pocket and stepped out onto the street.

"Driver," said Consuelo as Binty walked around to open her door. "Here's something special for your wife."

She dropped the irritating compact onto the front seat. It never hurt to give to one's fellow man. One day you might need someone to give generously to you.

Consuelo entered the Alliance Française ahead of Binty and walked through the foyer to the members' desk. Behind it, ancient Philippe bent his brittle frame to speak in an undertone to a uniformed teenage boy. His voice rumbled like distant thunder across the foyer. "That's her. She tries every few days. Remember, Monsieur doesn't allow—"

Consuelo interrupted with a clap of her hands.

"Good evening, madame. You kindly grace our lobby again." In this place where the default language was French, Philippe always spoke English to Consuelo. It was a comment on the quality of her accent, she was sure, and proof of his disdain for her Central American roots. More than that: it was just another way these *émigrés* tried to deny that she was the wife of the world's greatest living Frenchman. She wasn't fooled by the stock deference in the old lizard's bow.

Philippe continued. "And good evening, sir. Welcome to the

Alliance Française. Your first visit? You have come for tonight's show?"

"What's on?"

The boy answered. "The Fabulous Felson Singers. They're fabulous just like they say. But if you don't have tickets, we're sold out."

"We will make an exception," said Philippe. "Complimentary box seats. All I require is that you follow me directly to the theater. Only the theater is open to nonmembers—as Madame well knows."

"The Felsons?" said Binty. "You couldn't pay me."

And at any rate, thought Consuelo, we're not here to see a show, but to make one. "We've come for drinks and dinner," she said. "We're here to join my husband."

"And his guest," the boy said, but Philippe pressed a hand on his shoulder, shutting him down.

The old man made a show of studying something on the desk. "Dinner? Then Mr. Binty is perhaps a new member?"

"I am a member," said Consuelo. "Binty is with me."

Philippe looked apologetic. "That is to say, as I have said before, your husband is a member. You are always more than welcome, provided he chooses to sign you in." He put his fingertips together and assumed a sympathetic expression. "I was just telling our new desk boy that our policy is very strict. Members may bring up to three guests at a time for dinner; however, guests may not bring guests. As always, I'm afraid I'll have to ask you to return with a cardholding member."

A sculpture of a nasty Gallic rooster was within reach on the countertop. Its tail feathers would look good imbedded in Philippe's skinny, speckled scalp.

Consuelo spoke to the boy. "What's your name?"

"Carl."

"Stand up, Carl. Look at me."

Philippe raised an unruly ashen eyebrow as the boy scrambled to his feet.

"You know what my husband looks like, Carl? Tall, wide-shouldered? The famous writer."

"Yes, madame."

"Go into the dining room and tell him his wife is here—with her boyfriend—to join him and his lovely friend."

"They're expecting you?"

"My husband should always expect me."

When the boy had gone, Consuelo turned to Binty. "Tit for tat," she said.

"Who's the tit?"

Consuelo began to sweat a little as she waited for Carl to reappear. Before their marriage, she and Tonio had exchanged a promise: if one of them proved to be unfaithful, no longer would they be beholden to each other. In body and soul, if not on paper, they would be free. They had left each other and returned to each other a dozen times or more—but until now, no promise had proven stronger than their vow of unending love. Freedom had always failed to break the bond that was Consuelo's destiny.

When Tonio had almost lost himself—besieged by admirers and flatterers, caught in the quicksand of Paris parties and cafés—Consuelo had been his lifeline, his handhold for his art. When he would emerge for a nap or a clean shirt or a fresh start, she would coddle him, assail him, commission him: demanding five pages of writing for each visit to her boudoir.

Of course other men had loved Consuelo, too. How could they not? She'd been a young beauty, a patient angel, a girl who tried so hard to be good. And always the threat of losing her had brought her husband home. He had turned planes around to stop her; showered her with presents; followed her across seas. He trained her over the years on how to reel him back. A crisis was always more effective than complacency.

She had never made an impenetrable secret of her dalliances. But never before had she resorted to such boldness as this. When entertaining a lover almost under the nose of one's husband no longer amounted to a crisis, there was no choice but to put all at risk.

As Carl reappeared, Philippe said, his voice heavy with implication, "It seems that Monsieur is not in the dining room after all; isn't that right?"

"He's coming out," said the boy.

Consuelo laughed. Philippe disappeared, defeated, probably telling himself he was only leaving to be discreet.

Tonio strode into the lobby, his footsteps firm. "What is the meaning of this, Consuelo?"

She straightened to her full height—five feet, two inches—and looked up at her husband towering a foot taller. There was no one and nothing more exciting than Tonio angry. Her heart might explode with the thrill of it. Her voice rose on the crest of it. "I am allowed to go out! I am not a dog to be kept in a cage!"

Just let him provoke her, and she would drop to her knees, barking and howling. Let him push her to it, and she would grind his last ounce of self-control into the ground. She would feel his large hands on her, yanking her to standing, his hot breath on her face as he shook sense into her and propelled her out the door. The stone steps would scrape her hands and bruise her knees—as Tonio and Binty, made mad by jealousy, exchanged blows over her prone and trembling body. Later, in the weak hours of the morning, Tonio would come to beg her forgiveness and she would collapse like Spanish lace, delicate and beautiful, unraveling in his arms.

But her husband's voice grew low, steady, and cold. "I don't care anymore what you do, Consuelo, or with whom. Only don't interrupt me when I am in an important meeting."

"A meeting! I am not so stupid! Show me who is so important that you can't even give a minute to your wife."

"I am conferring with a general who has come from Washington. He is an extremely busy man. I have only an hour of his time. Good night."

"Tonio, wait!" Consuelo took Binty's arm. "Aren't you going to say hello to my boyfriend?"

"I could say hello, or I could continue to pretend that your friend is invisible, as I have these last few weeks: it is all the same to me."

"How refreshing," said Binty.

The men considered each other.

Then the taller of the two held out his hand. "I wish to you," he said in awkward, heavily accented English, "a good evening, monsieur. But . . . *pas ici*. Not 'ere."

Consuelo said, "Don't tell us where we can or can't go! I'm not your pet lapdog!"

Her lover removed her arm from his. He grasped and shook her husband's broad hand. "Jack Binty," he said.

"Antoine de Saint-Exupéry."

7

I was craning my head to glimpse the Alliance Française as it came into view. It was a square marble building, just two stories high but with solidity and dignity in its design. Its second-floor balconies were bright with flowers. American and French flags hung above the sidewalk and the limestone steps. On the main floor, the soaring windows were positioned to let members look out and to stop passersby from peering in. My father had designed it to elevate its members above petty worries and weariness, into the realm of comfortable intellectual camaraderie and cultural pleasures. He had wanted it to be a place where one could enter and feel removed from the worries of the world.

When I came here as a child, several times a week, it had seemed to me in every way the refuge Papa had sought to shape. He used to hurry Leo and me from home to its lobby, then leave us to do as we pleased. A good part of my adolescence had been spent playing on this building's grand staircase, under its desks, spinning on the stools of the bar, falling asleep in droning lectures, falling in love with sons of the members—and later, when as a high school and fashion school student I had tutored here part-time (English to the expats; French to their children), falling for certain members themselves.

I hadn't been to the Alliance for a year. A long time, but not long enough to become inured to what waited beyond the oak doors. No loved one would be there to greet me; my father had been gone for almost two years. Uncle Yannick was still an adviser to the dining room, but God knew how he could manage that now with his own busy restaurant to run. Leo still frequented the bar now and then, but as for tonight? Full of the whisky I had brought home, he had hopped out of the taxi a few blocks away and sent me forward on my own.

"Order for us both," he had said, "and I'll be right there. Just need to take care of some quick business."

"Here?" The block comprised upscale shops and a small hotel.

"Opportunity is on every corner, if you know where to look."

I exited the cab and climbed the stairs to the Alliance's door. I had been nineteen when Papa's memorial service was held, and twenty-one when I joined Mother in Montreal. Now, at twenty-two, I was living with my brother in a basement, eating his food, taking his only bed. My return to the Alliance was to celebrate a job that promised endless hard work for a boss I couldn't trust—and only a remote chance at recognition. I wilted on my feet.

Buck up: people are looking.

A petite, buxom woman with a fine Latin complexion stood in the foyer. She studied me while her companion cleaned his glasses with a handkerchief. She was perhaps forty, and exotically pretty despite her frown and red-mouthed pout. Her eyes were large and attentive. Her curves, in a stylish, unadorned burgundy dress, had a voluptuousness that American women could never quite convey and that the Frenchwomen of the Alliance would likely spurn as earthy and unchecked. The dress seemed to float along the lines of her body in a fashion I had never before seen firsthand. Valentina, I thought; I had seen pictures of something like this. It was obviously well made. The very craft of it was reassuring.

I could design something like that. If I let myself. I could sew it, too. I could do anything: Madame Fiche probably had a mile of such fabric stashed away.

I approached the reception desk and smiled at the boy who sat there. He looked sweet, but what had happened to Philippe? All those years, it had always been Philippe.

"I'm Mignonne Lachapelle," I announced. It was the first time in all my life that I had given my name at the desk.

"Good evening, miss. May I see your membership card?"

On the wall beside the desk hung a portrait of my father. Below it was a plaque. *Émile Lachapelle, 1882–1940. Visionnaire, fondateur, architecte.*

"I don't have a card. I've never needed one."

The boy shifted in discomfort. "Maybe some other desk boys were more loosey-goosey, miss. But now we're very strict and all that. You need to show a card or come with a paid-up member."

"I have a sort of honorary lifetime membership."

The boy hesitated. "I'm not sure we have those."

Where was Philippe? I said, "I'm Émile Lachapelle's daughter."

"Oh. All righty. So Monsieur Lachapelle is a member?" He checked a list on his desk. "Because if he is, it doesn't look like he's here yet. You can wait for him on the sofa, if you like. I just can't let you in without a member."

I felt ill. I closed my eyes.

I opened them to a touch on my arm. The dark-haired woman was standing next to me. "Darling, don't mind young Carl. I will vouch for you, daughter of Émile—and are you not the niece of my great friend Yannick Lachapelle?"

"I am." I smiled politely, a little on guard. Every New Yorker with the means to dine at Le Pavillon seemed to think that its owner was his or her closest friend.

"You know," said the woman, "I believe you were my husband's tutor last year. He wrote that he was taking English lessons with the daughter of the founder of the Alliance Française. Of course you remember Tonio."

I glanced toward the man who remained standing near the entrance door.

She said, "Not him. My husband."

"Tonio?"

"Yes—de Saint-Exupéry."

Antoine? My guard dropped with my stomach. This woman

was his wife? He had told me they were long through living together, that one of the few compensations for being moored in New York was that she was not here. But here she was. And if she was here now, then surely Antoine was in New York, too.

I barely found my voice. "Your husband."

"I am Countess Consuelo de Saint-Exupéry." Even drawing herself up in proud posture, she was several inches shorter than me.

"Mignonne Lachapelle." I swallowed awkwardly. "How is your husband's English these days?"

"Rotten as ever. Let's go in, and you can see for yourself." Consuelo addressed the desk boy. "We're going to have a drink at the bar in the dining room."

He stood up. "You can't!"

"Tell your boss that you tried to turn away the daughter of the man whose blood built this club. And that Jack Binty and I are her guests tonight." She took my arm with one hand and held out the other for the man with the round glasses and well-fitted suit. "Coming, darling?"

"To spend the night talking about tutoring? Too exciting for me. I'll see you tomorrow."

Consuelo waved goodbye. She turned back to Carl. "Be a little useful. Ring the bartender. Tell him to mix us two very large, very alcoholic Bloody Marys—on the house—and maybe I'll keep quiet about your boo-boo." She waggled her hand at him. "Go on."

I looked about anxiously as we made our way to the bar and settled on our seats, but Consuelo kept up an animated patter, switching capriciously between English and French—the former guttural, the latter speedy and with a grammar that was Consuelo's alone, both languages raspy with heavily rolled Rs. The Bloody Marys appeared. I drank quickly. Consuelo poked at her ice cubes with her fingertip and drilled me on my interests and pursuits, barely waiting for a response before moving to another topic.

She spoke so swiftly it was hard to keep up—and I found myself wondering if maybe my ears were drunk. "So you and your brother are native New Yorkers? How funny! Your father such a figure of all things French, and his children and wife as American as can be."

I tried to explain that my mother was Canadian.

"Then you're a bit of everything, halfway British, too, yes? Me, I am a pure child of my land. I was born in El Salvador. Prematurely, in an earthquake. Of course, you've probably never felt an earthquake. Have you felt an earthquake, Mignonne? This one was like a dervish gone mad! It turned our house on its foundations, spun me into being like a baby genie, and swallowed my mother whole."

I interrupted. "Do you know what happened to the old doorman?"

"That overstretched gecko! He's training the new staff to be as despicable as he is." Consuelo scanned the dining room. Her expression had gone sullen, but now she perked up. "There he is."

"Philippe?"

"Tonio. Over there, at the corner table, touching his forehead. My God, what is he promising now?"

I put my drink down carefully, as though it were my glass that was in danger of spilling over, and not my heart. There was Antoine, in conversation with another man, sitting as he used to sit with me. I had but a minute to take him in—and to do so with the most reserved of expressions, his wife peering at me from the corner of her eye, measuring my emotions as I looked at him.

He was bent forward, listening closely, elbow on the table, two fingers crooked to his temple with a cigarette burning lazily between them, his pinky resting near the scar alongside his mouth. His guest must have said something discouraging, for Antoine dropped his hand to take a draw of his cigarette and leaned back. He looked to the ceiling momentarily, then moved forward, his torso rigid and his expression intense as he launched into argument. I couldn't hear his words, but I recognized the signs: the unblinking gaze, the grip on his cigarette as his hand tapped the table, the lips moving quickly from point to point as though everything he could ever need to express had been laid out in advance in his head.

His mind, like his character, was complex, accomplished, infuriating: it was that of a dedicated storyteller and a natural mathematician, of a highly religious man who didn't quite believe in God, of an inventor of magical worlds and of patented mechanical gizmos, a war pilot who would never take up arms, that of a man whose greatest pleasure was friendship and whose greatest needs demanded solitude. He was a bear who would sooner charm than roar. He didn't yell; he never had with me, except in exuberance and delight. He rarely leveled an accusation without a meandering justification that would come in a pages-long letter the next day if not in the heat of the argument. He was too stubborn—too determined—to give in without solid reason, but he constantly induced himself to keep his mind open in order to learn something daily.

I wondered what he was saying so ardently now. He had too much discretion to center his arguments on personal issues and too much self-respect to pander, though by this point even he might be sinking to unaccustomed lows in his bid to return to the war. After all, he was still grounded, still in New York, after a year and a half.

He must be miserable.

Consuelo slipped off the high bar chair, her wooden heels clacking. "Wait here. I'll say hello from you, if he remembers you."

I turned away before she reached him. If he remembers me? I had thought about him every day.

It was Yannick who had introduced us in January '41. He had dropped by to ask me to give a few lessons to a Frenchman who was in town for a few weeks.

"Fair warning, Mignonne: he's resistant. His publishers want him to learn what he can while he's here. I said we'd give it a shot."

"How bad is his English?"

"I'm told it's better than he lets on. He refuses to use it."

"Sounds like a tough nut to crack."

Yannick chuckled. "That's why I want you for the job. He'll love you. And I know you'll like him. He's older, but it's good for a young woman to be with someone older."

"Yannick!"

"It works in France. And Saint-Ex isn't your typical forty-year-old."

"Old enough to be my father!"

"Actually, even your father would approve. Take a look."

Reaching into his inner jacket pocket, he produced a clipping from the society pages. It showed a man tall as a tree, expensively dressed in what appeared to be impeccable bespoke, following on the heels of a polished blond beauty who was entering a theater door. *The French author, immaculate in a black topcoat and white silk scarf, brandished his ivory cane with characteristic authority and élan.*

Not typical? I could meet fancied-up men like that every day. They were nearly indistinguishable: snooty, smooth, self-absorbed. To the masses, they were caviar; to the Alliance Française, bread and butter. I handed back the clipping. "Not my type. I'm not interested in the least."

"All right, okay." He held up his hands in surrender. "Forget

I suggested it. Take the job and I promise I won't mention it again."

"He's a writer?"

"Famous. And a pilot." Yannick retrieved several books from his bag and stacked them before me on the table. On the cover of the topmost one, an airplane angled through a ruptured indigo sky. "He flew airmail through northern Africa in the '20s. It's a miracle he survived—with the primitive planes back then, and almost nothing known of the land. If you went down, the natives were likely to— But he'll tell you. He has a million stories about the mail routes. And the French Air Force. He flew spy planes until Hitler took France."

The next night, we were on the grand staircase of the Alliance Française when the front door opened. "That's him," whispered Yannick as a tall, amiable-looking man came in from the freezing rain. "Saint-Ex."

Antoine shrugged off his coat—tawny in the dry uneven strips below the arms, but otherwise darkly wet—and draped it haphazardly over his forearm. His suit would have fit him well enough if he had cared to stand straight and still in it, but as it was, one moment the wool hung too loose from his wide, well-built shoulders, then it strained at his neck and across his chest as he leaned and slouched. It wasn't that the size of his suit was wrong or the cut sloppy; it was a fine and fitted suit, yet somehow it didn't fit him at all. He seemed to be poignantly mismatched all over: his feet in their polished leather shoes too big for even his expansive bearing, the hands and long fingers overly broad, the large eyes too youthful and inquisitive for his age.

Antoine removed and shook his hat, spraying droplets that made Philippe jump back in surprise, which made both men laugh. He had a delightful smile, impish, a little shy.

I slipped into the dining room to steady my nerves, leaving Yannick to greet my newest student. A few minutes later, he delivered Antoine to my table—and "Into your capable hands, Mignonne, courtesy of Reynal & Hitchcock."

Antoine pulled a face. "My publishers think they know what's best for me. Sometimes I wonder if they believe I know anything at all."

I blurted, "What *do* you know?"

"Pardon?"

My cheeks grew warm. "Of English, I mean. What words do you know?"

"I can say . . ." He switched to English. "Allo-I-want-a-taxi. I like zee orange and I like zee apple. Zee bread, 'e is good." He rushed through the words with no thought to the correct inflections, pronouncing them as though they were only slight variations of French. His accent was reminiscent of my father's—but Papa had spoken English at a normal speed and with care.

"That's a start," I said. "Let's review *être*. In English, to be. Please speak much slower this time. I am; you are; he is; they are; we are. I am what? You are what?"

Reverting to French, Antoine brushed away the questions. "This is silly. I have no need of English."

"It can't hurt to learn a little of it."

"I am still trying to master my mother tongue. Why do you laugh? In writing, the syntax must be very precise. It is no different than flying: introduce one word too many, a bit of clumsiness, and one may crash. I have no wish to put my own language at risk by habituating myself to another one."

"I'm not suggesting you master English, only that you become comfortable carrying on a basic conversation. My French isn't perfect, but at least I can converse."

"Like a child," he said petulantly, then caught himself. "Please forgive me, mademoiselle. I am a cur. Your French is charming. I cannot believe I have insulted you, and hurt you, and all because I am afraid of a few English words."

I sniffled. "All right. To be. I am what; you are what?"

The extreme effort of dragging English words from the depths showed on his face a little too convincingly; I lifted a hand to conceal my amusement.

He concentrated. "I am 'appy. You are sad. I am a man. I am . . .'ere. You are zare."

" 'I am *here*. You are *there*.' "

"You are zare. You are . . . beautiful." His fingertips touched mine.

I moved my hands to my lap.

"It is what I know," he said with an apologetic shrug.

I tried to glance at him surreptitiously as a waitress filled our wineglasses, but I found him contemplating me. She set down a platter of cheeses and olives, slices of green and red apples and hard pears, hazy purple grapes, and a generous basket of warm, fragrant bread. I busied myself with slicing and arranging cheese. An olive plucked from my plate was rich and sharp in my mouth; it piqued my tongue and made me feel reckless—so I drank deeply and subdued my palette with smoky brie.

I was sitting across from a man who could fly, who had experienced war, whose writing prompted accolades in every country in which it was read, who had lived in barracks and deserts and grand estates. I had spent my entire life on a single path in a single city. My travels had never taken me to another time zone, never mind another continent. And I was supposed to teach him?

The things he could tell me. What was it like to detach oneself from the earth, to know the sky, to approach the sun? My face felt as ruddy as Antoine's looked—but his had been engraved by the life he led. Scars arced through an eyebrow and near one side of his mouth. The skin of his forehead bore lines drawn through worry and weariness. At the corners of his eyes, pale rays were remnants of laughter and days spent squinting into the sun.

Now he squinted at the inquisitiveness of my expression. "What is it you want to know?"

I had stayed up half the night finishing *Courrier sud*, his story of a mail pilot flying from France to North Africa, the very route my uncle told me Antoine had established and maintained. The pilot had flown through the unforgiving night and through the pain of a broken heart. Had Antoine, too, been suffering the pangs of unreturned love? Why else would he have taken a lonely posting in Morocco, where he had written the book?

Reading, I had thought it impossible that the man of the newspaper clipping, in his elegant silk tie and his expensive suit, his hair combed back, his demeanor so at home in this restless city, had lived as simply as a nomad in the desert. But now I pictured him waking in the morning to feel heat rise through the soles of his feet, opening his eyes to a painful brilliance, opening his door to parched winds that stole the moisture from his mouth. I licked my lips. They tasted of salty heat. What had it been like to pass every day in unrelenting silence and sultriness, encircled by shimmering horizons, directionless without buildings or streets? What a torpor, heavy and sensual, would invade the spirit and weaken the principles. Where could one go for relief?

How could I pose a question, any question, without telling him that I felt his heat?

"Is it hot or cold in the sky over the Sahara?"

That first lesson, if it could be called a lesson, had stretched well into the night.

The kitchen had eventually closed, though drinks were still being served at the bar. The waitress had gone home, first bringing to the table, unbidden, another bottle of wine and two plates heaping with fried seafood and potato crisps. English was forgotten. At the center of a sea of empty tables, we ate with our fingers as Antoine told me story after story. He spoke of wartime marvels and misadventures—of falling planes unfurling smoke like the most exuberant of bridal trains; of darting like a fish between streams of fire; of the time he had played a joke on his navigator, lighting a flare port-side to convince the man that the plane was in flames and they had best jump. He spoke of the unwarranted fear of ascending to barely known heights; of failing to connect his oxygen and heat lines at 35,000 feet and minus 51 degrees. He described fingers so chilled they took twenty minutes to close the buckle on a strap, and clocks ticking away hours until it became clear that a pilot would not be coming back. He spoke of descending to a barely lit runway in the night when an obstacle appeared in his path: he pushed the nose down to ram his wheels hard into the ground, bounced over the truck and its terrified driver, and revved his engine to gain the altitude he needed in order to land.

He told me of his experiences in the North Sahara, opening the virgin territory to air postal service for the first time, of his education at the hands of his mentor Guillaumet in the tin barracks that had been the Aéropostale quarters.

"Guillaumet spreads a contour map on the table before my flight from Toulouse to Dakar. There is a lantern on the table. Everything is very quiet beyond our walls and within. Then the flame begins to pop. The map comes alive. First my friend points out a false clearing where the ground is said to lure pilots and hoard their remains. He sneers, but the landing has taken the shape of a Minotaur; I gape in awe."

Antoine pinched the tablecloth to define a path. "Guillaumet says, 'The trail gets very wide just here, after a red-roofed barn, but look carefully; often it is crowded with sheep.'"

His hands cajoled a napkin into a rising series of peaks. "'Here the mountain plays with your compass, so watch that both you and it do not spin like skirts on the stage. There, if you come down, the nomads will find you, but perhaps not until your lungs are drier than your feet and a tenth the size.' He says, 'Best drink well now, Saint-Ex. *Salut!* Just keep everything in the air until you pass this big black mark.'"

The table between us had sprouted salt-shaker towers and

cheese-knife runways. An ashtray that had done duty as a relentlessly ticking clock was overwhelmed by cigarette-butt hands. Lakes and rivers were marked by water glasses and wineglasses, though the latter repeatedly moved and ran dry. Pages pulled from a notebook had been creased into tent-like mountains and crumpled into impenetrable clouds. Other landmarks had been drawn by Antoine's fingertips on the tablecloth: a hut where an old wrinkled man gave him shelter, the place where the trees grew crimson and seemed on fire in the sunset; the pass where a comrade, presumed perished, was finally found.

Antoine had lived his life by such maps, had flown through such drawings for two decades. At my prodding, he spoke of his first flight as a youth; of lessons marked by broken bones, crash landings; how the desert sands and dark seas were no softer, to a plummeting plane, than the bombs that blew craters into his country's churches, roads, and homes. He spoke of silent flights lit by fire, of missions over enemy lines, his aircraft a heaving camera mount, no gun or gunner aboard. His hand moved again to mine, and it was all I could do to pull away.

"Mignonne, do you know how it feels to fly over one's own country and see it smoldering?"

"I hope I will never know."

"I hope that too, for you."

"But to fly—that's something I would like to feel."

"One day you will. Leave the ground, leave your troubles, be alone within the sky. It is something perfect."

"If you don't mind my saying so, you don't strike me as someone who yearns to be alone."

"The solitude of the cockpit is not like that of cities and towns. It's as though all of mankind is holding you up in the heavens. Loneliness is only possible on the earth, among men. I began to know it intimately only when they grounded me." He moved a salt shaker next to its pepper-shaker mate. "To lose one's duty and calling, to have it taken away, this is a special sort of torture."

The bartender called across the room. "Bar's closing, Mig. You folks want anything before I lock it up?"

When I turned again to the table, Antoine was rushing a hand along the corners of his eyes. I could only say, "I'm sorry, we should really end our lesson."

Antoine folded his napkin. "You must tell me something before we part. Your uncle informs me you are a designer as well as an excellent tutor."

"I'm in my last year at New York Fashion School."

He nodded, thought for a minute, then started twisting the napkin into a coil. "You know, Mignonne, just before the Nazis marched into Paris, I sent word to my wife to flee south to the Spanish border."

His wife.

"I instructed her to pack only her official papers and the bare necessities of survival. I should have been with my men. Instead, I hurried to Consuelo to check that she was properly prepared for the ordeal. There were many people making the exodus, and it would be difficult and dangerous. I arrived just as she was about to drive off. I had brought water and many containers of gasoline for her, for she would have a long trip and there would be no gas available at any price." He laid down the napkin. It shifted as it loosened, a snake coming to life. "Do you know what she had packed into the Peugeot, from front to back?"

"No."

"Ball gowns. Minks. Dresses. Hats. The finest creations of the best couturiers of Paris."

The image was disturbing, thrilling.

Antoine scooped up the napkin and flung it onto the table. "I pulled the clothing from the car and dumped it onto the street. Into the mud, to make room for the gas cans. Neither cars nor people can survive on pretty silks."

I was gutted for a moment. But when I breathed in, the breath fed a fire that would not be snuffed. "You make it sound as though I'm betraying my country—and yours—by pursuing a career in fashion."

"I only tell you—"

"You think it's frivolous. Or worse."

"I am just trying to—"

"Fashion is an integral part of a people. When you fought for your country, what do you think you were fighting for? The land? The roads? It wasn't the churches or the buildings—you'd gladly take France back with those gone. You'd take it with the roads blown out. You fought for the people."

"Of course."

"And if the spirit of the people is gone? If everything that makes life worth living were thrown away—then what would be the point of saving the life? You don't fight for the shell of the person."

He sat back, listening, as I continued.

"You tell me about the car filled with fashions and, yes, a part of me is horrified. But think what your wife was doing. Think what any woman does when she picks a nice dress over a few loaves of bread."

He put his elbows on the table. "Please, go on."

"She shows the world, in her own way, that it doesn't matter if the roads are bombed and the gas has all gone into German tanks: she'll live beyond the necessities of life. She'll live in the spirit, in beauty, in silks and minks, because if she's going to live she wants to feel—and not just be—alive."

For a minute, then, we sat listening to the sound of glasses being washed, our eyes on the scant inch of tablecloth separating his hand from mine.

He rose and came around to my side of the table. I stood as he slid back my chair. Suddenly he was leaning in close to my ear. I smelled his cologne as his cheek grazed my hair.

He said, "The sky everywhere is cold, Mignonne, if you fly high enough."

8

It finally occurs to me, a quarter century on, that I had started aiding Consuelo—*Spare your wife's silks and minks, Antoine!*—before I'd even met her. It's eerie how she always knew how to get her way.

9

Consuelo maneuvered through the Alliance's dining room toward her husband. The girl had gotten her into his hideaway. Consuelo had already hatched a plan to make it happen again and again. She glanced back to make sure Mignonne was staying at the bar.

She barely greeted her few acquaintances on her way to Tonio's table. Not that they were friendly to her either. You'd hardly know she was a famous writer's wife. These pretend-elite Frenchwomen were probably used to seeing her husband with any of a parade of girls. So much for arriving in America and taking her rightful place at the head of the socialite table. They didn't even want to let her into the room.

Tonio's brown eyes flitted to her and narrowed. He bent forward for a quick word with his guest before straightening in his chair.

A decent husband wouldn't feel the need to warn his companion of the approach of his wife. A decent husband would glow, not press his mouth closed as Tonio was doing now. But at least he had told the truth earlier: he wasn't with a woman after all, but with a man who was every bit an American general—hard and handsome, and polite enough to welcome Consuelo on his feet and in passable French.

Tonio stood up too, albeit with reluctance. "How did you get in here?"

"I'm delighted to meet you," Consuelo said to the general, holding out her hand.

"Consuelo, General Albertson. General, my wife."

"Madame," said the general.

"Countess, actually."

Tonio's guest said, "No kidding, Saint-Ex? You never told me you're a count." He smiled at Consuelo with gleaming teeth. "My sincere apologies, Countess. Has your husband told you about the fine work he's doing, helping us prepare our invasion to liberate France?"

"I'm afraid he doesn't tell me anything."

"Consuelo, I beg you. Could you go home now, please?"

"I wish I could obey you, darling, but I can't. I've been invited for a drink with a friend of yours."

Tonio looked disbelieving. "Who?"

Consuelo swiveled and pointed. "Your old English tutor. You didn't tell me she was such a pretty little thing." When she turned back to face her husband, he was still looking toward the bar. "You'd like me to reintroduce you, Tonio?"

"No."

"Just as well. She has completely forgotten you."

The general cleared his throat. "English tutor, Saint-Ex? You should keep up those lessons. It could help you get that posting you want, that's for sure."

"My English is good enough."

"He does understand many things," said Consuelo. "Don't try to pull something over on him by speaking in English. Believe me, I've tried!" She laughed. The men did not.

Tonio said, "I know the commands. 'Roger.' 'Clear for landing.' "

"Anyway," said Consuelo, "Mignonne isn't teaching anymore. She's working for Véra Fiche, the fashion designer. Isn't that wonderful?"

The general—such good breeding—did a fair job of looking interested.

Consuelo said, "I'm thinking of making Atelier Fiche my signature look. Of course I'll have to get to know Mignonne and her ideas a whole lot more. I'll be arranging to meet her here regularly to chat."

"Here?"

"You bring your guests; she is entitled to bring hers." Consuelo held out her hand. "Enjoy your stay in New York, General. Maybe I'll see you again at the Alliance. I know I'll see my husband here, if nowhere else."

Back at the bar, Consuelo picked up her Bloody Mary. Such a rewarding evening it was turning out to be. Everything seemed laid out expressly, enticingly, for her taking. Even the ring of condensation on the polished bar looked good enough to drink. Now if Mignonne would only relax a little, open up. She jumped when Consuelo put a hand on her back. "I invited Tonio to join us, but he's completely unenthused. We'll enjoy ourselves uninterrupted until your brother comes."

Mignonne said, "He's been here for a while."

A long-limbed young man was flirting with a table of young ladies near the entrance. Something tough about him. Interesting. The Lachapelles had a savage in their lineage after all, one whose swagger was disturbingly, deliciously, at odds with the manners of the father's club.

Consuelo said, "Jot down your telephone number. I need a new look. We must meet here again so you can tell me more about your work."

In an instant, the girl's expression transformed from dejected to keen.

So that's how it is, thought Consuelo. Fine then—a kindred spirit. Consuelo had ambitions, too. It was always the women who ached with hunger. Especially the wives.

10

The next morning, I walked with Madame Fiche to the subway, the reflections in shop windows of her unbending silhouette making me appear gangly and ungainly.

Taking the subway instead of taxis, Madame had proclaimed, was her newest personal wartime sacrifice. "Rubber rationing," she said, though I suspected it had more to do with cost. "We don't have dog sleds as you do up north, Mignonne. On the other hand, we have culture—such as it is."

Weighted down with two bags filled with fabric shears, thread snips, a tobacco tin of straight pins, a measuring tape, and other sundry tools, as well as the two muslins I had made to the client's measurements as dictated by her former designer, I pointed out the way to the right train.

Our destination turned out to be an old, sturdy apartment with a square black awning that arched over the sidewalk. The haughty concierge had us wait while he checked with Mrs. Brossard, then he sent us to the elevator, where the operator was equally dismissive.

At the client's door, it was another story altogether. A uniformed girl answered with a shy and respectful smile, taking Madame Fiche's coat, offering coffee—which Madame declined on my behalf—and seeing to it that we were settled comfortably in the parlor. Before announcing our presence, the maid scuttled closer. "Madame Fiche," she said, "you are the designer of the Butterfly Collection?"

"Indeed I am."

"I heard it was magnificent, Madame. Excuse my boldness, but if I may tell you . . . I made this myself." She held out the skirt of her simple uniform.

I braced myself for Madame's cruel response. But she took the skirt in her hands and considered it, her seriousness a gift to the girl.

"Very good," said Madame. "Carry on."

The maid beamed and tripped away with a smile broadening her shapely lips.

A moment later, a rotund woman entered, a small white poodle squirming in her arms. "Good morning, Madame Fiche." She bent to release the dog onto the carpet, wheezing softly at the effort, but upon touching the ground the poodle stood on its rear feet, its front paws stretching toward its mistress's sturdy calves. "Tsk. He has no respect for stockings, and no idea how precious they are." She scooped up the dog and nuzzled its nose with her own.

She had inadvertently lifted the front of her dress with the dog; her dimpled knees winked at us.

"It is lovely to meet you in person," said Madame, no hint of amusement in her voice. "I have brought with me my assistant—"

In that moment, I realized that this was Mrs. Brossard, the woman whom I had to fit into the muslin. Even with the generous seam allowances in the larger of the two sizes, there was no possible way.

"—and we have prepared a preliminary garment for the fitting."

"Monsieur Vaudoit gave you the sizes?"

"Indeed he did, thank you. The measurements he provided were . . ." With a glance I saw that she was reaching the same conclusion as my own. "Most generous of him to share. And Atelier Fiche is honored to be chosen as your—"

"Vaudoit is a moron," said Mrs. Brossard. "You tell me,

Madame Fiche, why would a designer show a dress that can't be made? Why put something on a runway and then refuse to make it for your client?"

"I trust you are not speaking of the coat I am making for you."

"I'm talking about a dress, a pretty summer dress! Why do you think I fired Vaudoit? He'll make the dress for Mrs. Mitchell; he told her he would. But I asked first, and he refused to make it for me. See if I ever wear a Vaudoit again!"

Madame Fiche looked shocked. "I have never heard of such a thing."

I began, "Maybe the style wouldn't suit," but the two women glared at me, and Madame's expression was chilling.

"The style," Madame Fiche said pointedly, "would be perfectly delightful on Mrs. Brossard. As would any. However, as we have heard, Monsieur Vaudoit is a . . . moron."

I asked, "Should I proceed with the fitting, Madame?"

The client was shaking the dog's face into her own. "Proceed," she sang out from behind the white fur.

But how to proceed? Both muslins were sized for a woman with a waist. I swallowed my reluctance and pulled them out of the bag. "The size," I began.

"Is based strictly on Vaudoit's measurements," said Madame Fiche.

The client said, "Everything he ever made for me has fit like a glove."

The coat muslin, however, was bound to fit more like a sausage casing. What could I do? I found the larger of the two cotton garments, shook out its folds, and held it up. It looked miniscule in relation to its target.

Now even Madame Fiche blanched. All was silent at first, then a mechanical whirling sound came from the mantelpiece, and a click. A clock struck once with a deep, reverberating gong. The dog in the client's arms squirmed and yipped.

Mrs. Brossard laughed. Madame Fiche forced out a laugh and gestured for me to do the same.

"Ha-ha," I said thinly.

"Ha-ha!" Madame Fiche answered brightly. "Such a lively household! It pains me to have to leave so soon to attend to some dreadful business. However, my assistant will stay on to complete the fitting. I will check on her progress at the studio later this afternoon."

Madame was leaving? The garment would not fit, and it would be all my fault.

The client brushed her hand through the air as if to say, "Yes, yes, off with you," and called her girl—"Celeste!"—to fetch Madame's coat.

As Celeste scurried past to catch up to Madame, I pulled out the measuring tape.

"Put that away!" Mrs. Brossard cried. "My God, how many times must a figure be measured? You designers are all the same! Give me that muslin."

I held it out.

"Oh, forget it," the client said as the dog once again refused to be released. "You put it on. Go ahead: let me see it on you. It'll give me the general idea."

I slipped into the smaller of the two muslins, adjusted the collar, pinned the waist closed, and smoothed the front panels with my palms. Though large, the piece hung elegantly enough from my shoulders, which were overly strong and wide thanks to my father's genes and my year of waitressing in Montreal.

"Good," said Mrs. Brossard. "That's it, exactly!" She squeezed the dog to her ample bosom. "That's what I want. Take it back and make it. Madame Fiche has the fabric already; you have the measurements. You understand I need it right away. Oh, it will be excellent. I have a good eye, I tell you."

Again she called her maid. Then, ruffling the dog's curly ears, she wandered away.

Celeste appeared, a bundle in her arms. "Don't forget your coat, miss."

I was bending over my bag, shoving in the useless muslins. "Thank you, Celeste, but I didn't bring a coat."

The girl glanced back at the doorway through which Mrs. Brossard had passed. "It's yours," she said quickly. "Keep it." She pushed the bundle into my bag and hurried me out of the apartment.

I walked stunned to the subway. Once aboard, I peered into the bag: Celeste had given me a garment of blue artificial silk. A present for Madame Fiche? A simple mix-up? I couldn't comprehend it.

Clutching the bag, I rode to the studio and climbed the endless stairs.

The day had been an exhausting disaster. At this rate, I would never prove my worth. I was unlikely to keep my job at all, never mind collect any pay. I would never make partner.

All I'd managed, so far, was to clean the studio, waste cotton, and lose Madame's newest client. I could cry. Instead, I let myself into the studio and curled up at one end of the sofa, pulling onto my lap a length of herringbone wool that had been draped across the arm. Leo was right: I ought to look for a real job, a way to be useful. I would wait for Madame's return to the studio, and tell her what had happened. Let Madame fire me as Mrs. Brossard had fired Vaudoit. I'd work in a factory: hard but mindless, logical work. It would be a relief.

The afternoon grew old as I waited. The sunlight that had streamed in so clear and bright this morning had dissipated to a haze. In its midst, a blade of white light, reflecting off the panes of some nearby building, quivered on the floor. I watched it tremble, my eyes tired.

It seemed just brief minutes later that an insistent pounding pulled me to consciousness. Madame was crossing the floor, each step as sharp as a hammer fall.

"What are you doing? Get up! Get off the sofa!"

My heart raced in my chest. The sky above the neighboring rooftops held a tinge of pink. "Is it morning?"

"It is night."

"Night?"

"Thursday evening! The day you measured Brossard. I have come to check your progress and I find—nothing! You should have cut the coat by now."

Right: the coat. Madame had left me there, left me to take the fall. Pain gripped the base of my skull. "I didn't measure her."

Madame swore. "Are you stupid? The measurements from Vaudoit were completely wrong!"

"She wouldn't let me. She hates being measured."

"*Merde!* That bastard!"

"I'm sure it was just a mistake on his part."

"Stupid and naïve! He would have known well her resistance to the tape. *Il est un serpent.* He sabotaged me."

Even in my tired state, I knew she was being ridiculous. "Vaudoit has no reason to do anything like that. Clients change designers. It's not personal."

"Oh, it is. Everything is personal. You have not seen what the French here are capable of; you were too long under the shelter of your father's wing. He could have told you, at least, that not one among us succeeds unless the others want him to do so. It is all to do with one's politics: all personal." She perched stiffly on the edge of the sofa. "You see what Vaudoit did to me today. He relishes the chance to break me."

"It's a competitive industry."

"Don't embarrass yourself. I am not speaking of fashion, but of country. Do you know nothing of what is happening under the German Occupation? The French government in Vichy has been working with great delicacy to ensure that France does not entirely disappear. But those who support General de Gaulle against Vichy are blind to the realities of diplomacy and survival; they mewl about collaboration with the Nazis. The Gaullists would lead a fresh invasion of France, spilling more French blood, destroying everything we have retained."

"I know what's happening there. I just don't see how it has anything to do with Mrs. Brossard's measurements."

"Vaudoit must be a Gaullist. It is this, above all, that sets him against me. As a point of honor, he must ensure my failure. I should have seen it. It is my own fault."

Madame bent forward in her chair as though she were in pain—or perhaps her script was written on her low-heeled, black shoes. "And your fault, Mignonne, even more so. You compound the failure, and I must carry it on my shoulders. Tomorrow, I tell Mrs. Brossard that due to your ineptitude, I have been unable to complete her coat on time. I will lose yet another client. You will have taken me, in four months, from *Women's Wear Daily* to a new level of defeat."

My mind was finally coming awake. "No." Fault or not, I would not let Madame think I had failed. "I'll make a new muslin tonight."

She gave me a baleful look. "And waste yet more fabric?"

"It will fit, I promise you. You can judge tomorrow if it's worth going forward with the coat. Go home now, Madame. In the morning, we'll cut the client's fabric. In the afternoon, we'll sew."

When she had left, I found the bag I had carried from Mrs. Brossard's apartment. I laid the muslin and the mysterious blue garment side by side on a table. The cotton muslin coat I had made was crudely sewn but sleekly shaped, its lines elegantly cinched, while the blue dress, though evidently designed for a body-hugging fit, was almost bulbous.

I turned the dress inside out. At the nape was an embroidered satin tag: "Atelier Vaudoit, Paris France, New York USA." Stitched into a side seam was a short loop of soft cotton ribbon. Handwritten on it were a code number, a date (03/42—the dress had been created just one month earlier), and a name: Brossard.

I considered working from the intact garment, manipulating the dress this way and that way on gridded paper to create pattern pieces from its various sections. I had done this sort of thing dozens of times—enough times to know it required a mind sharper and more focused than mine tonight. The alternative was tiresome, but I felt incapable of doing the job any other way. I would separate the garment into its segments, tackling one simple piece at a time.

Into the night, I picked at the seams of the client's dress, my eyes stinging with the effort of finding blue stitches in blue fabric, my lips twitching with satisfaction each time a few judicious snips released three or four inches of thread into my pulling fingers.

Soon, or later—there was no point in marking the time—the sleeves, the bodice, each section of the dress was detached and smoothed, and rested like a blue island on the brown sea of the table. I gathered the pieces without labeling them—I could read their shapes as easily as one reads words—and unspooled a roll of paper.

The new muslin I designed and sewed wasn't exactly as the coat Madame had planned for the client. I had interpreted the form for a woman of girth, drawing the imaginary waistline at a higher latitude, closer to the bosom—a trick that had been employed in the Vaudoit dress—and extending the V-neck lower to exaggerate the vertical effect. The narrowness of the coat's line, a necessity of the times, would skim the client's ample curves without accentuating them; I had planned it so.

When I retrieved the herringbone wool and reclined on the sofa to complete the short stretch until morning, my shoulders were tight, my back sore. My facial muscles were clenched as though I still held straight pins between my lips. But soon enough my lips and my hands fell open, and I was asleep.

11

A couple of weeks later, on a changeable April afternoon, I was hunched over hand-sewing while Madame Fiche sat sketching: a satisfied Mrs. Brossard had requested a dress to match her coat. Madame blew a stray hair off her forehead, her upward exhalation less a solution than an expression of frustration. It was pleasing to see her with at least one hair out of place.

Someone knocked on the studio door.

I could swear Madame growled. "The landlord. Son of a pig." She bent her head lower over her paper.

Pity the man who had to try to squeeze rent out of her.

The knock came again. Madame curled her lip and put down her pencil. "Enter," she yelled without leaving her table.

The door cracked open. "Excuse me."

I stood up so quickly, I almost upset my chair.

Madame Fiche's carriage was perfectly erect as she stood, her hands clasped tightly, the knuckles sharp peaks. "Count de Saint-Exupéry," she breathed. "What a remarkable surprise. Please, do come in."

Antoine had met my eye with a boyish, amused look. Now his expression took on a formal mask as he faced Madame Fiche.

She minced around her table, her hand extended, her fingers arched. "It is such a tremendous honor to make your acquaintance at last, my lord."

Antoine obliged with a chivalrous kiss of her hand. "My wife has been speaking highly of your enterprise."

"Has she, now?"

"Please forgive me my whim," said Antoine. "I wished to see your studio for myself. It is good for the spirit to be in a working space. One's apartment isn't always conducive to creativity. But I see that your studio . . ." His voice drifted off, then rose in excitement. "But what a studio, Mignonne!"

"It is Madame's."

Instantly, he caught himself. His visage was again that of a refined and formal military man.

Madame said, "It is a place for only the crudest elements of our profession. The cutting and sewing; the fight to the death with one's sketch pads. The most important part of our work happens in the salon, where we see our clients. It is there that the magic happens, where even the ugliest of society ladies is given the opportunity to be beautiful."

"I admire your perseverance. I too battle to put pen to paper in a way that, if fortune smiles, might have a chance of withstanding the test of time. But allow me to say, surely this is the sort of studio that brings creativity to life. The openness and the light . . . The light is profound."

It was true. At that moment, the light had a clarity that made me wonder if by some trick I was seeing through the eyes of God.

Madame asked, "Are you searching for studio space of your own?"

"Searching, no. But I do find myself working in a few favorite places where friends are kind enough to indulge me."

Madame put a hand on his arm and said with a coy smile, "You might like to sit with us for a while, and write. It's very jolly to have many creative hands at work."

"He works only at night," I said, then cringed as Madame eyed me.

Antoine's expression betrayed nothing. I thought, I must learn to be more like him.

Madame said, "The space is fine at night as well. I imagine

you would find it inspiring. You should try borrowing it in the evenings, when we are not here. You could have your own key." She tilted her head as though a thought had just occurred to her. "Bring your wife to see our studio! She will know what is best for you. Wives always do. I would be delighted to show her the space, as well as the wonders we create here."

Antoine bowed slightly. "I will let her know. Thank you." He turned to me. "Would you be so kind as to guide me to the exit, mademoiselle? The elevator seems to be broken, and the route to the stairs is somewhat confusing."

He opened the door to the hallway. As he followed me out, I caught a glimpse of Madame Fiche watching from the middle of the studio. Her mouth was set. She was raising one eyebrow—or would have been, if she had had any eyebrows.

Even with his inflexible leg—a souvenir of a crash—Antoine moved swiftly, pulling me along the hallway with his hand cupping my elbow. We reached the stairwell and braked to a stop.

He said, "So you have not forgotten me as Consuelo claims."

I shook my head.

"You even remember my work habits." His smile hadn't changed: it was quick and candid, full of playful mischief. "I'm glad I found you. I scoured the city! I asked your whereabouts of every person I met!"

"That must have been difficult given that you don't speak English."

"My point exactly. My tutor abandoned me."

"My student rejected me."

A pained expression crossed his face.

A year ago, he had told me that he and Consuelo had long since agreed to follow the dictates of their own hearts. He had kissed me—on a studio rooftop, in the back stairwell of the Alliance, in the inexplicably empty foyer of the Central Library, behind a shelf in a musty used bookstore while the aged proprietor napped. He had touched me, his mouth descending to my breast, his hands pushing aside my dress. I had told myself every time that this was all I would allow, that it was enough.

But Antoine bested my restraint with his own. Before I could protest, he would be fixing my blouse, pulling away, apologizing for his thoughtlessness, his recklessness, his distress. If he had wanted to leave me pure, he had succeeded instead in leaving me feeling deprived, depraved, and ashamed.

I continued. "He told me that he, too, was about to leave New York."

"I remain hopeful. The minute Roosevelt approves it, I will join the American Air Force and be gone. My plans have not altered; I only expected it would not take so long. I wish I could say otherwise, but nothing here has changed."

"Nothing?"

There was an awkward pause.

He said, "I should have warned you about Consuelo."

"There was no need. You're entitled to be with your own wife."

"But you're wrong, Mignonne. The need is clear. If I'd known you were back, I would have told you to be careful of her. Look how she has already gotten her hooks into you. She is using you to get closer to me."

I was wary of discussing fashion with him; it had never stopped being something of a sensitive topic between us. But surely he hadn't tracked me down simply to resume our old argument. Last year he had insisted I should be doing work that contributed to the war effort, though at the time the U.S. was still rabidly isolationist; it had not yet been attacked and was eight months from declaring war. He had told me, "With your language skills and allure, you could get into places a man could never go. How can you throw yourself into a fashion career when you could be working for the good of the entire world?" In Montreal, I had begun to ask myself if he had been right. But now I was working for Madame. I was on a path; I was finally on my way.

I said, "Consuelo is not using me to get to you. She's interested in my work."

"She is only interested in things she cannot or should not have."

"I should get back," I said. "Is there a purpose to your visit? Or did you really come just to see our studio?" It wasn't impossible. He used to tell me about his friends' apartments and studios, where his creative juices flowed more freely than in his own home.

"There is something I must ask of you."

"Yes?"

"I am glad to see your career is going well."

He didn't look glad. I said, "But?"

Antoine tucked his hands under his armpits, which raised the shoulders of his suit jacket unnaturally; he looked like a hulking brute. "I wanted to speak with you about the Alliance Française."

"The Alliance?"

"I would like to continue to frequent it regularly. But it has changed. And now you threaten to take from me its last remaining virtue."

"What have I done?"

"You can have your pick of clients, yes?"

Not a single high-worth client had darkened Madame's doorway since I had joined the atelier. Women came with sewing jobs or low-paying, straightforward commissions. Madame had bragged to me of the interest of this or that socialite, but no one of significance had come on board. As for my contacts, only Consuelo had hinted that a commitment might be coming. I said, "Maybe."

Antoine lowered his voice. "Then you will not mind if I ask a favor of you. If you still harbor any affection or compassion for me, I would like you to stay away from my wife."

The hallway was so quiet, my ears were nearly ringing. Somewhere down the hall, a door scraped open.

Antoine peered toward the bend of the corridor. He took my arm and led me down the stairs, all the way to ground level and out onto the sidewalk, into the cacophony of the street and the strange pressure of an imminent summer storm.

"You must think I'm crazy," he said. "The truth is, I desperately need my bit of refuge. The Alliance is not what it once was for me. Its members misunderstand me. The things they say— your father would be outraged. The community has turned on one another with the worst sort of gossip and lies."

"So stop going to the Alliance." Immediately, I regretted the words. God willing, Papa wasn't listening.

"I could not; not simply on account of being maligned."

I nodded. The club needed its members.

"But there is one thing that would change my mind. May your father forgive me, but I will cancel my membership if I am forced to see Consuelo there."

A man had been passing by, pulling a cart stacked with newspapers that were weighted down with a rocking brick. He had clunked and rattled along the uneven sidewalk. Surely I had not heard right. "You don't want to see your wife?"

A playbill somersaulted toward us and pressed itself against Antoine's ankle. The sidewalk beside it sprouted droplets like small dark mouths.

Antoine said, "I have forbidden Philippe to grant Consuelo membership status. Please, Mignonne, you must not let her come with you as a guest." He removed his hat and put it on my head. "I would like to see you at the Alliance, very much so; only not with Consuelo."

Is that what this was about? A rendezvous place for us? Or maybe there were others in his life now, girlfriends he hoped to entertain.

I brushed a drop from the end of my nose and retreated into

the shelter of the doorway. "Believe it or not, I'd like nothing better than to have never seen or heard of your wife. But you're the one who wanted her here. You can't have it both ways. Unfortunately, I'm not in a position to turn down a prospective client. Where would you prefer I meet with her, if not at the Alliance Française?"

Antoine worked the muscles of his jaw. He said, "Anywhere else. Your salon."

"That was a fable Madame pulled out of nowhere. We have no salon."

"Then your studio. It is the perfect place."

"Unless you're a discerning client."

He huffed. "Where do you generally see clients, then?"

"If they're the sort we want, Madame goes to them."

"All right. Fine. Come to the apartment. But come alone; do not bring Madame Fiche."

Drivers were starting to turn on their windshield wipers. A metal handrail just beyond the overhang was growing goose bumps. I ran my fingers along it, displacing water down its sides.

Come to his apartment. Let Consuelo see me mooning over Antoine in their own home. Let Antoine see me humiliated again by my desire.

"You prefer not to?" he asked.

"What do you think?"

"I am sorry if it is uncomfortable to have to make arrangements that exclude Madame Fiche. Only, I hardly know anymore whom I can trust with the details of my life. Every week there is a new scandal at the Alliance or in the newspapers over something innocuous I have said or done. There are some who would be happy to see me disgraced. There are also those who would rather I do not disappoint them."

"Not everyone is caught up in creating make-believe about you. Some of us just go about our daily lives, thinking about our own troubles."

"I don't say everyone or anyone should think about me. I wish people would not. And yet there are articles, and open letters published. Both Vichy and de Gaulle claim positions in my name; they ask the world to judge me as though I were a calf in a fair. I want only to attend to my work and my duties. And to be with my friends. Are you telling me you no longer count yourself among them?"

"All I'm saying is, not everyone is a scandal monger. Some of us are capable of seeing you as simply a man doing what he thinks is best."

He took a deep breath. "Thank you. It has been far too long since I've heard someone come to my defense, and with such a noble statement. I knew you would understand." He held my hand. "I wish to tell you something that I would prefer not become widely known: Consuelo and I do not live together as man and wife."

Could this be true? "She said you were happily reunited."

"You see how she torments me? Since her arrival here, she has been relentless in her machinations to either discredit or ensnare me, even as she flounces around New York on the arms of other men. I beg her to be discreet. Yet she thinks nothing of showing up at the Alliance with her boyfriend!"

He eased into the doorway and pulled out his notebook. "I don't demand that you do not see her, Mignonne. I understand that you need clients, and I realize that Consuelo desperately needs friends. But please, come to the apartment. I have let two units. Consuelo's is on the same floor, but entirely separate from mine." He scribbled down the address and telephone number, tore the paper from the spine, and handed it to me. Last year, he'd been ensconced in the Ritz-Carlton, now he and Consuelo were on Central Park South. "It's funny, you have just returned, and I myself must go to Montreal for a few days. I have to give a few lectures up there. In fact, I would be pleased if you would spend time with Consuelo in my absence. You will visit her in her apartment, won't you?"

Business with one Saint-Exupéry need not have any bearing on friendship with another. Their past was in the past—hadn't Antoine told me that long ago? And see: they didn't even live together. He wasn't really her husband; she wasn't really his wife. Besides, he was a writer, an artist; he was treating me as an artist, too. Artists were supposed to be open-minded, not stuck in traditional expectations. Only an artist could ask without a shadow of hesitation that a girl strike up a friendship with her lover's wife.

Then, too, Antoine wasn't even my lover. Not really, not yet. All that was between us was an understanding: he would abide by my wish to make Consuelo a client if I would ply my trade somewhere other than at the Alliance Française. It seemed reasonable when I thought of it that way. Antoine had a knack for making the oddest things seem quite reasonable.

I said, "Yes, I will. I'll try."

"Please do. Someone needs to keep an eye on her. She tends to imagine the worst when she is left alone."

Madame was still standing in the middle of the studio when I returned. "Well?"

"I walked him out. It's raining."

"You could have told me you are an intimate of the Saint-Exupérys. The Saint-Exupérys, of all people! How could you keep this from me?"

"I tutored him for a few months last year. That's all."

"And the wife? No one seems to know anything about her—except that her closet is said to overflow with Parisian couture. Who is dressing the countess in New York?"

"I know she wears Valentina."

Madame looked as though she had just tasted something putrid. "Valentina Schlee is not a real designer."

Who was, if not Valentina? Her clients were few, but they were as wealthy and as loyal as they come.

"If our main competition is Valentina, we should have little difficulty. We will make it our number one goal to dress the countess. Everyone is abuzz about her fashion sense. If she champions Atelier Fiche, I guarantee that others will follow." She rubbed a long-nailed finger below her lip. "*Le Comte* de Saint-Exupéry is the only one of the lot who has made a strict point of neutrality. All sides are furious that he won't give his name to their flank."

"And that will be a problem for us?"

"It couldn't be better for us. I myself think he is secretly for Vichy—he is an intelligent man—but I have heard rumors that he is a Gaullist, a royalist, a Nazi spy . . . everything but a Bolshevik, and it wouldn't surprise me to hear even that."

"A Bolshevik!"

"The point is, it doesn't matter what they hate him for; all that matters is that he and his wife remain publicly neutral. I assume that is likely?"

"Antoine's very steadfast."

"It's 'Antoine,' is it?" Madame indulged in a smug, sly laugh. "We will make the wife of *Antoine* our showpiece, and no one will have a reason not to emulate her: neither Vichyites nor de Gaullists. I will be the only designer whose clientele is on both sides of the line."

"But people know which side you're on."

"As of today, I am neutral—and so are you. Make sure to mention it when you are next at the Alliance Française."

"But Madame—"

"Why do you fight me? You have access to the richest soil in Manhattan. The expats should be clamoring for Atelier Fiche."

I started closing windows. "What is this salon you mentioned earlier? You said we see our clients there, all the society ladies."

Madame muttered as she pulled fabric from a flat bolt. It thumped onto the table with every rotation.

"What did you say, Madame?"

"I said, '*Laissez-moi tranquille!*' Leave me be! How am I to pay for a salon as well as a place to work and a place to sleep, when you cannot even bring in a sale? Do want me also to buy a membership to your father's social club so I can do your work for you?" The bolt smacked down onto the table. "What is the point of having a bilingual protégé? You don't use your connections or your French to help me."

"My French!" Napoleon Bonaparte himself couldn't force the elegant ladies of the Alliance into the godforsaken stairwell of this building, not unless Coco Chanel was waiting upstairs and holding a fire sale.

"I heard about your recent visit to the Alliance Française. Oh yes, Mignonne; everything gets around. People talk. It is your job to make sure they talk about Atelier Fiche. I made that perfectly clear from the beginning. But did you tell the ladies at the Alliance of your new position? Did you make the rounds of the dining room and encourage the socialites to visit the studio or commission a gown? I heard that you sat at the bar with your drunk of a brother and showed no interest in even one woman in that room. Where is your drive? Where are your connections? Have you or have you not *le sang de* Lachapelle?"

My face was burning. Of course I had my father's blood. That didn't mean I could ever hope to live up to his name.

Madame continued: "Did you see how I entertained *le Comte* de Saint-Exupéry? With just a wise word or two, I had him agreeing to send his wife to visit us. That is how one brings in commissions. When the most celebrated and privileged of wealthy New York intellectuals happens to drop by, one must give him an irresistible reason to return with his high-fashion wife in tow."

"He came because Consuelo and I talked about Atelier Fiche. I was with her at the Alliance before my brother arrived. She said she loved the Butterfly Collection."

"I did not hear that *la comtesse* was with you. If she knows about the atelier, all the more shameful that you have not yet brought her here." Madame smoothed her hair tight to her scalp. "I should be the countess's designer of record. She should be relying on me, confiding her desires to me—not throwing away her money on that pompous Russian fake."

"She loves Valentina's work."

"She also loves Fiche's work; you just told me so yourself. I am not asking the world of you, Mignonne. I don't expect you to bring me all of America or even Manhattan, only the *crème de la crème* of a small niche. Frenchwomen who are starving for real fashion. Women who admired your father, or whose husbands did. You should be able to do that with your eyes closed. Your father knew everyone who was worth knowing in this town; this is the legacy he left for you. It is why he created the Alliance Française: to position himself and his children at the center of the wealthiest, most influential French population outside of Europe."

"You're wrong. He did it for the sake of the community."

"This is what you prefer to believe? Let me ask you, then: how long did it take for your father to make his dream a reality?"

"Twelve or thirteen years."

"A dozen years of nights and weekends working on his project in addition to his architectural practice, instead of spending that time with his children, as a loving father would."

Didn't every father fill his evenings and weekends with work or a pet project of some sort? It had almost been the definition of fatherhood at our home. But as Madame spoke, an uneasiness seeped into my memories. It was true that Papa hadn't always been tied up with the Alliance. There had been a time when he had taken us, his little ones, to the park or to the pretzel man, a time when we'd sat down for meals together every day. What was so important that he let our closeness slip away?

Madame said, "You do not believe he acted in pursuit of profit. You say he followed the dictates of his heart. If so, it's quite clear: a group of rich, elite countrymen were more important to your father than his own flesh and blood."

She placed her hands flat on the fabric and straightened it on the table. Then she picked up her shears, snipped the fabric once at the edge, and, in a swift, resounding motion, tore it into two along its weft.

12

A few days into May, with Antoine expected back at any time, I still hadn't ratcheted up my courage and contacted Consuelo. But at least I'd completed an outfit to wear on my visit. A new outfit could be such a confidence builder. This one had better be.

When Madame left to see a client in the afternoon, I went downstairs and knocked on the landlord's door. In a minute, he opened up and gave me a head-to-toe glare. Deep lines creased his cheeks and his fat earlobes. He held a cigar and a worn fedora in the same hand. "Yeah?"

"I'm from 428, Madame Fiche's studio."

"So?"

"I was just wondering if I could borrow your telephone."

He grunted. "Make it snappy."

I dialed Consuelo's number and kept our conversation brief before pressing the cradle to end the call.

Though I had spoken in English, the landlord asked, "You're French?"

"I was born here, but yes, my father is from France." I started for the door with the landlord on my heels.

"You know it's on account of you people that we're going to war." He pointed his cigar. "Frenchies put their tails between their legs and ran. Now Hitler and his Japs think everyone's a pushover. You seen what happened. Boys died at Pearl Harbor because of you people. Good American boys." He opened the door. "Tell your madame if she doesn't get me the back rent fast, she's out of here."

I hurried from the claustrophobic apartment and was glad for once to step into the dirty elevator. Back upstairs, I changed from my smock into the outfit I had designed and sewn precisely with Consuelo in mind. I headed for the subway, a butcher paper–wrapped parcel under my arm, an umbrella overhead. Folded within the paper was a genuine silk scarf cut from yardage I had found at the studio, the edges of which I had carefully rolled and hand-sewn, a half-dozen stitches to the inch.

At Mrs. Brossard's apartment, I gave the parcel to the concierge, saying, "This is for Mrs. Brossard's housekeeper. Not for the lady herself. Only for Celeste."

He took it, and a tip for himself.

I walked to Central Park and followed a meandering path through it, humming nervously in the rain, half wishing to get lost and be forced to abandon my mission. But the path gave way onto Central Park South, and I found the Saint-Exupérys' apartment just a few steps from Columbus Circle.

A doorman was smoking on the sidewalk. He watched me approach. When I turned in to the walkway that bisected the small garden fronting the building, he jumped into action, opening the door just before I could reach it with my outstretched hand.

The concierge looked up from his desk. "What can I do for you, miss?"

13

On the twenty-third floor, Consuelo listened to the concierge mangle Mignonne's name. "It's pronounced 'La-sha-pell,'" she told him, "not 'Lash-pill.'" And people complained about her French!

In the bedroom, she threw off her house robe and pulled on a blue ski outfit and leopard-print boots. Designers these days were too inclined to produce pap for the masses; all the more so since the government had stuck their fingers into the business. Let the girl get a taste of a true, instinctual, untamed fashion sense. Besides, the ski pants hugged Consuelo's shapely derrière like nothing else could.

"I'm sorry," the girl said when Consuelo finally answered her knock. "You're about to go out?"

"Not at all. Join us for coffee." Consuelo opened the door to reveal her sitting room. The apartment had come furnished, unfortunately, by some stodgy and sincere secretaries—or some such thing—of Tonio's American publisher, women whose selections had been so tiresome and mundane that Consuelo's eyes had bled dry. It had taken her weeks to purge the worst of the furniture and take delivery of a few good pieces, the sort that made a room: furniture worth spending money on.

She gave Mignonne time to take it all in: the expensive modern sofa and chairs, the carefully chosen antiques that she was still in the process of arranging to best advantage, the long clear coffee table bearing a silver carafe on a tray, a couple of half-full cups, the remains of that morning's croissant on a plate, and Binty's open notebook. He sat on the sofa in his double-breasted pinstriped suit and his small round glasses, writing, his knees spread, his elbows on his thighs.

"Remember Mignonne?" Consuelo asked him. "We met her in the lobby of the Alliance. She had just returned from Montreal to conquer *haute couture.*"

Binty glanced up and went back to his notebook. "Great. If there's one thing this city needs, it's another model."

"She was Tonio's teacher."

"Oh, right. The tutor."

Mignonne said, "Actually, I'm a fashion designer. Or I will be."

Consuelo joined her lover on the sofa and linked her arm through his, leaving Mignonne standing. "Remember that name, Binty: Mignonne Lachapelle."

Binty extricated himself. "Minion? As in slave?"

He was such a sharp wit.

The girl said, "Mignonne. It's a French word."

"Meaning?"

"Pleasant."

Consuelo corrected her. "Charming. Delightful. A pretty little thing. And isn't she just?" She patted the sofa beside her. "Sit, Mignonette."

Mignonne chose a chair to Consuelo's left, low to the ground, with a simple dark iron frame and white leather cushions. It looked good with an attractive girl in it, especially one dressed in such an understated, refined ensemble—a ravishing ensemble, actually; deceptively simple. And the choice of chair put her and her outfit on eye level with Consuelo for a change. Smart girl. Worth a closer trial.

"Mignonne is a girl of many talents," said Consuelo. "A student of fashion. A deputy of her father's esteemed cultural club. A former teacher." She curled her hand into a loose fist and clicked the ends of two long, pastel-green nails against each other. Watch the girl carefully now. "And perhaps a *petite amie.*"

"English," said Binty.

"Girlfriend." As if he couldn't tell that by looking at Mignonne—those outrageously blue doe eyes, the unconscious grace with which she moved. Tonio must have been half in love with his beautiful tutor. But Mignonne, sitting so composed in the low chair, hadn't reacted to the suggestion. Maybe he hadn't been. Or maybe she had rebuked him. How dare she rebuke him? Only Consuelo understood how fragile and insecure Tonio could be.

The girl was quieter today than she had been at the Alliance; even somber, without the excitement with which she had told Consuelo about her prospects with Véra Fiche. But she was still guileless, still unguarded. Those eyes. A bit of sadness suited her. A woman was more attractive when her pain rose a little to the fore.

14

I focused on sitting up straight in the low chair. My pale gold dress and its matching jacket each wrapped across my front to form a collarless V neck and would gape in a most revealing way if I slouched. I had telephoned Consuelo, and had come all this way via Brossard's and through Central Park without arriving at any conclusion on how to make my pitch. If I had no words with which to sell Atelier Fiche, at least I could try my best to do so using the clothing on my back.

Consuelo was continuing her report to Binty. "Tonio says she was a good teacher. But he's through with all that. They're just friends, is what he says. He tells me they have barely spoken since her return."

"The man is in another country, after all."

"Before that, Binty. What a pest you are. Tonio is a paragon of self-control, or so he tells me: too busy writing and lecturing and meeting with his endless generals to even think about *l'amour*! His poor darlings. Up and down Manhattan, all the beautiful girl toys are weeping into their satin sheets."

"Look who's talking," said Binty.

"Oh, yes, I weep too, now and then. But I have my consolations." Her gaze swept over me. I was listening, trying to make sense of her claims and to balance them against Antoine's insistence that his wife told lies. She had a way of talking that sometimes bounced off my ears or confused my thinking; it took far more concentration to follow her unique logic than it did to listen to her clear illogic. Besides, my mind was wandering: I kept wondering whether Antoine's apartment was as magnificent and stylish as this one.

Consuelo yanked my focus back. "Why are you here?" she asked coldly.

It was an interesting question. How complicated the answer could be. "You said you like the work of Atelier Fiche."

Consuelo looked away, toward the Central Park view. Though the rain had stopped, the overcast sky was heavy and dark, the bulky clouds cumbersome.

Was I boring her? Consuelo had seemed glad to have me there when I first arrived, but now—should I leave?

I thought, I'll just stand up and go.

But instead, Consuelo rose. She walked to the wide window, the sway of her hips exaggerated by the clacking heels of her ankle boots, the swishing of her nylon pants. I had never created something quite so form-fitted, so blatantly, purposefully gauche. Madame Fiche would have a tantrum. Yet, on Consuelo, it worked; it was irreverent and fun.

Or, at least, it had seemed fun before this sudden change.

"I like Atelier Fiche, and you are with Atelier Fiche," she said. "Blah blah blah. What of it?"

Binty said, "The minion wants your business. Isn't it obvious? Here comes the spiel."

Without turning around, without trying to catch my eye in the reflecting glass expanse, Consuelo commanded, "Get up."

Was she talking to me?

I looked at Binty. He closed his notebook and crossed his legs. I stood, and immediately wanted only to disappear. But Consuelo had turned; she looked me up and down. She motioned with raised fingers: Come to me.

I tried to cast myself into the bodies of the models I'd seen in fashion parades and in the pages of *Vogue*: hips forward, walk a line, pose with front foot turned suggestively out.

I forgot about Binty, I forgot about the lushness of the apart-

ment and the vertigo-inducing view. I saw only the calcula-
tion and commanding desire in Consuelo's eyes. With careful
posture, with unhurried, even steps that belied the choppi-
ness of my breath and the racing of my heart, I crossed the
parquet floor.

15

Nice.

Consuelo was tempted to make the girl turn around and do it all over again: watch her beguiling movements from the back as she retreated, savor again the languid ease with which she approached from across the room. It had been a long while since she'd had someone she could play like a Pinocchio. Binty was mostly amenable to her whims, but only when it suited him. He was his own man, with his own caprices.

"Do you know why I adore Valentina?" asked Consuelo, letting Mignonne remain standing before her, ready for inspection, beginning to tremble a little on her feet.

The girl asked, "Because of her draping?"

"Because she appreciates the body. Not as a receptacle for color theory or formal construction techniques, but as the most raw and intimate thing that exists in nature."

Oh, the girl was a much better listener than Tonio when it came to discussing design. For him, concrete details existed only to convey the abstract, to vault the reader to some higher or inner realm. The man could write, but he was no sculptor or designer. Just try to tell him about the feel of a fabric, about the way it communicated with the skin. This girl, though, look at her hang on Consuelo's words! Such concentration and anticipation. This was why Consuelo loved to instruct. She should have been a teacher! Not a stuffy professor, though; a mentor.

The first rule of mentorship was to discompose one's most self-possessed student.

Consuelo went on. "Valentina works with only the most exquisite, most sensual fabrics, and shapes them with the sparest of seams. There is no interfacing, no padding of the shoulders, nothing to obscure the beauty of the material or the woman on whom it is draped. When I speak of real design, this is what I speak of. One can only submit fully to it. Under a Valentina, one must wear nothing, only bare skin."

The girl's cheeks had grown flushed in the centers. Now a delicate rosiness sprung up on her chest, within the valley of that deep, layered gold V.

Very nice.

Consuelo touched the edge of the fabric that crossed the girl's chest, steadying the hem, her cool fingers sensitive to its trembling and to the warmth of Mignonne's skin. She thrilled to imagine the emotion that would overtake Mignonne if she were to nudge the fabric aside. Her fingers itched to provoke it. She said, "Don't be alarmed, darling. We are daughters of Eve. We were made to live naked, to take pleasure in one another. Clothing is an aberration. It's a punishment from the Lord."

Binty stretched and yawned.

God, he was irritating. He knew nothing about fashion, or sensuality, or the intricacies of sex. Rut like a chimpanzee, that was all he knew. Not that Consuelo minded some rutting now and then. Better that than nothing. But still, a woman of her beauty, her life force, her drive, was entitled to some variety. Consuelo's tastes ranged beyond the simian and the silver dollar—though the ready combination had its obvious appeal. She was a woman of refined and diverse tastes. And what one appreciates, one should pursue: it was a duty to art and soul.

Consuelo asked, "Did I tell you about my earliest foray into fashion, when I created the most beautiful dress in the history of the world?"

Mignonne shook her head. Her hair gleamed.

"It is precisely why the Butterfly Collection caught my eye. I was just a child, as wild as the tropical forests of Central America. When the cook had her back turned, I snuck into the pantry and stole an enormous jar of honey. I took it into the forest and shed every stitch of my clothing, leaving it on the ground for the snakes and the rats. Then I ran through the trees until I found a patch of sunlight that tunneled down from the canopy. I stood there"—she trailed her fingers through a strand of Mignonne's hair—"as you stand before me now, and let the honey drip over every inch of my body. I can still feel it oozing down my shoulders and the tender buds of my chest."

She laid the lock of hair between Mignonne's collarbones. "I ran through the forest, dripping and sticky. With every step, a dozen butterflies alit on my skin and stayed there swaying, riffling their wings. When I emerged from the darkness I was wearing a brilliant garment made of shimmering butterflies, of every size and color you can imagine."

Binty guffawed. "Honey? Sure."

Mignonne said, "And that's why you're so sweet."

Spunk. Where did that come from? Fickle bitch.

16

I tried to keep my eyes and focus trained on the view, over Consuelo's shoulder, as she inspected my outfit. I tried to not read too much into her touch. I tried talking myself through it, to distract myself. I made myself imagine what it would be like to live here, twenty-three floors above the city, Central Park unspooling endlessly below. Just let Consuelo do what she must, I told myself. Let her take her time. You did the work to make this piece as perfect as possible; do nothing to stop her from discovering that for herself. I told myself it was no different than how a designer handled a model: objectively, hands on fabric, unintentional fingers on skin.

Consuelo fingered the fabric of my unlined, collarless jacket where it crossed my chest on a diagonal, following the line down to the single covered button at the left side of my waist. "I should have taken your jacket at the door. I'll take it now."

Deftly, she undid the button and held the coat open. It slid from my shoulders. Under it, I was wearing a matching, sleeveless dress, a narrow wrap style that mimicked the lines of the cover-up.

Underneath that, almost nothing.

I knew the tenets Valentina imposed on her clients. I had dared myself to create an ensemble that would justify following them myself. But it was one thing to walk in a veil of steady rain, with an umbrella held low and a parcel pressed against your front. It was another to stand inches from a client, from someone as curious, sensuous, and bold as Consuelo, with only a swath of silk like a watercolor wash separating the skin of your breasts from your interrogator's eyes and hands.

I willed my shoulders to ease down, my arms to hang loose and relaxed at my sides. I told myself to learn what I could from Consuelo's expression as she studied the design.

A second time, she ran her hand from the top right to the bottom left, now turning the edge to assess the width and bulk of the hem. The light-woven silk faille yielded to her touch.

Her face softened as she handled the fabric. She seemed to lose her hyper self-awareness as she gave over fully to the experience of touch.

"You mentioned that you make art," I said. "You're a sculptress?"

Consuelo looked up, surprised. "How did you know?" Her brown eyes narrowed. "Did Tonio tell you?"

"I asked because of how you use your hands."

"How do I use them?"

"Like an artist with clay. How a writer uses words."

"Oh God," Consuelo laughed. "With agony?"

"With sensitivity and confidence."

"You really haven't been talking to Tonio, not if you think writers feel confident as they work."

"I don't know about writers, but I know what it's like to be someone who works with her hands."

"You do indeed. Your work isn't like that of an apprentice. Not at all."

She placed her fingers on my shoulders and slowly spun me around until I was looking at Binty's profile. He paid us no regard. He'd put his notebook aside to read a newspaper. Through the supple fabric, I could feel Consuelo's touch on the nape of my neck, on my spine, and then on the small of my back. Her hands moved to my sides and probed for the seam allowance, testing the fit. Then her palms slid down my rib cage, igniting a thousand nerve endings as they travelled.

I swallowed a gasp.

Consuelo's fingers curled around my torso and slipped down until they rested on the bones of my hips. She said, very close, "The draping here"—her fingertips pressed—"is superb."

"Thank you," I said, my voice uneven.

Consuelo chuckled softly and breathed a word into my ear: "Brava." Then she released me, moved past me, and rejoined Binty on the sofa. "There is no label at the neckline of your dress. Your ensemble is, of course, designed by Véra Fiche?"

I hesitated. Madame had never even seen this dress.

"Naturally," mused Consuelo, "you wouldn't try to woo a client wearing anything else. A countess, for example, can't be expected to wear something some unknown assistant thought up."

"Of course."

"I admit I'd no idea Atelier Fiche had such finesse."

"But now that you know . . ."

Binty flung his pencil over his shoulder. It hit a wall, bounced to the floor, and rolled to a stop. "For God's sake, spit it out, Minion."

"Would you like to come to the studio and see what else we've been working on?"

Binty applauded. "Finally. Okay, Consuelo, say yes and put the thing out of her misery."

"As you wish, darling. Mignonne, tell your boss I'll visit the studio sometime in the next few weeks."

"Ta-da," said Binty. "Mission accomplished." He took his pencil from my outstretched hand. "Ciao, pleasant one."

I pulled on my jacket and fumbled with its closing as I walked to the foyer.

Consuelo waggled her fingers goodbye. She was barely repressing a laugh.

17

Rainstorm over for the moment, the street was fresh and clean. I crossed to Central Park to gather my thoughts among the trees. The park seemed to be opening up, its benches washed of grit, its oaks and roses still silently soaking up the welcome drink. I could walk its paths again, or I could walk the sidewalks for a while; the last thing I wanted now was to go underground.

I chose the streets. Let people look at me, look at my outfit, at how I walked. I had done it! With hardly a word, I had earned Consuelo's commitment to visit the studio. Madame could do things her own way, sell fashions through smooth-tongued guile; I might never master that skill, but today I had proven there could be another way. Consuelo would come to the studio sometime in the next few weeks.

What on earth could we show her? Had I come up with anything, beyond the dress I wore now, that I'd be proud to call my own? I did a mental inventory of my sketchbooks as I walked. The drawings melted together, one forgettable piece into another. Was there nothing striking and memorable, nothing that could make Consuelo leap up and take notice?

I replayed the events of the last hour: how she had been captivated, even captured, by the simplest of garments, an unadorned wrap. And yet this same woman had loved the ornate Butterfly Collection. How much of it was about the clothes, and how much was about how they were worn?

I emerged from the park and set off down the sidewalk. People were standing in open doorways, sitting on stoops, anything to try to catch a fresh breeze. I was walking past a shoe store when a few buildings ahead something white tumbled down from the sky. It landed on the sidewalk with a muffled thump.

A pillow. I looked up. Three stories up, two young boys were peering from the rooftop, guffawing. At street level, a door flew open. A boy in bare feet and pajama bottoms scrambled out. He grabbed the pillow and held it at arms' length as he stood catching his breath.

"We're going to sleep on the roof," he said.

"Isn't it wet up there?"

"Who cares!"

What was stopping me from pouring out ideas? How had I done it before? Week after week, as a student, I had produced and produced. Where had all those concepts come from?

I needed a trigger, something strong and distinctive. Did I expect something to fall like a pillow from the sky?

The rain started and stopped twice by the time I made it back. I was sodden. In my flustered state, I'd left my umbrella in a stand in Consuelo's lobby. I hoped to slip into the studio, grab a garment from a rack, and get changed in the bathroom down the hall without too much attention. But when I entered, Madame was there in a black raincoat, hanging her key on a nail by the door. Her stark brow lifted and furrowed.

"I've been at the Saint-Exupérys'," I explained, beginning to shiver a little. "I have good news: Consuelo said she'll come to the studio to see our work!"

"This is a revelation? Did I not already arrange this through *le Comte* de Saint-Exupéry?" Her lip curled as she took in my clothes. "You are completely soaked to the skin."

"Not quite." I looked down. The fabric was clinging provocatively to my arms and thighs. Even the extra layer of the jacket couldn't completely obscure the form of my nipples pressing against the dress. I crossed my arms.

Madame spoke in a tone of severe distaste. "One generally

wears more than a nightgown to visit a count and his lady." With two squeamish fingers, she lifted the end of my damp sleeve. "What is this?"

"I made it with the countess in mind. I was thinking we should develop a couple of variations to show her when she comes."

Madame dropped the sleeve as though finding it repulsive. "You tell me she likes clothing that is theatrical, then you try to entice her with this? You are wearing"—she moved her hand through the air as though struggling to find words—"a sheet! You are like a child who takes from the bed a sheet to wrap herself and pretends she is a goddess of ancient Rome."

"It's faille."

"I know it is faille, and from my own supply. *Vous pensez que je suis stupide?* I don't care if it is gold leaf. You haven't made something notable of it. You've just hung it from your shoulders."

"That's not true. I worked very hard on this outfit, and I learned a lot making it. I designed it with hardly any seaming. I cut the jacket on the bias—"

"I see very well what you did. You minimized and rolled the hems. You completely eschewed interfacing and lining and other critical elements. Do you think I could not do this if I wanted to? You haven't invented anything new."

"No, but I don't believe it's widely done."

"Of course not! Who would wear something like this? A lady needs a properly structured garment—and properly structured undergarments," she added pointedly, "if she is to feel properly dressed."

"It is highly structured—in a different way. The fabric does the work. You have to see how it moves when it's not wet. You'll love how it drapes. You're the one who taught me to pay close attention to how fabrics perform."

"It is one thing to understand the idiosyncrasies of a textile. It is quite another to be under its thrall. One doesn't sacrifice dignity for the feel and drape of the fabric on the skin. A lady does not get dressed in order to feel naked."

Maybe that was true, I thought, but was that so different from dressing to feel like a woman?

We had argued so long at the door that the damp fabric had begun to dry and anger had heated me through and through. I stood sketching at the closed windows, my drawing board propped against the long ledge. I would rather catch influenza than give Madame the pleasure of seeing me slink off to change and come pussyfooting back in something she deemed respectable.

The fabric, as it released its dampness, lifted away from my skin. It shifted as I drew, even as I filled my pages with harsh and rigid strokes.

Occasionally as I swiveled to pluck a piece of conté from the box on my worktable, I caught Madame watching me. Once, I heard her sigh.

Eventually, Madame swore quietly, got up from her table, and disappeared into the depths of the bulging racks and overstuffed shelving units that crowded her end of the studio. I could hear her restacking things. I heard her sliding wooden crates. When I paused in my sketching I thought I could hear her fingernails rub against cardboard as she dug through boxes. In the long pauses between movements, I pictured her running her hands over fabrics, lifting them to test the weight, feeling their movement in her grip and on her wrists—for I didn't believe that even Madame could escape their thrall. Surely no one becomes a designer without a sense of wonder and want.

Madame Fiche emerged with a rectangle of white material folded neatly in her arms. She crossed the studio to stand on the other side of my worktable and held the fabric out to me. "Here."

I wiped my hands on a rag. "What do you want me to do with it?"

"It is Japanese silk chiffon," said Madame. "Perhaps the last piece in all of New York."

"And?"

Madame cursed, low and filthy. She grabbed the top layer of fabric, lifted it, and in a swift and forceful motion snapped the entire yardage into the air.

The power of her movement passed like a wave through the weave, sweeping it open in a rippling flash of white. The silk captured the air below it and floated down, shimmering, falling as silently as snow, blanketing my table and streaming from it onto the pitted floor. Through the fabric on the table rose the form of my scissors, the screw at the joint of the scissors, my box of conté, the sticks of conté left lying outside the box, my key, the hole at the head of my key.

The chiffon was so delicately woven that it took on the finest imprint of whatever it touched, clinging like a lover to a lover. Yet where it draped from the table, it seemed made to caress only the air and to seek only its own soft folds.

"Oh," I breathed.

Madame took several steps back. "*Eh bien*. Make something." She crossed the studio, pulled her raincoat from the hook, and left.

The studio was magical in the moonlight; I hadn't seen this before.

I had put down my sketch pad when the rain finally ceased for good, and opened the windows to let in the night air. It drifted in, past me, releasing the faille from my torso where the postures and perspirations of work had pressed it to my flesh, reminding me of that afternoon's soaking and of warm honey on Consuelo's skin.

I stretched my aching arms, left my table to extend my legs, and took in the smells of my workplace as I walked: the heavy scent of humid wool, the acerbic edge of chemical dyes, the decades of thick, oily lubricants that permeated the wood and the air.

My table was directly across from the door. Behind my chair was the long bank of windows, almost floor to ceiling, divided with bare metal frames. It was here that the silver moonlight came in. It bent over the radiators below the ledge, curled over the back of my chair, and reflected in the varnish of my table-top. It arced across the floor and flowed as far as the sofa and the upholstered chairs, leaving Madame's worktable on the other side of the studio in leaden darkness.

Somewhere in the depths of the building, rhythmic sounds of machinery changed their tune: a low background rumble was joined by a circular rise and fall. If I were a dancer, I would move to such sounds—iron cogs and creaking gears, turning belts, pistons rising and falling, toiling away.

I crossed the moonlight to my table, to my sketch pad. I thought of Antoine lifting off in his envelopes of silver metal, mere air holding the churning, laboring motors in the sky. I thought of Consuelo's slender hands on my sheath of silk, the sliver-thin chrysalis between my body and the world. I thought of the body, of my own body, and I drew through the hours of the night. The paper was damp under my fingertips. The pencil was slick in my hand.

18

Waiting, like being kept from one's calling, can drive a person mad. Here at the airport, it has driven the mother and twins away. Three hours in, I feel like I've moved up three spaces in line. There is no line, of course; there is no flight. But if a single plane taxis up to this airport, by God, I'm going to get on it. I wasn't even sure I wanted to go to Expo; the whole idea of a world's fair makes me sad; but now that the heavens and Pan Am try to stop me, I will not allow the chance to be taken from my hands.

Two young sweethearts peel themselves off the floor and off each other. They mosey over (all the time in the world) to take the empty chairs, chatting drowsily in Quebecois accents. Their parents will be worrying. Even my mother still frets.

In New York, I had grown up largely out of her sight, growing unbridled—but not out of control—at the Alliance. In Montreal I outgrew Mother's capacity to understand me. For the first time, I was something of an expat: lonely, reeling, grieving, and aggrieved. In the mornings, I would sit with my father in the cemetery. In the afternoons, I would join Mother for meager biscuits and tea. I came to live for the evenings at the café in Old Montreal, waiting on tables, pleasing customers, moving, always on, always wanted. All eyes on me.

In the darkness at the end of my shifts, doors locked, tables clear, I would remove my apron in the clattering, spattered kitchen, and the dishwasher—a wounded veteran at thirty—would tell me tales from the battlegrounds. Soon all but the final threshold of my chastity was being eroded by his chapped hands.

Mother knew I had talent but would not have been disappointed to see my ambitions pushed aside for a normal life with a good man. But now I was not only unmarried but undomesticated. In Montreal I was becoming unfocused, uncontrollable, un-Canadian. Better if I'd stayed in New York, where it wasn't as frowned upon to see a girl act so free. By the time she brought home *Women's Wear Daily*, Mother had already asked when I might be ready to leave.

It had been weeks since Antoine told me he'd be going to Montreal for a few days. I sat near a window at the Alliance Française, staring out at the northeast corner of East 52nd and Second Avenue, having a drink. Was this what it had been like for his wife when his plane had been late returning, when his radio had gone silent, when the missions he flew took him halfway to his grave? All the while knowing that—no matter how great her despair, how many her tears, how her heart grieved to imagine her husband lost or dead—if he were to be found, if God guided him home, he would return undeterred to the cockpit again.

No wonder Consuelo was a mess: tormenting Antoine while professing her love, playing at a simpler life with Binty, amusing and soothing herself with fashion and (I took a long swallow of wine) with me.

I had been dropping by the Alliance regularly after work. Sometimes I came with Leo, mostly I arrived alone. I had to be seen by the membership; I needed to be remembered and respected here. But the conversations I had initiated had done nothing to advance my career. The expats couldn't think of me as a fashion visionary: I was my father's little angel, a good little teacher, the girl Émile had carried on his shoulders, who had steered him by the ears.

Little girl. They wouldn't think that if a certain famous author, an older and discerning man, could be seen dining with me, *tête-a-tête*—not to conjugate the English for *avoir* but to collaborate on our own translation of *amour*. Little angel? If they could see what I used to get up to with Antoine!

The room grew warm. I crossed my legs at the knee.

Usually these days I ordered a first drink and jotted notes about my day to look busy while I waited to see if Antoine would show up. Sometimes I ordered a second or third while I watched East 52nd Street. Antoine could steer clear of the Alliance to avoid me, if that was how it was, but eventually I was sure to glimpse him visiting his friend Bernard Lamotte.

I had been to Bernard's once, a year ago. By then, my meetings with Antoine had become more frequent and less productive, and I had become progressively more impatient for the next. Often we would take our lesson outside, strolling the streets. We would watch pigeons crowd against each other in the squares, Antoine giving each bird a name and personality, speaking their parts in pigeony tones. Once he cajoled me into a game of hide-and-seek with the squirrels in Central Park. I squeezed some English into each of our adventures. After all, I was his tutor; I could hardly pretend our outings were dates—until Antoine asked me to accompany him to an upcoming soirée.

"How can you say no to one of Lamotte's parties? He is the sweetheart of the artistic community here. Your own uncle has commissioned him to create murals for his restaurant. You must meet him. You will like him; it is impossible to dislike Bernard Lamotte. You will come?"

I hesitated. Should a tutor go to a party with her student?

"I shouldn't push you," said Antoine. "Forget I asked. We will keep our regular lesson. Let's meet at the side entrance."

On the appointed evening, at the Alliance's East 52nd entrance, he hooked my arm and led me directly across the street. We stood in front of a graceful old building with a restaurant on the ground floor.

"We're having our lesson over dinner?"

He grinned. "We are going above the restaurant, to Le Bocal."

The Fishbowl?

"It is what I call Bernard Lamotte's studio. It's just here." He pointed out the name beside the door. "The party has started."

"But I'm dressed for teaching."

"Then come as my teacher. You would do me a service to translate at my side. So many of Lamotte's friends are American." His argument would have been resistible if not for his boyish pout.

The door at street level was not locked. Antoine led the way up the narrow staircase and around a bend. Emerging into the finely conceived main room at the top of the stairwell felt like entering the outdoors: the space was so harmoniously designed as to seem a creation of nature. The ceiling was high, the walls white. At the building's southern face, three soaring arched windows crosshatched with metal frames caught the oblique lights of Second Avenue in their panes. Everywhere I looked, there was another half-hidden pocket of space: the juliette balconies with wrought iron details revealed through the two open windows; the intimate mezzanines along each of the brick side walls—internal balconies where one might sit to take a long, quenching view of the art that lined the walls. Through the windows I studied the view of the Alliance for a while, then turned to examine the back of the room. To the right of the door through which we had entered, a wide central staircase led to an open second level capped with a large skylight. Spaces layered here, too: an elevated walkway rimmed the floor, leading forward to the mezzanines and back to corner stairs and a shadowed door. As Antoine came up behind me and put a hand on the small of my back, I caught a glimpse of yet another room, on the far side of the grand staircase: its door was being closed on the sight of a man kissing a woman, her head bent back, her throat arched. It could have been a picture, or real, or a projection of my own absurdly hopeful heart. I took a glass from Antoine. We touched goblets, red to red, and brought them to our lips.

The party was in full swing. Jazz swooned. Men and women mingled and laughed. Some were beacons of beauty my age, in their prime; all seemed magnetic in their charismatic uniqueness. They propped against tables that were crowded with cans of brushes and layered in dabs and blobs of paint, as though unconcerned that their clothes could become ruined. They moved across the room surrounded by paintings on every side, arms draped over each other's shoulders, bright cigarette pinpoints reflecting in the windows that fronted East 52nd. Dried sausages hung from a painting above a table that was laden with cheeses and breads, olives and antipasto, and carved with initials and autographs. Another painting was festooned with a string of garlic. At a small metal table near the fireplace, a solemn man in an expensive European suit leafed through a stack of illustrations while, not three feet away, a woman in a tuxedo stood against a wall, arms akimbo, as a similarly outfitted man carefully traced her outline onto a large sheet of paper tacked to the wall, layering his androgynous lover's shape into numerous others that peeked from behind her form.

The host came over, wearing a neckerchief and a Greek sailor's hat, smiling a charming gap-toothed smile. "So this is Mademoiselle Mignonne," he said. "I am Bernard—or Lamotte, as you prefer. I know your uncle, your mother, and your father, may he rest in peace. I have heard much about you and your brother. I am astounded that we've never met."

Antoine said, "Mignonne rarely goes out. She is always hard at work. Can you imagine, Lamotte? She hardly knows the meaning of play!"

"Ah, then it is good that she has come on the arm of a child.

You know, my dear, Saint-Ex only looks like a mastodon; he may be older than you and I, but he is really just a boy."

Antoine beamed as Bernard veered off to greet new guests. It was true, what Bernard had said: in many ways Antoine was more youthful than I was. I spun the wine in my glass and imagined the room swirling, too—with my date and me in the center, gazing into each other's eyes.

I thought: I will kiss him tonight.

I took his arm and he led me around the room to make introductions. André, Celina, James, Kathleen . . . The names were numerous. Some were familiar: several were well-known artists, and there was a recognizable actor or two. Someone had brought their child to the party. I was crouched chatting with the little boy, Norman, when a perfectly polished red-haired woman approached Antoine and Bernard. She faced Antoine, staring brazenly up into his face.

"I've wanted to meet you for an awfully long time," she said in English.

"Netta Corelle," said Bernard. He explained in French, "She is an actress."

Netta turned to Bernard. "Tell Mr. Saint-Exupéry that I am in love with him."

Bernard smiled noncommittally.

She put a seductive hand on Antoine's lapel. "Tell him I am inviting him to take me home."

"Married to a powerful director," said Bernard in French. "Don't be a fool, Saint-Ex."

"Did you tell him?" the woman asked.

Antoine's face had flushed. His expression seemed half confused, half intrigued, and just a little too pleased.

I drank down the rest of my wine and stood up.

Netta Corelle shot me a dismissive glance and turned back to the men. "I mean it, Bernard. I've read everything he's written. Tell him I love him."

"Antoine," I said, "I hear there's a terrace. Will you show it to me?"

With an apologetic smile at the actress, Antoine took his leave.

Grasping my hand, he said, "It is a rooftop with a garden. Wait until you see it!" He brought me to a door half hidden by a curtain in a corner. We made our way up steep stairs, my hand small in his, and through a glassed enclosure with a wind chime hung on its door. On the rooftop, I made out the outline of a brick barbecue or broad chimney in a corner. Other shapes were chairs, a table suitable for a café patio, and fat metal structures—rounded and squarish conduits and pipes—that gleamed dully in many angles of moonlight. Bernard was growing things in pots and narrow beds. Plump shrubs ringed the roof's perimeter. Across the street were the windows and flags of the Alliance Française.

"Come to the edge," said Antoine.

The air was crisp and clean. Dozens of stars glimmered overhead.

" 'A sky as pure as water bathed the stars,' " I quoted—the first words of Antoine's novel *Southern Mail*.

"I didn't realize you were so familiar with my work."

"The funny thing is, of all the strange landscapes you describe in your books, that's the one that made me think, 'This is something I may never see.' Sometimes I forget there are stars above New York."

"If you look at them long enough, you can forget there is a New York below. But here, with you, I do not feel the need to forget. The view is magnificent, is it not?"

"This?" The ductwork and fire escapes, the stuff of heating systems, the neighboring houses with their ventilating funnels, the silhouettes of skyscrapers and the peaks of rooftop water towers, the chairs on Bernard's rooftop spread haphazardly, as though they refused to gather as a set?

III

"Absolutely. It is one of my favorite places in the whole of Manhattan. These metal channels and workings like a mechanic's shop, the buildings pieced together like a puzzle, and the sky wide and beckoning so far above . . . I feel I can breathe when I come out here." He inhaled deeply. I did the same, and felt my anxieties releasing with the long exhalation of our breath.

The sky wasn't far at all; it was too close, the stars unabashed, the night air dangerously soft.

Antoine stroked the back of my hand, and when I did not move, he reached up to touch my face. My legs grew weak. His fingers glided along my cheekbone and lingered on my lips that parted slightly to his fingertip. His touch drew down to the arc of my neck and around to my nape.

I turned my face up in anticipation of his kiss, but he only stood looking at me for what seemed like a tremendously long time.

He said, "Tonight you are more beautiful than ever. I have heard of flowers that blossom fully in the starlight. I have never before met a woman who does so." Still he did not reach for me.

My blood was drumming. I wasn't a statue or a painting to be admired. Could Antoine not see my desire; did a woman have to speak of it? I couldn't say the words. I put my hand on the front of his suit jacket as Netta Corelle had done.

Antoine removed my hand and said quietly, "In the daylight it is far easier to remember that you are still a young girl."

My face grew hot. "I'm not young." Nor was I entirely inexperienced, even then. I'd had brief romances with high school boys, and interludes with cute French boys in the shadows under the Alliance stairs. I'd had boyfriends at NYFS before my workload got in the way—one brawny and sweetly tentative, the next sharp and hard to please.

"It has been a long time since I have lived in the stars, Mignonne. You don't know how I envy you your innocence and promise. If I so lament the loss of my own youth, it would be unconscionable of me to fail to honor yours."

"But I'm not young! I'm old enough to be married. I'm old enough to know that life is short."

"Life is sometimes short, yes; but youth always is. You ought to do everything in your power to hold on to it. Don't let it be taken from you by someone like me."

Frustration lit through me. I pulled his head down and kissed him until his mouth softened and opened to mine. His arms encircled me and drew me close.

Bernard's voice rang out from the depths of the stairwell. "Saint-Ex! You're needed here."

Antoine released me reluctantly. His jaw clenched. He called brusquely toward the open door: "What is it?"

"They're hollering for you and your tricks. Bring the magic inside."

Back in Bernard's studio, Antoine lifted little Norman into a battered old wing chair, and I perched on the fraying arm beside the boy. As the partygoers gathered around, Antoine pulled a deck of cards from his shirt pocket and shuffled them in flamboyant ways, then ran through three quick tricks, one after another without pause, drawing laughter and applause.

At first he sat in a paint-splattered wooden chair, but the more he dazzled the guests, the more animated and restless he became. He sprang up to perform in the center of the room, shuffling, spreading, smacking the deck into place and sliding its slices one over the other, yanking his cigarette from his lips before he had finished inhaling, so that smoke drifted around his eyes and swirled past his eyebrows, setting his hands waving briskly before they resumed their giddy games. He turned as he performed, presenting his cards first to one side of the room, then to the other. I was mesmerized by the brightness of his eyes when he faced me, and took delight in the reactions of the audience when I watched from behind his back.

He slouched and chuckled as he assembled his tricks, his cigarette jiggling in the corner of his mouth. He gave orders by pointing fingers and singing encouragement. "Pick a card, any card" was understood in every language.

As one or another of the guests ventured forward and made their choices, little Norman laughed gleefully. He pressed his small fists against his mouth as the sorcerer's fingers spun above the depleted deck.

Antoine triumphed every time, and celebrated with hoots and leaps that made Norman laugh out loud. Liquor glasses danced on side tables when he landed, and were quickly clutched and emptied, and refilled with increasing abandon. Bottles were placed on the floor and shoes slipped off. Someone cursed in drunken disbelief: tricked again. In the aftermath of one particularly spectacular and unlikely win, Antoine threw his arms around Bernard and another man, and his back shook with laughter. When he let go, the man was blinking back tears, sniffling, slurring, "My friends. My fine, good friends."

Then the boy was snoring softly. Antoine stood in a haze of cigarette smoke in the center of the room.

Seated on a purple velvet ottoman, Netta Corelle leaned forward. Her eyes followed Antoine's hands. He stood facing her. His hands made magic—folding, fanning, hovering, now gesturing at the audience, now sweeping toward the actress and pausing there, cards palmed, fingers plying and caressing the air as he set up his tricks—hands fluent in their own compelling dialect. His suit jacket had been tossed aside, his tie loosened. His shirt was rumpled and coming untucked. Yet he moved smoothly, with the confidence of one who never fails, and smiled with the easy generosity of a man who always gets what he wants.

The actress fingered the pendant at the base of her throat. Antoine's hands played for her.

Leaving my third drink unfinished, I left the Alliance, crossed the street, and found Bernard's name still listed beside the door. I pressed the buzzer. His "Yes?" came through the intercom.

"I don't know if you remember me. I'm a friend of your friend Saint-Ex. Mignonne Lachapelle."

"Butterfly!"

"Pardon?"

"It's really you? Don't move! I'm coming down."

Butterfly? Had Antoine spoken of the drawings I had labored over before I'd gone to Montreal? What might he have said—and to such an accomplished artist as Bernard Lamotte? *The things she designs! An explosion of embroidery and sequins—applied to butterflies, of all things—the simplest, purest creatures that ever floated above the earth.*

Bernard pushed open the street-level door. "Mignonne! What a pleasure, after all this time. Come up. I'm sorry I used your nickname. I blame it on my surprise!"

I followed him up the stairs. "I didn't know I had a nickname."

"Truly? Then I apologize again, and with more sincerity, to boot. I heard Saint-Ex call you this. 'Mignonne, my butterfly.' It must have taken hold in my mind. I have thought of you this way ever since."

So Antoine had not been referring to the ornate ensembles I had designed. He had called me his own butterfly. But why? The last thing I resembled today was a creature of lightness or liberty. I had prepared the weakest of excuses for my visit to Bernard's, a question about marking Antoine's birthday at the end of June. Now I realized that excuses would make me seem even more pathetic than I felt.

Bernard poured two cups of coffee. I circumnavigated the studio nervously, looking at the paintings on the walls. I paused at a pen-and-ink drawing that was pinned to a board; it stood on the floor, propped against a radiator next to a painting of the same subject, a vase spherical at the bottom and fluted above, stuffed generously with flowers.

"That ink drawing is wonderful," I said as I returned to sit with Bernard. The oil painting, with its dull background and pastel-hued blooms, was much more somber and subdued. It was elegant but unremarkable, while the ink drawing shone with light.

"It's just a study for the painting, which was commissioned by De Beers—it was used in an advertisement for diamonds. They made me paint out the window for better contrast with the jewels. One has to make a living. Not that I'm complaining. Maybe someday I'll be able to afford the things I help my clients sell. But if you like the drawing, you are welcome to take it."

"Thank you. I love how the sunlight comes through from behind and pools on the table. It must be beautiful here in the daytime."

"Drop by anytime to see for yourself." He pulled over a wheeled tray table that held sugar and cream. "You haven't changed a bit."

"I'm sure I have. It's been quite a year."

"I know you were away, of course—and Saint-Ex says you've made a terrific start on what promises to be a busy career."

"You've seen him since he's been back, Bernard?"

"He's back?"

"Isn't he? He was supposed to be gone for just a few days." If he wasn't back, he had disappeared. Or he wanted nothing more to do with me.

"I'm assuming he's still in Montreal. He was spending a lot of time here before he left. I would have expected him to visit straight from the station, or close enough. But you know Saint-Ex; I've learned to take things as they come. Maybe he's holed up somewhere writing. You've tried calling him at home?"

Antoine had not given me his number; he had only given me his wife's. Imagine, thinking I had any claim on a man who hadn't even given me his telephone number. What right had I to hope that he might want to contact me again? I was a blockhead, coming over to interrogate his very patient friend.

"I'm sorry, Bernard."

"Why?"

"I shouldn't burden you with my concerns."

"I understand how you feel. Saint-Ex is like a brother to me."

"That's why I came." I turned my coffee cup around on its saucer. "I thought you might know if he's okay."

"I'm sure he's fine. His wife phoned me looking for him, as she is wont to do from time to time, I'm not sure what's going on up in Canada"—he pointed toward the high ceiling, as if to indicate north—"but Consuelo seems sure that our friend is still there."

"Aren't you at all worried?"

"When it comes to worrying about Saint-Ex, it's best to pace oneself. You know he has had at least thirty broken bones?"

"Thirty!"

"So I've heard, though not from him. Some of them several times."

He told me that Antoine rarely spoke of his injuries, except incidentally while eulogizing his adventures. What Bernard knew had come mainly from newspaper clippings, snippets from Consuelo's stories, and speculation by friends. Antoine's crashes had been numerous, and some legendary—like his Guatemala accident in '38. Antoine and Consuelo were separated at the time. He had begun a New York–Patagonia challenge; she was sailing to her Central American home. When his monoplane crash-landed, she returned to his side. He was an unrecognizable monster moaning in a hospital bed—or so Consuelo had often told Antoine, who had groused of it to Bernard. Broken bones had contorted his body and punctured his liver. His hand had barely avoided removal. Bandages soaked in colorful disinfectants made a pungent quilt of his skin. One eye was inches lower than the other; his lips hung close to the apparatus that caged his jaws. His head, Consuelo claimed, was several times its original size.

Bernard said, "He's been put back together more often than I can keep track of, and not always well."

"How can he even want to fly again?"

"It's a calling."

"It's dangerous!"

"He's very brave. Anyway, he's probably safest when he's facing danger. They say he's a genius when the stakes are high, but otherwise he's a menace to himself. He forgets to wear his oxygen mask. He writes or draws while he flies. And even now, when he's grounded, he has . . ." Bernard trailed off.

I had no idea what sort of confidences men shared with each other, or what would cause a man as carefree as Bernard to admit concerns about his friend. I only knew that Antoine had looked older and wearier than a year ago, and he had already been sad and frustrated back then. I could help him if he would let me, if I knew where he was. But maybe Antoine had told Bernard he was involved with some other girl.

Bernard seemed reluctant to continue, and I wasn't sure I wanted to hear.

He dropped a sugar cube into the dregs of his coffee. A brown stain crept up the sides of the crystal square. He spoke carefully. "There is one thing that may be keeping him in Montreal, Mignonne. Saint-Ex has some kind of mysterious, unpredictable illness. It started after that terrible crash and has been plaguing him on and off for years. He has described it as a burning knife plunged into his lower gut. The doctors can't seem to fix it; they just medicate the pain and have him wait till the fevers pass. It could come on anywhere—even in the air. It has happened here as we sat drawing together."

He paused, a glance to see if I understood. Much was written between the lines of that look: Bernard's love and care for his friend; his insistence that I know and accept what I was getting into; his unease in weighing the latter against the necessity of betraying confidences.

I could have hugged him then, and shame on me: he was telling me that Antoine was plagued by pain, and all I had listened for was that he wasn't in another girl's arms. To be sure, I asked, "You think he's sick and alone in Montreal?"

"He may be ill." He picked out the half-melted sugar and brought it to his lips to suck the liquid out. "But I'm sure he's in good hands."

"Whose?"

"Try not to worry. Despite what I've said, he is absurdly indestructible. And aside from maliciously depriving his friends of sleep, he is never knowingly cruel." Bernard popped the softened sugar cube into his mouth and crushed it between his teeth. "Eventually he will reappear as you have, out of the blue. He knows where to find us. When he needs someone near him while he works, or someone to tell him at three o'clock in the morning that his writing or his drawings aren't an embarrassment, I may call him nasty names, but he knows I will open my door. As you'll open your studio to him if he needs you. Am I right?"

I nodded.

"You are an artist, Mignonne. You know how it is."

Before I left, Bernard insisted on having me sign his table—a work of communal autography. I had studied it when Antoine had brought me here a year ago; I'd been fascinated by the signatures written deep into the wood. Tyrone Power . . . Max Ernst . . . Natalie Paley . . . Charlie Chaplin . . . Greta Garbo . . . Marlene Dietrich . . . Salvador Dalí . . . and Antoine, of course. The surface was more crowded than before; Bernard must have hosted some memorable parties in the last year. Among the names, stains, drawings, and a few inset coins, one thing jumped out as new: a doodle in Antoine's distinctive, effortless hand.

Bernard pushed aside some papers to reveal it in its entirety. "Saint-Ex's little fellow."

"I've seen this little guy on napkins and on the edges of letters and menus and all sorts of things. Antoine used to scribble him when I was trying to get some English into his head. I'm not sure he even looked at what he was doing."

"Exactly. Our missing friend is rarely short on words, but when he can't find a way to say something precisely right, inevitably he doodles this boy as he speaks. I have pointed it out to him many times. It's a funny thing, Mignonne. Ask him what he said a month ago and the words will be fresh in his mind, but bring his attention to what his hand has just drawn and somehow he manages to be ridiculously surprised."

19

Consuelo picked up her suitcase and moved forward a single step as the line advanced. Tonio had finally called. Consuelo had been waiting almost three weeks. Three weeks for a phone call from one's own husband! He had telephoned her a few times after his first few days away, and then nothing. When he thought she could be of help, he had sent telegraph after telegraph—*Contact the embassy! Call General So-and-So! Have Hitchcock or Reynal write to all the governments involved! My God, Consuelo, make something happen, please!*—as if she were a modern-day Athena who could rush spears through the chests of any bureaucrat who threatened to get in her way. She had done what she could, but what could she do? Paperwork was paperwork; it moved at the speed of trees. Tonio refused to hear that it was his own fault for crossing into Canada with only verbal assurances that he'd be allowed to return to the States. As if the spoken word were worth anything these days.

Her own documents were all in order; her train ticket for Montreal was in her hand; she needed only to ask the agent if there would be a club car open to civilians and to ladies traveling alone. She might have to find a uniformed gentleman to buy her rum-and-Cokes.

Modern-day Athena—that was a good one! Now another deity was nudging her memory. What was her name? Amphritite . . . or Amphitrite . . . another goddess they had discussed in the artists' colony at Oppède where she had settled upon fleeing from the Nazi rule. Oh, those golden, suspended days of eating vegetables from their own gardens, making art from whatever they touched, endless exhilarating talk, gestures of adoration made guiltless and gorgeous by loss. Amphitrite, that was it. Wife of Poseidon. The men had voted the goddess, by raucous ballot, the perfect wife. That was men: they had lauded the sea queen for her ready acceptance of her husband's affairs. Only a man would imagine that "acceptance" summed up the tides of loathing and love that good wives like Consuelo navigated every day.

Tonio's call had come a full twenty-four hours after that of his impeccably refined and wealthy older mistress, Madame Demarais. It was not the first time Consuelo had received such a message as this phone call of courtesy and concern from Tonio's other long-entrenched beloved. Women put aside their differences when the need is great enough.

Madame Demarais had reported that her agents had found Monsieur de Saint-Exupéry under medical care in Montreal. (As always, Consuelo wondered what she called him when they were alone.) First he had been held up by border issues. Then his fever had hit with rare force, and he had been hospitalized. He had been too incapacitated by medication to send a telegraph or make a phone call. Madame Demarais had flown to his side and was awaiting his imminent release into her care.

Consuelo had thanked her and had let her return to her vigil. It wasn't a question of acceptance or nonacceptance. It was something more than sharing a husband or overlooking an affair. Only Madame Demarais could come close to understanding Consuelo's burden. She had been sharing Consuelo's ministry for at least a dozen years.

Montreal was quaint.

Consuelo smiled as she dug a few Canadian dollar bills from her purse. She amused herself, she really did. To think she had felt like royalty during her year in the deserted village of Oppède—

with only a kingdom of rocks—but after scant months of living in New York, already she was judging a small metropolis to be provincial and unevolved. Well, but why not? The fact was, the citizenry here didn't even know how to nab a taxi outside the train station. They waited politely in well-behaved lines; that was fine, it calmed Consuelo's nerves. As in New York, the handiest cabs were reserved for men in uniform. The complacent Canadians, in their sensible shoes, had evidently accepted that they would walk to their destinations. Good for them; let them walk. Consuelo, on the other hand, had perfected a technique.

When a soldier opened the door to a cabbie's backseat, Consuelo pressed a handful of bills against the driver's window. "After you drop him off," she said, "continue on with me."

It was a trick that could transport one through any country of the world—and it worked flawlessly here, outside the Montreal station. Soon Consuelo was passing through the noble old streets she remembered from her last visit to the city. What she had forgotten was the ready courtesy of the young men here. The soldier who shared Consuelo's taxi had insisted that the cabbie deliver her to her destination first; the young man would pay the entire fare. For his trouble, Consuelo put her delicate hand on the fellow's smooth cheek.

But his response was less than genteel. She hoped it came of an abundance of formality, and not horror at the touch of a woman twice his age.

She had told Tonio to expect her that evening at his Hotel Windsor suite. It went unsaid that Consuelo would find his mistress with him there. Although the two women generally avoided being in public in the same room at the same time, they had certainly seen each other often enough. Back in Paris, the older woman had often called and even visited their various homes. In North America, Consuelo had somehow expected to be beyond the reach of Madame Demarais. Stupid thought. Nothing was beyond that woman: no borders, no encounters, were a match for the forces of her grace and wealth.

Not the slighted trace of discomposure showed on Madame Demarais's elegant, narrow face. The woman's ancestry was in metals and in oil, while Consuelo could claim only coffee plantations, an inheritance of limited depth. Of course, it wasn't just about the well of the woman's bank account (though that was important enough—and necessary for treating Tonio to gifts on the scale of his own airplane). There was also her ability to live life as she chose. The Madame Demaraises of the world had so little to worry about. Their ability to get what they wanted wasn't threatened by the appearance of a few wrinkles on the forehead or by the erosion of their claims on the heart of a famous man.

Indeed, Tonio's mistress bore her status with a quiet, dignified pride. She seemed content to be a shimmering shadow in the periphery, ever ready to come to Tonio's aid. Ready to the end of time and from the beginning, yes, for Madame Demarais was no young chinchilla scampering after the tails of this season's celebrity. She was several years older than Tonio and had been a fixture—and occasional godsend—from the start.

Tonio had long submitted to Consuelo's insistence that the woman be deemed a mistress, not simply a friend, though he assured his wife that he and his female supporter had never shared a bed, rarely so much as shared a kiss. "What does she get from you?" Consuelo had asked him, to no avail—but she had known the answer then and she knew it ever more piercingly now. Tonio allowed the woman to help him. Others might fool themselves that the arrangement seated all strength in the hands of the recipient, but Consuelo knew firsthand how barren and devalued it made one feel to have one's aid scorned. To help was to hold power. Madame Demarais had been helping for at least a dozen years.

Madame Demarais didn't rise from her armchair on the far

side of Tonio's bed. "Good evening, Madame de Saint-Exupéry. It is well that you've arrived. I have a flight to catch, and it's best that Monsieur de Saint-Exupéry not be left alone for long."

Tonio was sleeping. He looked peaceful and well rested with Madame Demarais at his side.

"How is he?" asked Consuelo tremulously. She wanted to throw herself over him and sob away what remained of her exhausting fears but she'd save that for later, when Tonio was awake and Madame Demarais gone. She sank into the leather chair at the desk. How she'd love to kick off her shoes and rub the tautness out of her arches.

"He's fine. Obtaining his discharge from the hospital was something of an ordeal. The attending doctor had arranged for him to be medicated quite thoroughly. Monsieur de Saint-Exupéry was unable to tell us whether he still had pain. I'm not certain he knew if he still had legs."

Ah, poor Tonio. He was the claim of every man and woman; he was to the world whatever his writings led them to believe. Whoever had him in their grasp wanted to keep him, to minister to him and fix him; it had always been so. Yet only Consuelo knew how to heal him for good. It was she who had brought him back to life with an ammonia rub when he drowned in his plane, she who had cured him with sips of warm milk when a crash made his head swell to five times its size. If he would only stay by her side, Tonio would be living a healthy and carefree life. Instead, he was forever being torn apart. One day France and America would be fighting over his remains.

Well, not if Consuelo could manage to survive him. She must start taking better care of herself. Eat more vegetables. Stop suppressing her voluptuary impulses. That was how one grew crippled from the inside out: by denying oneself the pleasures that kept one young. For Tonio's sake, she had to remain beautiful and brave and strong.

Madame Demarais pulled on her ivory kid-leather gloves.

"He was recovered enough to explore the city today, though the effort took a toll. I've given him a pill to help him sleep." She permitted herself to briefly touch the back of Tonio's hand. "You will take him home soon?"

"I'm going to take him to stay with a colleague in Quebec City for a while. And then . . . it depends on when there are tickets available for the train."

Madame Demarais unsnapped her purse. She delved into it and produced a checkbook. She signed a check, made out to Tonio, and placed it on the blanket for Consuelo to retrieve. "Allow me to insist. Please take Monsieur de Saint-Exupéry home by airplane."

Tonio awoke in the night to find his wife warm and naked in his bed, planting kisses in the thick forest of his chest. Consuelo wished she had gotten the name of the sleeping pills, which were wondrous. Not only had they allowed Tonio a most satisfying slumber, upon waking he only sighed in relief and said her name and rolled over to return to sleep. Consuelo sighed, too—in happiness. What a precious gift it was, this shared night of intimate privacy and peace. They were together at last, away from all that kept him from her. There was no need to rush. She could tell him in the morning where her hands and lips and hungry hips had been.

20

Tonio had never been voluble in the mornings, but this morning—after hearing Consuelo's gleeful confession and responding with a disgusted "This is how you would tame me?"—he had become all but mute.

Checking out of the Windsor Arms required a minimum of words: a bill settled, a car and driver arranged, an umbrella accepted, a tip proffered. Fine. But surely to God a woman could expect to hear her husband's voice at least once during a monotonous three-hour car ride, and not just the abrasive progression of his pen.

Rain flopped around the Cadillac's exterior, dreary as a string mop spreading effluent on a floor. Give me lightning, thought Consuelo. Thunder. What we need is a good, hair-stiffening storm.

The city outskirts gave way to highway, and the highway to only more highway and more rain. "How do you expect me to amuse myself?"

Scritch, scritch.

Why the hell had she married a writer? Self-indulgent. Stony. Telling secrets to their treasured bits of paper with their scratchy pens. "You're writing about me, aren't you?"

His mouth was tight and silent. His pen fell silent, too. He was staring through the side window as the car approached a bridge. They passed under it; the rain slapped down hard, all at once, and Tonio startled, his arms jolting up like a baby's at the sudden sound.

Consuelo laughed. So he was alive, was he? There was hope yet. She wriggled her bottom closer to his on the seat. "You can't still be mad about last night, my love. It was entertaining for both of us. How you could be anything but amused is beyond me." Amused and honored. And gratified! Most men would think they'd gone to heaven. But Tonio? Fussy as a woman these days. Everything had to be analyzed, required a decision, was contingent upon an assessment of right or wrong. As though there could be anything wrong with wanting intimacy with one's husband. His attitude was the problem. That and his depressive silence. It couldn't be good for Tonio to bottle everything up; no wonder he was so often ill. If he could only get his head out of the clouds, he'd see the cure right next to him.

Slowly the rain abated. Tonio found a fresh page and again began to write.

The landscape around them lifted into soft hills, quite lovely in the emerging sunshine. Remarkable Mother Nature: she knew best how to buoy the heart. Consuelo could break this impasse. Tonio seemed keen to stay huddled in his corner, but it was the job of a wife to be gracious and bend. "What are you writing now, darling? May I see! I'm sure I could help."

Scritch—Damn him! Consuelo made a grab for the notebook on his lap. He pushed her back. With his free arm outstretched to keep her at bay, he bent his body into a protective arch over his work. His pen moved quickly, furiously blackening a word or two at the top of the paper, then all at once he tore out the page.

"Read, since you insist," he said. "See if I still amuse you as you seem to think I should."

It was a letter. She held it up to the window, but his frenzied scribbling had fully obscured the addressee's name.

Quebec City, June 3, 1942

Dear XXXXXXXXX,
After all our time spent apart—each in our separate coun-

try, growing into our separate strivings and grief, sharing only silence—still in my voiceless hours my thoughts go to you who once taught me to speak.

"I want an apple. I am a student." How crude our early words were—mine truant, careless, childishly cruel; yours the unvarnished speech of a half-orphaned girl.

Concuelo checked the defaced salutation again. His oldest sister? Half orphaned, yes, for their father died when Tonio was three. With the mother raising the children alone, no doubt Marie-Madeleine would have been called upon to perfect her brother's speech.

Simple words were the first kindness you showed me. Only simplicity is honest and beautiful: the worker's uniform, the naked mouth, the unadorned breast.

Breast?

It is rare (as much in language as in fashion) to hide nothing, to promise nothing, to strive for truth and not simply to impress.

She skipped back. What naked mouth? Whose unadorned breast?

It is rare, yet there is nothing more vital. For how else can one human trust another, or know love? No milestone, no invention, no great love, no great life, is built through any but the simplest and most unambiguous steps.

I asked you to do something for me before I left. Another might have read cruelty into my words. But you took them for what they were, a plain and practical request.

For this I thank you.

For I have grown very tired of being misunderstood.

I wish words had proven to be as simple as you made me hope they could be. Even now there are things I cannot put into words . . . or not into speech . . . Memories of your young body,

Consuelo frowned.

and mine—young again with you. For a year, we were two children chasing squirrels, tossing whirligigs, wishing on stars . . .

An older schoolgirl, then? An early, never-forgotten crush?

he with his mind dominating his body and his heart; she all heart, at home in herself, as sure of her eager body as he was awkward and insecure in his own.

Who was this girl—middle-aged woman, now—to whom he would write so freely, confessing embarrassments that were so at odds with his adult facade and physique? This was not her Tonio; he never talked to Consuelo this way!

The girl had to be a memory and nothing more. He hadn't intended on delivering this letter, but destroying it. He only wanted for his wife to see him this way—more vulnerable even than a man drugged to sleep. He was testing her, daring her to make light of his troubles again.

Answer me this: How is it that one can believe the body to be sacrosanct, inviolate, the image and creation of God . . . and yet know it to be more destructible and error-prone than lowly structures created by man?

My brother died at the age of fifteen. He had been wise as a king, as diligent in the care of our friendship as a lamplighter in the tending of the flame. He had been my anchor, the angel to my devilry, my mirror in a household in which only sisters and mother remained. My brother had called me to his death-bed, not to speak of his pain but to soothe my own. His body, he confided, would die and be gone . . . but the rest of him would stay.

How can a child know himself as other than body? How did my brother know what he would be in both our world and in the world that waited?

What am I to do with the secret he shared?

You spoke so wisely of the spirit and the body on the day we met. What is this body, like a soul in its power to torment and exhilarate? Mine so worn now, fickle, creaking in heavy weather, limbering to life with the return of sun . . . or with the thought of sunshine such as you have been to me.

When I remember your blond hair holding light—just as did mine as a boy—your undimmed innocence as intoxicating as perfume . . . It pains me less to think of us growing apart than to think that your light might one day grow weak.

These are dark days in the country of our fathers. They will grow darker still, and colder, before the threat subsides. You asked me once if the sky was cold . . .

Enough. Consuelo couldn't turn back time. She couldn't become the little blond friend he had long left behind. Did he want her to return to the soil, to her mother, and arrange to be rebirthed?

All she could do was change the atmosphere of the moment. All he needed after his month of lethargy was to do a job and to do it well, as well as Consuelo did her own.

There were times when a wife had to grovel and bend; there were times when a wife had to snap.

"Give me the sleeping pills. Let me kill myself!" She tore at his jacket, batting away his hands. The car wobbled in the road-way as she pushed his head into the window. Her long nails caught the skin of his forehead and ear.

Tonio yanked her to him, locking her flailing arms against his chest. She showed some resistance; no more than was necessary. She cried a little. Tonio spoke to the driver, who had adjusted his mirror to frame the scene, and swayed Consuelo into silence.

She had had to whip up a proper storm to give him a chance to calm the seas. He would be fine now; it was like letting a toddler fight his way to sleep.

Tonio touched his fingers to his forehead, checking for blood. "You'll kill us all," he muttered. "Rabid cat."

"Don't call me that." She slid away from him, indignant as a flower standing straight in a chilly wind. "You know I hate cats."

The De Koninck home in the historic old *quartier* of Quebec City was a *grande maison* of quiet grey limestone. Staid, thought Consuelo. Sedate. But Tonio loved its leaded windows, its heavy banisters and soaring ceilings; he examined it like a doctor with a patient and happily proclaimed it constitutionally secure.

The hosts were similarly well settled. Charles De Koninck, in his mid-thirties, had already been a Dean of Philosophy for years. His wife . . .

What was the damn wife's name?

The fuzzy drone in jet planes these days: it's like sitting in an aerosol can. Makes it impossible to think. She'd rather have a 1930s propeller plane, whose massive racket numbed the ears and extremities but left the mind free to soar and to think . . . To think of nothing but the exciting suitor in the pilot seat beside her . . . His hands on the controls but his eyes on her . . . Her thoughts turning wild as she reads his moving lips . . .

She is there.

Then: turbulence; marbles strewn across a courtyard; her mind trips.

It was June. The wife introduced herself when Consuelo disembarked from the Cadillac. Charles De Koninck and . . .

Who cares! Only the boy mattered. Little Thomas De Koninck with his blond curly hair. Tonio's little prize. Little Tonio's lost twin. The small, blond boy who would become a little prince.

21

Their stay at the De Konincks' had been shaping up to be the usual: impeccably gracious hosts, elaborate meals, engrossed attention paid to Tonio, polite questions put to Consuelo. She was obliged to represent her husband at breakfasts and spend the mornings with Madame De Koninck while Charles put in time at the university and Tonio slept. "It's what your husband needs," the wife said approvingly each day, proud to give him succor and rest. But each night, dawn had been near the horizon before Tonio joined Consuelo in their bed. He claimed he was staying up only to write—not on paper but in his head. It infuriated her to realize he might never put his thoughts onto paper in her presence again.

Finally, it was Friday morning. The last day to endure chitchat over coffee and eggs Benedict, the last afternoon of sightseeing (yet another folksy gallery, another battle monument, another reverent reference to where Quebecois blood had been shed), the last evening in which they would sit four at the dinner table, the hosts fussing over Tonio's every serving and every word, as though without their ministrations and their guestroom the man would have been dead.

Consuelo roused him early. "I told the De Konincks we'd go with them to fetch the son from boarding school." It was a bit far, Charles had said, but a lovely drive; the scenery would do Monsieur de Saint-Exupéry good. She got Tonio up and dressed. Then she faked a sudden headache to claim a few hours of freedom—to read and sketch in the luxurious bed.

Lunch arrived—via the cook, on a silver tray—but Consuelo's

husband and the De Konincks did not. The afternoon passed in foul tedium. By the time she descended from the bedroom to take her pre-dinner cocktail—alone—Consuelo was nauseous with boredom, furious at being abandoned. The injustices that had been served upon her this holiday! They ground like sand in the teeth.

Dinner for one was served and rejected before the party finally returned. Their spirits were as elevated as the color in their cheeks. Their words were contrite but their tone was too carefree. *Père* and *mère* De Koninck spoke quietly. Tonio said not a word, nor did he raise his eyes. Asleep in his arms was a golden-haired child.

While the mother put the son to bed, Tonio and De Koninck settled down to smoke and tell Consuelo about the day. The school's headmaster had entreated Tonio to rally the boys with an impromptu talk, which evolved to a magic show, for which they rewarded him with a song. Tonio had responded with his favorite childhood tune, and needed no persuasion to teach the students to sing along.

By the time Thomas mastered the chorus, he understood that his new friendship with this big, funny man would elevate his status among his eight-year-old peers. That was the only explanation Consuelo could think of for Charles's claim: "It's the first time he's ever begged us to stay on and take in the pleasures of his school."

Thomas led a tour, holding tight to Tonio's hand. Even the teachers marched behind them, and soon teachers' wives emerged from the residences and were following along. They had a picnic and a boat ride; there were seagulls and sunshine and swans. Thomas taught Tonio clapping games. Tonio led a roving lesson on constellations, using resident pet turtles for stars.

When they said their goodbyes Saturday morning, there was great reluctance in Tonio's voice.

In the airplane, he opened his notebook. Consuelo asked no questions; there was no need; she could simply watch to see what he wrote. But all that he scratched out were doodles. A boy chasing butterflies. A boy playing with string. A boy with a stick or a scepter . . . with a sword . . . with a snake . . . with wings.

A boy-man pining for the boy he had been.

22

Leo leaned against the kitchen counter, spooning cornflakes into his mouth. "Did you see this? It came yesterday." He plucked an envelope from the counter and tossed it my way. "It's from Mother. She complains that you haven't visited our dear uncle."

"I've been busy."

"How's he supposed to report to her on the status of your safety and virtue when you're avoiding him? She can't trust me to tell her. She needs a respectable snitch."

I skimmed the letter. "For Pete's sake, Leo. She's not looking for information from Yannick. She's worried that he's working too much. She wants us to keep an eye on him."

Leo brought the bowl to his mouth and slurped the remaining milk. His bowl clattered into the sink, where last night's dinner dishes still waited. "Yannick can handle himself. He always knows best."

When Leo had started skipping high school and drinking, it had been Yannick who had convinced their father to kick him out of the house. When my brother moved out, Yannick reported to my parents that Leo was earning a reputation as a heavy gambler, and Papa immediately stopped sending him money. It had been left to Yannick to convince Mother to stop her secret cash-laden letters, too.

Even Papa hadn't known of Mother's covert actions, I was sure. His younger brother Yannick had a way of finding out everything. Everyone loved Yannick—in a way different from how they loved Papa. Papa had been respected and admired;

Yannick had always been everyone's best friend. People confided in him and looked to him for advice. Maybe Yannick always thought he knew best, but others thought so, too.

Leo turned on the tap.

"I'll wash up," I said. "You go."

"That's what I like to hear."

He disappeared down the hall, then returned a few minutes later to blow a kiss and grab his lunch box. He waved as he pulled the door shut behind him.

I took my time in the kitchen, savoring the warmth of the dishwater on my hands. June had begun with a fury. So hot, just outside the door, yet Leo's place in the early morning was still clammy and cold. When July came, and intolerable August, the basement would be either a cooling refuge or dreadfully humid and close.

But now there was Yannick to think about. I couldn't entertain him at Leo's. I tried to remember what I had done with him in years past. There had been musicals and cinema nights, occasionally a museum day. And, of course, the frequent, hilarious spying on competitors under the guise of enjoying dinners in fine restaurants all over town.

Yannick working too much? It had always been him hounding Papa to take a break. It was Yannick who had pressured his brother to visit Grand-mère in Montreal, to take the family south, to take up an instrument as Yannick had mastered the oboe, to learn to relax. He helped Mother plan vacations that never came to pass. But he did manage to get Papa to the New York World's Fair in the summer of '40; sometimes my uncle's efforts led to the worst that could come to be.

Yannick was running the restaurant in the French Pavilion of the fair, and he vowed to get his brother out to see the spectacle. I'd been eager to see it myself, but Papa had promised we'd go as a family, so I waited until he could take the time. His weekdays were overrun by meetings with clients, city officials, and staff.

Weekends were for developing and drafting ideas, a responsibility he said he couldn't delegate or deny. Around the edges, in the evenings and late into the nights, he fit the already-fraying Alliance Française community—dining with its members, drinking with the stalwarts of its splintered factions, pleading his case for a united, nonpolitical collective. I had been waiting fourteen months.

Leo was coming for a visit, a rare event, so Papa vowed to come straight home from work. Mother and I had made a casserole that could keep. We listened to the news, a comfortable threesome around the kitchen table, until the phone rang and Mother took the receiver from the wall.

She was hanging up when Papa came through the door. "Clear your schedule for the Fourth of July," she said. "Yannick's taking you to the fair."

Papa was trying unsuccessfully to get his shoes off without bending to untie them, one foot pushing sluggishly against the other.

Leo walked over to Papa and slapped his arm affectionately. "About time you got here. They're drowning me in tea." He took the hat off Papa's head. He considered his face. "God, you're old," he said.

They both smiled. Leo knelt down, loosened Papa's laces, and eased the shoes off his feet.

"Thank you, son."

"Anytime."

I placed a trivet onto the dining room table and Mother set down the casserole dish. A rich, cheesy cauliflower scent wafted from under the steamy glass.

Papa hung his overcoat on a hook, the lining swishing against the plaster wall. He eased into his dining room chair. "What did Yannick say?"

"You know how he is. 'Tell your knucklehead husband that if the owner of the most popular restaurant in the fair can go AWOL for the entire Fourth of July, an architect can leave his drafting table to see the greatest show in the world.' Really, all Yannick cares about is the foods of the world. He wants to eat his way through the pavilions. Better put aside a whole day for it, Émile. Don't make that face."

July the 4th, 1940, was Superman Day at the World's Fair. Mother hated crowds and Leo was not pleased with Yannick's interference in those days, so in the end it was just Yannick, Papa, and me.

Papa read from the official pamphlet as we waited in line for the Futurama exhibit: "'Here are the materials, ideas, and forces at work in our world. These are the tools with which the World of Tomorrow must be made.'"

Yannick said, "They forgot about cheese. Materials and ideas are good, but who wants to live in a world without cheese?"

All Yannick noted at the Italian pavilion was "They've got cheese as big as tires." He cursed the inability to order perogi at the Polish pavilion, which had closed due to the war, and praised the sausages in Switzerland. In the Belgium pavilion, he had a fat waffle piled with strawberries and whipped cream—and pronounced the dessert good enough to serve at Le Pavillon, the restaurant he planned to open after the end of the fair.

As we waited for the fireworks at night, just before the pavilions closed, Yannick ran back into Belgium and returned balancing more plates of waffles, one for each of us. While the last streaks of sunlight faded, we pulled plump, red strawberries out from under mounds of cloud-puff cream. We let the sweet juice spread across our tongues and trickle down our throats. I was completely exhausted. We had seen electrical displays; enticing and outlandish predictions for the future; an entire world of fashion extravagance and modern chic. We had waited in line for hours and walked for miles. But I laughed as we wiped white trails off our faces and as Yannick unwittingly pushed cream into his hair. The towering concoctions became soft lumps, and the soft lumps dwindled into bite-sized islands. I devoured my last piece slowly, savoring the cooling air and the first flashes of fireworks, the mosaic of carnival sounds, the sweetness that lingered in my mouth.

"Papa," I said, "we'll have to plan a visit to Le Pavillon next year to see how Yannick's waffles compare to these."

Against the wail of a rocket that screamed up and exploded in a shower of sparks, I could only read my father's lips. I thought he said, "All right." But his face, lit by crackling light, looked grey and pained—not right at all.

There were things I have imagined so many times that they have melded irrevocably with what I know to be true. Papa didn't go into work the next day. This is true. I imagine him waving Mother off with a drowsy hand when she tried to wake him, and Mother wondering if he and Yannick had drunk themselves blind after she went to bed. Yannick's idea of what was best wasn't always what was conventionally right.

She had let Papa sleep. He is worn out, she would have thought. I would have thought it, too.

Papa got out of bed at noon, moving listlessly.

"What's the matter with you?" Mother had asked.

He clung near her in the kitchen.

"Émile, I can hardly move. Go read. I'll join you when I'm through." She had taken the newspaper from the kitchen table to hand to him. "Oh my Lord. There was a bombing yesterday at the fair."

He took the paper and closed it on itself, not wanting her to worry—he'd take care of all the worrying on his own—and headed toward the front room, his slippers shuffling on the hardwood floor. She was drying the dishes when his voice rose in the hall.

They said it was a stroke. A stroke, like the swell of a paddle in water, like a twig of charcoal moving on a page, like Papa's hand smoothing my hair, soothing me to sleep when I was young and he had time.

Mother would have held on to the thought, the word, through the hours at the hospital, the discussions with the doctors, the taxi ride home alone. She held it through the worried silence in which Yannick opened our apartment door. Behind Yannick, my anxious face, Leo's bewildered eyes.

Mother had stood in the doorway, looking frightened and frail. Leo's rough and trembling hand took hold of mine.

Yannick asked, "What was it?"

Mother whispered the word. "Stroke."

The funeral had not been in New York, but in Montreal. The Lachapelles had a family plot in Sacré-Coeur Cemetery, and Papa was laid alongside Grand-mère and Grand-père. There was a place on the monument where his dates were inscribed. I had put my shaking fingers into the granite wounds.

Yannick had taken control, telephoning the funeral home and the church, arranging the train tickets, sending telegrams.

"How long are we staying in Montreal after . . . everything?" Leo had asked as we sat at our dining table in the hours before we would all board the train.

Yannick came out of the kitchen. His forehead shone. "As long as it takes."

Leo asked, "As long as it takes to what?"

Mother said, "To get Grand-mère's house cleaned up and make a start on moving in." She glanced at me. "Then we'll come back here to finish packing up and get Mignonne settled in with you before I go back to Montreal for good."

We had been fighting about the plans: Mother wanted me to move with her to Canada, to quit New York Fashion School, to go to Collège Lasalle in Montreal if I insisted on going to school at all. I had refused to consider it; I would graduate in New York. I clutched my fork in my lap, the tines digging into my knee.

"Try to eat," said Yannick, but neither Leo nor I touched our food.

"Mignonne," said Mother quietly. "It won't be easy for you to stay here. There, we have a whole house just sitting empty, waiting for us. You won't have to work. I won't have to work. We can take in a boarder."

"Won't you want to have boarders either way," asked Leo, "whether she goes with you or not? If she stays in New York, you can rent out more of Grand-mère's house. And it isn't going to cost her much to stay here if she's going to live with me."

Mother pushed aside her plate. "We would have all moved to Montreal anyway, as soon as Papa could finish with his projects at work. It's something he wanted for us. For you, too, Leo. It's a quieter life there."

But I knew that my father never would have finished; he never would have abandoned the Alliance. He would not have made the move.

"What Papa wanted was for Mig to be happy," said Leo.

Yannick had been standing at the head of the table, his fingertips on the back of Papa's chair. Now he walked over to stand behind Mother and rest his hands on her shoulders. "Think of Émile," he said gently. "Let him watch his children succeed."

So I had completed my diploma in New York, with a promise to join Mother in Montreal at the end of it—for a visit, not to stay. But I had stayed a whole year. What was in New York for me to rush back for? From the day I had met Antoine he had been vowing to return to Europe, and Madame Fiche had very efficiently stolen my confidence in my dream.

Cunning woman. Thank God that Yannick convinced me to come back and try again.

I put away the last clean plate and dried my hands as I walked to the phone. I asked the operator to let the number ring a long time. The restaurant hadn't yet opened for the day, but Yannick would be there.

"Le Pavillon."

"Yannick, it's Mignonne."

"The famous fashion designer? I have tried phoning you, but no one is ever home. When can I see you? Come to the restaurant."

"Let's get you away from work. We should do something special. Is there anything in particular you'd like to do? Something for old times' sake."

"Bite your tongue—you're too young to say 'for old times' sake.' But you're right. I'll tell you what. Let's fly the family banner at the Alliance Française. I haven't been in a dog's age."

"Really? Shame on you."

"Exactly." He laughed heartily.

We made plans to meet at the Alliance. I would ask him there for news of my former pupil—in the most offhanded, casual way.

23

Early evening. The ladies of the Alliance would be having aperitifs or finishing their late-afternoon gin. I had arranged to meet Leo and Yannick at the dining room tonight. I would arrive early, troll for clients. Maybe Antoine would be there.

I bathed in the shared bathroom down the hall. The hot water felt good on my body. In my closet I found a tailored jacket and a maturely dignified dress. I chose simple pumps, pairing them with a clutch purse. Wouldn't Madame be pleased if she could see me looking so proper for once? She would probably think I was being true to my bloodline. I fixed my hair and made up my face, tamping down the thought that Uncle Sam might want the metal of my lipstick tube for bullets or bombs. If he really needed it, he would have gotten to it first.

At the Alliance, it took less time for me to down a martini at the bar than it had taken the bartender, Eddy, to make it. The dining room was almost empty, I didn't know any of the members present, and all the ladies were intent on their own conversations. I couldn't bring myself to interrupt them with a sales pitch. But Eddy and I had grown up together. We had even had our time under the stairs.

He said, "You should see it from Monday through Wednesday. You could run the Polish cavalry through here and be lucky to bayonet a hat." He wiped a glass and flashed an arresting smile. "Did you bring back a Canadian boyfriend, Mig?"

I shrugged and rubbed my nose with the back of my hand. "Why is the place so empty? Is the membership down that much?"

"Not on paper. People just don't come in. It's no more one-big-happy-family around here. There's been no holding back the knives since your dad passed away." He tucked the end of the bar towel behind his belt. "Not that you've been around to see it."

I slid the empty glass across the bar. "So now it's my fault that the community's falling apart."

"I don't blame you for taking off. I wouldn't be here myself if I had a choice. I keep going back to the draft board asking them to take me. I got a punctured eardrum, that's all. But they just laugh and say I should go home. My friends are out training to kill while I'm mixing sidecars and drawing beer."

"It must be boring when business is slow."

"Honestly? I'd be just as happy if no one came in. The members who come are worse than the ones who stay away." He lowered his voice. "All they care is that their money's safe. They aren't going to get their hands dirty fighting Hitler. They do their fighting here, over whisky sours and escargot."

I swiveled in my seat, trying to imagine it. "What kind of fighting?"

"Cattiness, nastiness. So-and-so is for so-and-so, so-and-so's a dirty such-and-such. From that to whatever viciousness you could dream up. It's just talk, but these days talk can skewer a man."

"And it's all made up." There was no way the things they said about Antoine could be true. How could they be, when half the talk contradicted the other half?

Eddy slid over another drink. "Can't say one way or another. Everyone spouts off like he's a hundred percent right and he heard it from the mouth of God. Tell you why, too: everyone's got his own guilt to work out."

"Whatever happened to 'Say Three Hail Marys and go in peace'?"

He laughed. "It would be a better world. And this room would be a much nicer place."

When Yannick finally arrived, it was with Leo leading the way and—joy!—towering, rickety Philippe following behind, a smile splitting his handsome, well-lined face. The ancient doorman looked away politely as I hugged Yannick hello.

"Something to drink?" asked Eddy.

I said, "I'll have amother martini."

Yannick frowned. "Leo, take Mignonne to a table."

Philippe stepped forward. "Allow me, please," He offered his lanky arm. "Mademoiselle Mignonne, so long I have waited to see you again! And so worth it. I am pleased that your uncle alerted me that you would be here."

"It's wonderful to see you, too."

As we began our slow progression, he leaned in close. "The boy at the door: I apologize, mademoiselle. I didn't realize that his training by our new deskman was so deplorably incomplete. I've had words with them both; such an omission is intolerable. It will never happen again."

We stopped at a table and, inch by inch, Philippe pulled out a chair for me. He looked back. Yannick and Leo were still at the bar. With stiff limbs, Philippe crouched down beside me. "I wanted to tell you: Every day I thank our Lord for your papa's time on earth. And every day"—his rheumy eyes watered—"I ask the Lord to bless him and his children."

"Thank you."

"Did you know he arranged that I may remain with the Alliance for life? An emeritus position." He lowered his voice to a proud confidential tone. "I am no longer required to work evenings; I am here only when I wish to be. Your father said I should be the Alliance's figurehead, as on a ship."

"I'm so glad, Philippe! I didn't know what to think when I came in and you weren't here."

"Ah. Mademoiselle, I am mortified by what you were put through. The boy is young and very new, but that is no excuse." He broke off as the others approached. With gritting effort, he rose to his feet.

"Philippe," said Yannick, "let me get you a chair. Join us for a while."

"You are kind, but I must return to my duties."

"You must have a lot to tell us about what's been happening here lately," said Yannick. "And you're probably wondering what our Mignonne has been up to."

"I know only what Monsieur Leo has told me when he has been in."

Leo nodded. "Same old thing. Fashion, fashion, fashion. Always working. Too busy for boys."

Philippe bowed. "I'm afraid I must wish you a good evening. But if you need anything"—he patted my arm shyly—"if you need anything at all, please only say the word."

I ordered a creamy whitefish bake with a side of *pointes d'asperges*. As we ate, I asked Yannick for news from Montreal, for although Mother and I exchanged letters and she had plenty of questions for me, she said little about herself. Yannick spoke of her good health, her backyard garden, her volunteering at the Ladies' Auxiliary. She had begun keeping company with a man—a fact that Leo couldn't stomach and Yannick skirted, though it resounded in every "they": "They went to a dance . . . they were driving to church when . . . they're thinking that maybe one day." He said to Leo, "She asks if you're okay."

"I'm better than okay." Leo spoke around his steak. "Got a job. Roof over my head." He took a drink of beer. "Got my little sister coming and going at all hours, as she pleases."

"Oh?"

"It's the business," I said, and refilled my glass.

"Late nights?" Yannick asked with pretend nonchalance. When it came to his niece and nephew, his instinct for potential troubles was like a collie with its sheep.

"Overnight," said Leo.

"Ignore him," I said. "He tells me he expects me to work all night, then he gets mad when I do."

"You do?"

"Just the once."

Yannick asked, "And you come home every night, Leo?" He dabbed at his mouth with his napkin. "Look, I know you worry about Mignonne."

"Of course I do!"

"Good. You lead me to something I need to say." His expression grew stern. "Your mother feels the same about you as you feel about Mignonne. You don't telephone or write; she never gets a word from you. If it wasn't for your sister's letters, your mother wouldn't know you're still alive."

Leo scowled.

"Start giving a thought to the ache in your mother's heart," said Yannick, "and you'll have the right to be concerned about your own."

Leo got up and walked to the bar.

"He's just being Leo," I said.

"And I respect that. He follows his own path. He knows what makes him happy. But your mother is entitled to be happy, too. You know, I was hoping he would straighten out if you moved back in with him."

I contemplated the irony of that.

Yannick asked, "Do you really work through the night?"

"We have deadlines. There's a sofa I can sleep on."

He checked his watch. "Speaking of which, it's getting late. Would you like dessert, coffee—nothing? Oh, well. Okay, we'll leave Leo to his snit and go home. You must be tired."

"You don't know the half of it."

"Such as?"

Such as drinking, drawing, waiting, conjuring Antoine as I lay in bed. No doubt my face was as red as my wine. I brought my glass to my mouth.

"Saint-Ex!" called Yannick.

Wine spilled over my lip and mottled the tablecloth.

Yannick grinned. "Of course you remember my niece."

"He does," I said.

Yannick looked back and forth between the two of us. His expression grew uncertain, but he said, "So I see."

Antoine was smiling warmly. "Mignonne has changed little since our tutoring sessions—except in all the best ways."

"I'm much much older," I said. Maybe I'd had enough to drink.

"And wiser?" asked Yannick.

I said, "That depends on what you think is wise. For example." I took another drink. "Yannick."

"Yes?"

"I'm 'splaining." When I turned my head to look at my uncle the room continued turning, and so I spoke directly to Antoine. "Yannick is so smart. Right? Everyone says so."

"He is," said Antoine. "He understands everything."

"So why did he introduce us?"

Yannick said, "You were a tutor. Saint-Ex needed a tutor."

"Right. And what did you think I needed—a married man?"

From the surprise on Yannick's face, it was clear that he finally really did see. He looked at his friend. He looked at me. His niece and Saint-Ex, after all, and since when? Saint-Ex and his niece—and Consuelo.

"I'll take you home," said Yannick.

"No." I was just getting started.

But now another figure came to join our party, an older woman whom even my father had disliked. She stood at our table, staring down at me. "Good evening, count, monsieur, mademoiselle."

"Good evening, Madame Lucrece," said the men in unison as they stood. "Won't you join us?"

"I wouldn't think of taking the seat. Surely the countess will be wanting it." She leaned down to pat my hand. "I trust you know there is a countess, mademoiselle. Of course you do! I keep hoping to meet her. Why, when I saw how the count looked at you when he arrived tonight, I thought for a moment you must be her. Silly me."

Yannick, bless his soul, jumped in before I could speak. "Mademoiselle knows the countess well. In fact, she is the countess's *couturière*."

"Is she, indeed?" The woman turned to Antoine. "I didn't realize you took such a keen interest in fashion. You continue to amaze us, Count de Saint-Exupéry."

As she left, my companions exchanged glances. Antoine picked up his drink and carried it with him to a table in a corner of the room. Yannick called for a pot of coffee.

What did he know of falling in love? He'd never been married. He used to joke that he was too good of a cook to get married. He never seemed to have a girlfriend. He probably didn't even date.

He spoke quietly. "I'm sorry, Mignonne. I didn't know about Consuelo until she showed up while you were away—and then I assumed there was no reason for you to care. Never in a million years would I have set you up to be hurt." The pot arrived, and he poured us each a cup.

"I'm not hurt, I'm drunk."

That got a laugh from him.

"He doesn't even want Consuelo. Why do you think she's at home and he's here with me?"

"You do realize Madame Lucrece was just asking the same thing?"

"She's a meddler."

"She's your clientele."

The truth of that, or the coffee, made my stomach churn. "You think I should break it off with Antoine."

"As your uncle, I should insist that you do so." He stirred his coffee and reflected for a while on the steam.

As my uncle. I wondered what he thought that implied now that my father was gone and the closest substitute was him. I was sure we were both wondering what Papa would have said. The truth was, my father had always gone easy on me. He'd wanted me to be an artist, whatever that took and whatever it meant. While Leo's mechanical aptitudes had been overshadowed by his unruliness, I earned favor for both my early creative attempts and my occasional defiance. When Papa was home he had indulged me, made excuses to Mother for me, telling us both that we had to be open-minded, that there were worlds within me struggling to emerge.

All I'd managed to create so far was a world of confusion.

Yannick's spoon clattered lightly into his saucer. "You know, Mignonne, I hear a lot of confessions, if I may put it that way; and what people don't tell me outright, I see in how they eat. Half my customers are in love with someone other than their own husband or wife. I'm not a priest; I'm a restaurateur. I don't trade in penance but in private tables. I shuffle reservations. I make people happy. Their happiness makes the filet more tender, the crème brulée more sweet."

"You don't want me to break with Antoine."

"What I want is for your heart to be glad. You tell me what that would take."

"Make Consuelo go away."

"Your biggest client?"

I groaned.

Yannick pushed my coffee cup closer to me. "How on earth did you end up designing for her?"

"I don't know. I think it was Antoine's doing."

"Then he can help us fix at least one angle in this mess." He waved him over. "Listen, Saint-Ex. In a few days, we're going to have dinner together at Le Pavillon, the four of us, my treat."

"Four?" said Antoine.

"You and Consuelo, Mignonne and me."

I snorted.

Antoine said, "And this is intended to accomplish what?"

Yannick spread his arms. "Just a friendly dinner. A dinner between friends."

"I owe my wife neither explanation nor charade, and she is hardly in a position to expect either."

"My niece has a position to consider, too. She has persuaded Consuelo to commission some fashion work."

"You really are her *couturière?*" asked Antoine.

"I went to her apartment, like you asked. No more meeting her at the Alliance, just like you said."

Antoine brought his hand to his chest. "Thank you. This means much to me."

"What it means," said Yannick, "is a tenuous position for Mignonne. How will it look if she is seen with her client's husband, and at other times with his wife, but never with the two together? You know how the ladies here gossip. I know you don't want Mignonne to lose all chance of building a clientele. We'll take a prominent table. If you still think it's a bad idea when the time comes, I'll cancel the reservation at the last minute. I have that privilege. In the meantime, check with Consuelo and give me a call."

Leo had gone missing at some point. Now I noticed him again on his perch at the bar. He was watching.

I drained my cup. "I have to go. Have to get to the studio in the morning."

"You will be there late tomorrow, as well?" asked Antoine.

"Early, late. All or nothing, all day long."

24

The next day's work stretched on into twilight as I planned the construction of another dress of my own design. Dusky light lit the windows, lending a pink tint to the bricks of the wall and door, then faded as I continued to draw.

I had folded the silk chiffon and placed it within reach on my table where I could consider it as I sat with my book. I had long since turned on the table lamp; my eyes stung as I bent into its glow.

I was hunched over, worrying a detail—the exact spacing of gathers at a neckband—when footsteps sounded from the hall. The footfalls ceased, but their rhythm continued in a folk song I recalled from my childhood. Papa had sung it in upbeat tones. This voice—the middle timbre, the tinge of melancholy—it had to be Antoine's.

I set down my pencil and sighed in relief.

The door opened; the singing stopped. The yellowish light from the hall cast him in silhouette.

He said, "You look so peaceful sitting there in your island of light, as though time does not exist."

"It exists, believe me. I've been sitting here for hours."

When Antoine closed the door, the studio seemed to plunge into greater darkness than before, despite the constancy of the desk lamp. Unlit above us hung row after row of dangling green metal light shades. I said, "The switch for the overheads is on the wall to your right, where the keys are hanging."

He ignored the suggestion and crossed the shadowy room

with an unhurried gait. "The solution is not to turn on the lights, but to extinguish your lamp." He switched it off. "It is not so dark now. You see?"

It was true: the sky's cool, blue glow filled the studio as my eyesight adjusted. Outside, the skyscraper towers were only black silhouettes, but across the street, in low-rise buildings here and there, candlelight and gaslight glimmered against glass and swayed on walls, and incandescent lights burned with a tireless, steady smolder.

Antoine was looking beyond the rooflines, at the sky. He spoke quietly. "I went to Montreal for only a few days—and returned after five weeks. Did you not wonder what had become of me?"

"I thought that you made up your mind you never wanted to see me again."

"I was a hostage in your old land of refuge, Mignonne. First the Americans told me I had not the paperwork to return, then my body turned on me. I was ill, so drugged that I could only sleep. I wish I could leave this old crock of a body. Since my crash in the Sahara, it only betrays me. Even yesterday, for perhaps an hour or two, I was again like a man on his deathbed. One minute nothing, the next, a fever of thirty-three." He glanced at me. "I don't know what it is in your Fahrenheit. This strange pain I have, this thing that comes and goes as fast as a rabbit in its hole, that has plagued me for years, I thought at last it would be the end of me. God's hand has crushed me into the ground many times and I did not fear. But then, a sudden fever, a sharp pain . . ."

"You should sit down."

"Death doesn't frighten me. I only felt sad that I might die with so little achieved and with no purpose ahead."

"Oh, Antoine, don't be ludicrous. Regardless of what happens with the Air Force, you still have your writing to do."

"I do have writing to do, in fact." His tone lifted. "And not just the unfinished manuscript I lug around. I have been working on an idea for something completely different: a sort of children's tale about a pilot and a boy, a young prince who appears from out of nowhere."

"Kind of how you like to show up at my door?"

"Perhaps—if I came from another planet and not just from uptown."

"Tell me about this prince."

"Come, let's sit where it's comfortable. If we're going to talk about a boy who lives on an asteroid, we should be looking at the stars."

"There are no stars tonight."

"Stars often require imagination." He took my hand and led me across the studio. As we settled on the sofa, he said, "When I fly, I imagine the stars as lights shining up from the earth, one for each person who waits for me."

How many waited for him—girls going through the motions of their business, keeping their hands busy, wrestling with their worries as they worked, the pinpricks of their lamps spread across the earth like storm lanterns placed on docks and door steps for the lost and the late?

This time he had been ill; another time he might be on a mission, or crashed, or traveling, or simply disappeared into the sitting room or the bedroom of some other patient girl. Did he really see all those burning hearts as coolly twinkling, infinitely distant stars? Had he never waited himself, never felt the ember flare and sting when prodded by the smallest thought? Waiting was tiring; it was taxing trying always to keep the pain at bay. Had he never learned this? Not even in the year I had been in Montreal?

I asked, "Who is it that waits for you?"

"There is always someone waiting."

As there was always someone in love with him. "Do they ever give up on you?"

His gaze went again to the window.

I asked, "Do they ever fly with you?"

"Do you know how long it has been since I have flown?"

He knew I did. I refused to soften to his ache. "You have told me, yes."

"Did I also tell you how I fell in love in the sky?"

"With the sky?"

"How I fell in love with the woman who would become my wife. Soon after I met Consuelo, I took her up for a ride. The plane was shaking as it clawed its way off the ground. I was crammed into the seat, my forehead almost glued to the window, the yoke close to my chest and the harness strapping me to the seat back that felt as though it could be snapped by the pressure of my spine as we lifted off—and when I looked over, there was Consuelo sitting as tiny as a sparrow perched on man's palm, her eyes wide, her body trembling from head to toe. As soon as we were at altitude, I said something with a great show of bravado, about having her life in my hands. I pulled back on the stick and threw the plane into loops."

"But that's awful!" Just the thought made me feel sick.

"The engine stalled."

"Oh my God."

"We started hurtling out of the sky."

I clutched his arm as though to stop him falling. I would never fly. I vowed I would never, ever fly.

Antoine covered my hand with his. "I had cut the engine on purpose."

"You didn't."

"I did. I stalled it, and told Consuelo I would save us both if she would grant me a kiss. We were falling to our deaths— imagine—when I leaned in to her and—"

I stood up. "Why are you telling me this?"

"I have nothing to give you, Mignonne. I cannot give you commitment or children. I won't abandon my wife. I cannot live with her, I cannot spend any length of time with her, but I worry for her; I cannot entirely abandon my post. I cannot think when she's near me, but neither can I leave her to struggle on her own."

"No one's asking you to leave Consuelo."

"Don't get angry." He too stood. He smoothed back my hair. He said, "I know how it is. You wonder why I married her, why I stay married to her still."

"You torture yourself."

"I cannot undo a holy sacrament."

"Sacrament or sacrifice? You're like a man who is offered a knife but insists on staying tied to his stake."

"And you are as free as a river." His eyes grew moist. "And as pure. Oh, Mignonne. You cannot know how I suffocate. You can't imagine how heavy I feel. I am drowning in uselessness. The Air Force doesn't want me. I fail at love. I cannot write or fly. For half my life, I was like a farmer with the clouds as my fields. I saw the true face of the earth. Am I to forget all this, and join the masses that spend their lives on meaningless tasks, driven by the tyranny of petty things, for no reason except that it is expected of them?" His forehead furrowed sharply, eyelids closing on a fleeting pain.

I saw then why he couldn't move forward with me. His whole life had stalled.

So I kissed him. I kissed his lips. I kissed his eyelids, his earlobe, his neck. I could save us both. I would take away every pain.

"I ought to leave," he said.

"Stay." I took his hand and slid it around me. I pulled the ribbon that cinched my waist. "Open my dress."

Antoine's chest was broad and solid, his arms muscular. His scars and imperfectly mended bones told of survival beyond the realm of hope. I had unbuttoned his shirt to feel his heart beat against mine. As his hands moved over my skin, as his fingertips slid under my corset to my breasts, my breath quickened and deepened, and I reached for his belt—but he captured my wrist and urged me to the floor.

I sat on the rug while Antoine propped himself on his elbow beside me. He caressed my ankles and calves, then nudged my arms away from my legs, his bracelet's engraved letters catching and holding the moonlight.

A minute ago I had felt so sure of myself, so unguarded, and now—

My breath caught. Antoine had licked my leg.

He arched over me, pushing my dress up, and his tongue grazed my knee. I started to tremble. His mouth mounted higher. I reached down, and his moist lips closed on my fingertips. His hand now moved between my thighs. A rivulet of sound unfurled in my throat.

Antoine raised his head to watch my face. Sweat gleamed on the hair of his chest. I tried to speak. The stars in the ceiling were shifting. How could this be wrong, this slide into emptiness and peace? For a long moment, everything seemed to suspend in a balance so perfect that it could only come from God himself.

Some long moments later, I inhaled.

I lay on my back on the rug, the breeze from the open windows stealing the dampness from my skin.

"There is something more you want, Mignonne?"

"Water."

Antoine groaned.

I climbed onto the sofa to watch him pad away.

"Don't fall asleep," he said. "I will take you to your home."

"No," I murmured. "Can't."

Leo would throw a fit if he thought I'd been out alone so late, in the darkness of the emptying streets. Better to be in the locked studio, safe. Leo expected me to work all night; he had said so himself.

25

The world was made for men, thought Consuelo, especially in America. Witness the peepholes in the doors: they were always too high, positioned to the comfort level of the men who installed them. Men set the rules of machinery, mechanisms, emotions, love. It was no wonder they always managed to get their way. A woman had to be strong and cunning. She had to have her wits about her and her full quiver of weapons at the ready.

Bah. First she needed a stepstool to see through the goddamn door.

There had been one here weeks ago, before Consuelo had thrown out the old furnishings and brought some modern life to this room. It was a curse to possess good taste. It meant one had to resort, now and then, to standing on a sturdy valise to watch one's husband return to his home.

Tonio sometimes had visitors at his apartment: the city's most interesting Frenchmen, his publishers or his translator, often his secretary to transcribe his notes or recordings, and probably, surely, a girlfriend—though Consuelo had yet to catch him at it. And that was not the only thing worth watching for. There was the timing of Tonio's return. If he came home late, Consuelo would be obliged to make a point of coming home even later on her next night out. If she had to worry until two a.m., let Tonio fret until five! There was the posture with which he stood at the door, a call to her suspicion or sympathy. And there were the sounds that filtered through the tiny tunnel and curved glass. Why would he sing or whistle? Why should he be so carefree?

Now he stood at his door, fitting in his key as though he

hadn't a worry on his mind. How did he do that again and again? So many times she had watched just this: her husband walking up to his door as if he had every right to turn his key, enter, and close his life to her gaze. She was tired of staring at a blank brown door, its frame curving like a comic book bubble threatening to burst in her face, tired of standing with her glossy lashes bent and damp against a golden ring.

She went into the hallway and knocked on his door, holding her dressing gown closed around her.

"Good evening, Consuelo." He looked as though his mind were somewhere else.

"How are your shirts?"

"Should I know something about my shirts?"

"I told the concierge to send a maid to gather them and clean and iron them."

"Thank you. Good night."

"Wait."

"Yes?"

"You'll crush my foot if you close the door that way." She had placed her bare toes across the threshold.

"I wouldn't want to do that. You have lovely feet."

How generous! How adorable. Whatever had brought about this mood was something worth repeating. "My feet miss your strong hands, Tonio. No one knows how to press out the aches like you do."

"Your feet ache? Poor Consuelo. Mine, too. Getting old is—"

Old! She shoved the door. Its angled edge smacked into Tonio's cheekbone. Her hand came up to batter him on the other side of his face. How dare he call her old!

"Quiet." He caught her wrist and pulled her into his apartment, closing the door behind them. "You are not the only inhabitant of this building, that you can stand in the hallway and scream. Do you want me to be evicted?"

Let them throw him on the street for making his beleaguered

wife cry! Just let them come and ask her why her heart was so painfully torn. She began to weep. "I have given my whole life to you, Tonio. And now you say I am old, that you are done with me."

"I did not say you are old."

Consuelo pulled open her robe. "Look at me. Touch me." She took his hands and placed them on her breasts.

He let his hands fall to his sides. "Where is Binty tonight?"

"Probably with one of your Fifth Avenue tarts!"

Tonio took off his jacket and hung it on the back of a chair. He strolled over to his desk, straightened a stack of papers, and pushed aside his bracelet to check the date on his pilot watch. He found the first blank page in his notebook, and uncapped his pen. "Good night."

"You still want me," said Consuelo. "You still love me."

"Love is like a scar. It is impossible to excise."

"You'd cut your arm off to get rid of it. You'd do anything to rid yourself of me."

"I will start by asking politely. I have a deadline. I need to work through the night and I need to begin now. Would you be so kind as to go home?"

"You are my home. I belong here."

"Do you know any other man whose wife comes to his office to watch him work? Please. You see I am at my desk. This is all I have"—he indicated the shape of the tabletop with two angular chops of his hand—"and the hope of quiet, and nothing else. Do not take from me even this. If I have no peace, I cannot write. If I cannot write, I might just as well cut off both my arms. Either way, we will both end up living in a ditch."

"I'm bothering you," she said humbly.

"God, yes."

"And your apartment is so small. You should come move into mine; I have more space than I can fill on my own."

"Give it time."

Consuelo rose up onto tiptoes. "Really, darling? You'll consider moving in?"

"What? I said, 'Give it time.' You will fill your space as you always do, then your apartment will not seem so large." He sat down at his desk, his back to her.

Her spirit deflated. He wanted her gone. Fine. She would leave him alone.

"I'll give you some time to yourself," she said.

"Thank you."

"How long do you need? I can be a model of patience. I'll wait for you in your bed."

"Consuelo, please, leave me alone!"

It used to be she who would turn him away—in punishment, in control, to heighten his desire. It had been forever since he'd made love to her, forever since he'd tried.

"I am giving myself to you, Tonio."

"Don't."

"We're not finished. I still believe in us. I believe in you."

"You believe in a memory."

"Prove me wrong, my love."

He ignored her.

She snatched up a picture frame and flung it. Tonio ducked as though he had foreseen its course. It hit the wall with a resounding crack that spattered into a tinkling shower.

"You think you're a man of duty?" cried Consuelo. "A real man would do anything he could to satisfy his wife."

But even as she said it, she knew only everything would be enough. She wanted the lover he had once been for her in full, unbridled force—his passion breaking in her, shattering her like ice.

26

I wasn't sure what I was seeing, at first, in the light of dawn.

I was still on the couch in the studio. Antoine was gone. The sun—great relief—was low in the sky. Madame would not arrive for hours.

I lay my head back down and tried to follow a pattern of white lines that stretched across the floor.

The floorboards were pocked and scratched, the varnish unevenly worn. It wasn't unusual for the light to catch here and there. I had often lost myself in daydreams gazing over it; often my eyes had seen a figure in the marks within the wood. Even now, I could change my focus and make the image disappear, make its pale lines blur into dashes of sunlight and nothing more.

But it returned, and, with it, realization: Antoine had made a drawing for me.

He had also covered me with a length of red wool. I pulled it around my shoulders and eased my feet onto the rug and beyond, stepping onto the floor with the crimson fabric a dragging cape.

At my feet there was a drawing made in dressmaker's chalk, some seven or eight feet tall. Its base was a circle, a planet. Rising from it was a single rose—a rose as tall as I was, as alone on its globe as I felt in the world.

The magnitude of the drawing compelled me. I grabbed my largest sketchbook and painstakingly copied the rose. I drew sketches of the entire composition, and page after page of its details. Then, with a rag of terrycloth in my hand, and a dress from a garment rack pulled over my head, I scrubbed Antoine's chalk away. Soon all that remained were flecks of white, deep in the old scratches, smears of grey where the drawing had found exposed, unvarnished wood.

I checked the studio for any remaining traces of his presence: ashes, lost hairs, errant papers. I sniffed for his cologne, his cigarettes. Then I stood in the strengthening sunlight, naked under my dress. My back and hips ached, yet I felt clean and alive.

I turned my sketchbook to a fresh page and drew the rose from memory.

The rose grew in my mind—appliquéd on flowing fabrics, swaying on skirts, arcing on women's shoulders, sparkling from brooches pinned to hats, painted on scarves, drawing attention to itself in shimmering sequins. I wanted her—the rose—to call out from every plane and curve of a woman's form, to claim attention and love, to be bold in sharing her beauty with the world.

Smiling over my book, my hand moving in unencumbered strokes, on page after page after page, I drew.

27

It was still early—the traffic outside was still building—when there was a knock on the studio door. I put aside my sketchbook and went to answer it.

It was Leo. I grinned up at him. "Well, hello!"

Relief shot through his expression but was quickly driven away. He pressed past me and scanned the length of the studio to his left and to his right. His gaze remained for a while on the target of red wool that I had tossed across the couch. "Where were you all night? Who was here with you?"

"No one was here."

"Who is he?"

I closed the door. "There is no 'he.'"

Leo considered my expression, the set of my shoulders, the stubbornness in my eyes. He watched as I turned away. Suspicion clouded his voice. "You haven't been home in days."

"You're guessing, and your guess is lousy. If you could manage to come home yourself sometime, you would see that I'm there. I come home late, but I come home. Exactly where do you sleep?"

"You weren't home last night."

"Then I suppose you were, for a change."

"You could have at least telephoned."

"Isn't it better to be locked in working late than to go out into the streets looking for a phone?"

His anger wavered. "You better be home early tonight."

"I might be. I'm not sure. I've got a lot to do. I'm working on sketches for an important client."

He slipped his hands into his pockets and cast around for something to focus on. "Those them?" He walked over to a large drawing board that I had left on the window ledge. A stack of Arches paper was held to it with a metal clip. He lifted the top sheet and looked at one after another of the pages, all the way down to the wood, then he let the papers fall. "This is what you do all day?"

"Among other things."

"Like what?"

"I sew. I study the fashions in magazines and storefronts. I think of ways we can get attention and business. I take things apart and put things together—just like you. I try to put everything I know into my designs. I try to learn what I can and come up with something new."

He wandered down the studio. "You designed this?" He was looking at the butterfly dress on the wall.

"That's one of the designs Madame Fiche stole from my portfolio. That's the piece that was in the magazine." The dress had lost its disturbing effect on me. When I looked at it now, I saw only color, fabric, and line.

But Leo seemed mesmerized. He squinted at it, and reached up to stroke the velvet with the knuckles of his rough hand. "Soft." His fingertips gingerly touched the jeweled beads at the waist. I wondered if he had a girl, if he was picturing her in such a dress. He asked, "Ever gotten a penny for this stuff?"

"No."

"Nothing? Is there just this one?"

"There are nine other pieces hanging on a rack."

"Ten in all. Then we'll call this ten percent, and call it even." His hand pivoted and gripped. "Fair's fair." He yanked the dress to the floor and gathered it into his arms.

"You can't do that!"

"Someone's got to stand up for themselves." The fabric trailed after him as he hurried to the door. "I figure I get a say. That bitch used your drawings, but you took the idea from my back." The door slammed shut behind him.

I did take the idea from Leo.

During the winter holiday in my last year at NYFS, I was home one night with my brother. It had been weeks since we'd spent any stretch of time together in the apartment—either I was at school or teaching at the Alliance, or Leo was at work or God-knows-where—and I was struck by the realization that he had changed. The pudginess that had long overlaid his muscles had faded away since the summer, since Papa's death, leaving him rangy and hard of limb, gaunt around the eyes and mouth. His jawbone had sharpened, and his cheekbones, like rock displaced at a fault line, thrust out over the valleys of his cheeks. I was used to his harmless, crude jocularity and defiant optimism, but now they seemed tainted with desperation. He had always been so determined to be independent— but from what? It was as though Leo no longer knew where to anchor his rebellion, or whether rebellion had been worth the strain.

He had been standing in the doorway of my bedroom, watching me pack a suitcase for a brief trip to Montreal.

"I wish you would come," I had said. "Mother really wants to see you."

"No reason she can't come here."

"She wants to do something at the cemetery on Christmas Eve. It'll be nice. We'll light candles and say some prayers together before midnight Mass." It had sounded beautiful to me: holding Mother's hand, candlelight flickering on the snow, puffs of white breath with each "Blessed are thou."

"You'll freeze to death," said Leo, and as I met his eyes I thought of Papa ice cold in his grave. Suddenly Leo's face reddened and rucked up, and I was alarmed to see that he was about to cry. But he groped for his cigarettes and matchbox, and waved away the moment. I locked my suitcase, closing my eyes against Leo's heavy streams of smoke.

"Oh, hey," he said as I slipped the key into my purse. He was cheery again: good old Leo. "Something I've been meaning to show you." He unbuttoned his shirt.

I winced in anticipation. His arms were already engraved with scars from his job building carnival rides.

He removed his shirt and his undershirt. "Have a look at my back. What do you think: is it a beaut or what?"

I drew in my breath. Spanning shoulder to shoulder was a butterfly, a tattoo set off by an aura of red. Its segmented body aligned to the ridges and furrows of his spine; its graceful wings—purple, blue, crimson—spread along the arcing muscles of his back. Black antennae stretched in a vee that curved to hook his neck.

It looked wet and raw, pinned down alive, rising and falling with his breath. I touched it. Leo's creature was a map of a thousand welts.

My final portfolio was due in three months' time, and I had nothing. I opened my sketchbook on the train. I took my brother's pain and used it, even as it settled fully into his skin. I made of it something stunning, extravagant, grotesque. What else are we to do with the things that sear our hearts?

Someone's got to stand up for themselves: that was what he'd said. And maybe he was justified. Maybe I should have given him the whole lot and been done with it; let him spread its opulence among his girlfriends or streetwalkers, wherever it was that he spread his seed. Maybe no justification was needed. If it hadn't been for Papa's death, for Leo's pain, for his tattoo, if it hadn't been for my empathy and desperation and envy, and for Madame's uncanny manipulative skills, there would have been no Butterfly Collection at all. Where did the credit lie, and where did the blame?

Madame entered without a word as I was sweeping the floor. At her desk, she pulled out her book of accounts and made a few notations.

I crouched to use the dustpan, and a wave of exhaustion seeped in. Was it just yesterday that Antoine had been here, that he had been with me? Yesterday he had drawn the picture on the floor. And then I had drawn, too, pages and pages filled with sketches of the rose. And then Leo, come to take his due.

And today was only beginning.

I knelt, fingertips on the floor, the parallel floorboards wavering like the rain wavers down the windows at JFK.

Madame crossed over and gave me her hand. It was small and bony, firm. When I was standing, she gripped my elbow and led me to the sitting area. We settled in the chairs.

She said, "It gets no easier than this. If you cannot manage the strain of these times, you do not belong anywhere near the helm of an atelier."

"I'm just tired. It's been a long couple of days."

"Every day should be long. With success, they become longer still."

My fatigued eyes wandered to the wall behind my boss, to the hook and hanger lacking a dress.

"You have not the strength I expected of you," said Madame, "nor the commitment you showed as a student. There was a time when you rose to every challenge I placed before you. You were desperate to learn."

"I still am. I'm here late most nights, trying things, figuring out things that we barely touched on in school."

"You play with textiles instead of applying proper techniques. You wrap; you twist. All of America is in tailored pieces cut high at the neck, padded shoulders, garments that make up in diligent workmanship what they lack in generosity—and you devote yourself to draping as though it is the foundation on which everything stands. You have the skills to give women what they want, Mignonne. I don't understand why you resist. You know better than most how to fit, how to perfect a collar, how to hang a facing, how to bind, which stitch produces which effect."

Yes, but I'd discovered a whole range of exciting methods and effects since I'd left the classroom. Through my own research, curiosity, and trial and error, I'd learned how to shape a garment with just an iron and steam. I'd learned to use hidden weights to affect draping—in ways more exciting than stringing a ball chain through a bottom hem. I'd been experimenting with soft harnesses that made a garment's structure virtually invisible to the eye. There were so many tricks for making the surface of the fabric perform.

I said, "Wrapping and twisting is craft, too. We shouldn't be afraid of adopting new techniques or making things of real lasting beauty. The less we tailor and fuss, the more life we can give to a garment. Instead of starting with some rigid concept and trying to make it work for clients, we can give women clothing that will be right for their own bodies."

"Listen to me, Mignonne—"

"We can be making pieces that outlive all the trends."

"*Écoutez-moi!* We are not gods in the heavens that we should imagine our work everlasting, and scorn society's direction. You believe you have a vision. It is not one I share. So: you will pursue it on your own. I will not be derailed by your base obsessions. Atelier Fiche no longer requires your talents."

For a moment I felt as though blackout drapes had been passed across my eyes. "But Madame. I thought we were working things out. You gave me the white silk."

She straightened in her chair. "I do my utmost to uphold proper ideals, Mignonne, but I am an *artiste*. The artist's eye is amoral. It doesn't care that some things of beauty are better left unseen. I abhor the baseness with which you clothe yourself, yet it is the artist's nature to be moved by the sight of a youthful figure sparely and provocatively draped. I gave in to impulse; I gave you the silk: more the shame on me."

"There's nothing wrong with being moved, Madame! You shouldn't regret it." Or punish me for it. I suspected she wasn't simply prudish; she seemed to feel that a love of inherent beauty was a weakness. And not just human beauty: she had whipped the white fabric in the air as though trying to snap away its powers of enchantment.

I thought of how it fluttered to the ground like petals or leaves. "Let me tell you a story my father told me."

"No, thank you."

"There were dandelions on my grandparents' lawns in France, and it used to make my grandmother mad to have to pay the gardeners to pull them when they could be tending the formal gardens. One day when the dandelions were white, Papa started picking and blowing on them, and his mother came out yelling. But when she went over to him, she saw how pretty it was—all those lacy floating seeds. She even blew on a flowerhead herself. You see what I'm saying? She just had to shift her perspective to see how powerful natural beauty could be."

"Very touching." Madame's mouth twisted. "Your father's mother paid the help to tend the gardens and the lawns and the weeds. My mother dug up dandelions with her own hands to have something to put on the table for dinner."

I felt sick. I had so much still to learn, and the means to learn it here. I couldn't start over on my own, with no studio and few tools, no reputation, no boxes of fabric stacked and overflowing, with supplies quickly getting scarce on the street. Talk of the birth of American design was starting to seem like mostly talk. Where were the jobs? I would have to resign myself to working as a copyist in a department store studio, anonymous and stagnant, as girls like me had always done.

And what about Madame? How would she survive? "What will you do on your own? How will you pay the bills and the rent? You can't build your name by taking in more sewing jobs. How will you create a new collection?"

"I hope you are not suggesting I cannot conceive of a collection on my own."

"It's a lot of work, a lot of time to invest without money coming in."

"Work can be shared. There are a thousand girls who would love to take your place." Girls who would build their own advancement upon the foundation I had laid. "And as of September money will no longer be such a concern. The school has approved my return to teaching. The rent will be paid."

"You can't teach and try to keep the studio going."

"Of course I will."

"You need all your energy for Atelier Fiche!" Madame's passion had to fire the work of her hands and eyes, not be spat away in frustration and cursing as she walked between students' desks. I needed this studio and this job. Madame needed to not throw it all away.

I jerked my head in frustration—and my gaze met the wall where the dress had hung. Thank God for Leo's sense of entitlement; he'd been right that I needed some of that myself. I took a deep breath. "NYFS won't hire a proven plagiarist."

Madame froze for a moment; only her nostrils moved. She said, "Ah, you play your card. Very amusing. However, your threat is empty. There is no proof." She stood up and held out her hand. "You may leave the studio now. Give me the key."

"I have the issue of *Women's Wear Daily* at home. It proves that you presented my butterfly concept as your own."

"It proves nothing. No artwork has ever been created in a vacuum. It would be entirely acceptable if your work inspired the profile of my collection."

"My work didn't inspire your collection, it *is* your collection!

The dress in that *Women's Wear* photograph matches the sketch in my portfolio in every possible way."

"You are forgetting that you did not retrieve your portfolio from my office. I had no choice but to throw your sketches in the trash."

"I don't think so, Madame. I found them gathering dust on top of a shelf on one of my first days here." There had been no shock in coming across them as I had cleaned the studio, nor had I been excited to see them again. It had been largely in pursuit of tidiness that I had taken them home.

Madame sat down. She cleared her throat. "You claim the resemblance is not general. Your argument has no basis. Whatever your sketches show or do not show, the photograph is no comparison; it is too small to capture the garment's details."

"I'll show them my sketches and I'll show them the actual dress."

"If you only had such a dress." Madame smiled. "It is entirely logical that a designer might destroy a garment of her own design if new regulations rendered the piece difficult to sell, don't you agree? These days, every sequin and notion is precious and must be harvested from stagnant inventory. Oh yes, there once existed a dress vaguely resembling a butterfly. It is true that some people have seen a butterfly dress, of some sort, displayed on my studio wall. But believe me, Mignonne, all trace of it will have disappeared from the studio before you even reach the street."

I pointed past her to the empty wall. "I'm not leaving Atelier Fiche. And you are not going to teach."

Madame spun in her chair to look, and for a long time she did not turn back.

28

Thank you for coming. I hope you are all enjoying this incredible fair. I'd like to speak with you about inspiration, and a man who has inspired so many: Antoine Jean-Baptiste Marie Roger de Saint-Exupéry. In fact, it's Antoine who inspired the name of my retrospective collection, Star Pilot—which we're standing in the midst of today. And although he was a stellar pilot, what I meant to convey with my title was that Antoine de Saint-Exupéry was a pilot not only of the skies but also of the stars.

His readers will like that, especially the fans who believe that Antoine is living on asteroid B-612. Soon we'll be sending men to the moon; maybe they'll see him up there.

If anyone could find a way to live among the stars, Antoine could. The sky was his playground and his workplace; when he couldn't be in it, he couldn't be at home in the world.

Once he came to one of our rendezvous carrying a box of whirligigs—helicopters of paper folded into T-shaped wings. As we made our way to the Empire State Building, he prattled on in an excited stream, explaining how rivers and skyscrapers affected the prevailing winds . . . predicting flight paths, percentages of whirligigs that would move this way versus that . . . musing about his research and what it could inform . . . describing inventions that seemed preposterous to me. On the observation deck, we tipped the contents of the box over the side. The whirligigs spun and spread over the whole of the island. The sight left me speechless. He owns Manhattan, I thought. Give him paper, give him sky, and he can do anything.

You've read his books. Maybe you haven't all read *Terre des hommes*—Wind, Sand and Stars—the novel from which Expo 67 takes its theme. But no doubt you have all read and loved . . .
  (Pause. Indicate with smile and gestures that audience should shout out name of book.)
  Which is precisely why we have all come together today!

I put my pen down. What an embarrassing attempt at camaraderie. And do Canadians ever shout anything together? I would ask the couple next to me, but they've snuggled their way back to sleep.

To begin at the beginning, my story of inspiration begins not with planes or stars, but with butterflies. Butterflies were in an early draft of the manuscript, by the way.

I throw down my pen. It bounces off my notebook, hits my neighbor's leg, and rolls away.

"Geez, Miggy, you look like hell," said Leo. "Maybe even worse."
  We had spent the previous night arguing over the butterfly dress. He wouldn't tell me where it was, or whether I could get it, or anything else. We argued; we talked; we drank. We had ended up talking about childhood and Papa, fashion, France, and war.
  "It's not fair," I said. "I think I only had three drinks."
  "Three glasses of Scotch isn't nothing, sister. And then the

wine. You know it's the weekend, don't you? If I were you, I'd go back to bed."

But there was Consuelo's upcoming visit to the studio to think about. I needed drawings to convince Madame that we should present something fresher than the Butterfly Collection. And it was already close to noon. I pulled my hair into a ponytail, though my roots ached in protest, put on my most comfortable slacks and an untucked shirt, and slipped my feet into casual slides.

Leo was in the kitchen spooning dumpling dough into a pot of boiling milk. "Off to inflict yourself on the innocent civilians of New York?"

"Going to the studio."

"Oh yeah? Bring me back something nice."

Riding the subway only increased the throbbing in my head. I made my way to Madame's building, opened the street-level door, and jumped back in surprise.

Antoine was sitting on the steps to the lobby, looking petulant. He closed his notebook, dusted off his trousers, and took his folder from a stair. "How am I to borrow the studio when no one has given me a key?"

As if I didn't have my own problems. For one thing, this miserable brain.

He said, "I spent the whole night in interruptions. I haven't written a word, and I haven't slept a wink." He began to climb the steps, but stopped when I didn't follow. "Well, come on. I've been waiting for you for an hour."

Audacious, rude man. I opened the door. "Leave."

Antoine clattered down the stairs, his soles making an ungodly noise, and stopped beside me. "Don't be like this, Mignonne! Good morning. I'm sorry. Please forgive me."

He tilted his head one way, then the other, ducking down

to my height, trying to catch my stubbornly averted gaze. "It is only that I am desperate. A million hornets are buzzing in my head. I need to work. My publishers, they will lock me up if I don't get them something soon."

"That's a lie."

"You are right; they will wait. But I cannot wait; I need to complete this manuscript. Every day it takes is another day in which I am chained to my desk in America instead of fighting to free my country. And the money, you understand. I cannot leave until I settle my debts, until the book is in my publishers' hands."

Chained . . . what? I was in no shape to argue or to understand.

"And my apartment," he continued. "It is unbearable. I cannot work there. Consuelo is killing me with her visits, her demands, her staying out to all hours with whomever suits her fancy, all night, without discretion or sense." He stood in front of me, jittery. "Please, can you let me in now? We both have work to do. We should get started. Please, Mignonne." He gave me a contrite, endearing smile. "Let's go upstairs."

I followed him, my head pounding with my feet. Let's go upstairs, indeed. This was not how I had hoped to someday hear those words. I asked, "Do you really think Madame Fiche was serious when she said you could borrow the studio?"

"Does it matter? Since she suggested I do so, she cannot blame me—or you—if I do."

Upstairs, I pulled out my key but did not slide it into the lock. "Bring me coffee, lots of black coffee, if you want me to let you in."

He examined my face. "Ah. Poor Mignonne. I did not realize that last night you perhaps had too much to drink."

Antoine returned with a full restaurant pot of coffee and a bottle of wine. "The waiter attempted to limit me to a single cup, and no bottle at all, in the interests of national defense. But he gave in readily when I explained the severity of the situation. Unfortunately, I had to do so with the most grotesque pantomime." He gave me a sample performance, staggering and cross-eyed, that left me guffawing painfully. "I'm afraid I may have besmirched your dignity a little." He held the bottle under his arm to lock the door behind him.

I had settled into a corner of the sofa with my open sketchbook on my lap.

"I'm sorry," he said, tiptoeing. "I am stopping you from working."

"You're not. I am working."

Antoine peered at the page. "Apparently everything next season, including the models, will be invisible."

I swung the book at him, and he laughed as he swatted it away.

"Come now, Mignonne. Surely it is not that hard." He took a blank sheet from his folder, filched the pencil from my hand, and in a few confident strokes completed a sketch of a lithe, sensual beauty in a clingy, off-the-shoulder dress and a featherweight cape that hovered above the ground.

It was stunning. I said, "You're a swine!"

"Ha-ha! You take yourself too seriously. Come, let us play for a bit." He pulled a deck of cards from his pocket.

"Coffee."

"I have it, hot, right here. You have cups?"

Of course I didn't have cups.

"No? It is just as well. What you really need, first, is a small bit of wine. In a moment, your headache will be fixed."

He roamed the studio looking for a tool, and finally reamed out the cork with sewing shears.

"Madame Fiche would string you up."

"Madame is all too serious herself. Now"—he sat down beside me—"just a little bit on your lips." He supported the bottle while I took a tiny sip. "Good. Are you ready for a short break? I will teach you a simple trick—how to make a card disappear."

He stood on the rug, cards jumping, eyes laughing.

I could hardly follow what he was doing, never mind memorize how to recreate the illusion myself, but it wasn't unpleasant to watch him perform. I drank from the bottle and began to breathe more easily.

He moved gracefully as he demonstrated the mysteries of the trick, very light on his feet for a man who had broken so many bones.

I had asked him about one of his scars at the studio the other day.

"I was flying a Simoun. Very simple compared to what we have today. When we crash landed, the nose curled like the toe of a sultan's slipper."

"How exotic."

"Just so. The sun was shining; I had my mechanic friend by my side; life was good."

"And your Guatemala City crash?"

"Broken collarbone—right here."

"As I heard it, the plane was smashed to smithereens and you were, too."

"One gets used to being reassembled."

"Bernard says the repairs haven't always been good."

"The mechanics'?"

"The surgeons'."

Antoine looked at me sharply. "What did he tell you?"

"He said your bones weren't always set properly."

"And?" The scar that ran from the corner of Antoine's lip to his jaw seemed to have darkened.

"That the crash in Guatemala was the start of your fevers. I'm sorry; I didn't think it was a secret. He spoke freely to me."

Antoine lit a cigarette with a long draw. "So you have been seeing Lamotte." Smoke seeped from his mouth and veiled his face. Then suddenly he was muttering: "Of course you are free—and he is closer to your age. Of course you should. You are right, you are always right. I knew you would like him. And if—"

I pressed my fingers to his lips. "Are you losing your marbles, Antoine?"

"Am I?"

"Hold on. I'll check." Brazenly, I dropped my hand to the front of his trousers. "Everything's there. You have nothing to worry about."

That had pleased and amused him. He said, "Nor should you worry, Mignonne. Lamotte speaks openly because he knows that I trust you. But he is not loose with secrets. I have known him for a long time. I would trust Lamotte with my very soul."

I refocused: we were alone in Madame's studio and Antoine was still talking. He was still standing in front of me holding out his cards.

"And that is all there is to it." He came laughing back to join me on the sofa and take a swig of wine. "You must try it on Madame Fiche."

"Oh God, no. Madame would turn up her nose."

"Consuelo too."

"Consuelo doesn't seem like such a serious type."

"She is full of fantasy, but she has lost the taste for simple play. Her imagination, though, is enormous. She could convince one that a hat is a boa constrictor that has swallowed an elephant. She sculpts. At times she paints. She draws. Mostly, she makes up fantasies. She wants to write."

"And does she write?"

"That is a good question. I have come across pages that are written in her voice but not in her hand. She may be dictating, or she may be relying on the talents of a literary friend."

"Fiction?"

"She calls it a memoir, and says I don't have the right to ask her not to tell the story of her own life." He sighed. "She has acted when it was the thing to do. In Oppède, where she lived with a colony of artists after the exodus from Paris, they had all sorts of ways to pass the time. Skits. Games of the heart. I'm sure she misses the drama of it all. She makes up for it by engineering her own."

I rubbed the edge of my sketchbook. "I guess sometimes you must wish for a life of peace and quiet."

"I crave it," he said huskily. "It is not easy to escape commitments one has made. It is not possible to shed the duties and demands one carries in the heart." He opened his folder, pulled out a drawing, and contemplated it. "So it is in my new story. I am calling it *The Little Prince*. I asked Lamotte to illustrate it, but he insists I am capable of creating the pictures on my own."

He handed me the drawing. Rising from the bottom right was a miniature planet in a sunset violet hue. On the planet stood a boy—the blond, wild-haired boy Antoine had been doodling for more than a year. Another planet, with a single orbiting ring, was visible far away. Robust stars sat like rivets in the sky.

The boy wore springtime green—a short-sleeved, buttoned shirt, and long pants that flared toward the hem, where pointed shoes stood sturdily on his planet's curving ground. Antoine had captured perfectly a child's softly rounded muscles at rest.

The red of his bow tie and belt were reflected in the slight flush of his cheeks. Golden hair fanned out from his head like soft flames. His face was simple and pure, sketched with a quick stroke for the bridge of a childish nose, the mouth no more than a brief bar—a mere hyphen—as though he held his emotions in check. His eyes were small ovals, defined with ink that swelled thicker at the bottom so that rather than being blank and empty, they looked longingly down—at a flower, a rose.

My rose, captured forever in Antoine's art. My whole body warmed with pleasurable surprise.

Carefully, reverently, I placed Antoine's drawing on top of the sketchbook in my lap. "Tell me the story."

"A pilot crashes in the middle of the desert with nothing but sand for thousands of miles around. He's awakened by the voice of a little boy."

"This boy."

"Yes. He is a prince."

"He's dressed very simply here, for a prince."

"Because he is going to be traveling. He comes to the desert from far away."

"From this planet?"

"Yes. The asteroid known as B-612."

"I see. B-612." We sat shoulder to shoulder on the sofa. I had my feet up under me. Antoine sat with his long-injured leg held almost straight.

I said, "He looks worried."

"It is love that does this to him."

"Because he's away from someone he loves?"

"In this drawing, because he is with her. But later in the story, in the desert, it will be because they are apart."

"Is it a love story, Antoine?"

"All stories are love stories."

I was transfixed by the expression on the face of the little prince. "Before you tell me anything more, I want to know the ending. I'm afraid your story will make me cry."

"Because it is a love story? It isn't love that causes pain, but ownership. And anyway, I don't know the ending yet. Much still needs to happen before the end. You must be patient, and let me work." He took his drawing from me. "How are you feeling now?"

"Much better."

"You will work, too?"

"I'm going to try."

"You draw. I will sit for a while and write. Later, you can show me your sketches and I will read to you."

He lowered himself from the sofa to sit on the rug, and propped his notebook on his bent knee. For a long time, he only looked at the paper. Then he began to write, his script small and imprecise, each letter half finished, the words spreading wide in even lines.

On the sofa behind him, pencil poised over my sketchbook, I hesitated longer yet. What could I design that would appeal to Consuelo? Beautiful, rude, sensual, hypnotic, fashionable, proud Consuelo: what would make her feel good?

Antoine began crossing out sentences. His pen stopped. He wrote again. He ripped out the page, crumpled and dropped it, and dove directly into fresh writing as though nothing had disturbed his flow.

"Antoine?"

"Mmm?"

"How would you characterize your wife?"

He barely paused, and didn't look up. "In large things, frail and humble; in small things, mean and vain." He crossed out a paragraph with a furious stroke.

The intensity and mystery of his actions made it impossible to concentrate on my own work. I couldn't stop watching him. He worked like a man unaware he was being observed, like a man unable to see anything but the world that was in his mind—springing to life in words, being obliterated with absolute conviction, rising again in a different skin—sentence by sentence, paragraph by paragraph, and page by page, what pages still remained.

When yet another balled sheet of paper had skittered across the floor, I forced my focus back to my sketchbook. Frail, vain . . . "You didn't say Consuelo is passionate."

"That is a given."

"Is it what attracted you to her?"

"Mignonne," Antoine said in warning.

"Sorry. I'll let you work."

"Don't bother me with questions you might just as well ask of yourself."

Long after I had exhausted my shallow store of inspiration, Antoine still wrote, oblivious to his setting, to the hard floor under him, to me. I felt I was watching a man possessed by a zealous ghost, so unearthly was his silent intensity.

Then, without warning, an invading imp dislodged the zealot from his head. He turned around to grab at my legs, pulling me onto him as I fought and squealed.

"What have you drawn?" he asked, laughing, when I'd made my escape.

I blushed. "I've designed a coat. For your prince."

"Really? Have you sketched a whole wardrobe for the Little Prince? I will ask my publishers to offer him for sale as a paper doll."

At first I thought he was serious. Imagine if my work could be produced on the scale of Antoine's—and with his blessing, too! But he had made a sound, a truncated laugh that was almost a grunt. He was joking . . . or he wasn't amused at all.

I said, "Better ask your prince what he thinks of the idea. He's the one who told me to make him a coat."

Now Antoine did laugh. He joined me on the sofa. "It's true that princes can be somewhat demanding."

"He's right, though. He'll be flying very high. Think how cold the air will be up there."

Antoine nodded. "You have designed for him a very regal coat."

"It's not too much like a dressing gown?"

"Not at all."

"I could put some ermine on the collar."

"He's just a child. Ermine is for kings." He pointed to the prince's shoulders. "You might add a little something here. Boys like a bit of glittery metal."

I gave him my pencil, and he added a few quick lines.

I asked, "How about giving him a scepter?"

"What for?"

"To show his royal authority."

Antoine thought for a moment. "I will write of authority, but not the prince's. He has so much to learn." He gestured for me to show him more sketches. "What else?"

"Nothing worth showing. I was trying to concentrate on ideas for Consuelo, but I couldn't get your story out of my mind."

"Is that so? Shall I read to you what I have written so far?"

"I would love it." I put my sketchbook on the table and leaned against him, studying the drawings that illustrated the text.

He began reading from his manuscript. " 'Once, when I was six years old . . .' "

Antoine read, his voice swelling like a springtime stream brought forth by the life he had created. And what a boy he had made. Antoine's unruly charm, my blond hair; so curious and touching; so vexing. So lonely and far from home.

Antoine's child. Yearning grew in me like thirst.

I was so taken with the story that when he broke off, I said, "Don't stop! It's not done."

"I told you so, Mignonne; that is why I came here. I still have much work to do."

"But I want to hear the rest."

He chuckled. "Then perhaps you should greet me more warmly next time I show up to write."

"You'll come back? You feel productive here?"

"It went very well, compared to my last couple of nights. When I try to work in my apartment, even when Consuelo isn't pestering me, the voice of the city through the windows has a distressing sound. There's no sense of that here. It is so empty and still."

"But not entirely quiet."

"The sounds are different, and the feel. This place was built for hard, honest work. One doesn't sense the piling up of people in their skyscrapers. There's dignity in this building's bones. You must feel the energy put out by buildings; I am sure your father did."

"I felt it when we went to Bernard Lamotte's."

"Le Bocal. Yes. It is a very good place. It is like a little piece of France."

"Is it? I've never been to France."

The contentment in his expression fell away. "And now you can never see France as it has always been. Soon there may be no France at all. Oh, Mignonne, it breaks my heart to think of what you will never see or feel."

I rubbed his shoulders. "You're so tense. Lie down for a while."

He stretched out, and I eased his head to my lap.

He closed his eyes as though to stop tears from escaping into the crow's-feet wrinkles that radiated toward his temples. "You are kind to me. And I am so alone. There is no one who shares my memories, not a single man left on earth. The men I have flown with, friends I have lived with . . . Guillaumet, Mermoz . . . the entire Casablanca-Dakar team with Aéropostale, every man on the South American route . . . they are all gone, every one of them. Disappeared with the mail, crushed, some of them melted with their machines. I am the only one still alive, the last who can still give his life to some greater good." His tone grew ashamed. "And I lie here in your arms, held to your breasts as soft as doves. I do nothing; I lie weeping. France is imprisoned and I am of no use."

"Don't say that. The tide will turn. You'll go back to France and see it free."

"I want nothing more than to believe you. All I need is one

signature. But I am shackled by spineless imbeciles who think I am too old to fly. At least I can believe that you feel there is hope. I knew from when I first met you: you are honest. You are not afraid to tell the truth."

The truth was, I had told him what he wanted to believe. As I touched his lined brow and traced the scar at the edge of his mouth, I prayed he would see his beloved France liberated—but also that he would never fly again. I had never known so abused a body, so anguished a spirit, so vital a mind. So many times he had been flung into the ground. He would rather be dropped by the hand of God than be banished from the skies.

In my lap, Antoine said, "Once, I was lost for four days in the Libyan desert, with my mechanic Prévot. We were desperate for water. One night, I spread out my parachute to try to catch the dew. In the morning, there was nothing; not a single drop. I just stared. I could not even make tears. I remember thinking that even my heart was dried out."

Moisture beaded on his lashes. They gathered in points like black stars. I touched them gently. "But look: your heart isn't dry anymore."

"But it is cold, like the heart of this city is cold. Talk to me, Mignonne. Make me love life."

In the darkness of the studio, I told him about my childhood, my brother's struggles, the death of Papa. He listened in silence, smoking on the sofa. I told him about my year in Montreal, what it had been like to live with Mother there, and to drink in the cafés, and to be reminded every day that the populace, unlike that of my home country, was fighting a war. I spoke of school, successes and stumbles, fashion and sewing, my trials with Madame Fiche.

Antoine blew a long, slow course of smoke toward the ceiling. "Raising a fashion protégé is perhaps not so different from training a pilot to be single-minded in delivering the mail. She pushes and kneads you to almost a breaking point, tempering you like steel. It's 'Those are the orders,' always and only," he said, quoting *Night Flight*'s high-minded aviation chief.

"Madame Fiche is not the Garment District Rivière!"

He chortled. "True. Her morals are firm enough but of questionable value. And her ethics are highly suspect. Still, she has you working hard for the success of her enterprise."

"It's for my own success, too. I need her, and though she doesn't realize it, she needs me."

"And you both place your fate in the hands of Consuelo?"

"And in those of all the expats. Madame Fiche has given up on American women; she says they dress to disguise themselves as nothing, but Frenchwomen still dress to be French. She thinks if we can get Consuelo to wear us, the whole community will notice."

"You agree?"

"Consuelo's our best hope to get our designs out there. I've been working on all sorts of ideas, but Madame doesn't want to take a risk. She wants to sell her an ensemble from our Butterfly Collection, the one I designed at school. I showed you my sketches, way back when."

"They were very dramatic and skillfully done—but I admit I am not fond of the ornate. For me, perfection comes not when there is nothing more to add, but when there is nothing left to take away. There is far less beauty in clothing than in the body's naked state."

"Consuelo said she liked the butterfly idea because it reminded her of an adventure in her childhood." Antoine nodded as though he knew the story well. "But that's all we have. I think I need to come up with something else that reminds her of better days. She won't wear just anything. It has to speak to her. It needs to reflect who she is. As you said: frail and humble, mean and vain."

"Did I say this? I'm not sure if I hinder you or help you. I give you the thoughts of a man who is fed up with the ways of his wife."

"Then think back to the young Consuelo. When you fell in love. What was she like then?"

He smiled. "Are you sure you want to hear this?"

Of course I wasn't, but I was sure that what Consuelo wanted more than anything else was to return to those times. And the most important thing, for a designer, is to understand a client's heart.

Antoine asked, "Are you not afraid that if I conjure it all up, I will fall in love with her all over again?"

"Do you really think you've stopped loving her? Because I don't believe you're capable of falling out of love."

He pulled out his wallet and removed a photograph. The young woman in the picture was an extraordinary creature, asleep, her dark hair tumbling down the side of a satin-sheeted bed. The peaks of her breasts were covered by a sheet, her face turned slightly away from the camera. She was elegant and tranquil, a pure and naked beauty whose complete serenity surely came of being well used and fully satisfied by her Tonio—by my Antoine.

I turned the photo over. In Antoine's writing, "Consuelo *chez* Greta Garbo, New York"; in what must have been Consuelo's hand, "Don't lose yourself, don't lose me."

He said, "When I met Consuelo, she was twice widowed already, at your age. She had an air of tragedy. Her face was delicate and precise. Her eyes were so large and expressive, one couldn't look away."

They were still like that.

Antoine said, "I noticed them immediately, along with her wrists."

As had I.

"Once when our money ran out, as it often did, she claimed

she would go to work scrubbing floors. I said, 'With your thin wrists!' and she said, 'Jesus Christ had thin wrists, too!'" He laughed. "She was not made for work. She has always been fragile. She would cling to me as though only I could save her from some terrible end. Early on, we were walking in the square in her homeland. We hardly knew each other then. There was a demonstration and gunfire, and she pressed herself against me. She was trembling like a flower that is about to be picked. I imagined her this way, too, when she was living with the refugees in Oppède and I was flying for France. Always, I worried about her. I wanted only to ensure that she was safe from harm. I would fly overhead and feel the pull of her heart on mine, calling me to her defense."

I made myself listen. I had to hear it. Let him say it; let me use it; then we would put it all away.

"But whenever she was angry—and anything could set her off—she would insist that she didn't need me, that she could take care of herself. And with what?" He shook his head. "She acted so fierce."

"She still does."

"And yet her weapons against the sorrows and demands of the world amount to nothing. No more than three or four thorns on the most breakable of stems."

"Thorns?"

"Just so. A few feeble little thorns."

Deep inside me, a hollow feeling grew. Thorns . . . of a rose. The rose is Consuelo. Not me. Consuelo.

How could he have drawn the flower for me, the rose that was his wife, on our most intimate of nights?

I pushed him from my lap and got to my feet. "Thorns of a rose."

He looked perplexed. "Just so."

"My rose!"

"What?"

"You drew a rose for me. And now you tell me that you were thinking of Consuelo."

"No, no." Antoine stood up. "It was not like this. There is not only one rose in the world."

"There is on the planet you're writing about."

"But Mignonne, you've heard only the beginning of the story! There may be other roses to come. You will see."

"I've seen enough!"

"It isn't fair that you ask me to speak of my love for Consuelo, then attack me for it."

"You think you know what's fair?"

"I do not mind being held to task for things I do wrong, but do not berate me for things I do well and at your bidding."

I bent my head into my hands, my fingers digging into my scalp.

Antoine continued. "You asked me to tell you how I saw my wife in the beginning. Yes, it was as the Little Prince saw his rose. She appeared like the sole representative of her species, a rare flower in a land of dangerous volcanoes and voracious trees—where a blade of grass sprouting from a crack in a sidewalk could become a rainforest that obliterates an entire village."

I couldn't listen to this barrage of words. I walked away, directionless across the studio, and found myself holding on to my worktable. Antoine followed, pursuing me with his tale of the young Consuelo, of the rose, assailing me with what I had asked of him.

"She coughs, she blushes, she pretends she needs nothing—it is all in service to the entrapment. She knows the weakness of man. Man needs to feel useful. The need is so great that even her lies lead one to say, Oh, she tells lies because of her pain that comes of not being what she wishes to be . . . And she lies so simply, so gracefully. One cannot help but be entranced."

I covered my ears.

Still he continued. "It is not a sin to be enthralled. It is the quality of a child who is not hardened to the world. When the—"

"What are you talking about?" I cried. "How can you tell me there is more than one rose, the world is full of roses—as if that should make me feel better!—and then admit, after all, that only the most devious one deserves your attention?"

"I am telling you that, in romance, I was only a child, enchanted by a spoiled coquette who seemed a child too. I knew nothing of the world. Before Consuelo I had been attaching myself for a night or a week to some pretty little girl I met in a nightclub or a bar. Silly girls who wanted only to dance and be told how adorable they were before settling into a life of darning my socks."

He banged his hand on the table, making my shears and jar of dressmaker's pins jump. He roared, "I cannot live with a woman who would darn my socks!"

I couldn't help myself: I began to smile.

He ceased upon it. In an instant, his anger was gone and his voice had grown plaintive. "Don't you see, Mignonne?" He ran a tentative finger up my arm. "I committed myself to Consuelo when I knew so little of her. And then, in spite of my efforts to the contrary, I grew up. It is painful to grow up. My eyes were opened to the nature of the pact I had made—and to the existence of other roses. Women as beautiful and more, as intelligent and more, with as fertile a mind as the first—but stronger. Women who were not so dependent on me for every little whim."

"You let your wife become dependent on you."

"I let her? She has made an entire life's work of accumulating needs and creating drama. I am the cause of all her unhappiness. She claims she cannot live without me, yet does all she can to humiliate and destroy me even as she demands that we reunite. She has entered fine restaurants and announced to the entire room, at her whim, 'My husband has just ravaged me!' or 'My husband cannot—'" He bit off his sentence, turning angrily away.

I said, "She needs to be the center of attention."

"Hers is not a need but an obsession."

Was I so different from Consuelo; was I not obsessed, too? I reached across the table to touch the featherweight silk chiffon.

Antoine said, "A man cannot but help a woman in need: his ego demands it. It means nothing, except that man is weak. But when one wishes to help a woman who is strong herself, someone like you, the wish is not born of ego but comes from deep within the heart."

"Do you wish to help me?" I picked up the neatly folded white fabric and held it out.

Antoine touched it awkwardly. "It is very soft, very nice."

"It's very fine silk."

"Good. That is—I'm sorry, Mignonne. I know nothing about fashion. I'm not sure what you want of me."

"Hold the fabric for a minute. Just hold it." I laid the bundle on his upturned palms. "Don't move." I walked around to stand behind him. As silently as possible, I slipped out of my clothes.

"What I need," I said, "is for you to fit the fabric on me."

He turned around.

The silk shifted. The layers began to slide, cascading from his hands in a whispering sweep. He bent and grappled to stop the flow. Then he straightened, spreading his arms open so the fabric spanned tall and wide.

He draped me in white, a wash of foam on my shoulders, a wake trailing from my breasts. He wrapped me with exquisite tenderness, smoothing the silk with merciless attention to the peaks and dells it caressed.

By the time he reached my hips, the cloth had fallen from

my shoulders and I was rocking on my feet. Whiteness pooled around me and flashed behind my eyes.

His hands were on the small of my back; he was down on one knee. I swayed. I begged hoarsely, "Hold me up, Antoine, please."

29

That Sunday morning, I was back in the studio—inspired, alone. I spread the silk on the worktable and examined it. I lifted it and moved it around me, seeing how it would hang as a cape, as a skirt, how it bunched and released in my grip. I held it to my body and wrapped it around my arms, watching how the fabric wanted to flow and bend, taking notes with every step. I pulled it along its warp and weft, and diagonally on its bias, testing its delicacy, its sensitivity, noting its remarkable strength. When I had worked out its basic properties and possibilities, I reviewed my notes, put them aside, and began to sketch.

I wanted something floor-length and flowing: an oversized hood like a shawl, an uncomplicated dress. It would be modest in style, yet distinct in its luxuriousness. A garment uninterrupted by details or fuss. Sleeves that bloused as they draped, cinched into tight cuffs; pearl buttons iridescent at the wrist. At the back, the lines of the hood would drape softly to my waist.

I knew which of the studio's standard patterns would fit me. I brought one out and placed its sections on a long expanse of paper, traced where the outline should be traced and altered the line where alterations suited my needs. I measured. I measured again. I folded the fabric and arranged the pattern pieces, holding them in place with a cast iron weight. I barely knew this fabric; if I only had more time, I could make something worthy of its delicate, graceful beauty and hidden strength. If only I had more experience, more skill. It was too soon to make a decision, to make cuts that I wouldn't be able to undo.

But it was always too soon to cut beautiful fabric. I couldn't keep this material intact for thirty-odd years as Madame had done. I might never know more than I knew today. I was almost sick with anxiety—but I might never have more courage than tonight.

The silk was insubstantial in the jaws of my shears. The blades parted it into segments, generously shaped, until each had been carefully cut.

Now I found myself impatient to start sewing—wanting to put the dress together before I could start questioning my choice of design and regretting having committed myself so irrevocably. But I would do no more today. The skirt portion was cut on the diagonal; it needed to hang for a day or two, to stretch to a natural shape that would let it lie smoothly without bunching or twisting, before I could proceed with the real sewing. I tacked its bias-cut seams together with a long basting stitch and carried the skirt into the dim storage area behind Madame's desk, where I hung it on a dress form before returning to my worktable. The pieces for the upper portion would wait, too. There was no technical reason not to proceed with them; they did not need to stretch or hang. I could baste the upper portion together and run it through the sewing machine right away—but it didn't seem right to do so, not while the rest waited in the dark.

I piled up the shapes that would become the sleeves, bodice, back, and hood. Tenderly, respectfully, I laid them aside to wait.

Then it was Monday, the morning of the day Consuelo would visit. Madame pretended it didn't matter a whit to her—she came in at her usual eleven fifteen, and tossed her jacket onto a chair—as though I had not been devoting every extra hour for weeks to transforming the chaotic studio into something organized, energizing, and clean.

"The countess comes this afternoon," I said as I picked up Madame's jacket and hung it.

"Roll out the collection. Dust what needs dusting." She walked over to inspect my work area—the drinking glasses I had brought from home and placed on the window ledge, the small vase of flowers beside them, the fine cut fabric dolloped on the table in soft mounds like whipped cream. She had not paid it any attention these last few days; she had been all but ignoring me for the past week.

She asked, "You are making something?" She poked at the silk.

"A dress for myself."

"You have hemmed Mrs. Englander's skirt, and let out the waistband of her husband's trousers?"

"Not yet. They're just sewing jobs."

"If I give you sewing to do, I expect you to do sewing."

"But doesn't it make sense to focus on our designs instead of adjusting other people's clothes? I thought if I made a dress, I could wear it when I next see Consuelo de Saint-Exupéry. We'll show her the Butterfly Collection today, then I'll wear something interesting every time I see her until she gets a full sense of what we can do. We'll win her over one piece at a time."

Madame narrowed her eyes. Her brow was meticulously plucked, her forehead taut. Her face looked as though she might have taken it out of a drawer and polished it before attaching it to her scalp, which had not a hair astray. "We will win her over with the Butterfly Collection. Your dilettante efforts are amusing, but unnecessary." She waved her hand above my table. "I don't want to see this silk again. Put it away."

I ignored her: I walked to the end of the studio behind Madame's worktable and desk. I chose a garment cart and rolled it to the center of the studio.

Madame stood waiting.

I removed the covers from the nine remaining garments of the Butterfly Collection, one by one, pulling off and folding each cotton wrapper; one by one, carrying each wrapper to a table to add to a growing stack. I disappeared into the storage area, taking my time clearing garments from a second rack. Then I emerged with the empty rack and distributed the collection over the two, ordering and spacing the clothing for maximum effect. When I was satisfied, I pulled both racks to the edge of the room.

Madame's fingernail tapped a staccato on my table. She was waiting for me to look over. What would be the point of dramatics if they were to go unseen?

All right, then. I looked.

With spitting fire in her eyes, Madame swept her arm into the pile of silk, propelling it off the edge of the table and onto the floor. It fell sumptuously.

I turned back to my task. I hummed as I brushed and fluffed the garments on their racks. What did I care where the silk lay for the moment? It wasn't anywhere it hadn't already been. It wasn't anywhere that I hadn't lain, too.

The white silk was still on the floor—neither Madame nor I had been willing to bend to pick it up—when two o'clock arrived and Consuelo did not. Two thirty passed. It was a little after three when we finally heard footsteps and a rap at the door.

Madame stood up. She gave the hem of her black jacket a firm, corrective tug and walked with monarchical bearing to usher in her guest.

Guests: Consuelo entered on Binty's arm.

"*Comtesse* de Saint-Exupéry!" Madame Fiche said, curtseying as she took Consuelo's hand. "I am Madame Véra Fiche. I welcome you to my atelier. And this is?" She tipped her head a little to regard Binty with a girlish, sideways gaze.

He shook her hand. "Jack Binty."

Consuelo said, "My paramour."

Madame Fiche's always-straight posture became rigid. Through tight lips she said, "Thank you for coming, Mr. Binty."

"Lovely to see you again," I said, holding out my hand.

Consuelo took it and touched it to her lips.

Binty smiled a wry, crooked smile.

Madame's piercing gaze moved from Consuelo's face to mine. She said, carefully enunciating, "We have much that is beautiful to show you, Madame *la Comtesse*."

Consuelo said, "Indeed"—her eyes holding mine, her voice rich with intimation.

In the next instant, unceremoniously, she dropped my hand. "Bring it on, then. I'm bored, I've had a rotten day, and I don't have a thing to wear."

Madame's mouth opened just a little—perhaps not enough for the guests to note, but with my knowledge of Madame's unfailing composure before clients, the opening seemed to yawn like a crevasse. I interjected myself between Consuelo and Binty, gently elbowing them apart and linking each of their arms with my own.

"Come on," I said. "Sit where it's comfortable, and we'll give you your own personalized Atelier Fiche show." I led them to the sofa, squeezing their elbows close to my sides until their shoulders bumped companionably against mine and their steps were comically misaligned. On the rug, I released Binty and spun the giggling Consuelo around so her back faced the sofa.

"Countess Consuelo," I said, "our studio is yours. Your wish is our command."

Consuelo sunk into the sofa and kicked off her shoes. She put her feet on the coffee table. "Excellent, darling. Let the show begin!"

In a dark corner behind racks and shelves, I wriggled out of my dress. Madame Fiche had taken a chair. Snippets of her stilted conversation reached me as I pulled an outfit over my black corselet.

"And of course the weather . . . Needless to say, one does not like to . . . A woman of your stature, *comtesse* . . ."

Neither Consuelo nor Binty had much to say in response.

I stepped out into the center of the studio, into the afternoon light, and all eyes turned to me. The dark velvet train followed my progression, in fluid steps, toward the sitting area. I paused before reaching the rug and walked a wide, graceful circle in the skirt, butterfly jacket, and black sleeveless blouse.

Madame announced, "Allow me to present the first item in my Butterfly Collection."

"Very glamorous for a red carpet entrance," I said, "and a dramatic departure in your limousine."

Binty watched dispassionately. Consuelo was rapt, Madame anxious.

When I was sure Consuelo had taken her fill of the heavy detailing, I slipped off the jacket and placed it on the remaining empty armchair. Now I was wearing only the black blouse and the long velvet skirt.

"Perfect for an elegant evening with your husband," I said.

Consuelo put her fingers together in a steeple and smiled from behind them as I rolled my hips to catch the light in the velvet pile.

Then in one smooth motion, I pulled the blouse straight off, over my head, and dropped it onto the chair. "Or a special evening with someone else's husband." I twirled in the velvet skirt and my sleek black corselet.

Consuelo clapped and laughed. "More!" she cried. Binty cracked a smile.

Madame's mouth dropped fully open.

She was right about the importance of good undergarments.

When I had modeled all the remaining variations of the butterfly line, I got back into my green dress and hauled the two racks closer to our guests. I met Madame Fiche's eye and gave her a nod.

Madame picked up the baton. "*Voila.* You have seen the collection. It is dramatic, extravagant, and bold—entirely fitting for a woman of your beauty and charisma. You may not know this, Madame de Saint-Exupéry: after its explosive premier and all the attention lavished on it by the press, I refused to take commissions for this line. I waited for just the right woman, searching for the very figure of drama and poise to take the butterfly into the world. Now, at last, she has entered my atelier. The collection has found its muse."

Standing by the racks, I awaited my cue. Consuelo seemed to be considering Madame's pitch. Binty was already restless; he got up and strolled to the windows.

Madame said, "It would be a small matter to adjust the design to accommodate the governmental mandate, if this is your concern. We simply reconfigure the sleeves, and shorten and narrow the skirt—unless you'd like to keep it formal length, in which case we are granted greater freedom to do as we please. Would you care to try on the jacket, to feel the luxurious weight and hand?"

I shifted the other garments to display the jacket more prominently. The size should be right—the cut would accommodate Consuelo's bust, which was larger than mine—but we would have to shorten the sleeves.

Binty called over, "Do you have anything to drink here?"

"Of course," said Madame. "Mignonne, make tea."

"Don't you have a bottle—of anything at all? Christ, I could use a slug of something." He was at my worktable, slouching in the chair with his legs extended in front of him and his hands dangling. He looked as though he could melt from boredom and slide off the chair to join the pile of silk on the floor.

"Attend to Mr. Binty's needs, Mignonne, *immédiatement!*"

I was easing the jacket off its hanger. Consuelo looked

expectant—but not for the prospect of trying on the garment. She was interested in seeing how willingly I would submit to Madame.

Now Binty said, "Aren't you done yet, Consuelo? Let's go. There's nothing more tedious—"

I rushed across the studio to serve him. "There's a liquor store just around the corner. Sit tight for a second, Binty. I'll be back before you can breathe."

When I returned with the bottle, Consuelo was standing on the coffee table wearing the first combination I had modeled, with Binty and Madame standing nearby. Madame was assessing the effect from every angle, her hands held up as though she were molding the fabric onto Consuelo from several feet away. Binty had been pressed into action to hold a full-length mirror, which he did with a scowl, as Consuelo directed him.

"A little lower and step to the right a bit. My right, Binty. Move that edge toward me. Will you concentrate?"

"Just decide if you want the damn clothes and let's get out of here."

I came forward with the bottle extended. "Let me do that. You pour yourself a drink. There are glasses on the ledge by the table."

Consuelo pouted at the mirror. She asked, "Why does it look the way it does on Mignonne, and on me it's dead?"

Madame Fiche said, "It is magnificent on you! Very suitable for a countess."

"It's true," I told her. Her coloring, her dark hair and eyes, gave the jacket's jewel tones greater depth. "It suits you very well. We just need to make a few minor adjustments so it will drape as it should. The size is basically right. We'll just take it in a little there"—I tried to point and almost dropped the mirror—"and around the waist."

"Come show me," said Consuelo.

I carried the mirror to Madame Fiche, who swore under her breath as she took it, and resumed explaining the alterations.

"Stop gesturing and pointing," said Consuelo. "Just do whatever it is you're planning to do, so I can see what you're talking about."

"I'll get my needle and thread." I hurried over to my table, where Binty was drinking.

As I was returning, I heard Consuelo say, "Higher, Madame Fiche. You're going to have to hold it higher and tip it back. I already know what my lovely feet look like."

30

Consuelo loved standing on tables. All the more so when her audience was Mignonne. The girl had a light touch, like that of a tentative kitten. Or a pickpocket.

"You have such lovely wrists," Mignonne said as she folded the butterfly jacket sleeves.

"As do you, darling," said Consuelo, and felt pleased by the kindness of her lie. Of course the girl's wrists were slender—everything about Mignonne was—but they weren't particularly notable; they weren't frightfully, delightfully delicate like Consuelo's. Nobody's were.

"Let's show them off with a three-quarter-length sleeve." Mignonne used a quick tacking thread to mark the desired length. When she had finished, she peered at the fit of the rest of the jacket.

It was delightful to have Mignonne reaching up to Consuelo's shoulders as though inviting her to dance. If it weren't for the probing glare of Véra Fiche, or the effects of the fumes from the hallway that were making her sinuses ache and swell, she would encircle Mignonne's waist and lead her in a tango across the floor.

The girl pinched the fabric atop Consuelo's shoulders and lifted it slightly, then let it drop back into place to see the jacket's natural lie on her frame. "That isn't bad at all. Just a few more minor adjustments."

Mignonne was certainly meticulous in her work. Consuelo tried to take enjoyment in the routine—the fingers sliding down the front center edging of the jacket closing, the girl checking how the sides aligned, inspecting for imperfections due to idiosyncrasies of structure or posture—but it was quickly becoming too much for one day. She needed a break from all this concentration. Too much standing still.

Why was Binty the only one with a drink?

Time for mischief. She leaned down to Mignonne and said, her voice low, "Visit me again in my apartment. It's a much more comfortable place to play with each other's clothes."

She was rewarded with the instant hot reddening of Mignonne's cheeks.

That was good fun, but it made Consuelo feel even more unsettled. "Forget the jacket. I don't know if I want it. I don't have all day. Just fix the fit of the skirt."

Mignonne spread her hands over the fabric at Consuelo's waist and hips, shifting the velvet until it lay properly against Consuelo's magnificent curves and eased smoothly into the waistband. She walked around the table to view the garment from the back.

"Binty," called Consuelo, "bring me a goddamn drink."

He came over with a half-full glass. Stingy bastard.

"Now help me down."

Mignonne said, "It's better to be up on the table when we do the hem."

"We're not doing the hem. I'll think about the skirt. Pack it up and I'll try it on at home."

"Mignonne," Madame Fiche barked, and the girl hurried over to take the mirror. "The skirt is outstanding on you, *comtesse*. Divinely inspired." The crow seemed to believe all could be set right with a little simpering. She went on and on, accelerating the spread of pain in Consuelo's head. "Should you wish to purchase it, Mignonne can make the alterations tonight. You could be wearing it as early as tomorrow, and decide on the rest of the ensemble at a later date. Or simply choose to purchase the skirt and the jacket; it is not necessary to pair them with this particular blouse. The skirt goes with so many things."

"As we've seen," said Binty dryly.

"Then we will indeed continue with the hemming?" asked Madame Fiche, clasping her brittle hands together.

Indeed we would not. Not here, not now. "Send Mignonne to my apartment with the skirt tonight. I can just as well climb onto a table there." Consuelo lifted the hem and started across the studio to change.

31

When Consuelo and Binty had left, Madame turned on me. "This is how you present my work? Clothing for the promiscuous? An outfit to turn a wife into a whore?"

"It was all in fun."

"You are an embarrassment!"

"How else was I to keep their attention?"

"A model does not draw attention to herself. She walks. She turns around and returns. It may be insipid, but that is what women expect and applaud these days. The girl does not open her mouth or throw off her clothes like a trollop—and yet somehow department stores sell truckloads at their fashion parades."

"That's all fine if you're selling copies of some other designer's work. But if we're going to make a name for ourselves and our own designs, don't you think we should try to be original?"

"Your vanity is unbecoming and unwarranted."

"Consuelo is used to being entertained. Valentina's shows aren't traditional. They aren't stodgy. They amuse people. She makes women laugh."

"*Oui*, I laugh at Valentina, too. She is precisely what I do not wish to be."

"It's the way things are headed. She turns fashion into theater, and her clients love it."

"Valentina Schlee prancing around her parlor is not theater! You think I don't know about theater? It was my life at your age."

"You worked on the stage?"

"I apprenticed to a costume designer."

"You went from costumes to *haute couture*?"

"That was my master's path and it became my own."

"It seems like a strange shift."

Madame looked disgusted. "There was a time when knowledge of costume and stage was still valued and in demand in the fashion world. We didn't just send out girls to walk up and down. Instead of parading, there would be a dramatic production, with a narrative. The story of Napoleon and Josephine. *The Golden Slipper. The Princess of the Peacocks.*"

Each collection would be about a story? An existing story. No wonder Madame struggled to develop concepts of her own.

"Fashion theater is hardly a new invention. Neither was your cheap spectacle. At least the fashion parades do not pretend to be what they are not. What you did today was nothing better than burlesque. I have had enough of you exposing and prostituting yourself in the name of Atelier Fiche."

Madame's face gathered like a drawstring handbag. Efficiently, decisively, she spat on the floor.

32

I spent the rest of Monday afternoon working silently on the alterations I had basted earlier. Then, with Madame's curt approval, I headed home for a quick supper before my nine o'clock appointment with Consuelo.

It was a different Consuelo who answered the door. Her eyes were puffy and pink-rimmed as though she had been crying. She was wearing seersucker pajamas and grey high-heeled slippers with ostrich-feather tendrils that oscillated as she walked.

"I've just been across the hall speaking with Tonio," she said. She sat on the sofa, and I took the same chair as before.

Consuelo pulled a handkerchief from a pocket and wrung it in her hands. "My husband doesn't want me here. He doesn't want me to take care of him and try to keep him safe. He won't let me. All he wants is to leave. He would rather die than be anywhere close to me!"

"That can't be true."

"It is! Look how he treats me. He puts me in a separate apartment, like a dog in a cage to be thrown a scrap once in a while."

"You have a very lovely and large apartment."

"Tonio gave me the nicest and biggest one so that I wouldn't complain. He wants me to have no possible excuse to insist that I have to move in with him. The superintendent colludes with him, too. Every time I have something wrong here, the man comes and tells me there's no problem. Just today I had him checking the temperature. Tonio's apartment is always comfortable. Feel how stifling it is in here. Tonio must be bribing the man to pretend that everything is fine in my apartment. That's where his money goes! It doesn't matter how much it costs, Tonio will do anything to keep me in my overheated, gilded cage."

"Maybe he thinks it's best for you to have room for your own projects."

"And why should he get to make that decision for me? Am I not a human being? He says his apartment is too small for me, that he would have no space to write, and he refuses to join me in mine. I need to find us a larger place where we can be together. This isn't the only building in Manhattan!"

But this one was extremely attractive: modern, thoughtfully designed, with pleasing proportions. The parlor was spacious and had high ceilings—and those big windows overlooking Central Park. "You have a view that is very difficult to come by."

"A bunch of trees. What do I care about trees? I grew up in the jungle. Trees don't give me what I need. Only one person can do that. And he wants nothing more than to torment me. He wouldn't even have let me come to New York if I hadn't forced him. He would have had me stay at the commune in Oppède while he enjoyed all the parties and celebrations here. I knew when *Wind, Sand and Stars* became a Book-of-the-Month Club pick that it was my ticket to America. My friend Robert said to me, 'Your husband writes of responsibility; if people only knew he has a wife, abandoned across the ocean, just waiting for his word!' I knew that Tonio couldn't deny me my passage then. His reputation would be ruined." She tugged at her pajama top. "But he just hides me away. He doesn't take me to anything. He goes to see his famous friends without me. They probably don't even know he has a wife! He makes me ill with his cruelty. Look how thin I am. I could die at any moment! He doesn't want to admit I exist, even here under his nose in Manhattan." She sniffled.

Then she ran her fingers through her hair and asked, her voice suddenly clear, "You weren't at the big fête in Montreal a few months ago? There was an enormous party in honor of Tonio.

I wore a stunning red dress, to the floor. Everyone was agog over it. They all wanted to tell me how much they admired me and my husband. It was a terrific evening." She lifted her chin defiantly. "The people have a right to celebrate having a count *and* his countess in their midst. Most of the time he doesn't even want to go out to these things himself."

"Maybe it's just that he needs solitude and space to write."

"An artist needs to be seen and to promote himself, too. You know this. Coming here, that first time, presenting yourself in a dress almost worthy of Valentina at her best." She smiled. "Then your naughty little fashion show this afternoon."

"I brought the skirt. I made the changes I tacked earlier. If they're fine, we just need to mark the hem. I assume you want to keep it at evening length? If we shorten it, we'll also have to narrow it. Shorter dresses are categorized differently in the regulations."

"Whatever you decide. Just make it whatever length you think is best. I don't care. Fashion doesn't mean anything to me."

What ridiculous things Consuelo said.

I pulled out the skirt and stood up, holding it in front of me enticingly a matador with a cape tempting a capricious bull. "Just wait until you see how well it will look on you now. No one will be able to take his eyes off you. I would love to see it for myself. You should really put it on."

Consuelo pulled on the skirt over her pajama bottoms, then maneuvered the bottoms off. Hoisting the skirt to the height of her knees, she stepped onto the coffee table. "Hem me."

First I had to check the fit of the alterations at the waist, back, and hips, assessing with eyes and hands. Consuelo lifted her pajama top high above the waistband to give me a clear view of the top section of the skirt. I tried to ignore the span of smooth olive skin, but Consuelo repeatedly glided her fingertips across her ribs, and it took a concentration of will to keep my focus where it should be.

"So we're agreed that the skirt stays long," I said, kneeling on the floor.

"Such a clean, simple design," said Consuelo. "It sets off the jacket perfectly."

I nodded. "After designing the butterfly dress, I realized that—"

"No, Mignonne." Consuelo put her hand on my head. "One wears Fiche. Not Lachapelle. You will ensure that the labels in this ensemble say Atelier Fiche."

I swallowed. "Yes."

"Fiche has a name, a presence in the industry. Good things are expected from her. You have a lot of nerve, trying to promote yourself to me. Loyalty is a virtue; you should learn it."

"Of course." Loyalty like Consuelo's to Antoine? Or to her paramour?

Consuelo crooked her fingers into my mane. "Keep doing what you do, darling, and one day you will rise above your mentor. One day you will be my designer."

It troubled me to feel the hope rise in my blood.

"I will be your muse," said Consuelo. "The Garbo to your Valentina. They are inseparable, you know." She hooked a lock of hair and coiled it around her fingers in a slow, lazy twirl. "They are at each other's side through the day, every day. And all through the night."

When I stepped from the elevator into the lobby, the concierge said, "Miss Lachapelle? Mr. Saint-Exupéry asked that I ring him if I see you. Would you mind waiting?"

In a few minutes, Antoine appeared, smiling broadly. He led me outside to stroll along the sidewalk. "Consuelo told me you were expected. I'm glad the concierge caught you. I wanted to ask: May we work together tonight?"

I needed to hem Consuelo's skirt. More importantly, I had to get the silk dress done and I didn't want Antoine to see it before our dinner at Le Pavillon tomorrow night. I was heading straight back to get started, and needed to have the space to myself. "I can't have you come to the studio tonight."

"You are going home? Then may I borrow your key so I can write? The book refuses to come to life in my apartment. I keep writing about the prince's disappointing encounters with men who are as stuck as I am. I cannot seem to transcend it, to make it go anywhere."

"I can't give you my key. I'll need to get into the studio in the morning."

"True." He rubbed his jaw. "I will slide it under your apartment door at home after I lock up."

"No. Leo gets up early. He'll be all over me with questions."

"You have not told him about me?"

"Are you serious?"

"I'm sure you have your reasons."

"Leo would go crazy. You're married and twice my age."

"These are trivial things! One an inconvenience and one irrelevant."

"Maybe if you're French. They aren't trivial to Americans."

"You can't live your life on the basis of what America thinks."

"You do. You told me you would never send for Consuelo. But the minute your reputation was at stake, you had her come to New York. Better to pretend you're a devoted husband, even if you're both miserable, than to have people think you deserted your wife."

He walked silently for a while. It was not easy to match his long strides when we were not arm in arm. Finally he said, "It is like that, then? She tells you her side of the story, and you forget everything I confided to you? Our marriage may be little more than paper, but I have signed my name to it. I do not entirely abdicate my responsibilities."

"But you don't even want her here."

"Of course not. We were estranged already in France. Try to understand, I didn't tire of her as a boy tires of licorice. She exhausted me in every way. It kills us both to be together, not just me. It is only when we are apart that we understand each other and long for each other. Everything is better when we are apart. It has always been this way."

We stopped to wait for a traffic light to change. I said, "So the more time you spend in my studio, the better for your marriage,"

Antoine only lifted his head stiffly to look at the sky, his expression growing cold.

I continued, "No wonder you're trying so hard to go away. Back to having heroic adventures and writing romantic letters to each other."

"Mignonne."

"And *longing* for each other."

"Listen to yourself! War is not an adventure; it is a disease. My people are starving in the streets."

I was silent.

Antoine said, "A man does not go to war for the purpose of reviving his marriage."

"Nevertheless."

He stood with me until the light turned green. "Good night." He bowed slightly and began to walk away.

"Antoine!"

He paused.

"Will I see you tomorrow night for dinner?"

"I would not wish to disappoint Yannick."

Along the way to the studio, I used a pay phone to inform Leo that I would be working late into the night.

Finishing Consuelo's skirt was a straightforward matter. I ran a long length of thread through a block of beeswax to prevent it from catching and curling into knots, then I bound and blind-stitched the hem, taking care to pick up only one or two threads of the fabric at a time with the needle, and not to draw the thread too tightly. When I was done stitching, the hem lay flat without rippling. I checked the heat of my iron and tested the steam, nerves speeding the blood through my veins. Maybe one never became inured to velvet's demanding, sensitive idiosyncrasies. I concentrated as I aligned the hem on the prickly needle board that would protect its pile, then steamed the fabric lightly, tapping the hem with the bristles of a brush to get a good, clean edge without bruising the gleaming nap.

With Consuelo's garment done and carefully put away, I turned finally to the white silk. I bent to scoop it up from the floor. As I straightened, a flurry of wisps detached themselves. They wafted to the floorboards and caught in the dark, splintered cracks.

I froze. In my arms, flimsy bits of fabric began to disassemble, skimming over each other in all directions at once. With a cry, I spun toward the table and let the yardage spill onto it.

It was a snake's nest of twisting, tortured planes. Slender swatches curled around my fingers as I spread the fabric across the tabletop. The bodice pieces had been cut and hacked. The long shapes of the arms had been pierced, and bore slashes. The broad swath that was to have swept along my shoulders and drape unbroken down my back had been hewn to barely connected panels of indiscriminate lengths and widths.

The cuts had been made without symmetry or pity. It was as though Madame had simply dipped the points of her shears into the fallen fabric, again and again, closing the long blades on the silk, reducing it to shreds, fraying swaths, and long, jagged strips.

33

I woke late on Tuesday morning, took a bath, and didn't hurry over breakfast. I had brought home all evidence of Madame Fiche's silk chiffon.

One o'clock: Madame would have arrived hours ago, and registered the absence of the fabric, and would be sitting unsettled at her desk wondering what would happen next. She would have noted my drinking glasses still on the ledge, and my cardigan still hung on the back of my chair, and—most of all—my thread snips and bent-handle shears, and would know that I would return. No seamstress, no designer, would abandon her favorite shears.

It was midafternoon when I entered the studio, taking care to smile as though I was not only untroubled but well rested, too.

Madame Fiche was indeed at her desk, her mouth an unbent line. She shifted her jaw as if to loosen a deadening grip. "You're late." Her voice was dry and choppy. I wondered if she had spoken since yesterday afternoon.

I asked, "Are you having a nice day?"

Madame watched warily as I continued to my table.

"Glad to hear it," I said, though she hadn't replied. "You need a break, after all the work you did last night."

There: a slight smirk. Madame could hardly wait to get into the ring with me.

I said, "I came in after you left. In fact, I was here almost the entire night."

"You expect me to feel sorry for you?"

"No, but thanks for offering."

"I warned you, Mignonne. I was very clear."

"I don't mind putting in the extra hours. That's how one learns: by making the time to try something new. Did you learn anything new yesterday? I noticed you played with the white chiffon."

"This is not a joke."

"I agree, Madame. You've taught me an important lesson with your shears."

"That was my intention." Madame waited, her expression tight as wire, until it became clear that I was not about to continue. "You have learned what?"

"That sometimes the only way forward is through destruction."

She slammed a hand on her desk. "The way forward is through discipline and self-control."

"I guess I'll have to learn that one some other time."

In the evening, Yannick came to the apartment and Leo let him in. When I walked out of the bedroom wearing the white silk dress, Yannick removed his hat. "Holy Toledo. I'll be the envy of every man at Le Pavillon."

Leo faked a dramatic stagger. Hand on his chest, he stumbled backward until he banged into a wall. "Jesus, Miggy! Will you put something on? You make Ready Hedy look like she's wearing a barracks bag."

A wide grin had spread across Yannick's face. "Leo, my friend, your sister would upstage even Rita Hayworth in that dress."

The dress I had built was a series of bands salvaged from the remains of what Madame had wrecked. I had snipped clean and rolled under the uneven edges, sewn swatches together into ribbons, combined ribbons into rivulets that wanted to curve and flow. I had studied how the long swaths could twist and move like water around stones. I had stood in the studio wrapping my body, testing the lie of the fabric on my breasts, across my belly and my hips. I had passed panels of silk over and under each other, trusting the fabric and my eye—drawing strength from my year of learning to make do in Montreal, thankful for lessons of resourcefulness.

The dress left my arms and shoulders bare, save for a rope of fabric that came curving down from my nape and bisected my collarbones before spreading open to sheathe my breasts. All down my midsection, horizontal bands drew in from each side and met in the center, where they linked together and bent back upon themselves, wrapping my rib cage in separate, softly pleating planes that left spaces between them where my torso was exposed. The skirt portion, spared injustice as it had hung stretching in a dark corner of the studio, draped straight down from my hips. It broke gently in an elegant wave where the fabric met the floor.

The long corridor of tables down the center of Le Pavillon was reserved for truly prominent guests—a couple of whom I recognized from the newspaper, and one legendary diva from the opera. Heads turned as Yannick took me past them to a table that had a banquette seat along one side and chairs on the other. I settled into the banquette and Yannick fidgeted in a chair, turning this way and that to watch the goings-on in his restaurant.

Bernard's murals surrounded us on the walls. They made it seem as though we had gathered to dine alfresco at a French seaside town. Sunshine danced on water. Seabirds perched on dock piles and sailed through blue skies. Their depth and perspective made Le Pavillon feel larger and more open than it had when I'd last been here. Good for Yannick for seeing what could be achieved through the use of artistic *trompe l'oeil.*

But even as the murals were bright and sunny, they were also slightly and inexplicably sad. I wondered whether Bernard, like Antoine, missed his homeland. Maybe he, too, was planning to go back.

At the front of the restaurant, the maître d' greeted Antoine and Consuelo and began leading them to our table. Antoine stopped several times to shake hands with this or that patron, while Consuelo either sidled up to or stood stiffly behind him.

As they neared, Consuelo was chastising her husband in a low, rapid voice. "Can't we go out without running into one of your girlfriends? It's like walking through a hallway in hell. No wonder you never—"

"Consuelo!" interjected Yannick. He took both her hands in his. "My God, you look stunning tonight!"

Her scowl fell away. She glowed as Yannick kissed her cheeks. I shook her hand while Yannick greeted Antoine.

Consuelo said, "Such a strong grip for a willowy girl."

I loosened my hold, but Consuelo's hand lingered.

"Your dress, Mignonne."

"Do you like it?"

"It's terribly alluring. Move over."

She slipped in beside me on the banquette. The two men were already talking. Antoine had not even looked at me. He was usually unfailingly polite, I thought; how livid he must be.

As the waiter was taking our drinks order, I slid my foot over and tapped Yannick's ankle. When he looked at me, I indicated Antoine with a tiny tilt of my head.

"Saint-Ex," said Yannick as the waiter left, "I am monopolizing you. I haven't even given you a chance to say hello to my niece."

Antoine turned mechanically. As his gaze fell on me, some sort of disjuncture—a disturbance or a thrill—rippled through his expression. His Adam's apple bobbed. His gaze slipped down the front of my dress, descending the triangles and diamonds of my bare skin between the bands of silk.

He said coolly, "Please excuse my lapse of manners. You have been well? Consuelo tells me that your work with Madame Fiche is progressing smoothly."

"Madame has been generous. She gave me this special silk, which is impossible to come by these days."

To any other observer, Antoine might have looked angry, his eyes intense and his nostrils flaring. But his lips opened as he inhaled, and I saw that he was remembering the intimacy with which he had moved the fabric—and me.

34

Consuelo took note of the effect Mignonne's dress had on the restaurant's patrons. Fashion at its best was the most subtle and complicated of aphrodisiacs, and the girl had a witch's instinct for the nuances of desire. Of course, every young flirt knew that dominance lay not in the ability to give people what they want but in making them want—but few knew how to govern their own power. Consuelo had known from a prepubescent age, and had perfected it over three decades. Now it was all she had. And Mignonne was besting her; Consuelo was on the other side. The girl's flawless skin half sheathed, her expression both dewy and determined, her blood pulsing too quickly where the fabric touched her neck: it all took the air from Consuelo's lungs.

These fleeting flecks of girl-lust that pricked like shards weren't the same as Consuelo's love for men. She didn't care if she never touched a woman's breast. She would hardly care if she never again consummated the sexual act with anyone.

But she would be wanted as Mignonne was at this moment wanted. To be wanted was everything. To make oneself wanted by those who think they are in control: this was ecstasy itself.

She reached over to feel the weight and texture of the silk. Tonio was watching surreptitiously as her fingers slid along Mignonne's collarbone and into the gap between the fabric and her skin.

She thought, He envies me my liberty. Even as he turns away, he finds it necessary to demand of himself that he mask his emotions and become stone. And the girl is no different—staring blankly around the room, crossing her legs and swinging a foot as though oblivious to the tornado of desire that swirls around her. Damn her.

Consuelo reminded herself to relax her face. It was unflattering to grit the teeth; it made the jawline uneven.

She could never have imagined a dress such as Mignonne wore now. She would not even have been able to commission it; she didn't have the vocabulary. Decades of mastering the politics of want, years of wielding clay, a lifetime of getting what she desired, of making miracles out of mud and a countess of a country girl, and Consuelo was reduced to this: child's words.

"I want it. Make me one."

35

A commission from Consuelo! Madame would be impressed; the rent would be paid; everything would be fine. I tried to keep my voice nonchalant. "Of course. When can you come to the studio again?"

"Christ. What's wrong with Véra Fiche, that she doesn't have a salon?"

"She had one before," I fibbed. I had practiced my tale. "It was the parlor of her ex-fiancé's apartment. He was an art dealer. Apparently he had a bit of everything, from the Pre-Raphaelites to Dalì."

"It's true that the right apartment could make a very good salon."

"I've heard that Valentina holds shows in her own parlor, very in demand."

A waiter came to take our food order. I chose *madrilène en gelée*—a cold clear soup—to start, and a lobster entree.

"Tonio." Consuelo reached across the table to tug on her husband's cuff. "I have too much space in my apartment. You know I rattle around in it."

He groaned. "Not here. Not now."

"But it's just occurred to me: Atelier Fiche needs a salon, and my parlor is the perfect setting." She tugged again. "Are you listening? I want to make my sitting room into a fashion salon. It will be marvelous! Ladies will beg to be invited."

Antoine pulled his hand away to rub his eyes.

"Tonio? You're always so busy, and I'm lonely without you. I could use the company of a few creative girls."

Anticipation was taut in every muscle of my face. Did Antoine realize what it would mean if we could use Consuelo's apartment? Madame Fiche would go there regularly, and he and I would have the studio to ourselves more often. It would be a chance to lift Atelier Fiche and my career off the ground. No doubt I would be made a partner for such a feat.

Consuelo said, "Darling? May I invite Véra and Mignonne to use my parlor? It will be so much fun."

Antoine refused to glance at me. He said, "You never tire of coming up with new tricks." Then he turned his chair toward Yannick. "How is the restaurant business these days? There appears to be no shortage of the ingredients for *haute cuisine*."

We had finished dessert by the time Consuelo finally excused herself to powder her nose. I glowered at Antoine. "Why can't you let Consuelo share her apartment?"

"She doesn't want to share it, she wants to give it away and move in with me. Should I stop writing to allow you and Consuelo to make your names in fashion?"

Yannick said, "One can't compare the value of one art form to another. There isn't a hierarchy."

"Tell that to him," I snapped. "His writing brings him respect everywhere on earth. As it should. But that doesn't change the fact that I work just as hard at my art."

Antoine said, "I have never suggested you don't work hard."

"Making it in fashion isn't like finding a publisher who will print and promote your words. You can look down your nose because I have to beg, borrow, or steal what Madame and I need to survive, but you'd be doing the same thing if you had to go and find a buyer for every copy of your books."

"You think I would borrow? Steal? A publisher does not make words appear in my manuscript. Why do you think I need to live as I do? You see what it does to me. I haven't written in days. It kills me not to write, yet writing is agonizing."

"All artists suffer for their art," began Yannick.

"I've watched you write." I met Antoine's eye and felt my

anger begin to drain. Images were pervading my head: his pen clipping across his notebook; words rolling across the page like stones kicked along a path; rock walls slashed to nothing with a hard stroke of his hand. The memories filled me with a hunger I couldn't explain. I could feel the silk of my dress straining against my rib cage and my breasts. "It isn't agony. It's power and compulsion. It's passion."

Yannick picked up his wineglass, pushed back his chair, and walked off.

"It's like a tide rises in you and a fire burns above your head. You go somewhere." In that moment, with all my being, I wanted to be with him there. My throat was growing hot and sore. Consuelo was approaching. "Come to the studio tonight. Come write. Read to me. You'll feel better. We both will. Please."

As Consuelo took her seat on the banquette, I glanced with trepidation across the restaurant. Yannick raised his eyebrows and his drink to me.

36

I waited, standing at the open windows of the unlit studio with my heart high in my throat. The bands of silk that encircled my body felt insignificant and weightless, so aware was I of the bare spans between the fabric, of the heavy summer breezes that passed over my skin without wicking away its dampness or its heat.

The door opened. In four long strides he was on me, his mouth on mine, his hands in the silk. The hot breeze stole across my belly as he unbound my dress. I grappled with his belt until my hands felt the strength of his legs.

The windowpane was cold against my shoulder blades, the concrete ledge rough. I pressed myself to it, willing Antoine to be as unyielding, tempting him with parted thighs. But he seemed to retreat into himself, and his expression grew pained. His fingers on my back and ribs grew gentle—the touch of a watercolorist, a writer, not of a war pilot whose survival was in the reckless confidence of his hands.

His forehead was damp. His eyes shone wetly in the moonlight. He drew long, uneasy breaths.

Not now. His old unforgiving illness couldn't hit him now. My own fever was strong and would not wait.

I kissed him and closed my teeth on his lip. My nipples grazed the wool of his suit, and I muffled a cry. He moved against me then, his hands tough and alive, rocking me, my spine scraping on the window's metal frame.

I wept on his shoulder. I had only wanted to give myself to him. Instead, he had shamed me with the crudeness of my desire.

When Antoine's pain passed, we went outside and sat by a fountain in Bryant Park. Light danced on the pulsating droplets and falling spray. People of all ages had escaped their stifling apartments for the less oppressive heat of the summer night. Children who would have been long in bed last week were milling about, splashing in the water, giddy with the arrival of school holidays. No one gave me a second glance, though I had hitched my dress up to my knees to catch any current of air.

Before leaving the studio, I had handed Antoine a key. Now he weighed it in his hand. "You know what this will lead to."

"I'm offering you the use of the studio any night you want; you can write to your heart's content. Consuelo's parlor would give me a chance to succeed at my work, too."

"Consuelo will insist on moving in with me. I will not be able to write. My publishers will lose faith in me. I won't finish the children's book, or the long work I have been writing for years. I will die useless and forgotten."

"Oh, Antoine. Don't be so all-or-nothing. Put yourself in my shoes. If I don't do something drastic, the studio will fail. Do you want me to go back to waitressing?"

"You could become a translator for the Intelligence Department."

"You've got to be kidding."

"Very soon the Americans will be in France and across the Continent. They will need all the help they can get. I know people who would take you on in an instant."

"I'm a fashion designer."

"And you are proud of this?"

I wiped a trickle of sweat from my face and felt the heat of my breath on my wrist. "No less than you're proud of being a writer. Or are you shocked that I would compare the two?"

"I do not put one creative form over another."

"You have no respect for what I do."

"Designing a story and designing a dress are not so different."

"No? Then why is it all right for you to take what I do and write it into a story, but it isn't acceptable for me to take from your stories to create my designs?"

"Who said it is not?"

"I drew that coat for the Little Prince."

"It was a fine coat."

"You were angry. You joked, but underneath you were irritated. I'd degraded your creation by bringing it into the world of fashion."

"Should I thank you for your interpretation? The world over, people take what I write and they read into it whatever they want to see."

"So my design was just one more example of people abusing your work."

"You are putting words into my mouth. It is you who are insecure about your career choice. How do you expect anyone to believe in you if you don't believe in yourself?"

"There are people who believe in me. Consuelo believes in me, more than you ever have. She respects my vision and my skills." I pushed away an uneasy sense that somehow—though it would have been impossible—Consuelo had engineered this confrontation in which I would hold her up to her husband as an ideal.

"Far be it for me to contradict Consuelo. God knows she is always right."

His sarcasm took my breath away. I hung my head to obscure his view of my face, but he reached out and tucked my hair behind my ears.

"I believe in you," he said. "And you have the prerogative to create what you must—no less so than I do if I write of a little girl whose eyes, filled with tears, are as deep as the Mediterranean Sea and make my heart ache." He put his arms around me. "Just don't cry. I need you to show me the good in life. When

I look up from your studio floor and see you listening to me read, with that look of wonder you have . . . when you allow me to kiss you and part the opening of your dress . . . I feel sunshine. The softness of your skin heals me. You are my peace and my pleasure. Let's not poison what we have with accusations we don't mean."

I didn't know what Antoine meant sincerely and what he said only to calm me. All I knew was that, after kissing me good night outside Leo's, he went home with the key in his pocket— so the salon at Consuelo's was all but clinched.

37

I rose early to have coffee with Leo, then headed into the studio, where I wrapped the hemmed velvet skirt in tissue paper and left a note saying I was off to make the delivery. If Consuelo didn't want to see me, I would leave the parcel at the front desk. Maybe I would sketch in Central Park, or at the shop windows of Fifth Avenue. I had a dress to design for Countess Consuelo de Saint-Exupéry, an important commission earned entirely on my own.

Consuelo greeted me with a sleepy yawn—no makeup, in a simple, ice-blue satin house robe, her unbrushed hair curling softly around her face. Whatever their age, people are as cute as lambs when they yawn. She really was like a small child, so vulnerable looking with her big brown eyes.

She said, "You brought me a present."

"The skirt. This here is just my sketchbook."

"Oh well. Come in."

I scanned the parlor. In the alcove on the right, we could put an elegant screen behind which clients could change; we could move the glass table to create an uninterrupted span for modeling; we could place a big, ornate floor mirror beside the window, where the light would be flattering and the view seductive.

I said, "I hope I didn't wake you."

"Everything wakes me. I hardly sleep. I have a horror of being alone." Her delicate face looked pinched and wan. Her gaze darted around the room. "There's a ghost that sits and watches me through the night. I can wake a hundred times, and always his eyes are on me. He doesn't move at all."

"Maybe it's your guardian angel."

She shook her head. "And another that comes to lie with me. Sometimes he's a man—with long filthy hair, clothes from a pirate's grave, and his thing like a stallion's, as hard and heavy as iron, that presses against my stomach and chest when he lies on top of me, so I can barely breathe. Other times he's a woman with wide folds of fat that smell like old milk and spread over me slowly. But it's the same spirit. It has the same hair. Sometimes I dream that I'm trying to get away from it. Its hair hangs in my face and fills my mouth, and I can't escape."

A chill crept along my arms. When Consuelo patted the sofa, I left my chair and joined her. Antoine was right: she was fragile. Her imagination was too self-destructive, her fears too close to the surface. It pained me to think of her keening in distress and disgust at night, wracked by the dread of lifeless watchful eyes, half suffocated by the phantoms of her harrowed imagination. I murmured, "You poor thing."

Consuelo's lids came down over her anxious eyes, and her expression eased. She exhaled. Her body inclined to mine as though only I, in all the world, could free the demons that lived within. She reached for my hands, lifted one to her cheek, brought it down to her throat, and leaned in to touch her lips to mine.

Even as I jerked back in surprise, a current passed through my spine.

This was nothing I had ever imagined. I could not fathom what was expected of me, or what Consuelo hoped to gain. Had I led her to anticipate something like this—to feel justified in bringing my fingers to her bosom, bare under the cool robe, to her nipple pebbled and firm? Was she already planning to cast it up to Antoine: *Your little tutor girl is quite an easy thing; I'm surprised you haven't had her yourself.*

And why had he not? Why wouldn't he? He had kissed me. He had kissed me in ways and in places that even now made me moist and disturbed to recall. But he had never fully taken me as a man could. Never seduced me as Consuelo was doing, by inches and strokes, fingers slow and sure, tongue tip at my ear, buttons tugged undone. I had had to beg him to come to me last night. It was I who had pulled Antoine's mouth to mine at Le Bocal, who had untied my own dress at the studio for him, who had stripped to the skin that he might bathe me in silk. While Antoine looked for permission to succumb to his need or to recognize mine, Consuelo was an abductress driven by desire.

I felt a fullness between my legs, and the fear that she would feel me there, too—and then it hardly mattered anymore. If sex was not love, and love not sex—if Antoine would not make love to me, and Consuelo's lovemaking had the intensity of hate—if I could be made wet and weak and ashamed by the touch of my own beloved's wife—what could Consuelo possibly say to Antoine that could be worse than this?

It isn't so much that Mignonne is easy, it's that you never wanted her enough.

The sofa was deep. We lay together on our sides, skin to skin. Consuelo drifted in and out of sleep, her lashes falling, then fluttering up. I disentangled myself, retrieved the satin robe from the floor, and covered her. But she pushed it away.

She smiled, one arm resting above her head, one knee bent, her wide hipbones framing the gentle roundness of her belly and the flaring thatch of black hair below it, her collarbones lit in contrast to the sweaty cleavage between her breasts, her nipples dark as bruises. "Draw me."

I bent to reach for my dress.

"You don't need that, darling. Just stand as you are and draw me."

I glanced nervously at the wide span of window, though it was impossible to be seen on the twenty-third floor. "My sketchbook is by the door."

"Then get it."

I walked over and picked up the velvet skirt along with my sketchbook.

"I finished the hemming." I pulled the skirt from the bag. The tissue paper disengaged and rustled to my bare feet. "Would you like to try it on?"

"Do you want to draw me or not?"

"Of course." I fiddled with the binding of my book. "It's just that it's not something I usually do."

"Draw women?"

"Nude. I mean, when I'm nude."

"Then, obviously, you need the practice. Maybe you can become an expert in the genre—nudist fashion design—and get tenure at NYFS."

I inhaled. Propping the bottom of my sketchbook against my hipbones, I reminded myself of Antoine's words: "You take yourself too seriously. Play for a bit."

As soon as my pen hit the paper, I felt different, freer. I wondered whether, despite everything—or because of it—I had found my muse.

After I had filled several pages, Consuelo pulled on her robe and took the sketchbook. I dressed as she perused my drawings.

"What's this?" She flipped through a few pages rapidly, then returned to the beginning of the sequence and went through them slowly. "What is this?" Her voice was barbed.

My mind raced. She wouldn't inquire in such a way about my sketches for the white silk. And it couldn't be the Little Prince's coat; I had torn out that page and given it to Antoine. What else was in there besides failed ideas for Consuelo?

"This," she said, jabbing. "How do you know about this flower?"

Oh no.

There was no use trying to pretend; the image was unmistakably Antoine's. "Your husband drew it for me."

I braced myself—but Consuelo's expression crumbled. Had she never suspected that Antoine and I could actually have been together? It seemed that despite her husband's dalliances, despite her infidelities with Binty and (though already I could not fathom how) with me, despite whatever other liaisons and diversions kept her out at all hours, she still believed that she and Antoine were in a marriage, albeit a marriage in which affairs were not as damaging or as intimate as the bestowing of a rose.

It seemed, too, that Antoine had spoken the truth: he and Consuelo did share some sort of unbroken faithfulness. Had he betrayed their complex loyalty by sketching the rose for me? Had he been aware, as he drew on the studio floor, that he was drawing me into this strange relationship of three? In laying his rose at my feet, had he been passing on some measure of his own responsibilities?

Consuelo's voice quavered. "Tonio drew this for you?"

"I asked your husband to tell me about the young Consuelo, the girl he fell in love with . . . so that I could create something worthy of you, something to make you happy. He drew a flower—just like that one. He told me it was you."

Consuelo looked hopeful. "You mean you designed this collection for me?"

"You are the prince's rose." I eased the sketchbook from her hands and shut it. I felt as though I were closing a once-promising chapter of my life.

38

INSPIRATION & ANTOINE

~~THE INFLUENCE OF ANTOINE~~

~~THE ART OF INSPIRATION AND~~

INSPIRATION & ANTOINE

Thank host & audience/reporters
Star Pilot spiel
Introduce Antoine—pilot of skies and stars, etc.

It's a world's fair. You can't count on every tourist knowing who or what he was.

List his books—or only W3&S & TLP?
Transition—

I've never been good with transitions. I tap my pen. The ballpoint leaves flicks of ink on my notebook page. Without thinking, I connect a few and doodle Antoine's rose.

I am immediately aghast.

All these years of refusing to recreate the rose, of weeding the impulse from my fingers, of burying my memories of Consuelo . . . and she springs whole onto my page the moment I let my defenses down. The drawing repels me. It seduces me.

Maybe it's time for a resurrection. I picture the image on latex bikinis, on painted cheeks and bellies, a sock-it-to-me, star-age rose . . .

I could rip up the sketch, and invite the curiosity of my bored-beyond-belief fellow nontravelers. Or submit to the lure of opportunity as I did a quarter century ago.

Consuelo sent me on my way with a gentle kiss and a vague offer. I took the first and brought the second to Madame Fiche. "Consuelo requests that you visit her this afternoon."

"A potential client is coming at four o'clock. Mrs. RJ Wilson of RJ Wilson Blades. I may visit the countess afterward. She probably wants to pay me for the skirt. It is a lot of money to entrust to an assistant."

"There's something else she wants to meet with you about."

"Yes?"

First, to frame the living arrangements without entirely giving away the marital situation. "The thing is, the Saint-Exupérys have two units in their building. He needs room to write, and she has a place for her creative work, too."

"How nice for them."

"One of the units has a large parlor overlooking Central Park. It would make an incredible salon for us. There's a big difference between inviting clients to a factory studio and entertaining them in the parlor of a countess."

"Is there any point to this story, or are you only trying to depress me?"

"Consuelo is considering allowing us to use the parlor, rent free."

Madame's forehead furrowed. "Why? What would she receive for this?"

I said, "A chance to be associated with you, among other things"—but I had overestimated Madame's vanity.

"Do not bullshit me. I am not altogether sure I want the countess's space, but if I do decide to enter into negotiations, I would prefer to be successful. You would be wise to tell me what you know. All of it. If having such a salon will make or break us, as you seem to think it will, then do me the service of facilitating our success—and reap the rewards of doing so—or take responsibility for our failure."

I sank my hands into the pockets of my dress and rocked back and forth a little, thinking. Finally I said, "You have to keep it to yourself."

"I do not share business information with a soul."

"Okay. First of all, the countess is lonely. She and her husband live separately; their apartments are across the hall from one another. She doesn't want to be alone. She doesn't seem to have women friends. There's Jack Binty, but that's not the same as having girlfriends. If we use the salon, she gets our company. She gets someone to listen to her."

"*Bon.* Continue."

"Second, she's creative—and she's bored. She takes drawing and sculpture classes. She spent some time in an artists' commune in France. I expect she wants to be part of a creative community again. She's probably hoping to collaborate with us."

"Go on."

"Well, obviously, she's extremely vain. She wants attention and admiration. We can assume she'll want to use us to attract notice, even envy."

"That is our job, after all."

"Except that she might push us to do something we maybe shouldn't do. Just because something's right for a client, doesn't mean it's right for the designer."

"Leave off the riddles. What will she want?"

It was one thing to pacify Consuelo with a story; it was another altogether to put Antoine's drawing on the table as the next direction for Atelier Fiche. I played with the bracelet on my wrist, turning it around and around.

Madame said, "Now is not the time to be circumspect. You are very close to achieving for Atelier Fiche something truly significant. Setting the groundwork for a salon, as you have done, is work worthy of a partner, not an apprentice: I do see that. What is the third thing Consuelo de Saint-Exupéry will want from us?"

I picked up my sketchbook. Still I hesitated and remained silent.

"Mignonne. Let's close this deal together on equal footing."

"She will want to be immortalized." I opened my book to the series with the rose.

At a few minutes to four, I stood on the sidewalk scanning the street until a butter-yellow Lincoln Continental convertible purred up to the curb, the driver craning. In the passenger seat, a svelte woman in a small, exuberant hat and sleeveless peach dress stared straight ahead through the curved windshield.

The driver caught my eye.

I called out, "You're looking for Atelier Fiche?"

The woman turned toward me, her face largely obscured by sunglasses.

"I'll bring you upstairs, Mrs. Wilson." I opened the car door, and the woman disembarked gracefully. When I opened the studio's street-level door, she reached for the greasy handrail, then caught herself and pulled her hand back.

"This is where Madame Fiche does her showings?"

"There's also the salon," I lied, "but occasionally we like to treat our clients to something a little bohemian."

She slid her glasses off. "You'll be familiar with the slogan of our company: 'Wilson Blades cut to the chase.' I have my own version. 'Wilsons cut through the claptrap.' Unfortunately, I'm not in the business of lending my name to help an untried label gain footing and cachet."

"You're not coming upstairs?"

"I'm afraid not."

"What will I tell Madame Fiche?"

"Tell her that I prefer to visit her at her salon, if and when she has one."

"Oh, she does. On Central Park South."

"Excellent. Have her pop a note in the mail. My secretary will be in touch."

As I entered, Madame looked up expectantly from beside the rolling racks that held the Butterfly Collection. "Where is Mrs. Wilson?"

"She doesn't want to walk upstairs or spend her afternoon in a filthy factory building or be the first big name to wear Atelier Fiche or any other label that doesn't even have a bloody salon, never mind a handrail she can put her perfect fingernails on."

"She's not coming?"

"She left. She'll see you on Central Park South." I wrenched the rack from Madame's grasp and propelled it toward the end of the studio. It bumped over the uneven floorboards and came to rest a few unsatisfying feet away.

"What did you say to her?" asked Madame, her tone accusing.

"I didn't have to say anything. It's a miracle she even showed up. We've been acting like there's a grey area where we can get away with an off-putting address as long as our designs are impressive. It doesn't exist. It doesn't work that way. God! It's not like you didn't know this all along! Why do we have to be one rent check away from disaster before we do something about it? We could be locked out by the end of the month!"

"I would be surprised if the landlord gives us the week."

"He's going to kick us out?"

"I have removed my important papers."

"How can you be so blasé about this? You're talking about me becoming a partner, and meanwhile you know we're this close to shutting down?" I grabbed my purse. "He can't change the locks if we're inside. I'm going home to get some things. I'm sleeping here until this gets sorted out."

"You would do better to start packing up garments and fabrics. I will bring them home for safekeeping. We will find another location. This city is crawling with space."

"You've done this before."

"It is how things are."

"Not in my world. I'll deal with the landlord if he comes tonight. But you have to get serious about Consuelo and her parlor. We need that salon. We need it right now."

39

It was one thing to work oneself to exhaustion and collapse on the studio's sofa or to wait in the dark for a lover to arrive; it was another to have locked oneself in and barricaded the door and be facing a long night in which every sound and every minute could be bringing the landlord with his locksmith and his anger. I busied myself with sorting and packing, but not as Madame had suggested. I collected items that would belong in a salon: tools for measuring and fitting, an adjustable, full-length judy, a selection of fabrics that illustrated a range of textures and properties to help a client narrow down her preferences.

I went through the garment racks, deciding which pieces were worth keeping. It was startling how thoroughly my aesthetic had come to differ from Madame's. Of the garments I selected to keep, almost all were pieces I myself had designed.

With hangers squealing and rattling across metal racks, with the effects of my own exertion, at first I didn't realize there was noise coming from the hallway. Then the sounds sunk in and I froze in place.

Maybe it was Antoine. Let it be Antoine. How perfect that would be.

But no—someone pounded on the door.

"Miggy! Are you in there?" Leo! I had left him a note at home. I unlocked the door and he barreled in—followed by Yannick. "Oh my God, Miggy, you're stupid. You want to be hauled off to jail with your head busted in?"

Yannick strolled around. "Nice space. It's like my first restaurant. The floor is fabulous: so full of history. You just need a few tables, candles, maybe some gas lamps."

I listened for Antoine with half an ear. "Look, I'm fine. You should both just go."

Yannick opened his bag and handed Leo a bottle. "We'll keep you company for a while. I brought beer. It's cold."

If there was one way to pacify Leo, that was it. He dropped into a chair and used his lighter to pop the bottle cap. "You're not pulling this stunt again after tonight, Mig. This is the last bloody time."

A collection of empty beer bottles littered the floor of the sitting area. Yannick was telling stories when we heard footsteps and the raking of the key in the lock.

Leo jumped up. "Get the hell—" he began.

We all stared at Antoine. His gaze sliced past the men and gripped mine. "My apologies. I did not realize you were entertaining tonight. I only came to pick up . . . uh . . ." He may have been a master of words, but voicing an outright falsehood left him stumbling. "My trousers," he said—and Yannick burst out laughing. "The trousers Madame Fiche designed for me."

"'Jacket' would had been better," said Yannick. "Or 'book.' That would work. Heh-heh. Ah, Saint-Ex, I bet you're a lousy poker player. I wish I'd brought my cards."

"Who is this?" asked Leo. I could tell from the set of his shoulders that his agitation was extreme.

I said, "Leo Lachapelle, meet Antoine de Saint-Exupéry."

Antoine held out his hand. Leo ignored it.

"Leo is my brother," I said.

Yannick said, "And Saint-Ex is my very good friend."

"I've seen him at the Alliance," said Leo. "Mooning over Mig. Why does he have a key?"

Yannick spoke up. "Antoine, do you have cards?"

"Always." He pulled a pack from his jacket pocket and took a step.

Leo blocked him. "Why do you have a key to my sister's studio?"

"It is Madame Fiche's studio."

I said, "And Madame invited him to work in it when it isn't in use at night."

"Just so. Which necessitates a key."

"Yeah?" Leo turned to me. "Is this guy paying rent? Because people borrowing your space won't stop the landlord from changing the locks."

"Which is why we're here," Yannick said. "The wolf is at the door, and all that. Mignonne is keeping him at bay. We are her reinforcements."

Antoine tossed him the deck of cards.

Soon the men were deep into poker. Antoine won the first game, then, after one loss each to Leo and Yannick, won three in a row.

"Wait a minute," said Yannick. "What happened to Mr. Trousers who couldn't bluff to save his skin?"

"Winning is not about bluffing."

"Lots of it is," said Leo.

"Not if one's definition of bluffing is to put on a mask and fool others," said Antoine. "The secret is to see yourself as others wish to see you, and to intuit their expectations of you. It has much to do with putting oneself into another's shoes."

"A writerly perspective," said Yannick.

I said to Antoine, "Not that you're above putting on a mask. Antoine shuts off, Captain de Saint-Exupéry comes on."

Leo folded. "Captain—as in the Marines?"

"The French Air Force. There are worse places to perfect one's poker skills." Antoine handed me the deck. "You be the dealer. Triple or nothing, no limit. Who's in?"

"Are you kidding?" said Leo. "I'm not suicidal."

"Then it's you and me, Yannick. The pot goes to Mignonne's landlord if I win."

"Then I guess it goes to Leo's if I win."

"Amen," said Leo. "But can we switch the teams around?"

Antoine grinned. "Ready? Let's play."

It was past three o'clock when Antoine and Yannick sauntered out in search of Bernard Lamotte and a supply of liquor. Antoine had won. Leo had settled in an armchair to wait out the rest of the night with me. I shifted onto my side on the sofa.

For a few minutes we were silent in the dark studio. Enough light filtered in to allow me to make out the planes of my brother's face. Every once in a while the tip of his cigarette flared bright as he inhaled. He said, "He reminds me of Papa in some ways."

If we had to talk about Antoine, this was not a bad way to start. "But years ago, right? Before Papa started being so exhausted all the time."

"Yeah."

"Papa would have liked him, I think. That's what Yannick said when he introduced us."

"How long has this been going on? You and Saint-Ex."

"You're not mad?"

"I guess not. You need someone like that. Older. Successful. He's already done his military service. He's sown his oats. I can see how he'd be more than ready to take a wife and settle down."

The studio fell quiet. "He's done that, too," I finally said.

Leo didn't hesitate. "Sure—guy like that. Course he's been married before. He's not going to get to that age without being hitched. No kids from the first wife, though, Miggy, right? Run from that. She keeps hers. You want your own."

I rubbed my eyes. "I can't marry him."

"You better."

A sort of laugh escaped my lips.

"Okay," said Leo. "He's a lot older. I get it. But he can still give you a family."

"I don't need a family."

"Sure you do. Little Antoine and Antoinette bashing around your knees."

He was right. Yearning swelled in me.

Leo said, "Just tell him you're not ready to give up fashion yet. The guy looks at you like you're a goddamn goddess; he'll wait. In a couple years . . ." He faded out.

Somewhere on a floor below us a machine rumbled. It picked up its pace, advancing toward a steady thrum.

"Hey." Leo's voice was gentle. "Things can change. Couldn't things be different in a couple of years?"

Could they? Maybe Consuelo would give up Antoine. Maybe I could find a way to make him want a life with me. If I could keep him in New York. If I could show him what could be. If there were a little one growing in me from his seed.

"You awake, Miggy?"

"Yes."

"I just want you to end up happy. Give it a few years. You'll be glad you picked someone settled and respectable—and with trunkloads of money, to boot. Not to mention he's a hell of a card shark. Holy Jesus! He's a bloody magician."

"That's true."

"You could do a whole lot worse. You could end up with someone like me."

40

I was sketching wearily at my worktable when Madame arrived. "Where is the stationery?" she asked. "I must invite Mrs. Wilson to our salon."

Despite my exhaustion, I sprang to my feet. "Fantastic! I've already started to pack. And I've arranged for the late rent to be paid."

"*Vraiment?* But this is incredible. You have my utmost appreciation. I did well to hire you."

"And to make me a partner," I dared to say, my stomach clenching.

"Yes indeed, perhaps one day to make you a partner. As for now, I have a partner. As you say, we need the salon, and immediately."

"You offered the partnership to Consuelo?"

"She wished it."

"You promised that partnership to me!"

"Are you so surprised? You astound me, Mignonne: you have absolutely no head for business. I have told you before and I say it again: it is fortunate for you that I have taken you under my wing."

We arrived at Central Park South with as much as we could carry on the subway, including a judy whose metal base had battered my ankles along the way. Already Consuelo had removed many of her personal items—and had added an eight-by-ten of the portrait of her reclining in Garbo's bed.

She said, "I'm so glad Véra and I could come to an arrangement. We are going to have so much fun."

"You think so?" I ignored the threatening look Madame shot my way. "Because Atelier Fiche hasn't been what I'd call a barrel of laughs."

"Aha," said Consuelo. "That's exactly why a rebirth is in order. Don't you agree?"

Did it make any difference whether I agreed or not? I said, "Sure," and pushed the judy into the corner.

"Then we are all simpatico. Wait until you see the sign for the door. I've commissioned Romescu, the Surrealist. Should I open champagne? It's never too early."

"It is certainly too early," said Madame.

I began to ease a heavy box to the floor.

"Oh well." Consuelo raised her coffee pot like a stein. "Here's to us: Studio Consuelo!"

The box landed with a loud thump.

41

Interesting. If Mignonne had been foul and sullen before, all at once she seemed as irate as a typhoon. So Véra hadn't filled her in on the arrangements? What fun! Consuelo settled on the sofa, prepared to enjoy the show.

Mignonne said, "Studio *Consuelo*, Madame? You've given up your name?"

Véra gave the girl an imperious look. "Keep your voice down, and keep some perspective. We are trying things out. If it would help you, feel free to think of it as temporary."

"Of course it's temporary—you can't commit to anything! You won't even commit to your own business without planning to teach in the fall."

Consuelo sat up straighter. *Teach?* Véra had said nothing about teaching.

"Even your studio is disposable," Mignonne went on. "Stiff another landlord. Fire me. Eventually you'll design your own collection, but in the meantime, you steal mine."

"*Ta gueule!*"

"It's all the same to you. And now you've actually given up your name!"

Goddamn it, Consuelo thought, Mignonne's got fire in her. The stubbornness and strength of a bulldog in the body of a whippet. A familiar craving moved through her as she watched Mignonne's cheeks and throat grow pink. She touched her own chest and found it too was warmly flushed. The excitement they would generate working together! Consuelo's very skin was prickling in anticipation of it.

"How self-righteous and ungrateful you are," said Véra. "If *la comtesse* is to support an enterprise, naturally it must bear her name."

"We'll see what happens to your partner's name when it's stuck to a stick-in-the-mud who only knows how to give women things they already have." Mignonne picked up her sketchbook, brushed off her skirt, and walked away.

"Get back here," said Véra, "or you're fired."

The door slammed.

Consuelo almost applauded the performance, but her hands were stilled by a dawning realization. She had done something almost unheard of: she had made a mistake.

42

As I slammed the door behind me, Antoine's apartment door opened.

He took my arm and pulled me inside. "Consuelo gave me the news about the salon. Congratulations." He touched my face. "You don't look happy."

The sleeve of his jacket was wet and cold against my cheek. I pushed it away.

"Sorry," he said. "I got soaked carrying out experiments with toy submarines." He made a rumbling engine sound as he leaned over an imaginary bathtub. "Consuelo ran the bath before she left. I didn't realize until too late that she added oils to the water. It changes the properties. All my calculations are off."

"Poor you," I said flatly. "Did you drag me in here to see if I have tricks for removing oil stains?"

He laughed. "I hope you're not planning to offer to darn my socks, too."

"I'm not expecting a proposal. I'm not that dumb."

His face fell. "There is no need to be harsh."

"No? I just think we should be perfectly clear about what we are to each other."

"I thought you would be happy. You have the salon; you got your way. Why such concern about us all of a sudden? Has something changed?"

"Everything. I've just quit Atelier Fiche. I have no income and no career. You can't come work at the studio anymore. I have no studio."

"Oh, Mignonne." He drew me into a tight hug. "The studio

isn't important. You have followed your heart. I am sure you have made the right decision."

My whole body felt tight and unbending, but he stroked my back and my hair until the tightness in my neck loosened and my head rested against his chest. I put my arms around him, savoring the closeness of his body against mine.

He said, "I was watching for you. I want to show you something."

"A submarine?"

"Something much better. Come." He took my hand and walked me to an adjoining room.

I stopped short in the doorway.

Antoine's bedroom. There was his bed, large and rumpled. His robe tossed over a chair. His slippers. Somehow, this all seemed a hundred times more intimate and serious than being with him at the studio. Already I had crossed a threshold today. Now another faced me. I was about to step into his bedroom. I would lie with him in his bed. I would know him as a wife knows a husband. Suddenly I wasn't sure if I wanted this. He would take me and own me fully; there would be no going back. Already I could feel the role settling within me: the missing him, the jealousy, the wanting him always at my side.

He let go and continued into the room, oblivious to my hesitation. "Here it is." He grinned as he crouched beside the bed. "Do you like it? It cost hundreds of dollars, but it was worth every penny. Shall we try it out?"

Tears welled in my eyes. This was how Antoine would take me, with a *Here's my bed, come and get it?* I leaned into the doorframe, letting my tears fall.

Antoine was there in an instant. "What did I say? I am trying to cheer you up, not make you cry. Come on." He pulled me into the room and made me sit on the edge of the bed. "You don't have to do anything; just listen. You'll feel better. I promise."

He returned to the bedside, where—I now saw—a boxy

brown device sat on a small table. "I bought it on 57th Street, near the art school, with Lamotte. I went in to buy a great big church organ. Can you imagine me thinking I could fit a twenty-foot organ in here? As it turns out, this is very much better. You see—you never know what will come of obstacles. There is silver and gold in clouds."

He moved a switch. Within the box, a disc began to turn. He hurried back to sit with me. "Listen now," he said, the words thick with excitement.

Then his voice was coming from the machine: a whole group of voices, all of them Antoine's, chanting in near unison. It moved into a spritely song of *voyageur* canoe paddlers—"*V'la l'bon vent,*" "Go, good wind"—then a poem that grew in dissonance as it overlapped rhythms and tones. After some minutes, the stream of sound evolved to a chorus of babble, a tumbling brook of nonsense words spilling over each other in delight, interspersed with laughter and the faint ringing of bells. Then the layering fell away, and one voice carried on, singing a suite of French folk songs, each one softer and more heartfelt than the last. A lump grew in my throat and refused to subside.

"Is it not magical?" asked Antoine. He began to sing along in a voice so hushed that it barely reached my ears.

I couldn't answer. I didn't want the music to stop. I didn't want to leave this room or this man. I wanted him to remain a boy forever, to stay with me like this, Antoine whispering the songs of my childhood, his eyes dancing as he clutched my hand.

43

Regret: that was the strange little ache Consuelo felt. She went to the door and peered down the empty hall.

Damn Mignonne! The girl had walked out on Consuelo, not only on Véra Fiche. Rejected her. Ignored her! Not only ignored but deprived her, sentenced her to tedium and mediocrity. Consuelo could never again wear something as sensual as the ribbon dress or as memorable as the rose. All she could wear from now on would be Studio Consuelo—and Studio Consuelo was just her and this dry, old bat.

Consuelo glared at Véra. "There's no need to wait out the trial period. I've seen all I need to see."

"Very good. Perhaps we should arrange a small celebration, after all."

"The partnership is dissolved."

"*Pardon?*"

"I will ask the concierge to call you a cab."

"What are you saying, *Comtesse* Consuelo? We have not yet even begun!"

"I'll have your boxes and judy moved to the mail room. It's really no trouble. Just try to have the last of the things picked up within the week."

Véra hissed. "Rot in hell!"

In the airplane, Consuelo coughs. Her head scarf has slipped down to block her eyes. She's hot, her breath tastes caustic, and she has lost a shoe under the too-high seat.

What was she just thinking about?

Véra. Hell.

There was a time when hell hadn't worried her. In those days, she could have tricked Satan into turning down the heat.

44

Antoine and I had left his apartment; now we sat on a bench deep in Central Park. The talk had turned to his frustrations— the acquaintances who passed judgment based on rumors, the accusations that refused to succumb to truth.

He dismissed my suggestion that the gossip sprang from jealousy. "We lost our country in an instant. They are like parents who have lost a child and are desperate for someone to accuse. I would accept their blame if I thought it would help them, but I cannot bear that they make me the symbol of what pits them against each other."

"They never were a tight group, not even before the war. My father really struggled to bring them together. He used to tell them constantly, 'We are all France.'"

"We will be one again—but not until the Americans set France free."

"And you think they will."

"They will, and I will be their witness."

My spirits sank. "You don't have to go with them."

"They will need my knowledge. They have little experience of the North African terrain that must be their staging ground."

"They've asked you to join them?"

"Not as of yet."

"Then stay."

"I am not staying."

"You'd rather die anonymously there than face criticism in the spotlight here."

"You need not criticize anonymity; it is noble enough."

"Not for someone like you, who can do so much with his name. You're running away from your problems. Look what you'll leave in your wake. Your wife has nothing but your reputation; you'll leave it in shambles. Your publishers set you up like a king here. You can't run out on them in the middle of things. And I . . ." I faltered. "Would you stay in New York if you could make a difference here?"

"There is no way to make a difference here." He plucked a tubular red bloom from a firecracker plant and spun it like a propeller. "I should have been a gardener."

I pictured the Little Prince carefully deploying his watering can. He was so alive to me. I could almost feel the water's diminishing weight in his hand, and the coolness of the stray droplets that clung to his shins. Who but a true gardener could create such exquisite life? Who but Antoine and his stories could plant such love in the heart?

And was that not a way to make all the difference in the world?

The fine hairs on my arms rose in goose bumps.

The Little Prince was like France itself, a child loved and lost, who finds a way to return to life and love again. All that was needed was for Antoine to finish the story and see it published. The story itself could unite the community. And surely, with all rallying behind him, Antoine could be convinced to stay.

I said, "I don't think you realize what *The Little Prince* is going to achieve."

"It will fail, as all writing must. With luck, I will not be here to witness it."

"You wouldn't leave before it's published!"

"My responsibilities to Reynal & Hitchcock do not take precedence over my duty to my people."

He placed the flower in my palm and closed my fingers over it. "I know you mean well, Mignonne. But *The Little Prince* will not be in bookstores until just before Christmas. You expect me to do nothing until then? The world as we know it may have already disappeared."

My mind was churning. The only puzzles I was good at involved shapely pieces of paper and bolts of cloth. Antoine was the mathematician who created number problems so diabolical that they had stumped his pilot colleagues for days on end. He was the inventor who had patented solutions before others had even begun to see problems. He was the writer with a lifetime's experience in helping characters overcome obstacles and find means to an end. It wasn't fair that I was left to figure out this conundrum on my own.

How could he insist that the only possible solution was for him to leave? I thought of what had driven me from New York to Montreal: despair over the failure of my portfolio, the withering of my dreams, the shame of believing myself unwanted. Is this what he was feeling? Was his insecurity about his forthcoming book driving his need to escape? Was it possible that, in this country where he was lauded as *"the French author with authority and élan,"* he could yet feel unloved? Maybe a writer who so respected his native tongue as to forever consider himself a neophyte in its use could not be satisfied by the praise of those who read his work in translation while he was excoriated by those whose language he shared.

I thought of the heroes of his earlier books. The pilots who survived had done so through obdurate will and the whims of fortune—and despite the fact that engines failed. They had the blind drive and forgiving bodies of tireless youth, whereas Antoine . . .

I pulled him to a stop. "When you go overseas with the Americans, will you be flying newer planes?"

His irritated expression disappeared. "Very much newer. Much more reliable! I should have told you that before. You'll have no reason at all to worry about me. Planes today are entirely different."

"And will you be wearing a parachute in these new planes?"

He smiled indulgently. "I should think so." He took my hand in his right hand, kissed it, and held it to his heart.

"And what if your plane is hit?"

"I shall float softly like the Little Prince—or like you, a butterfly—down from the sky."

I didn't smile. "And how will you get out of the plane in midair?"

His voice dampened. "How?"

"You have to open something, don't you? A hatch or a door? Where is the lever or the pull cord? Which hand would you use?"

Reluctantly, he turned up his left.

"Show me how you would bail out of a burning plane."

His expression became grim. He began reaching up as though attempting to access a handle. His arm froze at a low pitch. His left shoulder was long seized, damaged with his broken collarbone. He couldn't bail out. He probably couldn't maneuver into a parachute. I asked, "Can you even manage to pull your flight suit over your clothes?"

He spoke through gritted teeth. "I have the mechanic help me dress."

My hand released the propeller blossom, a pulp of red.

If I could only believe some good might come of him leaving. If I could only hold on to hope that he would save not only his country but also himself. I would let him go, for the sake of his spirit, if I thought his body capable of safeguarding his soul. But who would protect him if he refused to protect himself? Who would keep him alive, if not me, if not now?

I said, "Maybe you don't want to change your plans for my sake." My voice caught. "And maybe the French here don't seem deserving of your help. I know they're not starving. But imagine how empty and bereft they must feel in their souls. Isn't that worth your concern? The French line in America will grow from these seeds. You said you wanted to be a gardener."

He lit a cigarette and forced a long, slow stream of smoke into the humid air. "You travel many avenues of persuasion. What other dead ends shall we go down today?"

Tears stung my eyes, but I refused to let them drop. He could say what he wanted to quell my efforts. He could dismiss the power of his storytelling, but I would not. If he insisted on leaving before Christmas, I would find a way to tell the story of *The Little Prince* before the book's official launch. I might be naïve, I might not have a job or a studio, but I was not going to let that stop me. He might find it as easy to ignore my pleas as those of the next girl, but I would not be pushed aside.

By the time we reached Central Park South, I had the beginnings of a plan.

We would work together. I would make the expats fall in love with him. I would make him fall in love with me.

45

Consuelo had spent a tiring hour directing and accompanying Elmore as he moved Véra's boxes to the mailroom in the lobby. She was at his desk when the doorman came in and gave Elmore a warning look. Consuelo immediately focused past him to the sidewalk.

Nothing. No Tonio giving a girl a goodbye kiss. No couples lingering in a cab at the curb. But when she turned back to the lobby, there was no mistaking the doorman's relief. She looked again.

There: in the park, on the other side of the stone wall. All she could see of Tonio were his head and his shoulders. All she could see of his companion was the back of her blond mane. Mignonne?

Whoever it was, she was getting nowhere. They were both gesticulating angrily. When the girl reached up, Tonio all but sprung back. Now he veered away and left her. There had been no kiss and unlikely even a goodbye. Consuelo chuckled as she returned to Elmore's desk.

Tonio came storming in from the street.

Consuelo joined him at the elevator. "Darling? Can I help?"

"Help your designer friend."

"Véra? We've decided to part ways."

"Not her. Mignonne. She has just tried to convince me I should turn *The Little Prince* into a fashion show."

So it had been Mignonne—with a business proposal. And such an outrageous one! No wonder she had been quick to drop Véra: the girl had a brilliant idea and no intention of sharing the rewards. "How intriguing. And you want me to help her with it."

"My God, no. Help her get her head on straight. Her idea is ridiculous. She thinks that by dramatizing my story, she can smooth things over at the Alliance Française."

Of course she would tell him that. How else was she to get him to agree?

He said, "Can you imagine the prince as a mannequin? The fox? The rose?"

Indeed she could. Mignonne had already proven the power of the concept with the rose-embellished pieces; a *Little Prince* show would bring them to life. What was more—ingenious idea!—Consuelo herself could model the central piece. It would show the world, in a way the book could never do on its own, that the prince's beloved rose was Consuelo, only ever Consuelo, for ever and evermore.

As they stepped from the elevator, she put a calming hand on her husband's arm. "Just think of it as another medium of expression. Besides, it wouldn't be fair for you to stop her. It was you who gave her the idea."

"Me?"

"Didn't you draw the rose for her?"

Tonio's face changed: it took on the unreadable veneer she detested. His voice became impassive. "What are you saying?"

"Mignonne told me that she asked you what you love about me, so she could design something completely unique to me. She said that you drew a rose and explained how it represented me."

He nodded slowly. "This is fundamentally true."

"If you directed her to design a collection using the rose as her muse and motif, you can't blame her if she went ahead and did so. And once you have a collection, well, a collection needs to be shown."

The facade dropped for the briefest moment: Tonio looked trapped.

46

"Lots of factories are looking to hire ladies these days," said Leo. He took my arm as we stepped off a high curb and crossed the street. "I'm thinking of buying a wig and nabbing one of them jobs myself."

It was midday, midweek, the day was bright, and we were taking a stroll. I had nowhere to go and Leo hadn't been going to work. He wouldn't tell me why or what had happened, but he admitted that no, he wasn't sick; no, he hadn't told Mother; no, he had no savings or prospects or brilliant plans.

"See that?" Leo pointed at a young man in neat clothes with a crisp haircut and a clean, honest face. "One of the best jobs you can get in all of New York. Fresh air, flexible hours, lots of folks helping you succeed."

"Doing what?"

"He's a slicker, the smoothest kind of no-good bum. He's out here stemming for maybe five hours a day. 'I just lost my job, I hate to ask but I have to eat, boo-hoo.' *Crème-de-la-crème*, sister. Ten dollars a day, that's what a good slicker makes. That guy probably makes enough to keep his girlfriend in a hotel in the 70s, take her to the El Morocco and have a maid."

"Why wouldn't someone like that be in the military?"

"Probably wrangled a deferment, like me."

"You have a deferment? All this time, I thought some sort of official was going to grab you off the street."

"Nah, I'm fair and square. I told the draft board I was eager. I knew the railroad was going to get me a six-month deferment, and then another. They could have kept getting me more and more."

"What do you mean, the railroad?"

"Working on a railroad's an important job. Can't fight a war without a system on the home front."

"But you were building carnival rides."

"For Carson Unity, owned by Carson Unity Railroad. I keep telling you, it's all about what you do with what you got." He stopped at an open window to order breakfast.

I wondered if the last of Leo's inheritance was now crisping his toast. My own nest egg was still stashed away. "We need a plan."

"I got a plan. You marry Antoine and buy a place in the Hamptons. I live in your garage."

"I'll look into teaching at the Alliance. And there's always Le Pavillon."

"I'll be your driver. Does Antoine have a car? Hold on—I can't live in your garage. Where are you going to put the car? I'll live in the servants' wing. Me and a feisty little maid." He rubbed his palms together.

"I've been meaning to call Yannick. You could probably wash dishes while I'm waitressing."

"You really think I'd go begging at Yannick's feet?"

"What are you going to do? Seriously, Leo."

"I'll find something in a war plant for a few months. By November or so, the draft board will come sniffing around."

At home, Leo slipped his lighter, his Lucky Strikes, and a flask into the pockets of his robe. "Nothing better for you than a cigarette in the bath. The steam opens up your lungs." He disappeared into the hallway.

I phoned Yannick. "Remember you said I could wait tables at Le Pavillon?"

"I heard about what happened."

Madame Fiche had been right: everyone did know everyone's business. All that talk about tight lips was just more talk. "You know I quit Atelier Fiche?"

"I had lunch with Saint-Ex. He was very worked up. Apparently, you want to destroy his reputation and ruin his name. Also, you're just like Consuelo."

"Oh my God."

"He said . . . Let me get this right. 'Your niece and Consuelo are birds of a feather. Why is it that when one loves a woman . . .'" He stopped. "I forget the rest."

"Yannick!" I slapped the wall beside the phone. "Who did he mean?"

"'One loves a woman.' You don't know who that would be?"

"I don't know what to think or do anymore."

"Do what is best for you."

"And what, in your wisdom, is best for me?"

"It isn't waitressing at Le Pavillon; I can tell you that."

47

Dear Mignonne,

Your uncle had the courtesy to telephone tonight to tell me not to worry, that he was sure you would be fine. Not being a family man, he didn't realize that a mother's worst phone calls all begin that way. It took some doing to convince me you were not disfigured or barely clinging to life.

If you had only written, I would have told you about the struggles your father went through in his career. He would say that success rarely comes easily, and when it does, it rarely endures. I would add that there is no failure in turning away from a fruitless path.

Don't be upset, Mignonne. It is a sign of maturity to know one's limits. You completed your education, you tried your hand at fashion. Now your only worry will be to find a fellow who doesn't mind a girl who has been around a bit. A few months' rest, and then perhaps a normal job here, will put that all in the past.

I have enclosed a check for the train fare. Your room awaits, as pretty and calm as when you left it. Soon you too will feel calm. As always, I look forward to your return.

Yours,
Mother

48

June 29th was Tonio's birthday. His publishers were throwing a party; he had told Consuelo she was expected to attend. She had feigned indignation—of course she was expected!—but secretly she had been thrilled. So often he went to parties and celebrations without her. She never knew if it was because he alone had been invited or because he preferred to go alone.

To be sure, many of his friends disliked her. From the beginning, they'd thought her overbearing and unreasonable. One had gone so far as to cast the opinion in stone—or on paper, which was more permanent in these bomb-infested days. He had written that Tonio had introduced him to two new developments, of which the friend far preferred the manuscript to the wife.

That was what Consuelo had been up against all these years! Well, she always got the last laugh. She would make an unforgettable entrance tonight, dressed in her best—and her best was impressive indeed. She chose a fuchsia gown, added a black lace bracelet sprinkled with slivers of white diamonds, and topped off the effect with a tiny, perfect tiara. Then she waited like a princess for her knight.

He didn't come. He didn't even answer when she rapped on his door.

Finally the phone rang. "Consuelo, where are you? I told you I'd be waiting for you downstairs."

She put on her fur stole in case it grew cool in the night, gathered her abundant hem, and escorted herself to the elevator.

In the lobby, Tonio regarded her gown, flawless makeup, and upswept hair. "No wonder you are so late."

She took his arm, and they walked ceremoniously to the sidewalk. "Stay close to me, darling. Protect me. I feel as nervous as a new bride."

"You will stand out like one, too." Instead of hailing a cab, he led her to the casual bistro at the foot of the apartment building, the little hole-in-the-wall from which he ordered lunch or dinner every day.

"Tonio, no! The party can't be at Café Pedro!"

"It was my duty to choose the venue. I like Café Pedro. Did you think I would opt for an embassy or opulent club? Maybe I should have put out a press release so the *Times* could announce that I'm getting old."

His friends had already seen them through the window; the proprietor himself had come out to usher them in; it was too late for Consuelo to go back upstairs to change. Fine then: she would simply make the others feel underdressed.

She spent the evening drinking heartily, laughing merrily, then raucously, saying who-knows-what about who-knows-whom, dancing between the tables, then on the tables themselves.

49

June 29th was Antoine's birthday. I had made him a simple white scarf from what remained of the ribbon dress. I wrote his name on the package and took it to Central Park South to leave at the concierge desk.

Elmore said, "They're just next door in the café, if you want to give it to him yourself."

It was a kindness, a warning: your lover's wife is with him nearby; you might want to watch your step.

But it didn't matter. I thought it unlikely I would ever see Antoine or Consuelo again.

50

"Thank you for coming," said Consuelo, as she ushered in a wan and tired-looking Mignonne. "It's been lonely here." The hours stretched on endlessly when there was nothing to divert the boredom. The apartment sounded hollow, Tonio had been refusing to answer his door, and Binty had gone out of town.

Consuelo walked toward the sofa, but the girl remained standing. "Sit down. I don't bite. At least, I don't think I do. Have I bit you yet?"

Mignonne didn't even crack a smile.

"All right, then. I'll get to the point. Tonio told me you're planning to use his *Little Prince* story in a fashion show."

Mignonne gasped lightly.

How everything showed on that girl's face! Consuelo asked, "True?"

"No. Not really. I didn't propose a fashion show. I suggested we collaborate on a dramatic production."

"With fashions."

"Costumes." The girl squirmed. "A production has to have visual appeal. It's not a reading. And the fashion aspect would have helped bring in an audience."

"Which Tonio could not do without your designs? He must have been thrilled to hear you say so. Do you think he has no ego at all, darling?" Consuelo put her feet up on the sofa. "Man is pride, Mignonne. If he appears humble, it's because he is proud of his humility." She chuckled. "Ah, well. He may never forgive you, but I think it's all terribly cute."

Mignonne's face had flushed. Now the pink had spread to her chest. Such an endearing thing, her familiar betraying blush.

"Your plan," said Consuelo. "It's all about helping Tonio—is that the pitch?"

"I want to help people understand him." Mignonne looked down at the floor. "To stop him from being attacked all the time."

"And why do you care if he is attacked?"

Mignonne turned her face toward the wide window and gazed out silently, long enough for the high color to leave her skin, long enough for Consuelo to see the answer. The girl's jaw held no defiance. There was no fighting spark in her eye. The planes of her face were smooth and still.

It was nothing new to see a girl in love with him. Every girl was smitten by Tonio. They were swept away by his writing. He wounded their hearts with his smile. Consuelo had come to expect that they would want him. But those girls wore entitlement like cats carry musk. They did not stand with sunlight and sadness rendering their features as lustrous and fragile as that of a marble Virgin. Consuelo had not touched them through their clothing, nor eased away the fabric to cool their skin with hers. She had not lain with them, nor lain awake aching to sculpt them, nor been unnerved by the softness of their mouths.

She shook off the memory. "Tonio censured you. You must be very disappointed. It would have been so handy to take my husband's art and money for your debut."

In a flash, Mignonne was at the sofa, leaning over Consuelo, her face close. Anger amplified the blue of her eyes and the force of her breath. "I am not taking anything."

It was as Tonio used to be, his shadow swallowing her, his body and his passion engulfing her. Let her want me, begged Consuelo silently. She lifted a hand to touch the girl's lips.

The aggression seeped out of Mignonne. "I just wanted to help."

"Hush. We will do the fashion show. And I will play the role of the rose."

The peculiar conjunction of fashion design and the momentous art of Antoine de Saint-Exupéry would not only sell out in Manhattan, it could pique the interest of the whole besieged world. And then the magic would begin. The audience would see for itself that—above all and above anyone—Tonio, the prince, needed Consuelo, the rose. The reviews would broadcast the message in advance of the book's publication. Reynal & Hitchcock would set in print, for all time, the legend of their love. Everyone would know that she and Tonio were one. He wouldn't be able to hide her away anymore. They would live together again as man and wife. Consuelo couldn't let this chance slip through her fingers.

Mignonne said, "I'll make you a rose dress if that's what you want. But we can't do a show, not without Antoine's approval."

"My husband doesn't always know what's good for him. We don't need his approval to help him—especially since all we're doing is promoting and honoring his art! You make the clothes and squeeze the old goat for a spot on the Alliance stage; that's all you have to do. I will put my sculptural talents to use on the sets. We'll round up some French-speaking lovelies, and block out some action around the story script."

"I'm not sure."

"Do you have better plans? Every designer in New York is scrambling to be first out of the gate, and you don't even have a studio. You can let the train leave the station without you, or you can make a huge splash in a few months' time and let the mayor himself treat you like a star."

Mignonne drew the tips of her nails back and forth on the

glass tabletop. "I don't have space, or fabric, or half the tools I need."

"I've told Binty already that I'll be starting a new adventure. He'll open his pocketbook. We'll work right here in the parlor." If that meant Consuelo was left with little room, all the more reason to secure a larger home where she and her husband could live together. "I'll get a copy of the manuscript. I know how important It Is for you to make sure every detail is right. You're a woman of integrity."

"I would have to get it exactly right if I was representing Antoine."

"Of course. We want to make sure that everything we do serves our goal. Including the name behind the designs. For example, we can't use 'Atelier Lachapelle.'" Imagine the ridicule the expats would heap on Consuelo if she tried to ride the coat-tails of their late, great, founding god.

"I agree: we shouldn't use the word 'atelier' at all. We'll do the show in French for the expats, but we should keep the door open for an English version down the road. It's better to go with 'Studio Lachapelle.'"

"You're not thinking, darling. We want something that supports our objective. Something people will notice."

"Lachapelle is a respected name."

"And respectable. It's too safe. There's nothing in it to suggest that something revolutionary is in the works. On the other hand: Studio Saint-Ex! 'A Night of Fashion by Studio Saint-Ex'—now that's a head-turner."

Mignonne tightened her cardigan around her. "It makes it sound like Antoine is putting on the show."

"We are putting on the show. But if you intend on letting the spotlight fall on him, you'll embrace the chance to present it under the Saint-Exupéry name." Under Consuelo's own name: it should be no other way.

She went to the bar cabinet and poured them each a drink.

The liquid shivered as she handed Mignonne a glass. Either the girl would splash the liquor into Consuelo's face, or Consuelo would control the show and the girl from here on in.

Mignonne looked down. She spoke quietly. "To Studio Saint-Ex." She raised the liqueur to her mouth and drank.

Stripping her of her name had been almost as satisfying as removing her dress.

51

I couldn't guess at how Consuelo managed to convince or beguile Binty, but he had come through. The parlor—Studio Saint-Ex—was crowded with fabrics, notions and tools, plus two antique, freestanding full-length mirrors of much better quality than Madame's mirror had been. Consuelo had arranged an easel and a table at the window to catch the natural light. In one corner, on a black lacquered tabletop, I had placed my sewing machine. In the other, a fully adjustable judy stood skewered on a brass base.

I moved about in stocking feet, pacing a route around boxes, chewing on the end of a pencil, running my fingers through my hair, stopping occasionally to add some notes or lines to my sketchbook.

Consuelo said, "It's such a comfort to have another body in here. Besides Binty. He really is getting a little uninteresting. And predictable." She examined her figure in the mirror alongside the window and walked to the second mirror to study herself in its more artificial light. "Let me know if we're still missing anything we need."

I nodded vaguely, distracted. The preliminary rose designs had come so easily; I hadn't expected the rest of the outfits to be a battle, based as they were on existing drawings. But that was the rub: how could I dare think I might match Antoine's creativity with my awkward, unyielding own? I had felt stuck now for days.

One morning, I had entered to find Antoine in the apartment, deep in a heated argument.

Consuelo was saying, "You can't complain about me calling it 'Studio Saint-Ex,' not unless you have a claim on fashion design as well as writing."

Antoine noticed me. "I suppose you, too, are content to exploit the Saint-Exupéry name?"

"I'm not. I wouldn't. I . . ." I looked to Consuelo for support. She lifted a box onto a table. "Come see what I bought. Sand for our desert!" She started pulling out bags. From each one, she poured onto the table a small mound of a granular powder, each a slightly different tone. "It took me days to find these samples."

Antoine had been moving toward the door. Now it seemed his curiosity got the better of him. He came back to peer over my shoulder. His arm brushed mine as he reached for one of the piles. I hadn't felt his touch or smelled his cologne in weeks. I had to stop myself from bringing my face to his neck to take in more of his scent.

He asked, "Cornmeal?" and ran his fingers through the granules. "The color is like the morning sun in early springtime."

I said, "It will reflect the brightness of the stars and the prince's planet in the sky."

For an instant, Antoine seemed to be about to smile. Then he said, "If you think you will win me over with cornmeal, you are wrong."

His indignation vibrated through every step. As he closed the door, Consuelo and I shared a look of amusement and triumph.

A day later, we were unrolling a bolt of ivory fabric on the floor and cutting out the first item for the *Little Prince* collection. Consuelo danced around as I snipped. I had promised her that the first outfit would be for the character of the rose, to be played by Consuelo herself. The fabric separating on either side of my scissors was only the base of the design; the flower would rise in appliqué from the floor-length hem, arching her stem up the front, and spreading her red petals across the entire bodice and on toward the shoulders. But even the base threw Consuelo into such excitement that she circled my operation, clapping, occasionally kicking up the edges of the fabric, and I had to tell her to sit and be still for a while or the dress would not get made.

By the time I had cut the pieces, my partner's patience was gone. "Are you done?" she asked again.

"This is only a fraction of the job."

"I just want to see it pinned onto me. Then I'll believe you're really going to make it, that I'll finally get to wear the rose."

No one had ever waited with such sweet anticipation for anything I had ever made. I took to explaining the steps to Consuelo. I wanted her to know exactly how much care and thought I was putting into this dress. "When you lay down the pattern pieces, you have to make sure you follow the direction of the fabric. See the weave? This is the warp; that's called the weft—or the woof."

"Woof-woof!"

"If you lay the pattern down any which way, the fabric will pull and drape incorrectly."

"You are a master of draping. Or 'mistress,' I should say." Consuelo was on her tiptoes, too excited to stand still. "Keep working, Mistress Mignonne."

I bent over the project. "If I'm your mistress, what are you to me?"

"Your masteress."

She is so silly, I thought. No wonder Antoine cannot entirely stop loving her; she is, at heart, a child.

Tiring days later, I finished the first dress. And what a dress! It fit Consuelo like a satin skin, caressing her shoulder blades, swelling with her breasts, hugging her ribs. Only after it had risen with the peaks of her hipbones did it begin to fall, plummeting straight to the floor from the contours of her hips. At the ground, the line broke just so. The ivory dress was stunning because it paid homage to the fine, full shape of Consuelo's figure, but what lifted the dress beyond stunning, making it unforgettable, was the shimmering red rose that dominated its front.

Consuelo walked the length of the parlor, back and forth. With each step, the rose moved as though bending to the wind or arching to hear a loved one's voice. She swiveled her hips and the rose sashayed with her. She was the rose, through and through, bright and shiny-eyed, glowing with beauty and pride. She said, "No one in New York is designing anything like this. There is nothing anywhere to match it."

"It's meant to be unique. Like the prince's rose."

"There are other roses in the story."

"I know."

"But we aren't going to include them in our show. Just one rose. Just me."

I put my hands on my hips. "We are not going to feature only one rose. It's a fashion show. We need to get clothing out there. We won't have time to make a whole garden's worth—we can take care of that by painting masses of them into the set. But we need at least a few good pieces."

"Oh, Mignonne. Why even bother? They'll pale in comparison to me."

"Not every woman can wear something like your dress. The other roses will be simple dresses and separates. I have a couple dozen things sketched out. Take that off and we'll go through them."

I was releasing the zipper down Consuelo's back when there was a brisk knock on the door and it began to open. Quickly, I zipped the dress closed.

Antoine came in. "Consuelo, where is my—" He stopped.

I could see from his expression, from the slight adjustment in his posture, that the image of Consuelo in the form-fitted dress warmed and loosened everything inside him. His eyes roved over the satin. My own face heated as I watched him take in the sight.

"Hello, Tonio," said Consuelo. "You like it."

It wasn't a question; there was no need for a question. Antoine had not even managed to tear his gaze away from her long enough to notice me glaring at him. How dare he come in here and ogle Consuelo? He never would have stared at me like that in front of his wife. My nails dug into my palms.

Consuelo performed a languorous spin. In the moment her face was turned from her husband, he finally glanced sheepishly at me.

He can't help himself, I thought. It's the perfection of the dress that does it to him. My God, how convoluted this has all become. I must not let myself resent that which I have created. This is success; I must not push it away.

52

Most mornings, I woke early and had coffee with Leo, updating him on the progress of the show without mentioning the relationship between my partner and the man Leo liked to refer to as my honey pie. Then I took the subway uptown and let myself in, letting Consuelo sleep on for another hour or two—if she was home. She and Antoine had rented a house in Northport, Long Island, for the summer. She continued to come into the city for lessons at the Art Students' League, but her sessions at the apartment had become sporadic.

Now it was almost September, with the show booked for mid-November. We were getting nowhere, complained Consuelo. "We can't have a show with one dress."

I gestured toward a hanging rack. "For Pete's sake. I've been blazing through the collection. But since you raise the issue, I don't think all your traveling back and forth has been good for your productivity." I didn't point out that her set design sketches lacked sophistication, sensitivity, and appeal.

"It can't be helped. Tonio is crazy about the Bevin House. It's a big white mansion, right on the water. He says he's never had a better place in which to write."

A pang gnawed at my insides, but I said, "That's good. I'm glad it's coming along. We can't finish what we're trying to do until he completes his manuscript. Even if we don't use everything in the story—"

"We can't use the whole thing!"

"We're not going to. We can leave out a lot of the early stuff—the men the Little Prince visits on other planets before he arrives on earth—but we have to get the rest right, everything having to do with the rose."

"And how all he wants in the world is to return to her and take care of her and show her how much he loves her."

"That hasn't changed in the manuscript, has it? You've seen the latest version?"

"Oh, Mignonne," said Consuelo, "that will never change." She reached up to run a cool finger behind my ear, down the slope of my neck. I shrank from her touch. "Don't look so anxious, darling. The manuscript is getting done. The essence of the story won't change. He'll just change words and change them back again before he delivers it to his publishers in the next three or four weeks. And then everything will go back to how it was: just you and me, nestled up here in our little creative cubby, and Tonio doing whatever he does across the hall."

"You're giving up the summer house?"

"Not yet. But have you ever spent fall or winter in a grand mansion? Of course you haven't. A home of that size is exhausting in the cold. Tonio isn't partial to furnace heat, and the fireplaces are a monster to feed."

She turned me around to massage my shoulders. "It's too bad I wasn't able to have you visit us there, darling. I begged Tonio all through August to let me invite you to stay for a week."

Could this be true? Antoine didn't want me near?

Consuelo's breasts brushed against my back. "It's nothing personal, darling. But as a count, Tonio does have social standards to uphold. Besides, you'd be bored—my husband always locked away working, me entertaining our famous friends night and day. What would you have done with yourself?"

With the Saint-Exupérys resettled into their respective apartments, Antoine had started dropping in now and then, watching and smoking, pacing.

Once, when Consuelo was out of the room, he said, "Do not let her push you around too much. She can be unbearable if you are not used to her, and even dangerous. She throws things."

"You think she'll throw something at me?"

"She may, and her aim is very good. She has broken plenty of furniture as well. Perhaps I should check on you more often."

But another time when I had let myself in and was working alone, he entered Consuelo's apartment and fixed upon his wife's photograph. He jumped when he realized I was there. He turned the image facedown on the tabletop and left without a word.

I picked up the portrait. How absolutely stunning Consuelo had been. Antoine had told me once that when a man is in hopeless love with a beautiful woman, he must destroy all his photos of her or he will never find peace. He had not been talking about his wife, or so I thought; he had mentioned it in the context of Madame Fiche's destruction of the white silk. But still . . . I stared at the door as though I could pull him back in. He didn't return that day. Neither did Consuelo show up, not that day or the next.

She had told me once that the only cure for the pain of love was flight.

Then came a morning when Antoine intercepted me in the lobby and pulled me outside, his expression grim. "My publishers want to ruin *The Little Prince*."

The wind picked up. I smoothed down my hair. "They don't like the story?"

"They want me to change the ending. They say it is unpalatable."

"It isn't unpalatable; it's unbearable."

His expression collapsed. "Truly?"

"It will break the hearts of everyone who reads it. It's exactly what it should be. You can't change it."

"Lamotte, too, insists I must not. I will not."

"You know, you've only told me what happens. You've never read the ending to me."

"And now, without the studio, I cannot."

"Read to me in the park. In a restaurant. Anywhere." I glanced back into the lobby. Both the doorman and Elmore had disappeared. "It's been a while. Do you miss me?" I touched his jaw; it was uncommonly rough.

"How can they think it is acceptable to pressure me? I put my faith in them. Have they no faith in me? They say they will delay the publication date to February to give me time to make the changes. They are willing to forgo Christmas sales—my best chance at royalties!"

I lifted his jacket collar against the cold. "Even if you changed the ending for the book, I would still want to use the original one in the show."

"You would?" He grabbed my arms. "Of course you would! That is precisely what you should do. You must do the show."

"Really?"

"We will work together. What do you need for the production? My God, Mignonne, how are you paying your rent? I will write you a check. I will give you a copy of the manuscript so you can get everything right. And I will insist that my publishers take orchestra seats. Eugene Reynal and Curtice Hitchcock will see for themselves, firsthand, that audiences agree with me: the ending should remain as it is."

I hesitated. "And if the audience doesn't agree?"

"Contracts can be broken. The book will not see print."

Keep Antoine in New York, alive. Avoid disgracing myself and my family name. Seal the fate of *The Little Prince*.

I thought, I'm not a savior; I'm not strong enough; I'm not made for this.

53

"Look at these drawings." Antoine brought Consuelo's sketch-book to my worktable. He flipped pages. She had reinterpreted the simple scenery of the story as enormous peaked and menacing sand dunes, pierced with rocks jagged as claws, frowned upon by a malevolent-looking moon whose teeth resembled fangs. "Look what happens when she gets her way. I cannot have these sets in the show. It would be an embarrassment. I need to do something about this."

"Would you please?" I whispered, unsure whether Consuelo could hear us from her bed.

"First show me what you have drawn and what you have sewn. You don't mind if I give you my opinion or contribute a squiggle or two? Let me get my supplies."

I followed him into the hallway. He looped his arm around me and kissed my nose. He said, "It has been too long since we have sketched together. What was it Madame Fiche said? 'It is fun to have many hands at work'?"

" 'Jolly.' "

"Very jolly," said Antoine, laughing, as he crossed to his apartment door.

At first I sketched tentatively, painfully aware of the creative genius of the man who worked alongside me. But soon enough, I felt myself transported back to the comfort of our long evenings in the studio. Antoine and I were collaborating. His hands were gesturing over my sketches, pointing out where this or that detail could be refined. This was not the fiery intense creativity I witnessed when he worked on his writing, but something sweeter, less agonized. We began to fill pages with lines in both our hands, wordlessly adding to each other's sketches, working as though we were two aspects of one mind.

One day, when I excused myself to take lunch in the café, Antoine also put down his sketchbook. He tagged after me as if we were two inseparable friends, as though Consuelo did not exist, as though it were the most natural thing in the world for him to follow me. We entered the elevator together, a capsule of quiet bliss. He was lost in thought, and I was content to imagine what might be developing in his head.

In Café Pedro, we took a table by the window. He devoured his steak tartare, then stared at the street and smoked. I found a pencil and a small pad of paper in my handbag.

Once upon a time, I thought as I drew his profile, there was a man with a nose as upturned as a smile, with a full and inviting lower lip. He sat in view of the world with the girl who was his secret love. He yearned to tell her his hidden dreams, unaware that she could see what was in his heart . . .

I was lost in the maze of Antoine's ear, my imagination and eyes as misty as if they already peered through a wedding veil, when a burst of internal excitement made him start in his seat. "I've got it! We give each soldier his own small, motorless helicopter, completely silent. Like a whirligig."

He jabbered about physics and mechanisms all the way back upstairs, where his wife greeted him with shrieks of indignity. Antoine was all innocence. "But Consuelo, you told me you would never again set foot in Café Pedro. Surely you don't expect me to eat my lunch alone."

On another day, in the midst of a rousing fight, Consuelo threw herself at her husband and locked her lips onto his, muting his criticism mid-word. Antoine pulled away in a moment, shaking his head and chuckling softly, the kiss having put a conclusive end to the disagreement.

I shut my sketchbook and went to my machine. I sewed furiously, head down, until Antoine left. The fabric cratered where the thread caught in the feed dogs. An ill-run, irreparable tangle bound it to its own machine bed.

54

Antoine arrived with Bernard at his side. I stood up to greet him, but a look from Antoine sent me back to my seat.

"Lamotte," he said, "you've spoken to my wife, Consuelo; I believe you've never met. This is her creative partner, Mignonne Lachapelle. Bernard Lamotte is a famous painter and illustrator. I'm sure you must have heard of him."

"At last," said Consuelo. "Such a pleasure, Monsieur Lamotte."

"Pleased to meet you," he said, shaking hands all around. "Call me Bernard. Or Lamotte. Saint-Ex has told me what you're up to. Interesting project."

Antoine opened Consuelo's sketchbook. "Imagine *The Little Prince* taking place in that."

Bernard's tone was noncommittal. "It is somewhat severe."

Consuelo said, "Maybe you'll understand my vision, Mr. Lamotte. The landscape is in contrast to the tenderness of the rose. It is harsh and unforgiving, while the rose is beautiful and soft."

Antoine protested, "The rose is not the star of the story."

"But she's the star of the fashion show," said Consuelo.

All heads turned to me.

I said, "The sets shouldn't be designed primarily as backdrops for the clothing. The most important thing is that they work with the story we're telling."

"Which is why I've brought in Lamotte," said Antoine. "Supporting a story visually is his forte. He is renowned for it."

Consuelo said, "Painting is two-dimensional; sets are not. And I am a sculptress. I don't need anyone's help."

"Lamotte is not here to help you, but to take over from you. He will bring the sets to life."

Bernard was going to design the sets! This alone would guarantee the attention of the press. I said, "This is great news, Consuelo! It frees you to do the work we should have had you doing all along."

She stopped whining. "What are you talking about?"

"I haven't had a minute to look at the photos from the modeling agencies. It won't be easy to find the right girls. They'll have to carry the designs and reflect the story. They have to be able to act, not just walk, and they need some French. Plus they have to look the part. It's a lot to ask, but you've got an eye for these things. Who better to do it than you? I hereby appoint you head of casting."

Consuelo straightened her dress. "If I have to take this on along with everything else, the rest of you had better start carrying your own weight."

"Aye-aye, Captain," I said gleefully. The whole silver-tongued, pulling-the-wool-over business wasn't so hard. I almost did a jig.

55

Aye-aye? thought Consuelo. There was nothing more infuriating than mock respect. On the other hand, the girl did have a point. No one knew better than Consuelo what made a woman beautiful—or what types of women to surround oneself with in order to seem the most beautiful in the room. It wouldn't do for the rose to be upstaged. "Where are the pictures?"

"I put the box in your bedroom," said Tonio. "Under the bed."

"Come," said Consuelo to Mignonne, and led her out of the parlor. When she threw aside the sheet that was lolling off the edge of the bed, the corner of the box was visible, almost touching Consuelo's feet.

"Get that. Be a love. Get on your knees."

"You can't get it? It isn't heavy," said Mignonne.

"I can, darling. But you will get it for me."

The girl looked confused. "What's going on?"

"If we're going to start assigning new roles, it's my turn to tweak yours. I need an assistant. What a face, Mignonne! You prefer the word 'helper'? Or 'minion'? Ha! I'll have to tell Binty he had it right all along."

Mignonne kicked the box. It slid further under the bed and hit the far wall.

"Temper," breathed Consuelo. "A little joke, that's all. I just wanted to see that sweet rosiness right here on your lovely cheeks."

Mignonne slapped away her hand.

Consuelo let the action send her sprawling across the bed. Yes, just like that, she thought, as the girl turned and fled.

"Tonio!" Consuelo cried out.

The silence that answered her arranged itself into a faint murmuring, in the slow way that one comes to hear the whispers of a distant brook. Mignonne's soft sniffling. Tonio's softer, soothing hush.

56

Antoine and Bernard could talk for hours about the visual impact of the set, the logistics, the qualities of the materials Bernard would employ. I sketched and snipped and sewed contentedly while, in the background, the two deep voices carried on—debating the value of simplicity, probing the aesthetics of nature, discussing engines or physics, arguing the pros and cons of building structures oneself versus bringing in experienced tradesmen. Occasionally Antoine would practice his cards or his juggling as they talked. Sometimes he kept up the conversation even as we collaborated, communicating with me through silent pointing or by taking my pencil to enhance or add to my lines without a pause in his discussion with Bernard. A couple of times he seemed to forget himself in the midst of a joke, and put his arm around my shoulders or his hand on my knee as he laughed.

But he never fully forgot himself when Consuelo was in the room. He couldn't entirely forget or forfeit who and what he really was.

Consuelo, meanwhile, flitted in and out as she immersed herself in the model search. The coffee table overflowed with eight-by-ten photos of beauties and less stunning girls. Most had straight blond hair. Many had unusual figures—a little bottom heavy, or overly broad shouldered, or thin to an ungainly extreme.

The stacks of photos grew. The parlor grew ever more cramped.

"Consuelo," I asked, "aren't we ready to audition these girls? I need some real bodies to fit the clothes on."

"That raises a problem." She turned to Antoine. "But I've thought long and hard, and I have a solution. There's no room to hold auditions in the parlor. We'll do them in my bedroom; I'll have the superintendent dismantle the bed. I'll just have to move into your apartment, my darling, until I can find us both a bigger place to rent. I'll keep my clothes here, and go back and forth."

"You are talking nonsense."

"A wife living with her husband is nonsense?"

"We'll hold the auditions at the Alliance," I said. "I've already cleared it with Philippe. He's holding a date for us. All he asks is that we use the back door."

"This should be easy," said Consuelo as we waited for the first of the models to arrive.

We sat in the third row, center, where we could scrutinize the features of each girl's face and the quality of her dramatic gestures, and have the perspective to assess how she moved across the stage. Antoine had volunteered to man the door. He had been given a list of names for each time slot, and had been instructed to note the time of each girl's arrival and point out the first of a series of scrawled arrows to follow to the wings where the girl would await her turn. He had been instructed, as well, to make a note of the girl's ability to understand his French.

After several girls had completed their audition, Consuelo and I listened again to the sound of dainty heels entering the wings. We heard Antoine's heavy footsteps following behind and his voice pitched in query. "Why don't you have a favorite author? Because you love so many, or because you do not read?"

He emerged on the heels of a thin young woman whose

alarmed expression made it clear that she wished she had never come. He asked her, "You have at least heard of Gide, have you not?"

Consuelo yelled, "Tonio!"

He walked calmly to the edge of the stage. "You cannot seriously be considering her."

"Leave her alone! I haven't even seen her. Will you please go back to your post and let me do my job?"

Antoine scowled and headed back toward the wings. Consuelo and I waited for the next girl to arrive. We had her walk the stage and strike a series of poses while we scribbled on our pads.

The audition continued through the morning. "Bold walk," I wrote. "Strong nose. Small gestures."

The next was a clear call. "Choppy stride. Can't act."

"Tell the next girl to walk on," said Consuelo.

The model left the stage, then returned. "Excuse me. There's no next girl here yet."

Consuelo huffed. "What is wrong with these people? Can't anyone ever be on time? I can't believe how many haven't even shown up. Go tell Tonio that from now on, any girl who is more than two minutes late is banned, no matter her excuse."

I made my way to the aisle and walked against the direction of the arrows to where Antoine stood at the back alley door.

His brooding expression brightened as he saw that I was alone. He took my hand, caressed it, and leaned down to whisper in my ear. "I never see you anymore."

"You see me every day."

"With Consuelo there. It is terrible working beside you and having to maintain such propriety. And yet I cannot wait to be with you. It is the only brightness in my day."

"When you start working, you don't even know I exist. I could be anyone."

"No one else could collaborate with me so well."

"You work well with Bernard."

"He is not so altogether enticing, or so maddening."

"I think it's your wife whom you find maddening."

"She is frustrating, not maddening. The two aren't the same."

"Your blood runs hotter when you're near her. All this time when you talked about your fights, I didn't understand that they brought you both such satisfaction. I never realized a couple could thrive on that sort of angry passion."

"Don't call us a couple, please."

"Husband and wife, then."

"Only on paper; you know that."

"It's what I thought."

"You misinterpret the situation. I receive no satisfaction from conflict. I cannot fathom why you think my arguments with Consuelo do me good. Perhaps it is only because I release the tension that comes of being close to you."

"Do you really believe that, Antoine? Because I'm pretty sure the same scenes have been going on between the two of you for years and will continue for years to come."

Just then, a young woman turned into the lane. "Sorry I'm late!"

"That reminds me," I said, "Consuelo said to turn away any girl who isn't on time."

"A bit of tardiness is the least of our worries." He peered at the girl. She was tall and blond, quite striking. "Tell me," he asked in French, "what do you think of Roosevelt's approach to the war?"

The girl answered in English. "Roosevelt what?"

"Thank you," said Antoine. "You are dismissed."

The girl's jaw dropped. She rushed off.

I stared at Antoine. "The war?"

"Surely it isn't too much to ask that a girl have an opinion regarding the war. Do you think she knows there is a war going on? She's even more obtuse than the others."

"What do you mean 'the others'? What have you been doing out here?"

"I don't want my story told by idiots who cannot even deliver the words."

"You've been sending girls away?"

"I am assessing how they talk. It is necessary for them to be able to deliver their lines in French. I don't expect their grasp of the language to be flawless, but I won't have my story garbled. And so I ask each girl a simple question. In answering, she reveals both her competency with the language and the quality of her thought."

"Antoine! They need to act, not teach."

"They do have to teach. It is their job to convey the messages in the story."

Consuelo rounded the last corner of the twisting hallway. "What is going on?"

"He's been sending girls away because they haven't been able to prove, in a second flat, that they're quite as smart as he is."

Antoine said, "Half these girls cannot speak a word of French! Where did you find them, behind the makeup counter at Barneys? New York is full of beautiful, intelligent girls and these are the ones you pick? I would rather rip up my manuscript than have it made a mockery of by a crew of misspeaking twits. I will not allow the story to be told by people who cannot even understand it."

"You're an idiot, Tonio. It only matters how the girls look and move. They need a basic understanding of French, but that's more than enough. They won't have any lines to speak."

Antoine frowned. "How so?"

"The story's told through a voice-over," said Consuelo. "We're telling your story, abridged, while the models act out the gestures."

"And who will speak the voice-over?"

I hesitated. "We assumed you would."

Just then we turned our attention to yet another young woman who was teetering down the lane on too-high heels. She reached for a garbage can to steady herself. The lid crashed down and rolled wobbling to a reverberating stop.

Antoine said, "You wish me to proclaim to the world that I have sunk to this: writing and reading macerated scripts for bumbling models?"

The girl reached us. She stood with one hand on the wall. "Is it okay if I just do the audition here? I wore the dumbest shoes. Gorgeous, but dumb."

"How apt," said Antoine.

Consuelo studied his list. "Not many prospects left." She turned to the girl. "You're hired."

"She cannot even walk!" protested Antoine.

His wife stuck out her chin. "Blame yourself if we end up with incompetents on the stage."

Antoine's face darkened almost to purple. He thrust the clipboard at Consuelo. "You are on your own."

57

Bernard's set design could not have been more different from Consuelo's. As I contemplated his oversized watercolors that were spread across the apartment floor, a wave of excitement flowed through me. For the first time, I saw how the stage could become a character in its own right as well as a vital backdrop for both the story and the costumes. Bernard had filled his pages with broad sweeps of color: gradations of blue-tinted hues from peaceful dove grey to brilliant turquoise, shades of yellow that ranged from warm and tawny to an acidic lemon, skies that transformed themselves from merciless ovens to cool, starry canopies whose beauty was as quenching as a spring. Most of the shifts would be achieved through lighting, he explained, some of extended duration and others lasting only moments. The harshest yellow, for example, would make a brief appearance only once, in a single flash near the end of the tale.

While Consuelo's designs had been hard and stagnant, Bernard's were something more like music.

"There's such a sense of movement," I told him, "even though the setting is a desert."

"Everything alive has movement, and natural elements give the perception of life to things that are dead as well. Sand, for example, is never still. The sky cannot be. When I paint a portrait, there's no point in asking the sitter to be completely motionless—not if I want to capture his or her essence in the work. And anyway, people can't be still if they try. The day my subjects stop moving is the day I'll put away my brushes for good."

He pointed to a series of sketches outlining the contours of a plane that had crashed in the sand dunes. "Even a piece of metal has to be shown to change in the course of the story. Nature and perception act upon it, just as the elements of the story act upon the audience."

Consuelo entered the parlor and gave the drawings a cursory glance. "Looks like it's coming along. What happens next?"

"Maquettes. I'll work up a miniature set based on the drawings. I'll need to work quickly, and they won't be perfect, but it's an important step. You'll want that as you're planning and blocking out the movement. You've started working with the actresses?"

"Models," said Consuelo. "The only actress is me."

Bernard wrinkled his nose. "You do know that gets under your husband's skin? Why not call the cast 'actresses'?"

"Tonio is just being immature. He was getting on board when it seemed to him that we were putting together a legitimate show. But as soon as he's reminded it's about fashion, he storms off."

I said, "To be honest, I'm not sure I could call many of them actresses, either. Some of them shouldn't even be called models."

Bernard looked worried. "Even for our own sakes, the show has to be of high quality. I know I can't afford to have clients question my creative judgment or integrity. I will continue to do the work, but perhaps the credits shouldn't mention my name."

"It will be fine," I said quickly. "The girls just aren't used to having speaking parts."

"Saint-Ex isn't narrating?"

"He's pulled out of the show."

"*Entirely?*"

"We're going ahead anyway," said Consuelo. "It's for his own good."

"Not if it flops," said Bernard. "The three of us will look bad if we fall flat on our faces out there. But for Saint-Ex, it would be a disaster. He is already so low. If this makes him a laughing-stock, it will be the end of him."

"Cut," yelled Consuelo. "Take a fifteen-minute break."

Sitting in the front row of the Alliance for yet another run through, I put my head in my hands and rubbed my forehead. What was the objective? I had to keep reminding myself: present the story, display the fashions, win over the hearts of the audience for their own benefit and for Antoine's. There had to be a way to do all three.

The girls were progressing beautifully in their movements and had begun to master the ability to flow their actions into expressive poses. But as soon as I had them add in their speaking lines, everything fell apart—the poses became stilted, the walking became awkward, the voices stumbled.

Bernard came from the back of the theater and crouched in front of us. "It's bad."

Reluctantly, I concurred.

Consuelo said, "They should all have their mouths sewn shut. They're ruining my scenes!"

I sighed. "We have to go back to a voice-over. It's the only way to do this without embarrassing us all."

"I've talked to Tonio. He's adamant."

"Bernard? Won't you reconsider?"

"I cannot, Mignonne. Saint-Ex forgives me for continuing to work on the sets, only because he's the one who asked me to get involved. But if I were to take over the narration, I'm not sure he'd speak to me again."

"He would if it went well, if it goes as planned."

"At this point, the chances of that are slim. Why don't you do it?"

It would be foolish to draw further attention to my relationship with Antoine. That a designer would design costumes was a given; to also narrate the production hinted of obsession. I said, "It has to be a man."

"Hire someone?" asked Bernard.

"With what?" Though Antoine's publishers had released some funds for the production as an advance against his future sales, the allotment had already run out.

Consuelo wrung her hands. "You must know someone, Bernard."

"Who would be willing to put in the time, and for free? Only your husband's most loyal friends. They are hard to find now—and none would be willing to take the chance of having this blow up around Saint-Ex."

"If no one will do it for Tonio, who do we know who would do it for us?"

Thoughts of Binty hung in the air, but were dismissed unsaid.

"Your brother?" asked Consuelo.

I shook my head. "Leo works long hours. We'd have to move rehearsals to late at night."

"We could do that."

"And get him to commit." That might be the most difficult thing of all.

"Recruit him," said Consuelo. "Start teaching him the lines at home. In the meantime, we'll go back to rehearsing with a voice-over. You speak it for now, and fill in for Leo at any rehearsals he has to miss."

I said, "As long as I don't end up having to do it for the actual show."

"If it comes down to that," said Consuelo, "the show will not go on."

58

Soon Bernard's posters and flyers started cropping up everywhere: at the Alliance, in bookstores and galleries, on the counters of shops all over Manhattan. It seemed that everyone familiar with the massive success of *Wind, Sand and Stars* and *Flight to Arras* was eager to promote this unorthodox preview of Antoine's new story. Bernard had not withdrawn his name from the production; both he and Consuelo had used their connections to spread the word in the press. Already I had heard announcers on radio programs discussing the upcoming show. Consuelo had been interviewed in print several times. No reporter had managed to elicit a comment from Antoine, but Consuelo had rhapsodized shamelessly about his involvement and full support.

The production was coming together. The sets had been built. Under Bernard's patient guidance, student volunteers were honing their skills at lighting. The entire collection had been designed. Most pieces hung complete under wraps at Studio Saint-Ex.

Philippe had insisted on supervising the sale of the tickets himself. He had asked, with dignified shyness, to join the show as the musical accompaniment on piano, while Yannick had claimed that the production required his expertise on oboe.

"How are the ticket sales going?" I asked two weeks before the opening night.

The old man had grinned. "Brisk, Mademoiselle Mignonne. I see an extended run in your future."

I hoped that age had brought him wisdom and not senility.

It had taken some doing to convince Leo to get involved. I had been walking him through the script after he returned from work, but lately he had become irritable and uncooperative. He'd begun asking, "Can't we do this at the pub?"

"If we pull this off, I'll buy you all the beer you can drink. Come on, let's go through it once more."

"I'm just reading the bloody thing. I don't need to keep going over it. I'm not memorizing it."

"But it's important that the inflection is right. It has to sound natural."

"You want natural, put a bottle in my hand and another in my pocket—or don't complain if I sound like an automaton. The tongue don't get loose on its own."

In the end, I began allowing him to drink while he practiced. Fortified, Leo's narration was warm and sincere. But the alcohol did nothing to extend his patience. He had come to most of the rehearsals—marching from the front entrance to the microphone backstage with put-upon grunts and rarely even a glance at Bernard, Consuelo, and me—but not once had we managed to get through the script in a sitting without stopping to deal with some frustration or request. His disruptions had made it difficult to judge the persuasiveness of his narration over the entire arc of the story.

With the exception of Consuelo, who seemed to get progressively stronger, the models had grown tired. Their fatigue lent a trace of melancholy to their movements, tinting their youthful exuberance with a richness that would have been impossible to prescribe.

Now it was the day before the opening. The models were arriving for the final dress rehearsal, laughing and chattering as they made their way through the halls of the Alliance. The weeks of hard work, and the resulting improvements and achievements, had created a bond among the cast. They were excited, certain they were ready to make a brilliant impression from beginning to end. And it was true, I thought, that even without the words, even if the show were simply a dramatic fashion parade set against the backdrop of Bernard's scenery, the presentation would be impressive. The emotions conveyed by the girls, the actions they mimed, the gestures they had finally embraced and mastered, worked to display the clothing to exceptional effect.

But it took the narration to make it a story. And Leo was quite capable of doing a fine job when he bothered to show up to do the job.

I had waited for him at home tonight for as long as I could. Please let him be at the Alliance already, I prayed. Let him have gone straight from work.

But when I arrived for the dress rehearsal, Leo was not there.

Backstage was bustling. Gleeful girls were fixing each other's makeup and their own, zippers were being zipped, giggles were rising. Consuelo and Bernard stood at the back of the auditorium, watching the set transform again and again in rapid succession as the lighting crew ran through their standard equipment tests. Philippe and Yannick practiced their music smoothly.

Only I was unable to focus on anything. I paced back and forth, returning to the hallway, looking for Leo in the lane and in the hallway that led backstage, peering out at the street front, checking with Eddy at the bar.

Bernard grabbed me as I reentered the theater by its lobby doors. "What's wrong?"

"Leo hasn't shown up yet. Did he come in the side while I was out here?"

"I don't think so."

"Okay. Don't tell Consuelo yet. If she pulls the plug on this now, we're done for."

"He's never missed a rehearsal without giving you notice."

"Right." I didn't mention that he'd missed plenty of our kitchen table practices, and that lately when he had shown up it had been with a good amount of drink already flowing in his veins.

"Still," said Bernard, "I wish we had a backup plan."

"Leo was our back-up plan. The only other option is you."

Bernard's look was apologetic, but his voice was firm. "Don't ask me to go against my convictions. I won't put my friendship with Saint-Ex on the line."

"I know. I just wish there were another way."

Just then, the door beside us opened and Leo burst through. "Hello, Miggy! Where's the show?" He gestured sloppily—and Bernard plucked a bottle of whisky from his outstretched hand.

"We've been waiting for you," I said.

"I was busy. I'm a busy man." He reached for his liquor, but Bernard moved it away.

"Start the music." Bernard took Leo by the arm. "He's full of beans now, but give him a few minutes and he'll be falling asleep." He called out, "Philippe, can you order up a pot of coffee?" He steered Leo toward the stage, up the stairs, and into the wings. "Everyone in your places," he yelled.

Within minutes, the piano was sending out the right notes and coffee was disappearing down Leo's throat. I pressed the script into my brother's hands and adjusted the microphone to his sitting height. "You remember your cue?"

"I remember everything. What's my cue?"

"After this comes the oboe, then it quiets down. When you hear the piano rise again, start reading. The girls will take their start from your lines. I'll be in the audience, watching and listening." It was such a relief to have him there. "I'm glad you came. It means so much to me. Now do a good job. Give it your all." I planted a kiss on his unshaven cheek, my nose objecting at a whiff of his breath, and hurried out to the seats.

The oboe began the opening passage, then faded while the notes of the piano rose to the fore. I bit my lip and rolled the script in my hands. I was just about to rise from my seat when Bernard, sitting beside me, touched my wrist—and the sound of Leo clearing his throat came through the speakers.

His amplified voice filled the room: "I had an accident in the Sahara Desert . . ."

The sky above the stage flared as the curtains parted. Lights flashed and illuminated the downed plane resting in fine sand. The sky seemed to hum with energy. Suddenly a figure appeared in the center of the stage. the Little Prince, the first of a series of Little Princes, each with golden hair and a waif-like physique, each simply elegant in a captivating, androgynous outfit of white or pale green.

This first prince wore a coat over her pantsuit—*his* pantsuit—a regal coat with golden epaulets and wide red turned-back cuffs. It was based on the sketch I had created months ago as I listened to Antoine's story the very first time; now it was the first item in the order book for the *Little Prince* Collection. The model wore it exquisitely.

As Leo continued his reading in a relaxed voice that was at once curious, thoughtful, and reverent, as the music swelled and fell, as Consuelo dazzled in the dress that even now still made me catch my breath, as the princes and the flowers and the animals played their roles through, I thought I would never again feel so glad, so blessedly relieved.

"It's going to be fine," I whispered to Bernard as Consuelo rejoined us following her scenes. "We did it, Bernard. Look at those girls! Look at your sets!"

He laughed quietly and put a finger to his lips.

59

Toward the end of the rehearsal, Consuelo got up from her seat. She moved to the side aisle away from Mignonne and Bernard and their precious little murmurings. They were happy. Good for them. Let them smile and nod at each other in their self-congratulatory sappiness. How quickly they had both forgotten that there would be no show without her. Soon they would be pulling out their handkerchiefs to weep at the ending and congratulating themselves for their tears, too. You'd think they had never heard the script before tonight.

Consuelo, of course, had heard all of it and more. Tonio had read the full story to her at the Bevin House; she had demanded it. The fact was, a wife shouldn't have to beg and cajole her author husband to read to her. A husband should involve his wife in every step of his creative work. But Tonio had long ceased coming to her with paragraphs or chapters, with ideas, with opening lines. So when he had finally agreed to read to her, he should have known Consuelo would not receive it in quiet servitude.

She had sat meekly as his opening lines soared up like a geyser, strong and sure. He had carried on, relaying the story from a place deep inside himself.

You can tell a lot about a man from his voice, she thought. With her fine ear, she had noticed every ebb in the forcefulness of his delivery. She knew that each almost-imperceptible hesitation signaled a word choice or passage that he knew, in his heart, was not yet quite right. Consuelo had taken it upon herself to guide him through the rough spots. She had done so with guileless comments that any writer might expect to hear. "How hilarious! Oh, I'm sorry—you didn't want me to laugh there?" . . . "I love how you made him so boring; you are absolutely brilliant at that." . . . "What a marvelous scene, darling! The only thing left to fix is the words."

Well, that's what he got for thinking he could disappear into other people's studios and homes, or into his own apartment or room, and come out with a creation fully formed without any input or advice from her! She had made her point. She had made it cleverly, with the innocence of a tot poking about in rubber boots. Tonio was incapable of faulting a child.

If Tonio believed in the story the way he had written it, let him defend himself. Consuelo would have been thrilled to engage him in debate. But he had not mustered the will to engage. Every time she had tendered an observation, the strength of his speech had weakened. By the end, the conviction in his voice had been reduced to a trickle.

That was Tonio now. All those years he had spent throwing himself fearlessly into the most dangerous of airborne circumstances, focused, forceful, accumulating a list of crashes that defied all odds of survival, disappearing into lands barren of shelter, food, or drink—making her sick with worry, hoarse with weeping, too grief-stricken to rise from the floor—she would take that all again over what Tonio had become in New York: a sad and sensitive soul. Once, he had been like a cannon. Now, reduced to nothing but his voice, with no clearance to take action, he had become a violin of a man.

Whereas Leo . . . There was no musical instrument that could symbolize Leo. He was a hammer: hard, unbending, uncomplicated.

Leo narrated the *Little Prince* story like a man with a job to do. He had a deep, straightforward voice; he took his time; his tone lifted and fell. He used his voice as a tool. No doubt he was good with tools.

His voice said other things about him, too. He had mastery

over himself and his world. He wasn't the type to be swayed or hurt. He didn't have a pathetic sacred fount inside his core that had to be protected. God, no! Leo would laugh at the idea. He wouldn't hesitate to laugh at Consuelo. He wouldn't put up with trickery or dissent.

He was—as she had sensed from the moment she had set eyes on him—a savage among the softest of elites.

She wanted a drink. And she wanted to have it with Leo.

By the time he came to the last page of the script, Consuelo was walking toward the stage, leaving those other two to their hankies and their glee. They probably didn't even hear the last few lines; they were probably weeping with relief that Leo had come through.

Not that Consuelo was really listening, either. She was on the hunt for her own sort of relief. It was on the other side of the curtain, up the stairs, in the wings—his long, lean body slouched at a bistro-style table, his mouth still close to the microphone.

He was young, of course, but he didn't look like he would complain about the age of any woman who would buy him a shot.

"Well done, darling."

"Thanks, doll."

Consuelo clicked off the microphone. "You know, Leo, Mignonne didn't think you would show up."

"I wouldn't miss it for the world . . . uh . . ."

"Consuelo."

"I wouldn't miss it, Consuelo. Mig's my sister, you know."

"I do. In fact, I was the one who asked her to bring you in."

He looked her up and down. "Aren't you the dress with the rose?"

She had changed into slacks and a black angora sweater with metallic detailing around the dropped neckline, but Leo's eyes had a good memory: they lingered where they should linger on the rose. She shifted one high-heeled foot in front of the other, assuming a stance she had held on the stage, one that accentuated the profile of her bust and the shapeliness of her hips. "Yes, darling, I am the rose. You can tell, though I've slipped out of my sheath?"

He grinned. "Yeah."

She could hear Mignonne approaching down the aisle, congratulating the actors and musicians. Somewhere further afield, Bernard was giving kudos and suggestions to the lighting crew. Consuelo bent down. "I can tell something about you, too."

"What's that?"

"You would love to go for a drink."

"You got that right, honey. Maybe two or three."

A handful of models had returned to the stage to demonstrate for each other their favorite moves. In the opposite wings, Yannick and Philippe were collecting their music sheets and pretending they weren't straining to hear Consuelo's conversation.

She twined her fingers into Leo's. "I can hardly wait. Let's go."

Leo, bless him, jumped to his feet. He led her toward the stairs with an urgency that almost cost her a shoe.

As they came around the curtain, there was Mignonne on the bottom step. "You were terrific!"

"Time to celebrate," said Leo.

"Just us two," added Consuelo, holding tight to Leo's arm. She fit her foot back into her shoe and prodded him forward.

"What are you doing?" asked Mignonne, catching Consuelo's arm.

"Someone is thirsty, darling. And someone," she indicated Leo with a meaningful look, "is awfully hungry. If you know what I mean."

"No, I don't. Just . . . No."

"Take it easy, Miggy," said Leo. "We're just going for one little drink. Come with us."

Consuelo said, "Don't be ridiculous, Leo. We're going for many drinks. Alone."

Mignonne lowered her voice. "You leave him be. Leo, stay here."

"Hey," he said, "you're not my boss."

Bernard was watching from across the theater. Yannick called from the stage. "Is everything all right?"

Leo gestured toward him. "Didn't Yannick say Mother asked you to keep an eye on me, make sure I didn't get into trouble with the ladies? Good job, Mig. You're finally doing what you came back to New York to do."

"That's not true! Mother wanted us to look out for each other. That's what Yannick said."

The siblings glared at each other.

It was time to bring the uncle in. The theater had excellent acoustics; Consuelo was certain Yannick would hear. "Now, children, stop your fighting." She shook a disapproving finger at Leo. "Naughty boy! Go to your room. Better yet, Leo darling, I'll bring you to mine."

She hadn't planned to do anything more than have a few drinks. Men like Leo were good to drink with. But his sister was forcing her to take it further. If Mignonne thought she could command Consuelo like she'd tell a dog to give up a prized bone, she was wrong. Consuelo was going to gnaw this boy down to the marrow.

Yannick was coming over, as surely as if Consuelo had pulled a string. Oh yes, she could cast a spell; she had the power. She felt engorged with it, a rose about to burst into bloom.

"Imagine," she proclaimed to the theater at large, "Mignonne telling her brother whom he should or shouldn't see. Given that she herself is desperately in love with a happily married man."

Mignonne paled.

Leo snarled, "He's divorced." But when his sister only looked stricken and reached for his arm, he reared away from her. "He's married? He's still goddamn married?"

The uncle's expression was pained, but not the least surprised. "Well, Yannick," said Consuelo, "I see I'm right about Mignonne and Tonio."

Leo said, "What? Who's Tonio?"

Consuelo continued. "If your niece wasn't so intent on clawing her way to fame—"

"Shut it," said Leo. "I asked a question. Who the hell is Tonio?"

"Tonio is the man whose work your sister used so she could have a show. The writer whose story you just read so well."

"Hold on," said Leo. "I thought you were talking about Antoine."

Yannick put his arm around Mignonne.

Consuelo said, "Also known as my husband."

Yannick nodded. "Antoine. Tonio. Saint-Ex."

60

When Leo left—with Consuelo—he had not been angry at her machinations, but furious with me. It was as though by allowing him to hope for the best for my future, I had betrayed his own hidden dreams.

"He'll be here," Consuelo assured me now. "You're damn lucky we called this business Studio Saint-Ex. I explained to him that it's my name on the line. He promised to show up—for me."

For the past hour, a steady stream of ticket holders had been arriving for the show. A few stragglers still chatted in the foyer while the usher showed others to their seats.

The student volunteers were poised over the lighting controls and the models stood awaiting their cues in the wings. Philippe and Yannick bided their time with a duet of a lengthy, low-key classical number. I resisted the impulse to run back and forth from the lane to the front foyer looking for Leo as I had last night. He knew the way in. He was either coming or he was not. The show would either start with him, late, or it would not start at all.

From the edge of the stage curtain, I scanned the crowd again, looking not for Leo this time, but for Antoine. He, too, had not appeared. Half an hour ago I had been hoping to see him, but now I prayed that he would not show his face, not see my failure. He would feel the effects of it soon enough.

Bernard approached, looking bleak. "I found your brother vomiting in the lane. I put him in a cab and sent him home. He can't do the voice-over. He's so drunk he can hardly see."

Bernard took my arm and steadied me.

There was barely enough time to rush to Antoine's apartment and return to the auditorium. I didn't worry anymore that the show would start late; I worried that Consuelo would cancel it before I returned. If the production was going to fail, I wanted it to be in spite of my best efforts.

"Wait here," I told the cabbie when he had pulled up at the curb. "I'll be two minutes, then I need you to take me back to the Alliance Française."

"You want me to wait, pay me for this part of the fare. It's a busy night."

"I'm getting something heavy."

"Give me the fare."

"I'll be right back!"

"Just pay me now, lady, so I know you'll come back."

I dug into my purse and shoved money toward him as I scrambled out of the cab. "Two minutes!" I yelled.

I hadn't dared take the time to ask Consuelo if she had a key and provoke a discussion I hoped never to have. I had chosen, instead, to have Bernard find and distract her and assure her that our narrator was on his way.

I ran to the concierge's desk. "Elmore! I need a big favor. I need you to let me in to Mr. Saint-Exupéry's apartment."

"I don't think he's in, Miss Lachapelle."

"I'm sure he isn't." Antoine would be out on the streets, smoking. He might even be circling the Alliance, obsessing over what could be happening inside. "I need something from his apartment, from beside his bed."

"Something you left behind in Mr. Saint-Exupéry's, um, room?" The concierge rose to his feet with reluctance. His expression betrayed both his embarrassment and affection for me, and his competing unwillingness to forsake the dictates of his post.

"It's not something of mine. But it's something that I need, right away, to get him out of a mess. Please, Elmore. I'm trying to help him. Will you help me?"

I followed him away from his desk. Never had an elevator seemed so slow to arrive, so reluctant to ascend. When Elmore had his key in Antoine's lock, I thanked him incoherently and pushed past him through the door and into the bedroom.

I pulled a blanket from Antoine's bed. I had only been in his bedroom the one, unforgettable time; now this second time would surely be my last. No matter what happened with the show tonight, Antoine would never forgive me for taking a piece of him and using it—his actual voice—without his permission.

I threw the blanket over the recording instrument and hoisted it into my arms.

"It's heavy," Bernard had warned me, "and somewhat delicate. Be careful with it—Saint-Ex could have bought a car with what he paid for it. But it works like magic."

I know, I had wanted to say. Instead I had given Bernard a grateful and appreciative smile, and the smile he had returned seemed to mirror mine.

In the lobby, I mouthed "Thank you" to Elmore, who was on the phone, opened the door with my hip, and was on the street.

The cabbie was gone. A number of taxicabs passed in the roadway, all of them carrying passengers. I caught sight of an empty one and yelled, but couldn't lift a hand without dropping the bundled machine, and the cab hurried past.

"I need to put this down," I said aloud. I swiveled, looking about for a platform of any sort on which to rest my load. A mailbox. A planter. Anything.

Pedestrians swerved around me.

Elmore appeared. "Taxi!"

A cab slowed.

"You're a lifesaver!"

He took the box while I slid into the back seat. "Not to worry, Miss Lachapelle. I figure my job is pretty safe." He settled the recording device carefully beside me. "Sounds like Mr. Saint-Ex is leaving anyway, if you can believe what he was hollering when he got his mail the other day."

I closed the door on Elmore's words and urged the driver on. From my purse I pulled cash for the driver, and a notebook and pen for the challenge at hand. The dry winter air or the wool of the blanket over the recording device was frizzing my hair. I pushed it off my face as I wrote frantically.

I checked my watch. Bernard had said he would meet me at the front door.

Let him be there. Let him be right. This solution had to work.

He had assured me: "Saint-Ex recorded the whole book. I heard it myself, read in his own voice. He played it for me to persuade me to join your project. It's an exquisite reading. It's what convinced me to sign on to your crazy plan."

At the Alliance, I paid the cabbie and slipped out, pulling the recording device out after me. God, it was heavy; my knees almost buckled.

Wordlessly, Bernard came up and took my burden. I followed him backstage to the table with the microphone.

"You have the discs?" he asked.

I felt the blood leave my face.

He opened the casing. The inside of the lid had a pocket, strapped with leather and lined with heavy pale pink satin. He reached in and pulled out a stack of discs, looked through them, and placed a selection on the table. On each, Antoine's handwriting indicated "*Le Petit Prince*" and a number: 1, 2, 3 . . .

Bernard fitted the first one into the player. Over the sound of the piano—tireless Philippe!—came a thunderclap. I peered through the curtains to see Consuelo, not yet in costume, trying to right a piece of wooden scenery that had fallen onto its face. Bernard left to attend to the problem.

"You try moving things in high heels," she complained. "Where's Mignonne? She's strong."

Bernard started dragging sandbags onto the stage. "More of these. Come on, Consuelo. Quick."

How to work this device? I pondered the mechanism and fit the first disc onto the spool. I turned a knob and the disc started spinning, its rhythmic hum not quite drowning out Consuelo's rant from a few feet away.

"Where the hell is Mignonne? And where is Leo?"

"Mignonne's finalizing the voice-over."

"Why does she wreck everything? We should cancel this whole thing!"

Bernard's voice was firm. "Remember who we're doing this for. Okay: the scenery looks great. Are the models in position? I will check on Mignonne. We're almost ready."

The audience was murmuring. Gingerly, I turned another knob. From the instrument Antoine's voice boomed, "*Le Petit Prince.*" I snapped off the device as a hush fell across the entire theater—except in my ears, where my own heartbeat roared.

Consuelo appeared. "Jesus Christ!"

"This is our Leo," I said. "Go tell Philippe to start playing the opening piece, loudly. Tell him to draw it out for a good few minutes. I have to figure out this contraption. I've got to find and mark the passages we're using so I can skip the ones we don't need. We'll start with chapter two and—"

"Where did you get this?"

"I stole it. Tell Philippe that he's got to play good and loud and lusty between scenes—so I can take that time to line up the next section we're going to use."

"You're deranged. I'll have your skin if this performance fails!"

"Go. And give the actors their final instructions. This won't take me long. I've already made a list of the scenes I need to find and mark."

61

When the lights had all been dimmed, and Philippe's playing had softened to a low background accompaniment, I threw the switch on the microphone and started the audio disc turning. Its spooky rhythm hushed the audience to silence, and into this silence the machine delivered Antoine's voice: "I had an accident in the Sahara Desert six years ago . . ." A bit of the tension left my shoulders. ". . . a thousand miles from any human habitation . . . You can imagine my surprise at sunrise when an odd little voice woke me up . . ."

Yannick's oboe lifted into its mournful warble, and the first model emerged from the wings: the Little Prince.

The voice continued, sure and persuasive. The models passed between the curtained panels on either side of the stage, coming together to enact Antoine's story in subtle gestures and evocative stances. When the text allowed, when the instruments held the audience captive and still like cupped hands can hold water long enough for a drink, the models held their poses—as motionless on their boxy heels as figures on a page, arms angled to showcase the clothing's drapery and elegant lines. Then they slipped back into the world of motion and the music of anticipation and action. Every once in a while, a spattering of applause greeted a design, but for the most part the audience was silent—whether in disdain for the creations or out of respect for the storytelling, I couldn't tell.

Philippe's piano played in the background all along, rising to take center stage whenever I needed to stop the machine and find the next usable segment, and Yannick's oboe pulled the listeners' emotions along the strains of every note. The story was not strictly in line with Antoine's tale: I had left out the prince's visits with the men who were so stuck in their ways: a money counter, a lamplighter, a king, and others. In tonight's story, a boy arrived and demanded drawings from a fallen pilot. He spoke of passion, love, and responsibility, and being bound by them to a rose. He would meet a fox and a poisonous snake, and choose his homeland over his new friends in the barren desert— gracefully giving his life for the choice.

In this story, the snake was a lean, tall young woman with icy blue eyes, the natural rosiness of her lips blotted and dulled with matte pastel lipstick. She writhed in a shimmering sheath that I had covered with transparent sequins over painted metallic scales. The model's long fingers reached for the girl with the messy blond bob who was the scene's prince. I pictured the cold hunger of the serpent eyes, the chilling elegance of the angular arms, and felt a pang of fright for the prince—not the one who turned beguilingly at center stage, but the young child who lived in Antoine's pages and in his heart.

The narrator spoke to the audience as openly as one does to a friend: Antoine did, his disembodied voice melancholy as the pilot who crashed in the desert, plaintive and innocent as the prince, cunning as the snake, and, as the fox, both charmingly exasperated and patient. As I watched the disc spin, I marveled that so intimate an aspect of a man could be captured in such a way, packaged for calling up whenever the desire arose. In a hundred years, I thought, science will replicate sight in a similar parcel, and perhaps imagination as well.

The rising of the oboe drew me out of my reverie. I put a hand on the machine and stopped its whirling. My heart was beating quickly. On the stage, as Philippe's notes clashed and peaked, as Yannick's oboe sounded its low warning, the snake returned. The model spun, and her cape of gun-grey imitation silk flared around her—its generous proportions an affront to the fabric restrictions—then she moved slowly toward the Little Prince, who sat unmoving and quiet on the wooden wall.

In Antoine's book, the boy gave himself willingly to death, his anxiety focused only on the pain it would cause the pilot. In Studio Saint-Ex's little fashion story, the child hesitated. Sensing the approach of the snake, he lifted his feet off the ground, one after the other in turn, then he climbed high onto the wall. He swayed as he questioned his decision, measuring the costs of first one and then the other action—to embrace his life here in the desert, with his new friends, or to sacrifice his new life to carry out his duty to the rose. The little model danced atop the wall, her gestures an homage to the land the prince had come to visit, and then, lifting her arms, to the planet that was suddenly lit overhead within a canopy of twinkling lights. As the planet stayed fixed in the sky, the blanket of star-lights grew, expanding lower to the stage, and the Little Prince's movements slowed and stilled.

The snake came close. As it lifted its cape, the stars trembled for a moment and the child slipped down off the sheltering wall. With a burst of light and a cry from the stage, the snake struck. The light flashed acid yellow. Immediately, all went black. Then, slowly, the spotlight was raised on the Little Prince, who was crumpled lifeless at the base of the wall.

A gasp escaped my throat—and I realized that all was quiet in the house. Where was the accompaniment? I couldn't find the closing lines without the music to cover my search. I moved to catch the attention of the musicians across the stage, where they hid in the opposite wings.

Philippe had covered his eyes; Yannick was staring at the fallen figure. As Yannick lifted his hand to wipe his cheek, his eyes met mine and he started—his hand now darting to his oboe.

But before the instrument reached his lips, a voice rose into the silence: Antoine's—not the recording, but Antoine himself, projecting from the very back of the audience.

"Now my sorrow is comforted a little. That is to say—not entirely. But I know that he did go back to his planet, because I did not find his body at daybreak."

The oboe breathed its deep bass sound.

"It was not such a heavy body . . . and at night I love to listen to the stars. It is like five hundred million little bells . . ."

In the theater, bells did not peal; instead, the response came in rustles and soft creaks—a delicate wave of sound that built up as one after another of the listeners turned around to watch Antoine speak. I had stepped from the wings to see it. Now Consuelo did the same. Bernard, too, stepped onto the stage. In any other production, it would be as though we were revealing ourselves in order to receive our praise—but all heads were turned away from us.

Applause had begun sporadically. It now joined note to note like a thread mending holes, until there were no discernable weaknesses in the fabric of the audience's response. Here and there, people stood in ovation. Antoine himself stood beside the rear doors, his large hands clapping slowly and pointedly as he stared at the stage.

His expression was inscrutable, from this distance, but his gaze seemed to focus on me. I felt suddenly that I was laid bare, exposed as a usurper and a thief. I stopped applauding Antoine, my hands falling to my sides, as more and more of the crowd scrambled to its feet. I was relieved then that most of the audience found the presence of the author at the back of the room to be more interesting than that of the clan of imitators clustered at the front—with a confused gaggle of models elbowing for position behind.

62

I couldn't convince Consuelo to change out of the dress. She wouldn't even cover it with her coat outside the Alliance Française, not with photographers pointing lenses her way. She handed her sable to Philippe and demanded that he lock it up wherever he had locked the recording device. Snow was falling steadily. Fat, spiky snowflakes glistened like crystal armor on Consuelo's shoulders and among the petals of the rose. I was shivering. My own coat had been left in the taxi to Antoine's before the show. Philippe draped Consuelo's fur over my shoulders and walked whistling down the street.

In the cab, as we raced to Le Pavillon, Consuelo fixed her makeup and kept patting Antoine's knee. Bernard was in the jump seat, bracing himself against turns with a hand pressed to the car's roof. In the front passenger seat, Yannick yelled joyously, "Left at the lights! Straight ahead! Step on it, my friend, we've been waiting long enough!"

It had taken ages to tear Consuelo away from the cameras and the fans. It was as though she thought all the kudos must be solely for her. I had watched some Alliance members approach her deferentially, shyly. They and Consuelo must have been aware of each other before, for they knew each other's names, but it was as though they were meeting her for the very first time.

And in a sense they were: the Consuelo they had known had been a spurned woman. But this woman, this rose-adorned star, was her prince's very lifeblood, a beauty worth the sacrifice of life itself. And her husband . . . They had thought he'd grown so bullheaded, when here he had been working on such a thoughtful and humane tale, a love story that one couldn't help but admire. Funny how such a small thing, a little story of a little prince, could put things in a different perspective. I read this all in their expressions, in their posture, and in their tone.

Audience members had approached me, too, to compliment my work. A publicist had given me a card. "I'm organizing something different for this summer—an extravaganza to introduce the press to all-American design. Everyone who ever reports on fashion will be there. Ring me tomorrow. Tell my secretary I invited you to show at Press Week."

I had been grateful and excited but demurring for the moment; this was Antoine's night. And look: there was warmth in his eyes. There was excitement in his voice.

The death of the Little Prince had returned Antoine to life.

63

Though the clamor outside the Alliance had been promising, Consuelo was not yet convinced. To impress that audience was something—but the real test would unfold at Le Pavillon, where every seat was reserved for the truly wealthy, the very rich, the moneyed elite, and those who were all three.

Arriving with the restaurant's owner was a delightful start; no other guests tonight would have had the privilege of bypassing the hoity maître d'. And even before Yannick escorted Consuelo's party to a table in the coveted center aisle, several patrons who had been in the audience turned in their seats to nod at Tonio with appreciative smiles. From here and there came delicate applause.

Yannick excused himself after seating Consuelo next to Tonio and across from Mignonne, who was sitting quietly next to Bernard.

Champagne appeared, and soon champagne appeared again. A number of bottles were uncorked; a good number of toasts went around. A toast for each patron who stopped by the table. A toast for each congratulation. A toast each time a glowing starlet or an aging socialite fawned over Consuelo's dress.

And Consuelo's silent private toasts, bubbly prayers of thanks for the much-proffered gift of that cherished word: "So nice to meet your *wife*" . . . "You and your *wife*" . . . "Your lovely *wife*" . . . "And of course this is your *wife*."

Tonio beamed, and drank, and beamed, even as his admirers came with tremulous concerns: "Please tell me . . . did the Little

Prince make it back to his rose?" Each time, Tonio gave a charming, noncommittal shrug.

Charming had its charms, but tonight the truth would be unmasked. Consuelo spoke with confidence. "The prince has returned to his rose, for evermore."

Tonio said only, "To the prince's rose," and drank. But when Consuelo lifted her fingers to her husband's face, he took them. In full view at the center of Le Pavillon, he kissed the back of her hand.

64

Afterward, Bernard left on foot and two taxis were called: one for Antoine and Consuelo, and one for me.

"Wait a moment, if you might," Antoine said to me. He went ahead to open the car door for Consuelo, then bustled back to say good night.

"I must thank you," he said, leaning into my cab.

"If you're happy, that's all the thanks I need."

"Very happy, and all because of you." He took my hand in his. "I have to tell you: my papers finally came in. But I couldn't sign them, Mignonne. You convinced me I should wait to decide until after the show. The more I waited, the more I thought about all the things you had said, the more anxious I became at the prospect of leaving—not knowing how things would be for you here, and for Consuelo, and for the Alliance Française. I starting thinking that I was needed here and not only overseas."

"Oh, Antoine, thank God you waited! And the production went well in the end."

"You were right: I didn't realize what the story of *The Little Prince* could do. I tell you, Mignonne, a weight has been lifted from me."

I felt a trickle of contentment. "And now you'll stay."

He peered into my face as though I were a curiosity. "You think I would stay? Of course I will not. Now I can go."

"Go?"

"You showed me with my own story that my worries were over trivial things—not the one conviction that drives my heart."

Go—such a small, surprising word, yet I could hardly contain the immensity of its meaning in my mind.

V'la l'bon vent. Good wind, go.

"And you showed me, also, that here all will be fine. I can see you will do well with your fashion business. Consuelo, I think, will find ways to get the attention she needs. My publishers believe they have something they can sell. The expat dance will go on without me; there is no need for me to stay here.

"I will sign the papers with my conscience untroubled. You always make everything so simple and clear and light." Antoine kissed my cheek. "Consuelo is waiting. Good night."

"Where to?" asked my driver.

Ahead, Antoine's cab left the curb.

"Where can I take you, miss?"

"I don't know. Just go."

Who knew a single spoken word could be heavier than a stolen box of ten thousand words? Its force on me was crushing. I was pinned beneath its weight.

65

In the morning, I walked into the kitchen and found Leo on the couch, his eyes bloodshot. "I messed up," he said hoarsely. "I'm sorry, Mig."

What could I say to my brother? He had allowed himself to be used by Consuelo, but I too had succumbed to her seductions as though I were helpless or hexed. And it was I who had let Leo go on imagining our future with Antoine—believing what I still wanted with my whole being to believe.

I wished my brother and Antoine had never met. The admiration of man for man was a confusing mystery. I knew nothing of how men might break or mend each other's hearts.

How could I be angry? By abdicating the narrator's role last night, Leo had almost put a stop to everything. It would have changed the course of my life if at the last minute we had canceled the show. If I had not found a way to make the curtain rise, Antoine might not now be planning to go.

I made coffee and brought Leo a cup. "Antoine is leaving."

"Leaving where?"

"Going overseas with the U.S. Air Force to try to join up with his old squadron over there."

"You've been saying for ages that that was his plan."

"I thought I could stop it. I thought that if things were better for him in New York, he'd quit obsessing about going back to the war."

"You've got to be kidding." Leo swung his legs off the couch, groaning with the effort. "I pegged you for smarter than that, Miggy. You should have read *The Little Prince* a bit closer."

A chill passed through me despite the hot mug in my hands. Leo said, "You were all swooning over it like it's a love story. Open your eyes, people. It isn't a love story, it's a war story. The prince goes back to his rose at the end. That's his country. He signs up to die for his prickly, pretty France." He took a long swig of coffee. "I might be an ass, but at least I'm not a dupe."

When I went up to Consuelo's later that day, I could hear her laughter and the mid-tenor of Antoine's voice coming from his apartment. I let myself into the parlor and commenced righting the chaos that had been created in meeting our deadline.

The phone rang. I stared at it a while; I'd never answered Consuelo's phone before. Maybe she would hear it and come over to answer it herself. But when I opened the door and listened, I heard no sounds from across the hall.

In a while, the phone rang again. This time, I picked it up. "Studio Saint-Ex; Mignonne Lachapelle speaking."

It was a reporter looking for an interview.

"With the Countess de Saint-Exupéry?"

"With the primary fashion designer of the *Little Prince* collection. Is that you?"

"It is. You're doing an article on the show?"

"It's about fashion—for the business section, if you can believe it. Apparently it's the start of a new era. Maybe you can explain it to me. What the heck do hem lengths and ladies' shoulder pads have to do with the economy of the state?"

A few days later, at home, I recognized Antoine's knock. He had never visited me at Leo's before. I opened the door, my hand lifting anxiously to my throat.

"Good evening," said Antoine, grinning. "I'm sorry to disturb you."

"Come in."

His gait was light. "You have heard? American troops have landed in North Africa. The push for France has begun!"

I smiled weakly. "I heard."

"I should ship out in a month or two. It could be sooner; one can't know. I am getting my affairs in order." He fished a rectangular item from his satchel. "I want to leave you with a couple of things. This is my watercolor set. It's what I used to paint the pictures in *The Little Prince.*" He contemplated it, turning it over in his hands, opening and closing it. "It has been used by Lamotte, too, as he coached me at his studio." He handed it to me.

"Thank you." Even my voice felt numb.

"I don't know if you will want to use it. But there is also this." He removed the thick bracelet from his wrist and released it into my palm, its bulk growing weightier with each stacking silver link.

The chain held a plaque engraved with an inscription. In capital letters, his name was followed by Consuelo's, and on the next line, the name of his publishers: all the things he had worried about, all the worries I had helped him let go of and leave behind.

I said, "You can't give away your identity bracelet." I refastened it around his wrist. "I can't let you be anonymous in the sky."

"Then you will have to remember me from my old paint kit alone. You know, Lamotte is quite a good mentor. If you ever need help with your sketches, you can always call on him."

As if the love of one man was exchangeable with another. Tears welled in my eyes.

Antoine said, "Please, you must be glad for me. I can finally do what my heart has always told me I must do."

"Damn your heart."

He laughed. "What? When it has always been so fond of you?"

Fond? I felt as though I were becoming unanchored from

the floor. Fond was not love. It was a word for a companion, an amusement. A pet. Fond was affection, not passion, not a woman he would never leave. "You were 'fond' of me?"

"Oh, Mignonne. Come here. You are my treasure. Do you not know this? You are my heart."

The heart that was cold and too dry for tears? Or the one that was so quick to push my heart aside to follow its own dreams? I said, "You told me you wanted to love life. You don't. If you did, you would have made a life with me."

He held me. "I have never hidden my intentions. You have always known I would not make my life here."

"We could have gone anywhere. We would have found a way."

He had been rubbing my back; now his movements stilled. "You pretend to yourself that you would have given up your fashion career."

Would I have?

Would Antoine have given up his dream and his duty for me?

"If we had a family," I said. "If one day we had a baby . . ." The thought hung unfinished in the air. Even I was unsure how it should end.

Antoine spoke softly into my hair. "Butterfly, there are some things that even you cannot fix."

I puzzled over that, thinking back. His insistence that I was too innocent and too young; his respectful, terrible restraint; his desire giving way to fevers or the deftness of hands and tongue. He and Consuelo had never had children. I had always assumed Consuelo refused to share him with a child.

He released me and fussed with straightening his bracelet and his cuffs. He would not meet my eye. "We are moving to a townhouse on the East River."

He and Consuelo. So in this, too, she had succeeded in bettering me. "Good for you. One last chance to make everything look lovely and normal to the outside world before you go off to show how brave you are."

His expression blackened.

I wanted his wrath. I wanted him to respond to me as he had so often to his wife, with impassioned words that brought their bodies close and her lips to his. But as he turned and stalked toward the door, I thought, What good would it do to stop him now? What would I get for my harsh words or my kiss or my pleas? Who would he be if he decided to stay? The only Antoine I had ever known was this man who lived to leave.

I felt I was suddenly old. I felt heavy, bereft of the buoyancy of my most hopeful, most childish dream.

In a way, it was a relief to give up and give in, to finally sink into this long-feared day.

He was almost at the door when something made him stop. From what already seemed a great distance, he said, "Things are much less complicated than you make them out to be."

He spoke as though I were a young girl. "You see, Mignonne, the work of the Allies requires a plane and the plane requires a man. I am going overseas to watch altimeters and tachometers. I will monitor pressure gauges and fuel gauges. Don't worry, I won't be very brave. Courage in war isn't always what you think it is. Sometimes it is chance in the midst of routine; sometimes it is anger and vanity."

He leaned against the wall and studied me. Without looking at the picture that hung beside him, he reached over to tap on its glass. "I am not courageous in the way this is."

Bernard's ink sketch?

"Of course we are all brave," said Antoine. "It takes courage to continue on, day to day—the farmer who pits his will against the weather, the mother who dares wager her child's love against the need to discipline, the girl who has the temerity to put her fashions on display. But I'll tell you something: I'm glad I was born a writer and a pilot, and not an artist. Imagine the courage it takes to create a painting or an ink drawing. Every stroke is irrevocable; it obliterates what one did before. You and I, we are able to move forward without being forced to destroy."

I nodded mutely. He could keep every draft when he rewrote. He could take photographs of his homeland and not crater it with bombs.

And I? I could choose to recut a pattern or to make alterations in a new one. I could rebuild as I had rebuilt the white dress. I could reimagine my career, my life without Antoine. My grown-up life.

"I had best go. I have a full day of visits ahead of me." He came over to kiss my forehead and retrieve his satchel before returning to the door. "You should visit us at our new home. Come for dinner—I will also ask Lamotte. I will have Consuelo contact you and choose a date. If it happens that I am gone by then, then I am gone."

Taking his heart and his secret away.

66

Consuelo checked the effect of her ensemble in the mirrors that lined the wall as the housekeeper answered the doorbell. The rose wearing a butterfly—magical! The ornate details sparkled in the light of the crystal chandelier.

Mignonne came in. Her eyes went straight to the jacket. "Where did you get that?" she blurted. Then, begging Consuelo's pardon, "Thank you for having me."

"Having you has always been a pleasure. How do I look?" Holding her arms out to show off her wings, Consuelo spun in place. The dark skirt twirled with her, wrapping softly and sensually around her legs as she stopped, then releasing reluctantly, falling sensuously back into place. "The jacket was hand-delivered this week by the designer herself. A gift to honor the success of our *Little Prince* show. Or consolation for the imminent departure of my husband. Or possibly a brilliant little reminder that I could still commission something or other from Atelier Fiche."

She led Mignonne up the staircase to a dark green library room. "See how my husband works like a king! I bought him this gorgeous table. It's a Spanish antique."

Tonio shook his head. "A complete waste of money. I told her I don't care what I write on, as long as it is stable. I have something much better to show you." He opened a drawer and riffled a stack of paper. "Print proofs of the text for *The Little Prince*."

Mignonne clasped her hands together. "It will be published in time for Christmas after all!"

"It is far too late for that, but the important thing is . . ." He flipped to the last few panels. "Reynal & Hitchcock approved my original ending without changing a word."

67

Consuelo bustled us into the sitting room for drinks and appetizers. The talk was small. No, Bernard had not been able to make it tonight. No, Leo hadn't been called up for duty yet. Yes, Antoine was all set; but no, he still didn't have a firm date.

"Get dressed for dinner," Consuelo told him, and he got up from his seat.

I shared the news from Montreal: my mother was engaged to be married this spring.

Antoine paused at the stairs. "You will come right back afterward?"

"It depends if history repeats itself. My mother wants me to stay in Montreal."

"But your fashion career," he said.

"Oh, Tonio! Not everyone has what it takes to make it in New York these days."

I set my glass down sharply.

"Consuelo . . ." Antoine began.

She assumed an offended look. "What? Did you think I meant you, Mignonne? I was thinking of your old mentor, Véra Fiche. The poor thing is going back to teaching in the new year."

I felt the hair rise at the nape of my neck. "No one should hire that woman. She steals her students' designs."

"Oh, that's right—Véra told me about your inane accusation."

"And my proof?" For Leo had recently retrieved it from one of his lady friends: the much worn and slightly torn, quite humbled butterfly dress. "It's not too late for me to take it to the administration at NYFS."

"Don't you realize they're not interested in your proof? Their illustrious professor has brought acclaim to the school with the provision of a showcase piece to the Countess de Saint-Exupéry—and at a time when all of New York has its eyes on me. We're going out for dinner; I've given the cook the night off. Tomorrow, everyone will be talking about the Atelier Fiche jacket I wore." She speared an olive. "You see, darling? Start making accusations and your own *alma mater* will laugh you onto the street. Véra and I shared a giggle about it ourselves."

68

In April 1943, Bernard and I joined a crowd that had gathered at Grand Central Station to say goodbye to husbands, brothers, and sons. Antoine's train idled, waiting to take him to a port from which a convoy of ships would plough the width of the Atlantic carrying thousands of men, one of whom had told me he was eager to till the clouds. My heart bucked when I saw him appear at an open window, but I kept my place. Bernard pressed forward and clasped Antoine's extended hand.

Antoine scanned the faces all around. As the train began to move, he swept his large fingers through the air in a broad, easy wave.

He must not have seen me, I thought. He would not be so cruel as to leave in such a way: with his face aglow with anticipation, his smile clear and wide.

69

If you enter from the east door, the work on your right is from Press Week, July '43. These six grey bolero jackets comprised the whole collection. No fuss: just gunmetal lining with a thin border of red binding tracing the edges of selvage inside. I paired them with grey chiffon skirts, short grey gloves, peacock-feather broaches on felted berets.

This was the first-ever Press Week, the first time reporters had come from across the country to cover a fashion event in New York. They were exhausted. They were glad for simplicity. So glad that they proclaimed this line the epitome of minimalist wartime chic—and I launched my first fashion house with commissions from all quarters. You never think you're ready to act until someone claims you've already made the leap.

I skipped the next Press Week, that winter. I was setting up my new studio and staff, I had a new apartment, my brother had just gone overseas. So my next collection—there's a sample in the revolving case—came in the summer of '44. That Press Week had a theme: the People's Fashion Show.

And what was people's fashion then? Women were wearing epaulets and insignia, eagle emblems, brass studs in the shape of bullets accenting sleeves or a yoke, Bakelite sailors pinned at wide, padded shoulders, cap badges on hats and scarves. Airplane-shaped buttons flew around waistbands or down from throats. The de rigueur colors had names like Valor Red and

Salute Blue. Women's fashion made men's uniforms seem like jaunty fun, and turned weapons of war into trinkets and trim.

Instead, I wrapped synthetic silk tight around my models' chests. Frothy, stormy purple-green clouds billowed around their waists and hips. You know the sort of sky that makes your stomach feel hollow and scared? The models looked as though they could be blown away. Underneath the clouds, their bindings hobbled them and stunted their breath.

70

Algiers, June 30, 1944

Dear Butterfly,

On my birthday yesterday, I flew again over France. I write to reassure you: the end is in sight. You will not see your country in flames.

My left engine malfunctioned and I missed the mocha cake back at the base, but as always, I returned. I return and I return. Once, when I delayed the lowering of the landing gear, I arrived to find an ambulance speeding to welcome me. Each time I land, I see in the expressions of my superiors that they will endeavor to make the mission my last.

Bit by bit, I am being pushed aside by time. Yesterday, on the morning I turned forty-four, I learned that my books have been banned in North Africa, where I serve. I have been reduced to a single letter by my American companions: they call me Major X. Even here, where I live out my purpose, it seems I disappear.

I am lonely, Mignonne, even in the air where I have always loved to be alone. Maybe there is a star where life is simple. My plane is something more like a city than a machine. The old Caudron Simoun and the Breguet 14 used to read my mind. Now my head pounds with migraine from the English that scrapes my ears while a hundred and forty-eight levers and buttons blink and blare at me. When one's plane has four cameras and no gun, one survives through altitude, fear, and speed. But I fly low to look over my country, and I no longer wish to speed. I am exhausted and I am lonely, but I am not afraid.

Do not be afraid for me.

Yours,
Antoine

71

They're tired, I thought. My second design assistant was quarreling with my apprentice about the translation of *peau de soie*. "*Peau* doesn't rhyme with cow," I told them, "but doe. *Peau* means skin. *Peau de soie* is a skin of silk."

None of them knew more than a few words of French. There was not a big demand for it; the émigré community was no longer the largest segment of my clientele. It had been twenty months since the *Little Prince* production. It had been a year since the first Press Week and Yannick's prodding had convinced me to put my inheritance to use.

I had presented my second Mignonne NYC collection just days ago. There had been no bright spot in the line, no giving women what I presumed they hoped to see. Afterward I had retreated into the studio, not ready to know the effect the designs would have on my career. When the girls tried to read to me from the newspapers, I declined to hear.

But one thing was unmistakable: the collection had been noticed. I had been forced to hire a girl to answer the everringing phone.

The new receptionist came in from the foyer. "A man to see you, Miss Mignonne."

"Give him my apologies, Esther, as with everyone. And if you have time, please type up the messages from the last few days."

"I've been trying to send him away, miss. He insists that I tell you he won't ever leave."

She led in Bernard. He was holding a newspaper.

"It's wonderful to see you," I said, closing my eyes to his broken expression as he kissed my cheeks.

"I know you're busy, my dear. I thought maybe you wouldn't have seen this yet. I thought you wouldn't want to read it alone."

I laid the newspaper down on my table. It was as though my fingers were not my own. They spread across the page, evening out its wrinkles as I would straighten a length of fabric, moving with slow precision as though smoothing a child's hair.

Final mission, I read. *Missing. Did not return.*

72

Consuelo is in a hotel room. The Hotel Windsor, her old favorite, in Montreal. She phones the desk.

"Any messages for Countess de Saint-Exupéry?"

"No, madame. Not since you last called."

Fine: she will make her way to the *Terre des hommes* fair without the help of the ungrateful mayor.

Consuelo enters the United States Pavilion. The crowds and lines are horrific everywhere. She is going to be late—if there is anything for which to be late. The weather here is calm; she's not sure about New York. She still doesn't know how to reverse tempests or time, unless by wishing it so.

She asks for directions to Mignonne Lachapelle.

"That would be the Star Pilot show, ma'am, just here on the map. Ignore the printed schedule. She's on a loop."

She almost asks, What is a Mignonne-on-a-loop? But she'd rather picture the possibilities.

The room is all windows and glass cases, and no Mignonne. Visitors wander through, taking photographs and pointing to clothes. The outfits enjoy the natural light, but where is the girl whose blush was rosier than the sun? There is no podium, no microphone; there are no reporters to set the record straight.

She walks among the cases, considering the displays. Such anger in these storm-cloud skirts. Who knew Mignonne had it in her? Who knew, in fact, that she had such an unconstrained sculptress's way?

A sudden turn. Consuelo finds herself in the 1960s—silver stretch suits with helmet-like hats. She shudders and decides on a counterclockwise path. 1950s: how decisively Mignonne had shunned the influences of the New Look. Her designs echoed the aesthetic of mechanics' uniforms, and garments to wear at play. 1940s: Consuelo slows down here. The awful awesome clouds. A clutch of nothing jackets—hems and lapels folded back to show piping as red as new scars. Then a mannequin whose dead-eyed form strips the life from a gold silken sheath.

Consuelo puts her hand on the glass. She is overcome by sadness. Sadness comes with age. She remembers touching this garment and almost weeps.

Then remembers another: the daring white dress of silk ribbons and skin. She turns in a circle. Where is the ribbon dress? *Where the hell is the rose?*

A click. "I'm sorry I couldn't be with you in person."

Consuelo looks around. The voice is older. It is louder. It is Mignonne's voice coming from the air.

"Fortunately, the wonders of world fair technology can overcome even the nastiest tricks of nature: I'm phoning from a rained-out airport to record my talk today. I'm Mignonne Lachapelle of Mignonne NYC, and what surrounds you is a selection of my design work spanning the last twenty-five years.

"It all began at an interesting time. The world was at war. On the fashion front, France was suddenly missing from the global scene. So the American industry was slapped into being—and it was slippery as any newborn, complete with awkward parts that couldn't be steamed."

Get to *The Little Prince*, urges Consuelo silently. Tell the world the story of the rose. A voice deep in her body speaks to the bodiless voice of Mignonne. Dress me with words, it says in the way memories speak to memories. Make me, it says to the memory of the girl.

73

Twenty-five days after Antoine's disappearance, France was set free.

I had breakfasted oblivious in my apartment, radio off, but I felt the change the moment the elevator opened to the lobby. The concierge met my gaze with unusual eagerness that floundered under my cranky silence. Outside, the world seemed to have tilted slightly, weakening the laws of gravity, allowing the spines of passersby to have straightened noticeably. Their heads swiveled, curious and light on their unburdened shoulders, as they amused themselves with the discovery that they could look strangers in the eye. It unnerved me, this being glanced at by all (and all acting as though there were something brilliant they wished to share), until I turned the corner and saw the line at the newsstand, and heard the proprietress singing her spiel while her young son pressed papers into hands and her younger son picked his nose. "What a news! France *liberato*! What a big news!"

Underground, the air itself could have powered the train. People read newspapers over others' shoulders and arms, dispensing with surreptitiousness, ravenous with the need to understand what it all meant for them, to know if their sons and husbands and friends would be coming home.

Had Leo been one of the liberators? Leo, whose parting words on the platform had been a reassurance that if the going got too rough he'd trade a minor body part for an easy discharge.

There was a whole country of people to be happy for—including distant Lachapelles; Madame Fiche's family; the relations of the socialites who supped at Le Pavillon and who could surely now begin to put differences aside at the Alliance; the friends and family and countrymen Antoine had worried for, for whom he had left me; the heirs of the compatriots he had returned to serve. I could be happy for my brother, who might see fit to reconsider aiming weaponry at his own toes. But I felt removed from the levity that had unlined the faces surrounding me, and immune to the frisson of optimistic energy that ran the rails.

I thought of what my brother said when Antoine decided to go: "He signs up to die for his prickly, pretty France."

The country had been liberated by the likes of Leo, with Antoine nowhere in sight. The man I had loved was not recovering in some makeshift field hospital, or living incognito on a tropical island, or choosing his moment to leave some sympathetic girl. He would not have missed this action if he were alive anywhere on earth. I had not realized until that morning that I'd placed so much on chance, not until the last card was played and the game lost even as it was won.

Antoine was not on the earth but within it, or deep within its cold waters. I couldn't know whether, in the end, he had given his life to fulfill the day's mission or had simply given up. Maybe Antoine's real secret was that the prince did not return to his planet or his rose, but gave himself to dust or the jaws of desert beasts.

Would that make *The Little Prince* a love story, a war story, or simply a pointless tragedy? If Antoine was the prince, which character might I be? The fox, dispensing counsel about responsibility to reconcile the prince with his rose, then weeping when the lessons took; the snake, scheming to solve every problem presto-magico in a flash; the heartbroken pilot, begging acquaintances forevermore to look for signs of the disappeared boy? I even saw myself in the businessmen and the old monarch who, having built their lives' work on questionable grounds, are unable to move on.

The prince was gone, and I was everywhere in his story. Every story needs a fool.

I arrived at the studio to find that the girls had set up a party of sorts. Bottles of soda and wine cluttered Esther's reception desk. The girls stood around, laughing about boyfriends and homecoming plans. They hushed as I approached.

I waved off the offer of a celebratory glass. In the depths of the studio, I gathered what remained of the *Little Prince* Collection. Many of the original pieces had been refitted to suit purchasers or sold outright to a collector of theatrical designs. Versions of several of the outfits had made their way onto women's bodies large and small, old and young. It had turned out that stylish grandmothers, no less than youthful girlfriends and all manner of well-positioned wives, liked to think of themselves as roses. Antoine had been quite right to claim that his wife was not the only one around.

Consuelo herself, lacking an actual rose dress, now inhabited that character in mind alone—in fact, in thousands of minds across the continent and beyond. When I had eventually pried the dress from her, I'd refused to give it back, not for any payment or favor, or for any promise that was sure to be proven a lie. It was mine, after all, if it was anyone's.

But that was the question. Based closely on Antoine's drawing, created without his consent, earning notice thanks to his name and his fame, was the rose dress really mine? Was the collection mine at all?

And what of the flourishing business that was Mignonne NYC, expanding as vehemently as a baobab tree? I'd never imagined I could feel even a modicum of resistance to accolades and acclaim, yet I was uneasy. I was being slowly strangled by regret that the roots of my reputation lay in the success and the wreckage of Antoine's *Little Prince*.

From now on, it would come from hard work alone.

I boxed up the pieces: the Little Prince's simple jumpsuits and two-piece suits, his cape that had done its job without ermine, the flower ensembles. On top of them all I folded the centerpiece of the collection, the ivory sheath that bore the rose. Perhaps every designer felt this way about her most significant works: that they were both triumph and travesty. Maybe the dichotomy itself was what made a work significant.

The rose had had its accomplishment. It would end there; I wouldn't let this dress come to mock me as the butterfly jacket had done. But I would not take my scissors to the dress as Madame Fiche had done. I could no more attack a gown than deface a book.

From the shelf above my desk, I took my copy of *The Little Prince*. It was not inscribed to me; it was unsigned. Its publication had come just a week before Antoine's departure. I opened the book to its title page. *Copyright 1943, by Antoine de Saint-Exupéry, 1900—.*

Where had he gone—this man who aspired to be as simple as a child? I imagined the boy he had once been, with golden hair as untamed as the Little Prince's and a spirit as unconfined. I imagined the child he would never give to me.

The book went on top of the rose dress. Its cover design was so modest against the scarlet sequins. The Little Prince looked surprised to find himself there. I closed the box, sealed it, and addressed it to myself care of my mother in Montreal. Mother would be accommodating. She would put the box in the dark on a closet shelf in her rambling home to wait for me, and the collection would all be forgotten one day.

I was drinking wine with the girls, and breathing more easily, when the entrance door opened. Bernard leapt into the foyer and swung me in his arms.

———

By dusk, a fine, feverish drizzle had sprung from the humid air. Night came, and with it, intermittent rain. Bernard and I sat on the roof of Le Bocal, tucked between ductwork, sharing a bottle of port. A blanket made a tent; its two rounded peaks were our heads.

Bernard handed me a letter that Antoine wrote on the day he left.

New York, April 13, 1943

Lamotte,

I don't say *au revoir*, for I cannot promise we will see each other again. I say only that I return to my first and most important duty, and I commend you for staying on to attend to yours.

I could add that one is no less honorable than the other, except that I am not sure there is any honor now in an expatriate Frenchman fighting for the remains of France. The concept seems to have gone out of vogue. Certainly few of our number in New York are scrambling to join the operation that has been my fixation for years. Still, progress has been made. If you were less industrious and more inclined to pass your evenings sipping champagne at the Alliance Française, I would not have to inform you that my reputation there has been elevated from that of "traitorous imbecile" to simply "imbecile." In fact, the latter is now occasionally spoken with indulgence, if not affection. Perhaps it is only sentimentality that warms our compatriots' thoughts: they once again associate me with the land they have loved, even as they tut at my assertion that France shall be regained.

I don't expect more from them, I promise you. Nor do I feel disappointed in them. One can hardly fault a being or a community for reaching the limits of its ability to hope. At any rate, their opinions are no longer of significance to me. To those who have claimed I go in search of glory, I reply that acclaim is assured only when one acts to please others—an aspiration I would be embarrassed to possess.

It was with cheerful heart that I found myself pulling on my uniform this morning, closing my bag, giving a final shine to my shoes, saying goodbye to my long-suffering wife (who has chosen to mark my departure with a day of vociferous squalling in bed), and looking forward to spying you on the platform within the hour. My eagerness to depart is wholly undeterred by the knowledge that honor and glory may never be mine.

I am content. It is as natural for me to give my life for my country as it is for you, Lamotte, to follow the dictates of your soul. With great relief I leave today in pursuit of freedom and peace—wherever I may find them, however I may help bring them into being.

But first to the station where, provided we find each other in the crowd, you will wish me a safe and speedy return (as a great friend must) and I shall wish you a long and happy life unencumbered by nostalgia, as must a man who is forever destined to leave his friends.

An ending always foretells a beginning. This is why I so love sunsets. Any day, one could wake to find oneself living on a star.

Saint-Ex

In a corner of the onionskin page was an ink sketch of the Little Prince's tiny planet, its knee-high volcano smudged by rainfall. I said, "If I hadn't gone to Montreal, he might be here celebrating with us today."

"I don't think so, my dear."

"At least he might not have asked Consuelo to come to New York."

"He didn't ask her. She told him she was sailing to visit her family in El Salvador. She said New York was just a few days' stopover—and then she stayed."

My lips parted in astonishment.

Bernard kissed me.

The rain picked up. It soaked our shoulders and our shoes. As we rose to go indoors, we pushed it from our eyes. I paused on the threshold. The wind chime on the open door was ringing in the rain.

Afterword

The Little Prince was published in New York in 1943 and in France in 1945. It became one of the best-selling novels of all time.

Antoine de Saint-Exupéry's whereabouts remained a mystery until 1998, when his engraved identity bracelet was snagged by a fisherman's net and pulled from the Mediterranean Sea. Two years later, his airplane was found in pieces, strewn across the seabed. His body has never been recovered.

Consuelo remained true to form until her death in 1979. It has been said that she moved in with another writer in New York upon Antoine's departure in 1943; that she allegedly forged a section of her husband's will to expand her entitlement to royalties; and that she banked heavily on her connection to *The Little Prince*, including opening a restaurant called *Le Petit Prince* where she wore a sailor's hat embellished with the same. Her memoir of unorthodox love was published posthumously as *The Tale of the Rose*.

Bernard Lamotte died in New York at the age of eighty. His life's work includes murals commissioned by John F. Kennedy for the White House pool. His artwork is still displayed at his beautiful old studio, which has been home to the *haute cuisine* restaurant Le Grenouille for the past half century. A plaque on the building's facade commemorates the creation of *The Little Prince*—directly across the street from the side entrance of the Fifth Avenue Cartier store, which locale for a short time did indeed host the Alliance Française, though not in the configuration described within these pages.

The very real (and self-invented) designer Valentina Schlee was largely forgotten until the 2009 publication of Kohle Yohannan's fascinating *Valentina: American Couture and the Cult of Celebrity* and the accompanying show at the Museum of the City of New York. Mignonne's white silk chiffon dress was inspired by the Valentina creation that graces the book's back cover. Mig's bold modeling of the butterfly ensemble draws on the words and actions of the inimitable Valentina herself, down to the corselet.

While the record shows that both Saint-Exupérys had close or intimate relationships outside of marriage, it should be noted that all aspects of the relationships within this book are fictional. The specific nature of Antoine's extramarital relations remains a matter of speculation, with some sources suggesting that his were exclusively platonic affairs. If so, his abstinence may not have been a matter of impotence but of a sense of responsibility: Saint-Exupéry biographer Stacy Schiff notes that her subject believed erroneously that he may have inherited syphilis, and worried (despite repeated test results to the contrary) that he was at risk of spreading the disease.

Whenever possible within the demands of this story, I have situated the Saint-Exupérys and their compatriots in historically documented places and situations at the historically correct times. I have attempted to give context to the better known of Antoine's written and quoted words, and have called upon my version of Consuelo to recast her documented tales and claims. Nevertheless, all elements of this novel—whether inspired by, based on, reflecting, or distorting the known facts—should be construed as fiction. Antoine de Saint-Exupéry's many biographers differ significantly in their interpretation of this complicated and contradictory man and his tempestuous wife.

Acknowledgments

Three remarkable women guided me through this story's final transformations and brought it to an international readership: I'm indebted to my editors Victoria Wilson and Adrienne Kerr, and to my agent Melanie Jackson, for their wisdom, enthusiasm, and grace. Thank you also to my publishers, my publicists Kathryn Zuckerman and Barbara Bower, and all who have worked so diligently in support of this book.

The manuscript benefitted greatly from perceptive readings by Barbara Berson, Cathy Marie Buchanan, Michael Schellenberg, Dianne Scott, and Roz Spafford. Sincere gratitude to them, and to University of British Columbia's MFA in Creative Writing program, where early drafts took shape.

Howard Scherry was generous in sharing resources and his vast knowledge of Saint-Exupéry's New York years. Stacy Schiff provided corroboration at a critical juncture. The Museum of the City of New York enthralled me with exhibitions on Valentina and on Paris and New York's design and fashion cultures; Jacqueline Chambord delved into the history of New York City's French Institute Alliance Française; the Color Institute unearthed 1940s fabrics and attitudes. Patricia Stewart and David Page provided Expo 67 materials and cast a careful eye over my French.

Among print sources, I am most grateful for *Saint-Exupéry: A Biography* by Stacy Schiff, as well as biographies by Curtis Cate, Marcel Migeo, and Joy D. Marie Robinson; *Saint Exupéry: Art, Writings and Musings* by Nathalie des Vallières; *Saint-Exupéry in America, 1942–1943: A Memoir* by Adele Breaux; *Valentina: American Couture and the Cult of Celebrity* by Kohle Yohannan; *The Tale of the Rose: The Passion That Inspired "The Little Prince"* and *Kingdom of the Rocks: Memories of Oppède* by Consuelo de Saint-Exupéry; *Émigré New York: French Intellectuals in Wartime Manhattan, 1940–1944* by Jeffrey Mehlman; *Don't You Know There's a War On?: The American Home Front, 1941–1945* by Richard Lingeman, *Forties Fashion: From Siren Suits to the New Look* by Jonathan Walford; *A Stitch in Time: A History of New York's Fashion District* by Gabriel Montero; *Over Here!: New York City During World War II* by Lorraine B. Diehl; and, by Antoine de Saint-Exupéry, *The Little Prince* and other works, particularly *Wartime Writings 1939–1944.*

Heartfelt gratitude to those who hosted me as I worked in Toronto, New York City, Massachusetts, Florida, Hamilton, Quebec, on the shores of Lake Erie and Lake Mississagua, in a wintery Killarney Park yurt, at Robert Wyatt's magical Woodstock home, and at Toronto Writers' Centre—my thanks to its members and its founder, Mitch Kowalski.

While writing this book, I was buoyed by the faith and creativity of Bruce Hefler, Ela Hefler, Luke Hefler, Daniela Draves, Celina Szado, Edward Szado, Cathy Buchanan, Miranda Hill, Ellen Irving, Eduarda Sousa, and Angela Thomas.

I thank the Ontario Arts Council for financial assistance during the tenure of this project.

To conclude where *Studio Saint-Ex* began: When I was eleven, I was given a copy of *The Little Prince.* I will forever be aware—and grateful—that the gift of a book can change the course of a child's life.

A Note About the Type

This book was set in Adobe Garamond. Designed for the Adobe Corporation by Robert Slimbach, the fonts are based on types first cut by Claude Garamond (c. 1480–1561). Garamond was a pupil of Geoffroy Tory and is believed to have followed the Venetian models, although he introduced a number of important differences, and it is to him that we owe the letter we now know as "old style."

Printed and bound by RR Donnelley, Harrisonburg, Virginia

Designed by M. Kristen Bearse